DINNER PARTIES AND DEADLY DISH . . .

As the hired help served the chicken, Bailey Bronson rose unsteadily.

"To Lawrence!" He raised his glass. "Underappreciated and now in the cat-bird seat." He swayed dangerously. "Renowned for his international epicurean flair and his parties, at which too many people drank too much and spilled their guts. May he take his secrets to the grave. The sooner the better."

Madame's gasp was the only sound. Even the cutlery stilled.

"My death would benefit no one," Lawrence said as casually as if he were ordering coffee. "All pertinent information is already in writing. As a vessel of secrets, I've been drained. But what abomination do you fear, Bronson? We'd love to know. I could hazard a guess, if you'd like. . . ."

Books by Carolyn Haines

BURIED BONES

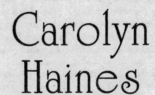

Carolyn Haines

BANTAM BOOKS
*New York Toronto London
Sydney Auckland*

BURIED BONES

A Bantam Book / November 2000

ISBN 0-553-58172-4

Published simultaneously in the United States and Canada

Bantam Books are published by Bantam Books, a division of Random
House, Inc. Its trademark, consisting of the words "Bantam Books"
and the portrayal of a rooster, is Registered in U.S. Patent and
Trademark Office and in other countries. Marca Registrada. Bantam
Books, New York, New York.

PRINTED IN THE UNITED STATES OF AMERICA

OPM   10 9 8 7 6 5

This book is dedicated
to the memory of Eugene Walter—
a tremendous influence even now.

Acknowledgments

With each published book I learn the value of good friends and good critics. No writer could have better friends (and critics!) than the Deep South Writers Salon: Reneé Paul, Stephanie Chisholm, Susan Tanner, Jan Zimlich, and Rebecca Barrett. They make me a better writer.

My agent Marian Young has hung tough through the lean times—and maintained a sense of humor that is very forgiving of mine. When she believes in a book, she is there one hundred percent.

Working with Kara Cesare and Kate Miciak at Bantam has been one of my best publishing experiences. And I can only praise the Bantam art department. Great covers!

I'd also like to thank the booksellers, particularly those specializing in mysteries, who work so hard to promote the genre. They are indefatigable.

1

Chasing the blues away is a talent Delaney women are still trying to acquire. Perhaps our melancholy *is* a sign, as Jitty insists, of some obscure womb disorder. *Regrettus Wombus*, a medical term for the regretful womb, resulting in the deep-dark, down-and-ugly blues.

Historically, Delaney women have been known to wallow in that place where loss takes up more space than any other organ. I fear I'm no exception to the family tradition.

There wasn't a radio station in the small Mississippi town of Zinnia that wasn't playing "I'll Be Home for Christmas." It is my belief that any song mentioning chestnuts, toasty fires, or sleigh rides for two should be banned from the airwaves. It's a fact, documented in my psychology journals, that suicide rates increase during the holidays. Due, no doubt, to the sadistic disc jockeys playing these songs.

With the conclusion of my first case, I'd received payment in full from Tinkie for my investigative services. Dahlia House had been saved, for the moment,

from my creditors. I should have been on top of the
world. Instead, I was in the front parlor, knotted in a
tangle of tinsel, and with a Christmas tree that looked
as if residents of Bedlam had put up the lights.

Turning off the radio, I tossed the tinsel in the fire
and was rewarded with a multihued flame. I picked up
all the magnolia leaves, holly, and cedar that I'd cut and
brought in to use as decorations. With a mighty heave, I
burned them, too.

As the last of the Delaneys, I'd inherited my mother's
incredible collection of great albums, and I sat down on
the carpet and began to go through them. I couldn't
control the radio stations, but I could find my own
music.

As my fingers closed over Denise LaSalle, I felt a
surge of renewed spirit. The album was a little
scratched, but there was no denying the feminist power
of the Delta-born blueswoman. It was perfect—fight the
blues with the blues. And Denise was putting it on her
no-good man. She had her Crown Royal, her car, and a
juke-joint band to dance to. She'd also given me a new
motto—"If you can't be with the one you love, love the
one you're with."

There were plenty of fish in the ocean. All I had to do
was find me a pole and throw in my line.

With my energy renewed, I crawled behind Aunt
LouLane's horsehair sofa, found the electrical outlet,
and jammed the prongs of the extension plug into the
holes. Maybe I wasn't the best with traditional Christmas decorating, but I'd found something even better.
Something that spoke to *me*. And I'd gotten it at a
bargain-basement price.

Peering over the back of the sofa at the mantel, I
smiled with satisfaction at what I had wrought. The
neon tubing slid to hot green with liquid light, creating

the perfect outline of a Christmas wreath. Mingled in the green curlicues that made the body of the wreath were red ornaments that blinked on and off. It was a masterpiece, a real find in Rudy's Junk Shop.

I picked up the second extension cord and poked it home. The reds, greens, blues, and yellows of old-fashioned Christmas lights flickered to life, creating a series of fascinating shadows on the high ceilings of the front parlor. Neon meets tradition! A successful Delaney moment.

Before I could stand up to see the fruits of my labors, I heard the harrumph that warned me Jitty was in the room.

"You've got this place lookin' like a Chinese whore-house," Jitty said. "And you not much better. I didn't know they made such a thing as a flannel muumuu. Girl, it's late afternoon. You been wearin' that getup all day? And look at those socks. Just 'cause they red and it's Christmas don't mean you should wear 'em."

Bracing against the sofa, I rose to my knees and traced her voice to the brocade wingback. She was sitting there, dark eyes reflecting the multihued Christmas lights that she disdained. Behind her, the neon wreath pulsed and throbbed, seeming to pick up the singer's declaration of freedom and at the same time give Jitty a hellish halo.

"Merry Christmas, Jitty," I said, brushing the dust off my knees as I stood. "I've been decorating."

"Honey, you need some serious help," she replied. "This ain't decoratin', this is vandalism."

I walked across the wide, polished oak planks of the parlor and viewed my handiwork from her vantage point. The thirteen-foot fir tree, trimmed with about a million lights, at least five hundred ornaments, some red-velvet bows, a few wooden toys and trinkets, and five packages of the real old-timey silver icicles looked pretty good to me. Not to mention the stockings hung by the fireplace with care, or the thorn branch that I'd laboriously studded with rainbow gumdrops. I turned back to Jitty. "I think it looks great."

"Don't get that hurt look on your face, Sarah Booth," she said coldly. "Some women got the touch when it comes to decoratin', some don't. You could improve yourself a little bit, though, if you'd take a few hints from—"

"Stop!" I would not allow the name of the decorating maven from hell to be spoken in my home. My home. The phrase gave me a moment of pleasure. I, Sarah Booth Delaney, had single-handedly redeemed Dahlia House. I still had debts aplenty, but I no longer had to peek from behind closed curtains whenever a car drove up to make sure it wasn't the sheriff and a repo crew.

"What you lookin' so self-satisfied for?" Jitty asked with tiny little snake rattles in her voice.

I looked at her. Really looked at her, for the first time today. Gone were the glitz and gaudiness of the seventies. Jitty had reinvented herself yet again.

"Where in the hell did you get those clothes?" I asked, pointing at her and moving my finger up and down to indicate the entire package. From the tight curls bound back by a turban-style scarf to the waist-cinched blue gingham dress and high-heeled pumps, Jitty looked like a negative image of Jane Wyatt on a rerun of *Father Knows Best*. My horrified gaze roved back up to her waist. My Lord, it had to be under twenty-three inches.

"Somebody around here's got to put a halt to moral decay. No more of this 'free love, if it feels good do it' bull. What we need are some family values." Jitty looked like a rod had been rammed up her spine. "Once we get us some family values, maybe a family will follow."

Her smug tone should have been a warning.

"You mean you're done with Gloria Steinem and moved into the camp of that fifties-throwback Phyllis Schlafly?" And I had foolishly thought nothing could be worse than bad polyester and metallic eye shadow. Her hair, normally alive with energy, looked as if it had been beaten into submission.

"You're leadin' a wild and reckless life, Sarah Booth. It's time you settled down. I thought I'd set you a good example."

I briefly closed my eyes, hoping this was all a bad, bad nightmare. Jitty, my great-great-grandmother's nanny, a ghost lingering in Dahlia House from pre–Civil War days, was going to set an example for me. A woman who fed off me—literally, figuratively, and spiritually—had found me lacking in moral fiber. This from the haint who only four weeks ago would have used a turkey baster to stuff me with the sperm of bachelor-banker Harold Erkwell?

"Hold on one second, there—" I began.

"Don't go pointin' that finger at me, missy," Jitty shot back, rising from her perch on the chair arm to stand on those slender little heels. It gave me a stab of pleasure to see her sway dangerously. She hadn't quite perfected the Loretta Young stance.

"Missy?" My voice rose an octave. "Missy? What's going on here?"

"You are a missy," she said, her eyes glittering now. "As in unmarried, over thirty, no prospects—you don't straighten up fast and act righteous, you gone be an *old* missy. And turn off that sex music. Listenin' to that stuff will get you—"

"Bred," I supplied, finally coming to the heart of the matter. "Which is the real problem here. You're mad at me because I'm not pregnant." It was unbelievable. "You're furious because my . . . encounter with Hamilton Garrett V didn't produce a viable . . . product. This is all some form of ghostly punishment you've devised. My God! I'm not living with a badass from the Mod Squad any longer. Now I've got Aunt Jemima acting out Donna Reed!"

"Child," she said carefully. "Not product. Child. That's what's wrong in this picture. You've lost your tender parts. I think it might have something to do with the Delaney womb condition. You let that man slip right through your fingers. You didn't even try to hold on to him."

The memory of my passionate—and doomed—Thanksgiving romance was enough to push every holiday emotion I had right out the front door and across the frozen acres of the Mississippi Delta. "Hamilton is back in Europe. He hasn't even sent a Christmas card. And you're upset because I'm not the vessel that holds his seed?" My hands went automatically to my hips. I could feel the red spread up my face.

"You need a doctor's appointment. If you didn't have some womb tilt, you might have held on to a few of those Garrett . . . you know . . ."

"Sperm, Jitty. You can say the word." I didn't like this new fifties modesty. Jitty had always been a ghost who called a spade a spade.

"If you'd tried a little harder, you might have conceived."

"What do you suggest? That I should have done it standing on my head? Or is that considered immoral in the land where *Father Knows Best?*"

"Have a drink of water," she said. "Your face is red and your eyes are 'bout to pop out of your head."

"Could it be that I'm angry?" My pulse throbbed at my temple.

She snorted. "Sarcasm is lost on me. And it's very unladylike. You want to get you a man, you gone have to give up actin' like a harpy."

"Hamilton didn't stick around long enough to see my harpy side."

She sat down on the chair arm, kicked off a shoe, and began to massage her foot. "If you'd gotten pregnant, Hamilton would have come back to Zinnia."

I was stunned. "You mean I might have trapped him into marrying me?"

She continued to rub her foot, unable, or unwilling, to look me in the eyes. "Lots of marriages start off that way. What difference does it make if you bait the trap with sex or home cookin' or a child?"

I waited until she brought her gaze up to mine. "I don't want a man I have to trap."

"Don't be a fool," she answered, a hint of the seventies Jitty showing through in the way she flounced to her feet, ignoring the fact that she had on only one shoe. "Men don't think of marriage on their own. None of them. Women got to put the idea in their heads. And if you'd hung on to that sperm, a baby would have been one unavoidable idea."

"Jitty," I warned.

"Make a doctor's appointment. Maybe there's a kink in some of your tubes. 'Course there's no rush. It'll probably be another five years before you slide out of your panties again."

"Jitty!" She'd gone too far. I couldn't tell if I was madder at the implication that I couldn't get laid or the prediction that I wouldn't. Truth be told, Hamilton's return to Europe had done more damage to my heart than I wanted to admit.

"I was thinkin' about pot roast for dinner," she said in an abrupt change of tactics. "You keep eatin' that fruitcake, you gone be too big to attract anybody 'cept one of those Shelby pig farmers. Now those boys 'preciate a woman with some poundage."

I saw her flicker, then begin to fade. It was just like her to start an argument and then disappear. "You come right back here," I ordered, even as the last trace of her form disappeared. "Jitty!"

"Answer the door," she said, her voice only a sigh in the room.

The chiming of the doorbell pulled me up short. It was Friday evening, the last weekend before Christmas. Who could possibly be at the door? Not Cece, the society editor of the local newspaper and my sometimes employer. It was deadline for her Sunday section. And not Tammy. Zinnia's local psychic was spending the weekend visiting her granddaughter, little Dahlia, over near Mound Bayou.

Harold Erkwell?

My thumb gave a little tingle at the thought of the distinguished banker who'd offered me a rock and a marriage—both rejected in haste. Was it possible I was still carrying some kind of torch for Harold? If not a torch, perhaps a Bic?

"Sarah Booth, yoo-hoo?" The bell chimed again, and there was a harsh rap on the door.

I hurried out of the parlor and into the foyer, noticing with a certain satisfaction the tinsel wreath I'd hung on the bust of Stonewall Jackson that had been in my father's family for almost as long as Jitty. Jackson was a hard-looking man—perhaps not hard but determined.

The glittering red wreath gave him a holiday air. Hah! Despite Jitty's cruel words, I did have a certain flair for decorating.

The bell rang again, this time with vehemence. The pounding was staccato and solid. A cane? I didn't know a soul who used a cane. I slipped to the window door and very carefully eased the lace sheer back. Two bright blue eyes, enlarged by black-rimmed spectacles and topped with a shock of snow-white hair, stared directly into mine. I didn't recognize the man at all.

"Open up, dah-ling, I'm here on official monkey business."

I did as he ordered and found myself face-to-face with an older man who'd escaped most of the trappings of age—he was spry. He made a courtly bow, sweeping low to the floor.

"Let me introduce myself. Lawrence Ambrose, a very dear friend of your parents. Your mother in particular. I adored her. She was every inch a real lady."

I was stunned. All of my life I'd heard about Lawrence Ambrose, the Mississippian who'd taken the Parisian world of letters by storm. He was also an artist and playwright and a host of other things. I'd known that Ambrose lived in Zinnia, a recluse on the Caldwells' large estate, but I'd never anticipated meeting him in the flesh.

"Please, come in," I managed.

"I do believe there's a bit of the monkey in you, my dear," Lawrence said, offering his arm to me. "There's not a Zodiac sign for the monkey, but there should be. Somewhere between the scorpion and the goat, don't you think? What sign are you?"

Leaning only slightly on his cane, he escorted me inside.

In the parlor, Lawrence Ambrose settled into the

club chair beside the fire and pointed at my Christmas decorations with his cane. "Lovely, dahling. Very SoHo, fifties. Andy Warhol would have absolutely coveted such a creation. That was before he became a caricature of himself, you know. At one point . . ." He lowered the cane and I saw his hand tremble before it closed tightly over the horse's head. He was too pale. "It's a sign of age when the past seems to dominate one's conversation. Forgive me."

He seemed so genuinely taken aback that I had to think of a change of subject. Food was always good. "Would you care for some coffee? And fruitcake?" If he ate it, I might be able to fit into my pants tomorrow.

"Fruitcake?" he asked, two shaggy white eyebrows arching. "None of that hideous store-bought gomm that they pass off as fruitcake?"

Though he was still pale, he'd bounced back. "No," I assured him, even more impressed that he knew the difference. "Homemade. From a secret family recipe."

"Dahling, there's nothing better in the world than a secret family recipe. Except for an afternoon in Italy with a skilled lover."

His reply stopped me dead in my tracks.

"You'd be surprised which Zinnians have indulged in such decadence," he added, eyes a wicked blue. "It's the most interesting thing, how something so wonderful at the time can end up being the source of such anxiety. I've lately become quite the expert on secret anxieties. And secrets in general." His smile was pure delight.

"I'll get us some. Coffee and fruitcake," I said, excusing myself and heading into the kitchen. Lawrence Ambrose intrigued me, but he'd also caught me completely off guard. What in the world was the writer doing at my house now? My mother had adored him.

She had collected signed copies of all of his work. She even had a photograph of him as Rita Hayworth's escort at the Academy Awards. Mother had loved his writing.

Years back, there had been rumors about his parties—bacchanalia with Maypole dances, original plays acted out in elaborate costumes on the lawn. There was even a story that he'd hung and burned an effigy of one of Mississippi's more infamous governors, Cliff Finch, and ended up in a fistfight with Zinnia's volunteer fire marshal. That was before he'd become something of a recluse. But he didn't seem at all reclusive. Just another example of how rumors spread in a small town.

I waited for the coffee to perk, pondering why he'd come visiting me. When the tray was prepared, I hurried back to the parlor with it. Lawrence accepted his coffee and cake with the ease of a man comfortable in a parlor.

"No doubt you're wondering why I'm here. It's a rather long story, and boring, as most long stories are. And naturally, it involves money. And secrets."

He was a verbal tease, hinting and dangling little tidbits. But he did it with such style and humor that I found myself intrigued rather than annoyed. "I love secrets," I said. "Generally they pay well."

"Ah-ha, I knew you were part monkey. Clever little thing. Facts first and then secrets. My last books were financial failures. No publisher will touch my work. They say my numbers are down and no one remembers or cares about what I *used* to be."

He took a bite of cake. "Heavenly, Sarah Booth. Who would have thought a pigtailed hellion would grow up to bake such divine fruitcake." Hardly taking a breath he continued. "I've now decided to publish my memoirs. Would you have a bit of brandy to liven up the coffee? Caffeine is bad for your liver, my child. Brandy counteracts the acids."

At first I'd thought Lawrence had reached the age where rambling and conversational rabbit trails were unavoidable, but his blue eyes belied such a judgment. He was in expert control of his faculties *and* the conversation. "Certainly," I said as I found the proper decanter and splashed a good dollop into his cup.

"Finding new talent is one of my greatest pleasures. I'm having a small gathering at my home Christmas Eve," he said. "There'll be some writers, publishers, a few movie people, an artist, and the usual suspects in the Sunflower County literati. Since you're writing a book, I thought you might enjoy the gathering."

"But I'm not—" I stopped my confession. The lie that I was writing a book had launched my career as a private investigator. As my mother once told me, sometimes it's too late for the truth. Besides, the party sounded interesting, especially based on Lawrence's past history of fetes. "It sounds lovely," I said.

"I'm reintroducing my biographer to her native soil. I believe you know her. Brianna Rathbone." Lawrence stamped his cane on the floor. "A dazzling young woman. She's been living in New York, but has now returned to the Delta to work on my book. My memoirs. This will signal a new era for me. Brianna is an international celebrity, yet Southern. I think the combination of my story and her celebrity status will push this book right to the top of the best-seller list. You remember her, don't you?"

The thwack of the cane combined with Brianna's name was like tiny little jolts of electricity in the reptilian lobe of my brain. I had the strongest urge to coil and strike.

"Yes." The word was a croak. My reptilian lobe was still in control. I remembered her perfectly. "I didn't realize Brianna had an interest in writing," I said, floundering for something to say. "She's a model. A jet-setter. One of the beautiful people."

"Brianna, as a *former* model and jet-setter, is the perfect person to add that zest to my story." Lawrence arched his eyebrows. "Don't you agree?"

"Can Brianna write?" I asked before I could stop myself. A better question would have been if she could read.

"I'm not in need of eloquence," Lawrence said. He sat taller in his chair. "The truth of the matter is that my light has faded. What I need is a biographer who can regenerate that spark. Like it or not, the world lusts for celebrity, not art. Miss Rathbone has been on the cover of *Vogue*. She's dating Gustav Brecht, the publishing magnate. She has the élan to capture the public's attention. She has a reputation."

No doubt about the reputation part. She'd slept with half the men in New York. And now she was dating a publisher. Was that a good thing? Brianna had always reminded me of a black widow. Mate-eater. Or at least maimer. I could see the benefits of a biographer who was in bed with the publisher, but what would happen when she gnawed off his leg? But I held my tongue.

"Can I expect you for dinner?" Lawrence asked.

As fascinating as the evening sounded, I'd rather spend an hour in a snake pit than sit through dinner with Brianna Rathbone. I was on the verge of declining when he pulled another directional shift in the conversation.

"I have two reasons for having this dinner, Sarah Booth. I found my favorite cat, Rasmus, dead yesterday. He was twenty years old. He *must* have died of old age. He loved my entertainments and would frequently perform kitty yoga on top of the guests. My only regret is that I didn't have one sooner, for him, but I'm having one now in his honor."

There was a hint of sudden desperation and sadness in Lawrence's voice that tugged on my heartstrings. He shivered then, even though he still wore his coat and the fire was hot. I had the sinking feeling that he was masterfully playing me, but I didn't have the heart to resist him. I got up and added another log to the fire. "What's the other reason?" I asked.

His eyebrows rose and the glitter in his blue eyes was both mischief and excitement. "Secrets. The second reason is that everyone there will have a secret. And I know them all."

"What time is dinner?" I asked, caught up in his spirit of devilment. Secrets were, indeed, good fun.

"I told everyone six, which means they'll arrive at seven because they all want to make a grand entrance. Seven would be lovely. Bring your opera glasses, dahling, the peacocks will be parading." The eyebrows rose slowly and held. "I intend to make them stampede. It will be great fun."

"It sounds wonderful, but why are you inviting me?" I had to ask.

"To bear witness, darling. You're the perfect choice—a writer and a detective."

2

"Leave it up," Jitty said, standing behind me as I poked a jeweled hair comb into my unruly mop of brown curls. I liked the casual elegance of the upswept do, but I was afraid it wouldn't withstand the rigors of the evening.

"It feels . . . unsecured."

"You're worried about hair? Take a look at your chest."

Jitty was opposed to the red-glitter cocktail dress that I'd bought at a tony little shop in Memphis during a shopping spree with Cece. True to her word, Cece Dee Falcon had provided entertainment during the trip—a nonstop babble of gossip and factoids she ferreted out and catalogued in her newspaper work. She also tossed out expert fashion advice. But trying on clothes with Cece was an experience I hadn't bargained for. More often than not, I forgot that Cece had once been a man. Long gone was the lanky, twitchy high school boy Cecil Falcon. In his place, an elegant, sexy, and very feminine woman emerged thanks to a talented team of Swedish surgeons. A cramped dressing room was an interesting place to play before-and-after.

Even as I fastened a diamond locket around my throat, I reassessed my image. Cece, with her lean hips and angular collarbone, could wear anything. But she was truly expert in dressing others, too. My dress was Parisian cool. Low-cut in front and daringly backless. The style did a lot to emphasize my décolletage, more defined since my fruitcake binge. Play your assets, my mother always said. My makeup was subtle, emphasizing the green of my eyes.

Jitty stepped back from me. "Honey, those fruitcakes are gangin' up on your waistline and looks like they're preparin' to claim squatter's rights."

Where I'd discarded binding bras and underwire, she was girded, girdled, heart-crossed, and granny-panted against even the tiniest jiggle. God forbid that she might be able to draw a deep breath. A little oxygen to her brain might allow her to think for herself.

"There's nothing in the detective handbooks that says I can't be plump," I offered, anticipating the explosion.

"Girl, you better pull yourself together! You talkin' like an old maid."

"I am an old maid," I reminded her. "But I have a good personality and I can make my own clothes," I added, to ward off the sting.

"Just keep makin' jokes," Jitty said. "Life has a way of followin' after the words we cast out in front of us."

Her philosophical statement caused a small cavalry of goose bumps to gallop up my arm. "Don't wait up," I said, picking up my purse and keys. I took off down the stairs and into the night.

It was perfect weather for a Christmas Eve bash. The

barren cotton fields were coated in frost, a tundra of silvery white that reached into the dark blue and star-spangled Delta sky. Though the night was clear, snow was predicted. I remembered a long-ago white Christmas. Dahlia House, decorated like a storybook home, had seemed to be a place where only happiness could live. I was four.

Still, a blanket of cold, white stuff would soften even the heart of a cynic. Let it snow, let it snow, let it snow. I kept the mantra going so that I wouldn't think about what was missing from the evening—a date—as I drove to the party.

Lawrence Ambrose lived in a cottage on Magnolia Place, one of the few estates that still functioned as a producing cotton plantation. The Vardaman Caldwells owned the property, but they traveled extensively and were often out of the country. Set back from the main house about half a mile, the spacious guest cottage was a perfect location for a writer, elegant and secluded— far enough from the main road not to draw attention should Lawrence decided to engage in one of his famous parties.

The drive was lined with live oaks. Huge and gnarled, they were probably two hundred years old. I pulled into a parking space beside a number of nice autos, and one silver Porsche, probably belonging to Brianna, since it was just like her—fast and high-maintenance.

The chatter of the party spilled out onto the wide gallery where several cats reclined in rocking chairs. Bottles of opened wine and clean glasses were on small tables beside huge brass planters filled with fresh spices. I recognized basil, dill, and rosemary. There were dozens of other plants I knew but couldn't name.

I helped myself to a glass of merlot, stroked a friendly yellow tabby, and listened to the mélange of voices within. Brianna's throaty laugh was hard to miss.

Ah, Brianna.

I opened the door and she was the first person I saw. Honeyed blond hair to her shoulders, black sheath, sharp hipbones—hungry. A walk like a caged panther, headed directly at me. For a few seconds I was back in tenth grade, staring at the perfect face that would grace magazine covers around the world.

"Sarah Booth Delaney," she said, coming forward to take my hand. "I never dreamed I'd see you here."

Interpretation—what's someone like you doing among these star-kissed people? Her tone made it clear that I didn't belong.

"Lawrence is interested in my book," I said. The lie rolled off my tongue like quicksilver. "He thinks I have talent."

"Amazing. But then, isn't everyone convinced that their pathetic little lives are of interest?" She flicked her hair over her shoulder. "I had no idea you could write."

"It's a skill I acquired in high school, while you were busy on your knees soliciting an A from the—"

Harold Erkwell appeared at my side, a striking figure in a black wool suit that emphasized his salt-and-pepper hair. "Stunning dress, Sarah Booth," he said, hands on my bare shoulders. "Luscious."

"Lush-us," Brianna said, mouthing the word with her collagen-plumped lips. "Another ten pounds, Sarah Booth, and you'll qualify as dumpling cute." She walked away and only Harold's hands on my shoulders saved her.

"I'm going to tear her throat out," I said sweetly.

"Too messy," Harold said, turning me in the opposite direction and giving me a gentle push.

"I didn't know you'd be here," I said, instantly realizing that he belonged here much more than I did. Harold was a huge supporter of the arts—in literature, visual, music, and drama. It was perfectly logical that he'd be among Lawrence's friends.

"I'm here to keep an eye on Lawrence. He's up to something." Worry furrowed his brow.

"What's going on?" I asked.

Before he could reply he was captured by Lillian Sparks and her campaign to outfit the first New Year's baby born in Sunflower County with a year's supply of cotton diapers. Homegrown cotton, of course.

The party swept over me and I found myself talking to a New York literary agent and a handsome actor who was hoping for his Hollywood break. Both were busy looking beyond me for a better connection. We were joined by a short, posturing man who enjoyed name-dropping and commandeering conversations. I thought at first his name was Dean, realizing only later that it was his title, which he'd soldered onto his identity by ceaseless repetition.

"Of course Joyce was never a social man," *Dean* Joseph Grace droned. "I once had lunch with William Burroughs, and it occurred to me that there were similarities between Joyce and Burroughs that no one had ever before connected. I thought instantly what a wonderful thesis that would make for some young scholar at the university. That's the problem these days, our students have no originality. No spark of creativity."

There was no doubt that he referred to the University of Mississippi, or Ole Miss, the Sacred Hunting Ground for Daddy's Girls to find suitable mates. I could have informed him that there was plenty of originality among the students when it came to snaring the suitable mate.

"You've read both Burroughs and Joyce?" His narrow brown gaze pinned me as a possible troglodyte.

"Who hasn't?" I replied gamely. To my horror the agent and actor fled, obviously better at self-preservation than I was.

Rescue arrived not a moment too soon. Madame Rosalyn Bell, former prima ballerina and Nazi dance mistress, took my arm. "Pull your shoulders back. It makes your breasts perky," she said. "There's someone I want you to meet."

I didn't want to imagine who that might be. So far the guest list, with the exception of Harold and Mrs. Sparks, seemed pretentious and fed on malice.

"Come along, dear. He's outside, smoking. Cultural thing, you know."

Before I could protest, her tiny fingers dug deeply into my arm and she pushed me out into the cold night. "Are you really a private investigator?" she said as she pulled me to face her, just as she'd done in dance class twenty years before.

"I've concluded one—"

"No prevarication, Sarah Booth. Either you are or aren't."

"I am." One thing about Madame—she didn't allow for waffling.

"You have a sharp eye for people. You must, if you're in the PI business. What do you make of Brianna's desire to write Lawrence's life story?"

Brianna had also been one of Rosalyn's students. She'd been a beautiful dancer with a superior attitude and the habit of never letting Madame forget that she was her employee. I had a vivid memory of the petite dance mistress lifting her hand to slap Brianna's face for an especially cruel remark she'd made to one of the chubbier girls in the dance class. But something had restrained Madame. She'd lowered her hand and walked away.

"I never knew Brianna had an interest in writing. She certainly never did in high school."

"You're hedging again, Sarah Booth. An unattractive habit I would have thought you'd outgrow. Brianna isn't interested in writing, she's interested in recapturing the limelight. Any. Way. She. Can."

The emphasis was clear, and the hair on the back of my neck quivered. Rosalyn was so tense she was almost vibrating. "Writing a book doesn't seem all that glamorous," I said, hoping to calm her.

"Lawrence has the goods on half the well-known writers alive today. During his Paris years, he knew everyone who was anyone. There are some secrets better left in the past, Sarah Booth. Some damaging secrets. Brianna is hunting for those secrets. Lawrence won't believe it, but she's been snooping in his house, plundering through his things. I've caught her twice. If she finds— The past is never dead. Lawrence doesn't realize how damaging, or how dangerous, it can be."

I remembered Lawrence's broad hints. Brianna would enjoy nothing better than digging up dirt on others and watching them twist in the wind. Still, I had doubts that Brianna would have the discipline to finish a book even if she started. Writing required solitude, and Brianna never liked her own company—for obvious reasons. "I wouldn't worry too much. I doubt Brianna can write anything, much less a book. Even if by some miracle she finished, it probably won't get published." That conclusion gave me a jolt of satisfaction.

"Layton Rathbone will buy his daughter a publishing company if that's what it takes," Rosalyn insisted. "Or at least that's what Lawrence believes. He thinks he's going to use Brianna, but there's one small problem. No one uses a Rathbone and gets away with it."

The sound of deep, sensual laughter was a perfect contrast to the chill of Rosalyn's words. We both turned our heads. I saw him standing at the edge of the light, a striking silhouette against the backyard torches—a tall man, slender, in an Italian-cut suit that emphasized his long torso and legs, lean hips, and broad shoulders. When he turned, I stopped dead in my tracks. Light from a dozen blazing lanterns caught in his golden blond curls, intensifying his hazel eyes.

Rosalyn moved toward him, leading me beside her. "Willem Arquillo, this is the woman I promised to introduce you to. Sarah Booth Delaney, *Señor* Arquillo."

He came toward me with two long strides, his hand capturing mine. He lifted it, then turned it over and bent back my fingers lightly to expose the palm. Very deliberately he kissed it. In the cold Delta night, his lips were very, very warm.

"You're even more beautiful than Rosalyn told me," he said. He continued to hold my hand as he turned to Madame Bell. "Exquisite," he whispered.

"I saw your paintings in Memphis," I said, beginning to see real value in cultivating artsy-fartsy acquaintances. Aside from the fact that he was a magnificent painter, combining primitive images with controversial politics, he was gorgeous. Lawrence had said an artist would be at dinner, but he hadn't said which artist. "What brings you to Zinnia?" I'd heard gossip, from Cece, naturally, that he was working to establish a trade partnership between Mississippi and Nicaragua—both Third World countries, as he so aptly put it. But that type of negotiation would take place in Jackson, the state capital, not little ol' Zinnia.

"Business *and* pleasure," he said smoothly. "Lawrence and I have some unfinished business. We've been friends for a long time."

Willem's melodious voice made my spine tingle. "I understand Lawrence collects art. Does he have some of your paintings?"

His gaze was sharp, but his voice was as warm as a caress. "Probably more than he realizes. But I'm bored talking about myself. I hear you're a writer. Are you helping Lawrence with his big project, his grand revelation of his life? He tells me he's going to zoom to the top of the best-seller list. I wonder how many bones will crack beneath his shoes."

The back door opened before I could ask him what he meant or answer his pointed question. Brianna stepped into the night. "So this is where you've stashed Willem," she said. "I should have known if there was a single man, Sarah Booth would have him out in the dark."

Before I could say a word, Willem cut in. "You flatter me, Brianna, but I came outside to have a cigarette. Now I must excuse myself. Lawrence promised to give me a brief education on the Southern baroque era."

He gave my hand a suggestive squeeze before he let it go. Moving with complete poise, he took Madame's arm. Brianna and I were left in the yard that was suddenly much colder.

"Too bad he's interested in Southern baroque," I said to Brianna. "If he liked Southern slut, he might want to talk to you." I headed for the back door, knowing that the battle lines were now clear. We'd each drawn blood.

Just as I reached for the door, it opened and a tall, slender man stepped into the night. He was backlit, his features hidden. "Sarah Booth," he said warmly, taking my hand and patting it. "How nice to see you. It's been years. I'm looking for my daughter."

He turned so that the light fell across his face. "Mr. Rathbone," I said in surprise. "I didn't know you were in Zinnia." Layton Rathbone and his wife seldom came home. He had extensive business holdings in Europe. Word around town was that Pamela Rathbone had gotten too good for her roots and preferred the rarefied air of "The Continent." It was beyond me how a man as nice as Layton had married Pamela and spawned Brianna.

"Just a pop-in visit to see my little girl." He patted my hand and dropped it. "Publishing is a new game for her. It always concerns a father when his baby takes on a new challenge, especially if you have a daughter like Brianna."

Layton Rathbone was a business genius, turning soybeans into gold, but when it came to his daughter, he was putty—to be molded by her every whim. Still, it wasn't up to me to point out that the idea of Brianna writing anything was laughable.

"My girl's out here somewhere, I believe," he said, looking beyond me into the shadows.

"Ummm," I said. "It was good to see you." And I darted into the house. I found a wall and eased around the cottage, scoping out the other attendees while admiring Lawrence's home—a place filled with art and objects of fancy. Every square inch of wall was hung with a sketch or painting. Books were everywhere, jammed in glass cases that also held sculptures and figurines, a mixture of fine and gaudy. A waiter took my empty wineglass and handed me a full one. I sampled a tray of hors d'oeuvres, delighting in the unexpected surprise of steamed collards stuffed with ground pork and pine nuts. Excellent.

Cece had arrived in a white dress that was simply dazzling: sleek, slinky, and sophisticated. I gave her a thumbs-up from across the room and indicated I wanted to talk to her when she had a moment. She'd have the lowdown on every guest. She was snared immediately by Dean Joseph Grace. He stood eye-to-nipple, continually smoothing back his silver-streaked dark hair as he talked.

Within seconds, their conversation grew heated. They both glanced across the room at Lawrence before they set to at each other again. To my surprise, Grace poked Cece in the chest with his little finger. Face red with anger, Cece drew back a fist, halted as if frozen, then abruptly walked away.

I was getting ready to check on Cece when I heard Madame's voice, raised high, from a corner of the room. She was arguing with a tall man whose silvery hair was badly in need of a cut.

Madame was clearly furious. She had to crane her neck to look at the tall man, and her expression was one of tight hatred. Even as I considered intervening, a hand on my arm pulled me up short.

"Sarah Booth, I need to speak with you."

Harold's gaze was intense, but there was the hint of amusement in his eyes. I felt a throb in my left thumb, the one Harold had suggestively sucked one cold November night in the magically lighted driveway of his home.

"Can we meet?" he asked.

"When?" I glanced over at Madame, whose face was beet-red. Lawrence had joined the group and was waving his hands, actually stepping between Madame and the tall man. Brianna and her father had also walked up. Layton held Brianna's shoulders, and I saw that he was no longer the dashing forty-year-old I remembered from my childhood. But he still looked good. Damn Brianna, she even had genetic advantages.

"Tomorrow is Christmas," Harold said. "Have dinner with me. I'm cooking a tur-duck-en. It's a turkey stuffed with duck and hen. Seven o'clock," he said. "I'm even making sugarplums."

"Fine," I agreed, anxious to see what vile thing Brianna was doing to Madame. In our little outdoor tête-à-tête, Madame had actually given me something to worry about. To my knowledge, Brianna had never written a word. But she did give interviews—to tabloids. And in them she took obvious pleasure in dissecting her past lovers. There was a cruel streak in her a mile wide, and if Lawrence was foolish enough to reveal secrets to her, she'd delight in telling them.

"Shall I pick you up?" Harold asked.

I surprised myself with the sudden anticipation I felt. "That would be wonderful, Harold. Now I have to check on something."

"Private eye business?" he asked, a worried gaze straying toward the arguing group. "Madame's upset. This whole book idea worries me. Lawrence's behavior worries me."

"I'll try and find out what's happening," I hedged, not wanting to admit to anything.

"You'll have to give me all the details tomorrow evening."

"We'll trade," I promised, slinking toward the arguing group until I was in eavesdropping position.

"Lawrence, tell them they can't do it," Madame was saying. She placed her tiny hand on Lawrence's shoulder. "Please. You promised me that the book would be about the Paris years. There's no point in going back to our youth."

"Cinematically speaking, the Delta era was the formative time for his character," the thin man said, nostrils flaring wide. "Those years must be included in the movie. As will the war years. Of course there may be cuts, but I will decide when and what to delete. Brianna has assured me that I will have complete artistic control. I demand that." His gaze seemed to dare Madame to resist.

Brianna clasped her hands in front of her hungry hipbones. She didn't need food; she fed on the suffering of others. "I've worked my tail off to get Sam to even consider this project, Lawrence. Gustav is expecting a movie deal. Don't be difficult."

"Artistic control isn't the same as good judgment," Lawrence said with the most reasonable tone I'd ever heard in the face of such bullying. "To stretch the story so long will only be tedious to the reader, or the audience, in the case of a movie. It's the heart of the story that deserves attention. Ramone Gilliard knew this instinctively. Look at his work."

"Gilliard is a pauper who couldn't get backing to make a film if he had a script written by God," the thin man replied. "And let me remind you, Lawrence, that you're far from a salable commodity. It's Brianna's name on the book and my reputation as a filmmaker that will pull this off. And so we don't have to have this conversation again, remember that in your day, when film was unsophisticated, there were restraints. We have cinemagraphic techniques, Lawrence." He patted the author's shoulder. "Leave it to the professionals. Now I need to freshen my drink." He walked away as if he were a captain who just dismissed his troops. Brianna was right on his heels.

"Lawrence," Madame said, her whispery voice shaking. "What have you done? What did you tell Brianna? Surely you remember we agreed that the past—"

"It's okay. Rosalyn, dahling, you know how those people are." He put a hand on her small waist. "Don't worry for a moment. I'm totally in charge." He took Madame's arm but it was Layton Rathbone he looked at. Brianna's father was standing beside a piano. He turned away abruptly and went after Brianna.

Lawrence's gaze swept the room and stopped on me. "Look, Rosalyn, you've caught the attention of our budding author."

"Is something wrong?" It would have been pointless to pretend I wasn't eavesdropping.

"A trifle," Lawrence said. "But how wonderful to see you, dahling. Red is your color. I made a very special treat for you. Stuffed okra. Let me help you with a plate. These modern women today, too thin. When I was in France working with Deneuve, we almost had to force the child to eat. Of course the director loved that ethereal look, those huge eyes. But I was always more of a Gina Lollobrigida fan. Rubens was right! A woman, not a twig. Fashion is so fickle, my dear."

His grip on my arm was firm but his hand was freezing as he led me away from Madame and in the opposite direction Brianna had taken. "Who is that self-centered bastard?" I asked him.

"Oh, a Hollywood type. Sam Rayburn. We want to bring out a movie simultaneously with the book. A big splash. That's the way it's done these days, or so I've been told."

I almost stumbled as the name hit me. "*The* Sam Rayburn? Producer of *Marilyn Goes Blonde*?" It was the blockbuster conspiracy movie about Marilyn

Monroe and her alleged murder with the use of Thorazine suppositories.

"Brianna assures me that he isn't an impostor. Very touchy breed. But don't take anything he says too seriously. Hollywood, dahling. Interest is like heat lightning, gone before you're even sure you saw it."

"What exactly *will* your biography cover?" I asked.

"Now if I told you, there would be no suspense. Look around. Everyone here wants to know what I'm including in my book. Tell me something, Sarah Booth. What's the most important element in writing?" he asked.

I realized he was talking to me as if I were actually writing a book. Now my lie would snap me on the butt. Still, I had to make a stab at it. "In nonfiction, the truth would be important. In fiction, I suppose it would be in creating a believable story."

"Dean Grace, our authority on everything, would give you an A for that answer."

"And you?" I was curious to hear his answer.

"Think a little harder. Why would I be motivated to publish my life history now?" He didn't wait for me to guess. "Revenge, malice, money. Or possibly truth." He let that sink in. "Good fiction is life laid bare, the actual emotional truth. Nonfiction is the illusion of truth. In nonfiction, detail is boiled down to a fine syrup. Truth is no longer a raw substance but a by-product of a process. The individual telling the story determines the process based on his own particular pathology. Right?"

I nodded, captivated by him and what he was saying.

"This by-product, labeled truth, has many uses. To sweeten, to flavor, to soothe, to tempt. To extract revenge." He waved an elegant hand around the room in a grand gesture. "They're all concerned what *my* truth will be." He laughed. "After two decades of being forgotten, it's wonderful to again feel the power of commanding attention." He selected a pickled mushroom and held it to my lips. "And for all of this fun, remember to savor the tiny pleasures, Sarah Booth. They're the only ones that truly count. Excuse me." He stepped back slightly and announced that dinner was served.

To my dismay, I was seated between a graduate student and the dean. They'd obviously come to the party together and chatted—over and through me—about books, authors, and Mississippi's place in the world of the literati. Of course they both knew everything about each subject. And what they didn't know, the bookstore owner across the table was glad to fill in.

During the delicious pumpkin soup, I learned of their importance in Mississippi in particular and the universe in general. The Chicken Muriel Spark was a treat, and I had a respite from the Ego Bowl while Lawrence explained briefly how he'd come to acquire the recipe. As the hired help served the chicken accompanied by beautiful crystal dishes of cranberry salad, Bailey Bronson, the bookstore owner, rose unsteadily.

"To Lawrence!" He raised his glass. "Underappreciated and now in the catbird seat." He swayed dangerously. "Renowned for his international Epicurean flair and his parties, at which too many people drank too much and spilled their guts. May he take his secrets to the grave. The sooner the better."

Madame's gasp was the only sound. Even the cutlery stilled.

"My death would benefit no one," Lawrence said as casually as if he were ordering coffee. "All pertinent information is already in writing. As a vessel of secrets,

I've been drained. But what abomination do you fear, Bronson? We'd love to know. I could hazard a guess if you'd like."

At that moment the waiters burst out of the kitchen with the cheese course. As they served, the tension grew. Only Lawrence seemed oblivious to it all.

When the waiters left, Lawrence smiled and nodded. "You're still not worried about that literary contest you organized. Some dazzling talent. I judged it, but the winner . . ." He arched his eyebrows. "There was some confusion, as I recall."

Bailey Bronson tried to rise but sat back down heavily in his chair. His hand trembled as he reached for his wine.

Time seemed to flat-line and stretch. I'd spent a few awkward weeks in a sorority house back in my younger days, but I'd never been in a room where the air seemed to itch as if it had been lightly salted. Everyone at the table focused on his or her food, except for Brianna. She blew a kiss across the table to her father. His smile was both tolerant and proud.

The kitchen door opened again and the waiters returned.

"Ah, the salad," Lawrence said, once again breaching an awkward silence. "Don't expect iceberg lettuce and pallid tomatoes. This is a fence row salad made from weeds gathered along the roadways and a hint of that wonderful plant that smells like an angel's armpit."

Beneath the clatter of china, individual conversations once again sprang up. I sat back in my chair and sipped my wine, examining the faces of my fellow diners. They were all practiced at the art of facade. Only Madame and Willem Arquillo made no attempt to hide their discomfort.

At last dessert was served, a persimmon parfait made from fruit Lawrence had gathered "at the Shelby hog farm. I had to fight the sows back." With the serving of the sweet, and last, course, the momentum of the party seemed to escalate.

Conversation rose in pitch and volume, and I was still left wondering why a man as charming as Lawrence Ambrose would choose to spend an evening with these tedious people. The purpose of the evening—the real purpose—and my role in it remained unclear.

Still, Lawrence's reputation as a chef was indisputable. I was captivated by the parfait, savoring the hint of Cointreau in the rich dessert. It was after my second spoonful that my tenure of boredom with my table companions paid off. The Dean dropped a blob of parfait on his lap and in the conversational lull that ensued as he tried to wipe it off, I heard Willem Arquillo talking about a new coffee bean he was developing on his finca in Nicaragua.

"So tell us, Arquillo, are you testing the new blend on the hapless Nicaraguan *campesinos?*" Bailey Bronson asked in a slur that was clear enough to stop all conversation at the table. "Isn't that what your father did? Some sort of testing on the Jews. Human genetics, I believe. Was it Auschwitz or Dachau? I hear Lawrence intends to spill his guts about your family in his book. That'll put the knife in your new political career as Nicaraguan Minister of Agriculture."

In the silence that followed, a thin woman I'd completely overlooked let out a choked cry. "Stop it! Just stop it!" The only color in the woman's face was a harsh flush that ran up her neck and into her cheeks. "This is enough stabbing and cutting. We all bleed!"

Beside me Grace expelled a burst of air, a sound of disgust.

"Bailey Bronson, you fool." Lillian Sparks rose to her feet. "You'd repeat any rumor that belittled someone else, hoping, I presume, to increase your own stature. You're pathetic." She reached over to the other woman. "It's okay, Tilda. Don't let them upset you. He's just a drunk, and Willem is far too cultured to even acknowledge him."

The bookstore owner sat taller. "I was addressing the Latin bean breeder, Lillian. But then you spent an awful lot of time down in the family barns, didn't you? Breeding is a big interest for you. Perhaps you think it's fine to experiment on beasts and humans. Is that why you never married?"

Willem rose slowly from the table, dropping his napkin in the parfait. "Bronson, if you wish to question my family and my honor, I suggest you stand up and do it like a man."

No one moved. Bailey tried to find his feet, but he was too drunk. He slammed back into his seat, tottered dangerously, then fell forward into his plate with a smack. The only appropriate thing seemed to be to toss my napkin over his head, which I did with flair. "Rest in peace," I proclaimed.

Lawrence stood at the head of the table and blew a kiss at me. "Dahling," he said, his blue eyes dancing with merriment. "I dub you Sissy Pom-Pom Ali. That's a combination of Mother Teresa and Muhammad Ali. You saved old Bailey's skin, though now that I consider it, that could be a crime against nature."

Laughter swept the table, and glasses were raised in my honor. Only Willem didn't pick up his glass. He was still angry, that Latin blood thundering. I could see it in his eyes, and it had a more potent effect on me than the wine, which I gulped down.

"Now that all of the excitement is over, let me tell

you some stories about the days of Henry Miller, Anaïs Nin, Hemingway, Fitzgerald—the Left Bankers." Lawrence recaptured the table with perfect grace. "It was a time of magic. We smoked Turkish cigarettes, drank, and ran wild in the more permissive climes of Paris."

While he talked I concentrated on using the private investigator's primary skill—observation. Harold sat with the attentiveness that marked his comfort with culture, and his pleasure in Lawrence. Layton Rathbone's gaze never left Lawrence, while beside him Brianna held a compact in her lap, studying her flawless face.

Off to my left, the Dean set up a buzzsaw of commentary. He was tipsy but able to enunciate clearly, and what he said suddenly caught my interest.

"Lawrence lived out in the wilds of Lula, you know," he said, talking still to the graduate student and an unconscious Bailey. I was getting worried that perhaps the bookstore owner had snorted his parfait and suffocated. But he gurgled, turned his head, and passed out again while Grace continued to talk.

"Lawrence worked as an entertainer and chef on a lake, a very interesting place. Tennessee Williams visited often, and others, but you won't hear Lawrence talking about those years. There was gambling and liquor. *And a murder*. I wonder if the old fossil will reveal that in his book."

"Sounds to me like something Ambrose made up to generate interest in his life." The graduate student licked the rim of his parfait glass. "I mean he was a brief luminary, wasn't he? This whole idea of letting a has-been model write his biography is scandalous. Strictly a publicity stunt. How else to reclaim a bit of spotlight?"

I felt a deep urge to shove the parfait glass down his throat. I was relieved of the urge thankfully when Lawrence adjourned the table. Coffee would be served in the European tradition, standing, so guests could move about, smoke, and mingle. I sprang from the table.

"A moment," Lawrence said, drawing everyone's attention back to him. "I have a brief announcement. I just want everyone to know that my book will be thorough and truthful." The room stilled. "Down to every little gritty detail. Those of you who are my old, dear friends—you'll all be stars." He smiled and I was reminded of the wolf in *Little Red Riding Hood*. "Each one of us sitting here hides something. I, of course, am included. I have my own shadow world where half-truths and base actions lie curled in a fetal position in the darkness. But I believe there is an accounting, and I prefer to have mine here. I hope you understand . . . and forgive me for whatever light I cast on your dark corners. Now let's have some coffee."

He walked away from the table, which suddenly erupted in a scraping of chairs as the guests evacuated. Madame had said Lawrence was playing out a dangerous scheme, and if his intent was to strike fear into the heart of his guests about what he might reveal, he'd done a thorough job of it.

I'd made it only a few steps from the table when I felt another hand on my arm, this one with perfectly manicured nails painted a glittering white to match her dress.

"Sarah Booth, I hate to ask," Cece said, "but could you possibly take me home?"

I turned to find her face blanched, her bottom lip trembling. "What's wrong?" I asked.

"I'm not well," she said, her voice shaky, eyes wild.

She didn't have to say it twice. She looked ghastly. "Let me get your coat and bag."

Lawrence spotted us and quietly escorted Cece to my car and carefully seated her. "I'll check with you later," he assured her. "We'll have a long chat."

When he turned to me, his eyes were lively in the moonlight. "Dahling, come to brunch tomorrow. We'll do something interesting with the carcass of this meal. And then we'll talk. Just you and I. Rosalyn is worried about me, and I want to set her mind at rest. I'm not the fool I might appear to be, nor am I an old crank bent on malice. The gloves must come off for the truth to come out. Come at nine."

"In the morning," I agreed.

I got into the car, where Cece was huddled in her coat, shaking like a leaf. She'd taken on a blue tint, but it could've been the moonlight reflecting off her glittery gown.

She groaned. "Why is Lawrence doing this?" It was suddenly like someone let the air out of her. There was a long sigh, and she slumped down in her seat.

I just looked at her and shook my head. I had no answer for her.

"Get me home, Sarah Booth. Just get me home."

3

Christmas Day dawned gray and gloomy. The promised snow had not fallen but seemed to hang low in the clouds, an impending, ominous pressure that made the drive to Dahlia House seem fraught with danger. In the Delta, there's only sky and land, and the sky rules. Against the lowering clouds, Dahlia House looked like a haven.

The weather perfectly reflected my mood. I'd spent the night at Cece's. Doc Sawyer had made a house call, giving her a shot of Valium and a lecture about the dangers of unchecked anxiety—work related, Cece insisted. When I left, she was sedated and asleep, the unexplained fear gone from her features. Now I needed strong black coffee and some rest. Unfortunately, I had time for neither. I was due at Lawrence's for brunch.

I was headed down the drive at a fast clip when a slant of sunlight broke through the clouds. Odd how an angle of light can evoke an avalanche of memories. I thought of my parents, sauntering down that drive on just such a winter morning, hand in hand. I could still hear my mother's laughter.

Or the Christmas Day that Eulalee McBride came galloping down it on Spartacus, an incredibly beautiful gray stallion that she'd gotten for a present. The light had caught her red braids and made her look like a Viking warrior.

Or Johnny Wells, walking down the lane toward the house, a box of chocolates in his hand as he came to pay a Valentine's call on me. I was twelve and mortified by his attentions. But it hadn't kept me from watching him come, black hair made sleek and brilliant as a crow's wing by the winter sun.

My life was captured in moments, some of them occurring in the lane that curved gently before me. But I knew that the past was so appealing only because the present was empty. I had diagnosed the disease; it was only the cure that eluded me.

Perhaps Jitty was right. Had I not slept with Hamilton Garrett V, the man I'd been hired to investigate as a mother-killer, I would never have known what I was missing. The feelings he'd awakened would have remained dormant. As my father used to tell me when I was a child, "You can't miss what you've never had."

As I continued—slowly—down the drive and through the flat land of the Delta, brown and barren after the cotton harvest but topped by a pink meringue of clouds so full of early light that my heart ached, I knew I wouldn't undo what I'd done. Fool for love or just plain fool, I would suffer the pain to pay for the pleasure. Thank goodness, though, I had no time for reflection. I was late for a very important date.

I made a mad dash up the stairs and into my bedroom where I jerked the first thing I could lay hands on

out of the closet and threw it on. Red was good.
Lawrence had complimented my red cocktail dress.
Clingy was not so good, but it would have to do.

"Try black. It's a minimizin' color," Jitty advised
from the doorway as I checked my reflection for un-
sightly panty lines under the beaded sweater dress.

My plans for Christmas Day had been starvation and
a form of physical abuse termed aerobics. Instead, I'd
signed on for two big meals prepared by gourmands.
Well, it was Christmas. Food was the one thing I had
left to enjoy.

In a pattern of bad behavior that codified the worst
of the Daddy's Girls, I'd opened every Christmas present as soon as it arrived. Instant gratification, the mantra of every red-blooded DG. End result—there was
nothing under my tree to slow me down this morning.

Jitty eyed me up and down. "You be sure and gobble
all the food at Mr. Ambrose's so that when you get
around to dinin' with Harold, you can eat like a lady
instead of a field hand."

"I thought you were watching reruns instead of
Gone With the Wind." Not for the first time I considered having the cable removed. Psychological studies
indicated that violent behavior on the little screen
warped the minds of children. Jitty was watching way
too many of the old black and white shows. She'd
bought into the theory that if she turned back the clock
on conduct to the fifties, then the era of moral prosper-
ity with families, mealtime, and cheerful children would
magically return. "Jitty, I might not love the way things
are now, but I won't ever be a Stepford Wife."

She ignored me completely and continued her tirade.
"No man wants a woman who can eat her weight in
cornbread dressin'. I found some back issues of *Bride's*

magazine up in the attic. I think we can fit you into somethin' decent if you don't balloon up another size. Those empire waistlines can hide a lot of—"

"I'll keep that in mind." I'd gained five pounds, not six dress sizes. As a ghost, Jitty never gained an ounce. I wanted to snatch her bald.

"Uh-oh," Jitty said and vanished.

I finished applying my lipstick just as I heard the sound of someone beating on the back door. Since Santa only used the chimney and I wasn't expecting any other guests, I hurried downstairs, curious as to who was knocking at my door.

I slipped into the kitchen and made my way to the window for a view of the back steps. A strange whine was coming from the back door. I eased open the curtains and found myself staring directly into the ice-blue gaze of Harold Erkwell. For the longest moment we simply stared at each other.

"Merry Christmas," he said, bent over in the strangest position. For all of his contortions, his salt-and-pepper hair was immaculate, his smile charming.

"Harold?" Just brilliant. Harold was a master of social intercourse, and I sounded like one of those sitcom idiots.

"I have a present," he said, not yet straightening up. "Open the door, please."

I did, eagerly. Harold was known for his exquisite gifts.

I never saw what it was that knocked me down, stepped all over me, and barreled through the swinging door of the kitchen. I only heard glass hit the floor and shatter.

"Sweetie Pie!" Harold cried out.

No amount of sweet talk was going to work now.

"You are going to die," I answered, all tender thoughts knocked slam out of me. What type of creature had Harold unleashed in my house?

A chair crashed over and more glass broke.

"I'll get her," Harold said, leaping over me as he ran across the kitchen and through the swinging door.

I remained on the floor, wondering if he'd remember his impeccable manners and rush back to help me to my feet. There was the sound of another crash and I leapt up, convinced that if I didn't get into the dining room, there would be nothing left.

"Sweetie, come here," Harold called pleadingly.

I was going to sweetie him! I pushed through the door and stopped dead still. A huge, raw-boned hound dog was standing in the center of the dining room table licking the hand-varnished oak. There wasn't a piece of china or crystal left on the table.

"What is *that*?" I asked, pointing at the creature that sat down on the fine oak table and scratched a floppy ear.

"It's Delo Wiley's hound. You said you wanted one. So I picked out the youngest, took her up to the vet, got all her shots, had her spayed, and here she is." His smile was amused, apologetic, and quite charming. "Merry Christmas, Sarah Booth!"

As usual, the purr of the Roadster boosted my spirits. The heavy gray sky met the dark brown gumbo of the Delta soil in the far distance. I sniffed the air and thought I detected the probability of snow. At least it would relieve the pressure, though it would do nothing for my blood pressure. I'd left Dahlia House entrusted to a ghost and a four-legged food disposal. After

Harold fled the scene of his crime, Sweetie Pie managed to open the refrigerator and eat a pound of cheese, half a dozen deviled eggs, the remains of a baked ham, and two California-raised tomatoes. Not exactly a balanced meal. Then she'd fallen into a food coma at my feet.

I cruised along the highway toward Magnolia Place and pulled down the lane to Lawrence's cottage. I loved that driveway. In the gray morning light, the huge oaks seemed tinted with melancholy.

The big yellow tabby sat on the front porch and meowed as I got out of the car. He held his ground when I knocked at the red front door.

When Lawrence didn't answer, I knocked again, a bit louder. I checked my watch; I was on time. The cat pawed at the door, demanding entrance. Inside, several other cats called out, strange eerie yowls that sounded like babies in distress. The yellow tabby answered them, a deep, guttural cry that made the skin along my spine tighten.

"Lawrence! Mr. Ambrose!" I knocked harder.

Yellow cat threw himself against the door.

I tried the knob and hesitated when it turned easily in my hand. All I had to do was push it open and walk inside. Lawrence Ambrose was the most gracious man I'd ever met. Still, he wouldn't appreciate an invasion of his privacy. I'd never actually met another SIGOOS (Southern Intellectual Gentleman of the Old School), but I understood instinctively that privacy would be a number one priority.

I cracked the door and called out again. As my eyes adjusted to the dimly lighted room I saw the cats sitting on the back of the sofa. They were motionless, silent, watching me. I had a sudden, vivid recollection of a photograph I'd seen once in some travel magazine, probably in the dentist's office. It had been taken in

Egypt. Great cat lovers, the Egyptians. The photograph was of a dead person—the corpse guarded by his cats.

The exact rightness of that image froze me at the front door. Three cats sat on the back of the sofa. Feline soul guards. The yellow cat bolted into the house and ran to the sofa. He disappeared for a moment, then reappeared on the armrest. With great aplomb he took his seat in the gloom of the still shuttered room. They all faced the interior of the house.

Stale cigarette smoke hung in the air, and I recalled that Willem had been the only smoker. But often after a few drinks, inhibitions loosened and good intentions fled. Almost everyone in the world was a partially reformed smoker.

"Lawrence!" I forced myself forward, walking past the living room and deeper into the darkened house. The dining table had been cleared and the party food put away, but there was no sign that Lawrence had begun to prepare our brunch.

"Lawrence!" No answer. "Mr. Ambrose!" I called. Perhaps he'd heard about Cece and gone to her house to visit her. But surely he would have called to cancel our date.

Beyond the dining room was the kitchen, and I went there. Wineglasses were drying in a rack, the only indication that there had been a party the night before. On the sideboard were two highball glasses, both dirty. I sniffed them. Bourbon. Not too difficult to deduce when a Jim Beam bottle was nearby. Glancing in the sink I saw a broken glass. Beside it was a pool of blood. Splashes of red spattered the yellow tile backwash and countertops.

It was an old-style house and a kitchen door gave on to a small, dark hallway which undoubtedly led to his bedroom and bath.

"Lawrence," I called, moving into the darkness. Something brushed against my leg, and I almost screamed before I recognized the yellow tabby.

"Meow," he cried. "Meow."

He darted forward. My eyes had adjusted to the light and I saw the foot and leg, sprawled at an odd angle. Feeling along the wall I found the light switch and flipped it up.

Lawrence was propped against the wall. His left hand was wrapped in a blood-soaked towel, his pale eyes staring straight ahead but unseeing. Beside him was the telephone, the receiver lying in a pool of blood that seemed to have spread over a large portion of the hallway. I'd never seen so much blood in my life.

The cat nuzzled at his foot as if begging him to get up.

I didn't know what to do. For a long moment I stood there and tried to force my brain to work. It looked to me as if Lawrence had been cleaning up the last of his party when he cut his hand on a glass. He'd obviously been trying to call someone when the blood loss became too great and he died.

As I tried to think what I should do next, I wanted to slide down to the floor beside him and simply sit. I held back the urge to panic. There was no hurry now. Death had robbed time of all importance. My only task was to act sensibly.

The night before, Lawrence had been fine. But death was like that—striking suddenly and without warning. I knew from personal experience. My parents had been driving through the long flat stretches of the Delta where oncoming traffic could be seen for miles. They'd been laughing and talking when a drunk plowed into them. In an instant they were dead.

I knelt down and tried to console the crying cat. He

kept batting at Lawrence's leg. I noticed there was a froth of blood on Lawrence's lips. Staring at his pale profile, the high aristocratic nose and the thick white hair, I felt tears threaten. It was ridiculous. I'd met him twice. But the sense of loss was real and not something I could deny. It was hard to explain, but I felt I'd been robbed.

Perhaps it was that motivation that made me linger in the semidarkness of the room with a corpse guarded by four cats. I didn't want to call 911. It came to me suddenly. I knew what I needed to do. Before strangers touched him, I wanted a friend at his side. I unplugged the line to his phone and found another one in the kitchen.

"Madame," I said when she answered. "It's Sarah Booth. There's no gentle way to say this. Lawrence Ambrose is dead."

I expected the genteel sound of sniffling. I was completely unprepared for the shriek of rage that echoed from the phone and made the cats on the sofa stand up, arch, and spit.

"That bitch murdered him," Madame cried. "I told him she was treacherous. Don't touch anything. I'm on my way."

The phone went dead in my hand.

I took a seat on the porch in one of the rockers and waited for Madame's arrival. Whatever official action needed taking, it would be best to let Madame do it.

I heard the crunch of wheels in the lane and looked out to see her oyster-colored Chrysler. She jumped out of the car, brushed past me with a tiny bleat of grief, and rushed into the house. I softly closed the door on her sobs.

The sky had dropped lower, it seemed, a pervading grayness that made my bones pop and crackle as I paced the front porch and tried not to hear the wrenching sounds of Madame's grief. The spike of truth that came to me was sharp and painful. Narrow, narrow is the view of a self-absorbed person.

Perhaps I had known her too long as the dance instructor who tolerated no foolishness or excess in her students. Dance was a discipline that required exactness. Lawrence, in his enthusiasms and generosity of spirit, was the antithesis of that.

I had seen only the contrast between the two, and not the emotion. It had never crossed my mind until that moment, her grief audible in the still morning, that Madame was in love with Lawrence. I'd seen it at his party and failed to call it by name. The way they'd communicated with looks, the regard they held for one another. His hand on her elbow, guiding and protecting; her concern for him. She had loved him for a long, long time.

It hadn't occurred to me that people of their generation still participated in romantic love. Had my parents not died when I was a child, perhaps I might have had a pattern for love through the ages. Now I found myself alone and too aware of the consequences of love as I sat out on the porch of the cottage staring down the moss-draped drive of old oaks and into the gray Delta that was both my home and my heritage. The first flakes of snow began to fall.

It seemed a long time before Madame came out. When she did, the cats followed.

"I called the police," she said. "That bitch won't get away with it."

I nodded as if I agreed. Loss is often followed by fury. It is part of the process.

"She murdered him. I don't know how, but she did."

I wasn't certain he was murdered, but I was positive

who Madame was pointing the finger at. "Is it possible he had an accident? Maybe when he cut his hand his heart gave out."

Madame's eyes were black chips of flint. The Indians used the hardest stones and deer horn to make tiny arrowheads for bird hunting. They might have used her eyes.

"Lawrence's heart was perfectly healthy. The old fool guarded it like Fort Knox. No fatty buildup and no romantic damage, at least none recent. It wasn't his heart that killed him. And no one dies from a cut hand."

I didn't want to argue with her. We stood side by side watching the snow fall. The flakes were big, piling down on top of each other. Beautiful. In a short time the Delta would be transformed.

"Last night Lawrence had a sudden change of heart. After the party had broken up, I stayed to talk. I finally made him see the truth and he told me he was canceling the book deal with Brianna." Madame's slender hands gripped the porch railing. The flesh was red from the cold but the knuckles were white with tension. "She didn't want to write about his life. She wanted to write a scandalous tell-all and reap the financial rewards of smearing Lawrence's name. She wanted to pick scabs and poke at scars. She's a greedy bitch. She'll try to go ahead with this book, but I won't let her."

Her assessment of Brianna was right on, but there was an edge of something else in her voice. "If Lawrence is dead, can she still write his life story?"

"She'll try," Madame said. Pushing off the rail she began to pace back and forth on the icy porch. "She'll try. You can count on that. She has the legal right to try. And she claims she has signed papers, a few tape recordings, ridiculous things like that. But she doesn't have any of the real facts—unless she stole them. Lawrence was smart enough not to trust her at all. And she'll never get anything else. I'm certain Lawrence named me executrix of the estate, and she hasn't counted on that."

I wasn't sure how effective that role would be in stopping Brianna, but I didn't say anything. Madame needed to vent her rage and sorrow. I could listen.

"She honestly thinks she can murder him and go back to New York to write her book. Well, she's wrong about that. Very, very wrong. She'll go to prison if I have anything to do with it."

"This will all work itself out," I said in an attempt to soothe Madame. She was chugging up and down the porch like a locomotive. All I needed was for her to stroke out on me.

"Listen, Sarah Booth." Madame took a seat in one of the rockers and began to fumble in her purse. She drew out a checkbook and wrote. She tore off the check with a flair and handed it to me. "Cece said you get ten thousand a case." She pressed the check into my hand. "There's ten. I want you to prove that Brianna Rathbone killed Lawrence."

I took the check and held it as if it were dangerous. "What if I can't prove it?" I didn't have the nerve to ask what if it wasn't true. It wasn't that Brianna wasn't capable of almost anything to push her own agenda. I just didn't see how she could have cut Lawrence's hand and held him down until he bled to death. And why would she kill off the source for all material for her book? It didn't make good sense.

"I don't care how you do it, just do it. Last night, Lawrence finally understood what I'd been trying to tell him. Brianna didn't care about the truth. She cared about money. He gave her the key to the kingdom, and she was about to destroy everything Lawrence held dear. She had no respect for his past or his future. She didn't have any New York connections and that Sam Rayburn is a tabloid opportunist masquerading as a producer. That's what Lawrence finally understood last night. That's why he told her he was pulling out of the book. That's why she killed him."

Madame had given me a motive. Sort of. "But you said she could still publish the book anyway."

"True, but it would be unauthorized. The other point is that the publishing world will be fascinated by Lawrence now that he's dead. Alive, they didn't have time to read one of his proposals. Now that he's dead, they'll fall at his feet and fawn over what a talent he was."

Sad but true, too. A corollary motive. The book would sell like hotcakes *because* Lawrence was dead.

"I'll get a copy of the autopsy report," I told her as I heard the approach of sirens.

"There are things missing from his house," she said.

The abruptness of her tone startled me. How could she tell? The place was jammed with paintings, sculptures, drawings, books, plants—artistic endeavors of every kind. Everything looked neat and orderly to me. "What things? How do you know?"

"Whoever was with him after I left took his journal, a scrapbook of clippings . . ." Madame's gaze slid down and away, "and the manuscript. He always kept them locked in a cabinet and they're gone. Maybe you can find some clues inside." She bent down and scooped up the yellow tabby cat. "If only Apollo could talk."

If only, I thought. As the sheriff pulled up, I dutifully

went back inside the house for one final look. Someone had cleaned up after the party and things seemed to be in perfect order. But how would I know?

I heard Madame speaking with Coleman Peters outside. She told the sheriff that she believed Lawrence had been murdered, but she didn't mention Brianna's name. I noticed a slip of folded paper at the edge of the sofa and picked it up. I was about to read it when the door opened. Instinctively I tucked it into my coat pocket.

Coleman and a young deputy I didn't know came into the house. For a few seconds they gazed at Lawrence in silence.

"He was that writer, the one who had the fling with Ginger Rogers," the deputy said with a proper note of awe in his voice.

"He was a wonderful old man," Coleman responded, his brow furrowed as he began to examine the body.

"I heard he could dance like—" The deputy stopped at the sound of Madame's sniffling. "Sorry, ma'am."

"He was a wonderful dancer," Madame said.

She left the room and I heard her big car start and pull away. I was left facing a curious Coleman.

"A new case, Sarah Booth?" he asked.

"You tell me."

He shook his head. "No sign of a struggle but an awful lot of blood. We'll see what Doc Sawyer has to say." He put his hand on my elbow and eased me out the door. Outside, his grip tightened, halting me. "I don't have to tell you that this could get crazy. Lawrence was famous in his day. If any hint of foul play starts to leak . . ."

"My lips are sealed," I assured him.

"I find it a little odd that you and Rosalyn Bell are

out here together with a dead man. What's going on?" he asked.

"I'm not sure," I said, eager to make my getaway. I liked Coleman, but I didn't want to be interrogated. "If I come across something, I'll get with you."

"Be sure you do, Sarah Booth. There's something troubling about finding you here. Something deeply troubling."

4

"Fetch, Sweetie Pie," I urged the lanky hound as I
tossed the Evan Picone shoe down the drive. It landed
under the first sycamore, a bright red splash against the
blanket of new snow. Unmoved by the sight, Sweetie
Pie flopped to her back and proceeded to do her doggy
version of snow angels by wiggling on her back and
wagging her tail.

"Get the shoe," I ordered. She'd already eaten the
mate. The dog had a distinct preference for Italian
leather. I'd hoped, using her fondness for fine footwear,
to teach her to retrieve. Or at least occupy her for a few
moments. In her brief tenure at Dahlia House, she'd
toted up a hefty price. Still, the light of joy in her warm
brown eyes whenever I gave her as little as a kind word
had to be weighed.

That it was Christmas Day held no joy for me. Not
even my neon wreath had been able to lift my spirits.
The death of Lawrence Ambrose weighed heavily on
my mind. Madame's check was still in the pocket of my

coat, another burden. In my heart, I believed Madame's reaction was emotional. There had been so much blood. Lawrence must have severed a major artery and then fainted as he was trying to call for help. I determined to hold her check for a few days and then return it to her, once the anger phase of her grief had passed. The harsh truth was that Madame didn't have ten thousand dollars to waste.

Chasing the shoe for Sweetie had made me warm and I took off my wool jacket and hung it over a tree limb. I returned my attention to the bounding hound. I had just retrieved the shoe when I saw a showy red car turn down my drive. No one in Zinnia drove such a car, a classic T-bird convertible. I stood up, wiping my cold, wet hands on my jeans. Sunlight had followed the snow, illuminating the solitary man in the car. I waited as the vehicle flashed red through the bare sycamores and finally come to a stop not ten feet away from me.

Willem Arquillo stepped out, the sun catching the golden highlights in his hair. His teeth were white and perfect as he gave me a smile that made it seem as if he had anticipated this meeting for at least half his life.

"*Hola, Señorita Delaney,*" he said, exaggerating his accent as he came toward me, a gift from a land kissed by sun, Spaniards, and some genetic component of tall, blond gods.

"Willem," I replied. "What brings you to Dahlia House?"

He lifted my empty hand and brought it to his lips, then stepped back, his gaze drifting to the red shoe I held. "Perhaps I've come to play Prince Charming to your Cinderella."

"I was playing fetch." I tossed the shoe again, but there was no sign of Sweetie. She'd disappeared.

He took my elbow and gently began to usher me to the front porch. "Perhaps you should go inside and warm up," he said.

His hand on my arm, even through my old green sweater, was extremely warm and supportive. Extremely. As if his fingertips had tiny little electric heaters in them whirring down to my skin. Had he said he was going to help me to the brink of hell, I would have followed his lead.

He hadn't answered my question and I was about to ask again when I saw the dog. She came out from under the porch, a blur of black, rust, tan, and big white teeth that had everything to do with the-better-to-eat-him-with line in the fairy tale.

"Sweetie!" I cried, thrusting myself against Willem in an attempt to save him from the hound.

Unaware of the pending attack from the dog and responding only to the attack from me, his arms came around me, one hand landing squarely on my newly robust bust.

Tearing myself away from Willem's embrace, I grabbed Sweetie's collar.

"What kind of creature is that?" Willem asked, stepping back from the dog, not in fear but in distaste. "I've never seen an animal so unfortunate-looking."

"She's a red tic." I was hanging on to her collar for dear life. Her normal tail-wagging charm had turned into Cujo. She barked in a deep, hoarse-sounding bay, and her ears flopped wildly as she lunged at Willem.

"I never realized there was such an ugly breed."

"Get inside." It wasn't exactly a gracious invitation to enter my home, but I wasn't feeling exactly gracious. He'd violated the code of conduct. In the South, be it the realm of wealthy Buddy Clubbers or the lowliest shotgun shanty, there's a list of things that aren't open for criticism. Dog is at the top, followed by pickup, gun collection, and shoe size—small for men and large for women.

When Willem was safely inside the front door, I released Sweetie Pie. "Guard the porch," I told her. "If he comes out with the family silver, eat him up." I gave her a pat as I slipped inside and found Willem admiring the bust of Stonewall in the foyer.

"I enjoy the fact that all Southerners claim some relationship to at least one Confederate general. If I recall my history, Jackson wasn't one of the really bloody ones. Too bad. Is he a great-great-uncle? A cousin?"

"Sperm donor," I said with the most charming smile in my arsenal. For all his handsome physical appearance, Willem had a way of getting under my skin.

"In my country, we also have strange blood ties." His hazel eyes actually seemed to darken before he turned his gaze away.

It was an odd comment after what I'd heard at Lawrence's dinner party. I fell back on the training of Aunt LouLane and simply made an interested sound. Overt interest can clam a man right up.

"But I didn't come to discuss history," Willem said, his long fingers ruffling the tinsel wreath around Stonewall's neck.

Remiss on both conversation and hospitality, I came to my senses. "Would you like a . . ." What should I offer? The day had gotten away from me, and I was at a loss to think of the proper libation for the hour.

"Brandy would be lovely," he said.

I opened the door of the front parlor. Willem stopped at the threshold, awed by the blinking neon and the huge tree that dominated the corner of the room.

"I thought I'd call the Daughters of the Confederacy and enter the holiday decorating contest," I said with some mischief. I had a sudden mental picture of Brianna Rathbone's decorations—all white twinkle lights, designer-tied plaid bows, ceramic angels, and matching gift-wrapped presents.

Willem had not moved. "I've never seen anything like it," he finally said. His hand, so fluid and sensual even with the smallest gesture, took in the neon. "A blend of traditional values and pop art. I'm envious. This must be photographed."

I'd anticipated horror, but his face reflected a deep interest in my handiwork. It occurred to me that he might be playing me for a fool. I got two glasses and poured us both a healthy brandy.

"What brings you to Dahlia House?" I asked again. Willem was taken with the decorations, but he was also carefully evaluating everything else in the room. After he accepted the drink, he took a seat in the leather chair that faced mine.

"To share the holiday sentiments of good cheer," he said with one eyebrow arching just enough to be devilish. "You left the party last night without giving me a chance to say good night."

He was smooth, and even though I was aware of it, I still couldn't help a tiny flutter. I dropped back to the safety of cynicism, my defensive trump. "Right."

His smile acknowledged my hard shell. "I came because I heard about Mr. Ambrose. You discovered the body."

Tiny little goose bumps trembled on my arms. "Yes, that's true."

"The shock, it must have been severe."

His eyes were a light hazel with golden flecks that seemed to shift in soft patterns. Perhaps it was just the effect of the blinking neon. "Yes." I lowered my gaze and waited.

"The sheriff certainly believes it was an accident, right?"

I shrugged, aware of his subtle implication that it might have been something other than an accident. "It would seem."

"And just when he was about to complete the book about his life." A pause. "Such a shame that the project is ruined."

"Is it ruined?" I asked. If Willem was pumping me, I decided to turn the tables.

Willem leaned across the space and touched my hand. "Perhaps I misunderstood. Will Brianna continue with the book?"

The touch of his hand distracted me with a flash of sensory neon, but something in his tone made me cautious. "I'm not certain what her plans are. Maybe you should ask her."

Willem chuckled. "You know Brianna, always so secretive."

I very slowly withdrew my hand. Willliem had come to pump me, but I didn't understand why. He could get better answers from Brianna. "I do know Brianna. How well do you know her?"

"Well enough. We parted friends."

"How nice," I said, wondering exactly which one had pulled the plug on the relationship. As far as I could remember, Willem had been spared the tabloid treatment. There had been no public recriminations in print. Now, at least, I knew why he wasn't asking her questions.

"This book, are you comfortable with Brianna writing the life of Lawrence?" He finished his drink and carefully put the glass on the table beside his chair.

It was impossible to determine the underlying basis of his question. He and Brianna had been lovers. What were they now? Had she sent him over here? "I actually don't have an opinion. You knew them both, what do you think?"

I watched his reaction and caught a flicker of something I couldn't define. "Brianna has connections in the publishing world, and perhaps the movies. I'm just not certain of her ability to get the facts straight. She has a very casual relationship with the truth."

"How deftly put." Brianna was a liar and he knew it.

"You didn't happen to see the manuscript in his home, did you?" Willem asked.

I was beginning to see the motivation for his visit. Disappointment has a metallic taste. "I wasn't looking for it," I said as I poured him another drink. "What, exactly, is your interest in Lawrence's book?" It was time to fish or cut bait.

He shrugged, that deliberate lifting of his shoulders that could mean almost anything. "I have my vices like all men. Curiosity is one of them. You left last night after Lawrence made his announcement." His smile was tinted with enjoyment. "Everyone was terrified of what he might put in that book. I suppose I've fallen victim to the desire to know the gossip."

I didn't believe that for a second, but the art of interrogation required that I resist the impulse to point it out. "I believe Lawrence was playing with everyone," I said. "You know, having his fun at their expense." His eyes held only mild amusement at the thought. If he feared something in the book, he knew how to cover himself. "How long will you be staying in town?" I asked, sipping my drink.

One corner of his mouth turned down. "Who

knows? Once I finish my negotiations on behalf of my country, I may stay for a while. I'm a farmer as well as an artist, Sarah Booth. The desolation of the Delta appeals to me. The land speaks to me. Perhaps I'll paint here."

I hadn't expected that response. "But your paintings are so political. I wouldn't expect you to find inspiration in a foreign land."

"An artist must grow, Sarah Booth. Besides, I've found something else that interests me." He stared directly into my eyes, and I felt the force of his charisma. There was no doubt he was a predator, and he was letting me know that I was the lamb of choice. At least for the moment. Though I had conflicting feelings about him, my body responded to the thrill. I shifted in my chair and saw him smile.

I had to gain control—of myself and the conversation. "You said earlier that you'd come to Zinnia to finish some business with Lawrence. If it wasn't the book, what was it?"

"Are you always so . . ." He turned both hands out, fingers fluid. "Direct?"

"Are you always so evasive?"

He laughed, a full-bodied sound of enjoyment. "Ah, a woman who understands the art of conversation. I like you, Sarah Booth, so I'll answer your question. My business with Lawrence did not originally involve his book. I didn't know of it until I came here. My friendship with Lawrence goes back to when I was young, back to my first days as an artist. It is for that reason that I came to visit. Of course, the book intrigues me." He finished his second drink. "Now, may we talk about other things. Why don't you tell me about the book you're writing?"

Conversing with Willem was a pleasure and a challenge, but I had another obligation. "Forgive me, Willem. I have plans." I wanted plenty of time to prepare for Harold.

Perfectly cued, Willem rose to his feet. "It was lovely to see you, Sarah Booth. If it's agreeable, I'd like to call tomorrow. Cece said you would be the perfect guide to show me the Delta. She said you could reveal the land's secrets. I need to explore, to learn."

"Tomorrow?"

"We'll take a drive." He made his way to the front door where he stopped, framed at the threshold of my home. "At two?"

"Okay," I agreed with my heart beating far too fast. Oh, the treachery of hormones.

He walked across the porch and was halfway to the steps when he turned back. "Lawrence didn't leave anything for me, did he? An envelope or box of some sort? He told me at dinner that he had something he wanted me to have."

"I don't recall seeing anything with your name on it."

He shrugged one shoulder. "Lawrence could be a man of mystery when he chose."

"I'll ask Madame. She's the executrix of his estate."

"Of course," he said, nodding. "Tomorrow at two."

His long legs took his tight butt down the steps and to the red car. With a languid wave of his hand he was gone. I was left standing on the porch. Sweetie Pie crept out from under the porch, her stomach groveling on the ground.

"Sweetie!" I'd never seen her so pathetic.

She licked the toe of my boot and whined. I knelt to console her, earning a full-fledged lick in the mouth.

I felt a whisper of wind beside me. Jitty had arrived.

"Better get you some new panties," she said in a dark voice. "I get the feeling that pair you're wearing is about ready to fall off."

"Nonsense," I said with as much starch as I could muster.

"Honey, you got the look of a woman who is seated at a banquet table after a two-week fast."

I tried to compose my face, knowing that if I looked in a mirror, I would see exactly what Jitty described. "He's very handsome," I acknowledged.

"Handsome, charming, sophisticated, talented, yes indeed, he's all of those things."

I was surprised she agreed with me. "So what's the problem?" I turned to face her. There was a small, black, furry creature clamped on her head, undoubtedly sucking her brain out through her hair follicles. I took a swat at it, thinking of body snatchers and other podlike creatures with . . . fur?

"It's called a poodle cut," Jitty said defensively. "It's the latest do. Judy Holliday was wearing one in this terrific movie where she pretended to be dumb to get men to do what she wanted."

Tentatively I examined what was obviously a hairdo masterpiece of anal retentiveness. "Does it hurt?" Even ghost hair couldn't endure such torture without a twinge of pain.

"It's the latest craze," she said, patting it lovingly.

"Jitty, you're overlooking one little thing in your quest for moral stability."

"What?" She gave me a sideways glance.

"The fifties weren't exactly the best of times for women. Especially women of color." Hah! I had her now.

"If you'd settle down, marry, and produce an heir, I wouldn't be forced to choose between my needs and yours."

With that zinger, she did a fast fade.

Sweetie's tail thumped the porch. She was looking perkier and had actually retrieved the shoe. I'd give her another five minutes of fetch before I got ready for Harold.

I went into the yard and threw the shoe. "Fetch, girl! Get it!" To my surprise she went right after it. But instead of bringing it to me, she hauled ass under the porch. No amount of coaxing could bring her out. On my hands and knees I went after her.

I heard her happy tail thumping and found her about ten feet under the edge of the porch nested in a pile of goodies, the shoe still in her mouth.

"Sweetie," I cried in dismay. She might not fetch for me but she'd been working overtime on her own acquisitions. She had a remote control—not mine—a catcher's mitt, and several tennis shoes, mismatched but name brand. The dog was a thief. I looked around the vast expanse of under-house terrain. No telling what else the dog had hidden.

"Sweetie," I whispered, gathering up the stuff. "They don't rehabilitate dogs. It's the gas chamber." I backed out from under the house and headed straight for the toolshed. I intended to bury the evidence before anyone else saw it.

5

The problem with getting dressed too early is that a woman is left with too much time on her hands. Coiffured, perfumed, made-up—there's not a single, solitary, useful thing she can do except look good. After two hours of labor, I had no intention of risking damage to the hard-won effect, so I found myself, nails aglitter with a dazzling coat of red, sitting in my neon pulsating parlor with a glass of Jack Daniel's. I decided to savor the moment and congratulate myself on having earned enough money to buy good bonded whiskey.

Sweetie Pie was lounging at my feet, content with her three cans of Alpo and a half of an apple pie she'd stolen off the kitchen counter. I rubbed my stockinged foot over her belly, feeling the swell of food. She wasn't a great dog, but she was one helluva calorie disposal unit.

The doorbell rang and I checked my image in the mirror that hung over the mantel. Harold would be suitably impressed with my dark green velvet dress with its mandarin collar and gold frogs.

I opened the door with a demure smile and found myself face-to-face with a short person completely covered in a black hooded cloak. The figure swept past me with a harsh command—"Shut the door! Quickly!"

I recognized Madame's tones and reacted as always. I obeyed and followed her into the parlor where she proceeded straight to the crystal decanter and poured herself a heaping amount of JD.

In a move that only a dancer could achieve, she swirled to face me. As the cloak billowed about her, the hood fell back. Madame's dark eyes sparkled with unshed tears. "What have you discovered?" she asked.

Though I wasn't much of a student of dance, drama was my love. I had to give it to her for theatrics. "It's Christmas Day," I reminded her gently.

She put a small fist to her mouth as she composed herself. "Someone murdered Lawrence, and you're only interested in a holiday!"

I picked up my drink and took a long swallow. The image of Lawrence Ambrose on his floor was clearly etched in my memory. The sound of Madame's sobs as she knelt beside him were also recorded in Memorex. "I'll check tomorrow," I assured her. "Nothing was open today." Besides, the autopsy had to be performed, dictated, and transcribed. These were details she didn't need to think about.

"The manuscript is missing," she said, pacing in front of the fireplace. "There's no doubt Brianna stole it. We have to get it back. We can't let her publish it."

This was a point that needed clarification. "How far along were they?"

Madame shook her head. "I don't know for certain. Lawrence had been talking to her for several months. He'd been working on the years he spent in Paris. That was what I thought the book would encompass. Those years of war and intrigue. Lawrence led a fascinating life. That would have been enough, a wonderful book."

She stopped, and for a moment I thought she was finished. When she resumed, her voice had lost all softness. It was as flinty as her eyes.

"At the party, that dreadful Sam Rayburn was talking about using everything, from cradle to Magnolia Place. It was like he owned Lawrence's life and everyone in it. And Lawrence didn't object."

I'd overheard a portion of that conversation. Rayburn wouldn't have been my producer of choice. "Lawrence wanted this opportunity," I reminded her.

"Yes, his plan." Her laugh was short and bitter. "He said that flies couldn't resist a fresh . . . well, you get the idea. He said the only way to sell anything was to create anticipation, a buzz, and that the best buzz came from a swarm of eager flies. He wanted everyone in that room to buzz. He knew that each of them, challenged with the possibility of revealing their dirty little secrets, couldn't resist talking. They would swarm and buzz, and the demand for his book would be irresistible."

I had so heartily disliked most of the people at the party that I understood Lawrence's motivation—on several levels.

Revenge has its place in the gamut of human needs.

"Surely, though, he didn't intend to torment you?" Madame had loved Lawrence, and though they'd never married, I was certain he cared equally for her.

"Oh, he assured me that everything was under his control. The problem with Lawrence, though, is that he underestimated the meanness and cruelty of his fellow humans. He was out of his league, and he paid with his life. And now his private journals are missing. His address book, all of his correspondence. That bitch Brianna has them and she'll publish a book if she can."

Sweetie Pie had settled at my feet, emitting the sound of soft snores of contentment in direct contrast to Madame's frenetic energy. "Can you tell me exactly what Lawrence was writing?" This was crucial. If the book was truly devastating to someone, then stopping it from being published would be a prime motive for murder.

"I honestly don't know," Madame said, her voice hardly louder than a whisper. "He hadn't been feeling well the past couple of weeks. His was pale and cold. And then the cat—he was distraught over Rasmus dying. Whenever I stopped by, Brianna was there, slipping in and out, pressing him about the past. She convinced him that her name and her connections in the publishing world would propel the book to the best-seller list. She claimed she was dating that publisher. Lawrence was completely blinded by—" She broke off abruptly and took a healthy belt of Jack Daniel's.

"By what?" I asked. My gut told me this was a vital point, and one that Madame didn't want to confront.

"By his desire to be read," she finished, her voice trembling. "You can't imagine what it was like for him. He was famous once, sought after, respected, consulted about literature and art. He was somebody, Sarah Booth. And the last years have just passed. He watched his contemporaries achieve great success. Tom and Truman and Nell, all of those powerful Southern voices finding people who read them again and again, while his wonderful books were forgotten, out of print."

I could easily understand, but there was a problem. "It would have been Brianna's book, not his."

"Not really," Madame said, finally looking at me. "Not at all. Lawrence was actually doing most of the writing. I know that for a fact. And if the book was successful, what would it matter? His books would be reprinted, his body of work revived. There would be new opportunities. He had it all figured out."

Perhaps. "And he really thought Brianna could deliver?"

"He did. And in a way, I think he felt sorry for her. Her career, too, was over. In another year no one in fashion would remember her name. He saw it as an opportunity to help her."

"Why?" The question popped out. Brianna Rathbone wasn't a woman who elicited my sympathy. She was a very wealthy woman, if not in her own right, then by inheritance. Layton Rathbone was a millionaire many times over.

Madame went to the decanter and tipped a splash of liquor into her glass. "I tried to tell him that she wasn't to be trusted. Now, if she has the manuscript, she'll publish it. I know she will. She'll ruin anyone who gets in her way. We have to get it back."

We were back at the original point. Madame had grown short of breath as she talked. I went to her and eased her down into a chair. What she said made just enough sense to trigger my neck-crepe reaction. The flesh at the back of my neck was prickling and drawing, a very unladylike behavior.

The doorbell chimed and I knew it was Harold. I started to the door as Madame's small hand caught my wrist in a grip that would have done Charles Atlas proud.

"You have to get the manuscript back," she said, "and then prove that Brianna Rathbone is a killer."

Staring into her black eyes, I could only swallow. Madame had always been demanding, rigid, passionate, and suffered no fools. But I'd never seen such iron as I did in her gaze.

The bell chimed again and she released me, but her eyes held me firmly in place.

"There's a lot at stake, Sarah Booth. Whatever you do, don't mention this to another living soul. Promise me."

"Not a word." I turned to go to the door, shaken by Madame's naked determination. Sweetie Pie almost bowled me over as she hurried forward. This time there were no growls, only a metronome tail that was as dangerous as a swinging blackjack. She whined fetchingly at the door.

"Harold," I said, opening the door, trying hard to sidestep Sweetie's baton tail. No matter how many times I greeted him, I was surprised by his handsomeness. His gray wool suit was perfectly tailored, offset with a red Christmas tie that sported a blinking tree. Odd that the foolish tie clip only made him look more distinguished. And desirable.

"Sweetie." He swept the dog into a big bear hug. "And nice to see you, too, Sarah Booth," he added as he stood and took my hand. His ice-blue eyes danced.

We hadn't made it past the doorway when Madame entered the foyer, her hood back in place, her face partially concealed.

"Good evening, Harold," she said before she turned to me. "Remember, Sarah Booth, I'm counting on you." She swept past us into the night, leaving a palpable void of silence.

"She's upset," I said, opting for the Daddy's Girl tactic of obvious understatement. This would, hopefully, put Harold in the position of assuming the tower-of-strength pose, which would then make him forget to wonder about Madame's presence in my home and her strange remark.

"Lawrence's death is a tragedy," Harold said as he stepped inside. "I'm certain she's devastated. They were best friends."

I cast a keen glance at Harold. He sounded downright emotional. "How about a drink?" I led the way into the parlor.

Harold stopped at the threshold, an abrupt movement that sent Sweetie Pie crashing into the backs of his knees. Red and green neon pulsed, washing him in rhythmic light. "Very nice," he said. "Very Elvis."

It was the perfect description. "Thanks." It hadn't occurred to me, but music was what I needed. I pulled out Mother's 45 of "Blue Christmas."

"Ah, Sarah Booth," Harold said with a grin. "Let's dance."

Though I'd never admit it to Jitty, Harold's stock rose once again in my eyes as he settled a firm hand on my back. He held me tight and slipped into movement with the music. It was exactly what I needed. By the time we left Dahlia House half an hour later, I'd forgotten Madame and her demands. It was Christmas Day, or the last few hours of it. A tiny bit of celebration wasn't unwarranted.

We carried our festive mood into the car and along for the drive. Harold's Christmas decorations were unexpected. Candles in red and green paper sacks lined the drive. I let out a sigh of appreciation. Terribly, terribly romantic.

Inside, there was the smell of fresh-cut cedar from the boughs that lined his staircase. Holly and wild magnolia leaves formed a bower, and from it hung the mistletoe. I had kissed Harold only once before. I'd been surprised, then, by my reaction to him. This time I was prepared. The restraint he used made me want to press for more. As before, though, he refused to accelerate the embrace.

"Our past indicates we should proceed with caution," he said gravely as he ran his hands over my bare arms and concluded the kiss with a brushing of his lips across my cheek in a tease. "You returned my ring, and I tried to recapture something that was long gone," he reminded me.

He spoke truth. I didn't bother to say that I could forgive him for taking off with Sylvia Garrett since I'd had my turn with her brother. I wasn't much of a scorekeeper in home runs of the heart, but we seemed to be even in the errors department.

He seated me and poured us both a glass of wine. Then he set the room ablaze in candles.

We ate in that rare light where everything gleamed and sparkled, even my conversation. We took champagne to the fireplace and sat down to listen to Beethoven. I found myself leaning against Harold, his arm around me, as I sipped the bubbly he'd poured into Waterford flutes.

"To the future, Sarah Booth. Yours and mine," Harold said. "And to Lawrence Ambrose, a man of talent and generosity."

It was an easy toast to drink to. "Tell me how you knew Lawrence," I said. Though the hour was late, I didn't want to go home. It was Christmas. Harold's arm around me felt just right, creating a 3.2 on the Richter scale in my right thumb as I remembered a moment beneath fairy lights.

"As an adult, I became reacquainted with him through his wonderful work. But I knew him when I was a child. He was a friend of my Aunt Lenore's. He encouraged me to pursue music, but it was mainly our love of art that drew us together in the past few years.

Lawrence was a fine sculptor. His work is in the best collections in Europe."

"Sculptor, too?"

"He was many things, Sarah Booth. It's one reason he never achieved the acclaim he deserved in this country. He refused to focus. That made him hard to categorize—and easy to dismiss."

"What was he like?" The champagne had made me warm and lazy, and I relaxed against Harold, enjoying his solid warmth, the beautiful music, and the flames of the fire.

"He'd come to visit Lenore, and sometimes he spent hours with me. He had the imagination to create another world, a place of enchantment for a young boy who craved attention from an adult."

I didn't know a lot about Harold's childhood, but I knew enough to know it hadn't been like mine. "He sounds wonderful."

"He was. And kind. He made me feel special, Sarah Booth." A log shifted in the fire, sending up a shower of sparks. It broke the spell of memory and Harold sat a little straighter. "Lawrence did what few people ever have the courage to do. He took life by his own terms."

"And he may have paid the price." The words were out of my mouth before I thought of the implications. Harold, though, was not as sizzled by the wine and candlelight.

"What are you saying?" He turned so that he could look into my eyes. "The cut on his hand was an accident. He died while trying to call for help—didn't he?"

I shrugged, hoping to end it there.

"If foul play was involved . . ." His gaze focused beyond me for a moment. "Last night, that party, it was all about the book. He wanted everyone there to worry about what he'd written, what he might reveal."

I could see Harold mentally going over the guest list from the night before. It didn't take him long to get to the Rs. "Will Brianna go forward with the book?"

"I don't know." I put every scrap of sincerity I could muster into those three words. I sipped my champagne and decided to shift gears. "Harold, what could have prompted trouble between Brianna and Lawrence?"

"What makes you think there was trouble?"

The habit of answering a question with a question was strictly male, and highly annoying. But Harold's pale blue eyes held real worry. "Madame says the manuscript is missing. She said Lawrence pulled out of the book deal with Brianna the night of the dinner party."

"Do you have any proof?"

I cleared my throat softly. "I'm not accusing Brianna of anything. Yet. I'm merely telling you what Madame said. Do *you* know of a reason someone might hurt Lawrence?"

"Brianna had no reason to hurt Lawrence. In fact, it would be to her detriment." Harold got to his feet and poked the fire even though it was burning fine.

"Okay, someone other than Brianna."

"There was talk that Lawrence left Paris for a reason. He had a falling out with some of the other writers there, and when he left, he broke all ties. But there was also a story before that." He hesitated just long enough to qualify it as a tease. "Something to do with gambling and a place called Moon Lake. Lawrence worked up at a casino near Lula when he was a very young man. It's all forgotten now."

"How do you know this?" Harold was a virtual encyclopedia of Delta gossip.

He gave me a look. "My Aunt Lenore ran away from home when she was sixteen and took a job as a guitar player in the same lodge. It was a gathering place for young artists. They worked at the casino and talked literature and art and music. It was 1940, Sarah Booth. Times were hard. Women had no freedom, and risk was a drug for the young."

Putting aside Harold's chivalrous defense of Brianna, this was the second mention of the old casino. "There was a murder there, right?"

He finished his drink. "I don't know. Lenore seldom talked of the past, yet she was trapped by it. She couldn't accept the restrictions of that time or her family's expectations."

Perhaps no one had asked the right questions. "What's she doing now?"

Harold shifted. His gaze dropped to the empty glass he held. "She hanged herself."

"I'm sorry." I felt as if I'd been slapped. The buzz of the champagne flattened, leaving the bitter aftertaste of regret. "Harold, really. I'm sorry. I had no idea."

"I was ten. She was still a beautiful woman, only forty-two. It's odd, now that I think about it. She never spoke of it, but that summer on Moon Lake may have been the only time of pure joy in Lenore's life."

Harold refilled both our glasses. "To my knowledge, she never accepted an invitation to any social event. She worked at the Presbyterian church. That was her life." His gaze found the fireplace and held to the flames. "She hanged herself from the wrought iron fence in the church cemetery."

I drank my champagne rapidly, but the bubbly had lost its magic. I had another glass, but the evening had turned as flat as my buzz.

"I'd better head home," I said at last. Harold, though perfectly mannered, had also slipped beneath the surface of the past. He and his dead aunt would spend this Christmas night together. And I would have Jitty.

He wrapped me in my coat and went out to warm the car. While I waited I toured his home, a beautiful old house filled with art. It was with some degree of surprise that I found myself gazing into a pair of piercing eyes that were familiar. The work was labeled "Self-Portrait: Lawrence, 1940." The image of the young writer was compelling, but the background also caught my interest. Behind the lanky young man who held a fishing rod was a huge lake. It was done in charcoal, a sketch more than a polished drawing. But far in the distance on the lake was a boat, and in it a young woman and a man were engaged in a clench. I was no art critic, but I found it interesting that Lawrence had chosen to include that little passionate scene in his self-portrait. What it meant was anybody's guess. Was it part of his view of himself, or something he'd witnessed that had affected him?

Ah, I wondered. What secrets had Lenore Erkwell brought back from Moon Lake? It was a question she'd never be able to answer for me.

6

The real problem with Christmas for Delaney women is the day after. The feast is over, the buildup has peaked, and all that's left is the decline into creative ways of disguising leftovers. Since I'd chosen to accept invitations to eat out, I didn't even have leftovers for entertainment. No bubbling pots of turkey soup. No turkey sandwiches made with dinner rolls and cranberry sauce. No chopping and dicing for turkey salad.

The only person more unhappy than I was Sweetie Pie. She moped under the table, warming my feet as I drank black coffee, as if she knew I'd let her down in the menu department.

"You know it's a scientific fact that people resemble their dogs," Jitty said from behind my chair. She stared over my shoulder at the crossword puzzle I was stumped by.

I didn't bother to respond.

"It would seem to me that Harold would have preferred somethin' with a little more bloodline and a lot less ear." Jitty walked around the table and glanced at my loyal canine. "That's a yard dog, Sarah Booth. At least your Aunt Elizabeth only let cats in the house."

"You thought it was fine for Chablis to be in the house," I reminded her. Chablis was my friend Tinkie's little Yorkie.

"Cha-blis was temporary. Besides that little dog had class."

"Back off, Jitty," I said, pushing aside the newspaper. "Sweetie and I have bonded." I looked up and almost choked on my coffee. Tiny pink donuts were all over Jitty's head. Spoolies! Aunt LouLane had used them once in my hair. It had taken three washings to get the kinks out.

"You'd bond with anything that stood still for five minutes," Jitty muttered, oblivious of my horror.

"I didn't sleep with Harold," I pointed out, not bothering to add that if I tried he probably would have said no. For a man who made his living manipulating money, he wasn't a risk-taker in love. "Did you leave your hair up in those things all night?" When she finally took them down it was going to be worth watching.

"You wouldn't sleep with Harold because he's already asked to marry you. Why should you sleep with him when you can chase down some other man who has no interest in makin' an honest woman of you? Sex isn't the measurin' stick to rate a relationship, you know."

I liked Jitty better when she was interested in pregnancy rather than matrimony and when the long, free hairstyles of the seventies better represented her attitude toward sex. Lately, she was as tight as those damn little hair curlers.

"Sex isn't the only critereon, but it is important." I decided to devil her a little, to see if she might shoot a

Spoolie across the room. "Anyway, Harold aside, there's Willem to consider. He looks like a man who wouldn't mind procreating."

"He's a dangerous man," she said, but with an obvious lack of conviction. "Lordy, he's fine-lookin'. That smile could blast the starch out of a girl's petticoats."

"Jitty!" She wasn't completely brainwashed by the fifties.

"That's all the more reason for you to steer clear of him. He's unemployed, from what I can tell. Of course that seems to be a drawin' card for you."

She was referring to several past boyfriends, none of whom I cared to defend. "He's independently wealthy," I pointed out.

"So he says." She cast me a worried look.

"He's eligible. And talented." I rubbed my hands up my arms for effect. "And he's on the market."

"Honey, a one-eyed armadillo can see he's not the marryin' kind. Better keep your libido down and your panties up." Her back stiffened and she set her mouth in that unforgiving purse. It was interesting watching Jitty hog-tie her own ardor.

"Latin men are excellent lovers. You know, a little hot blood for a cold Delta night—"

"Probably got a passel of chil'ren and none with his name." She was about to wear a hole in the floor with her pacing.

"We don't really care about a last name, do we, Jitty? Just as long as the Delaney blood runs true. Look at the bright side, he'd probably be more than glad to escape the bonds of matrimony and leave the two of us to raise a child." I scooted back my chair. "I'm going to the hospital to check on a few things."

"Forget that artist. Now a single doctor would be

ideal," Jitty said. Her dress billowed on crinoline petticoats. She actually swished as she paced back and forth. I caught the fragment of a TV memory—Gale Storm concocting a plan with Esmerelda Nugent to foil Captain Huxley?

"Nah, doctors are so . . . clinical." The little devil on my shoulder was having an excellent time. "But I hear cowboys stay in the saddle just a little bit longer."

"A doctor," she said, ignoring me. "Compassionate, healing, dedicated, smart, a man with all of the right qualities."

"It's the twenty-first century, Jitty, not Beaver time. Try on the concept of an HMO."

"The problem with you, missy, is all you want is the playboys. Loose livin' and fast times. You better listen to me or you'll end up payin' the wages of sin."

I paused in the doorway. "If someone offered some sin, I'd hop right on it and ride into the sunset." I couldn't fade like she could but I darted out the door before she could respond.

In Mississippi, the position of coroner is elected and requires no specific talents or educational background. In my last case involving the Garrett family I'd managed to get myself in dutch with the current coroner, Fel Harper, who was now under investigation by the state for his role in body swapping.

Technically, though, he was still coroner until he was formally indicted. Figuring Fel would not be real happy to see me, I decided the best plan was to go straight to Doc Sawyer at Sunflower County Hospital.

I pulled into the parking lot of the low-slung, yellow-brick building and went through the emergency room door, hoping to avoid answering any questions from prying receptionists.

Doc Sawyer had an office off the operating room. He'd been there since I could remember, a retired general surgeon who did emergency work and also served as pathologist on the rare body that came in and required an autopsy. In Zinnia, most people died of plain, uncomplicated things. Lawrence was viewed as a potential problem.

I found Doc at his desk, feet propped up and hair wild and white about his head. He had a thick mustache and looked a lot like Mark Twain. He talked like a cross between Atticus Finch and Billy Bob Thornton on one of his bad-character days. He'd been our family doctor since I was a child.

"How's it going, Doc?" I asked.

"Good." He pointed at the coffeepot. "It's about like cooked mud, but help yourself."

I poured some into a Styrofoam cup and waited a few seconds to see if it might dissolve the cup. When it didn't, I loaded in some sugar and Cremora. After five spoons of the white powder, the coffee was still a murky black. "Doc, thanks for coming over to Cece's. She's going to be okay, isn't she?"

"Panic attack. She needs to take a vacation from her job. Maybe you can talk to her. But you're here about Lawrence Ambrose, aren't you? I heard you found the body."

"Yes." I took the seat he indicated. "What did he die of?"

"It's an interesting case," He dropped his feet to the floor and sat up, riffling some papers on his desk. "The natural assumption is that he bled to death."

"The assumption?" Doc's nose was red and I knew

he'd been drinking, even though it was only nine in the morning. Hell, a bit of brandy wasn't a bad idea. It would probably evaporate in the coffee anyway.

"An artery in the back of his hand was severed. That was, technically, the cause of death."

"So you're ruling it an accident?" I was relieved. "There was a broken glass in the sink."

"It was an odd cut. And he bled out mighty quick. It might have been a tragic accident." He shook his head and I didn't doubt his regret, but there was also a hint of excitement in his voice as he continued. "There are a couple of things that trouble me. I'm running more tests, but right now, Lawrence's death is something of a mystery, Sarah Booth."

It was exactly what I didn't want to hear.

"The test results won't be back for several days. Until then, I don't have a verdict. You'll just have to wait."

After Doc's coffee, I needed something absorbent in my stomach, so I took myself over to Millie's Café for some biscuits and a bit of history.

Millie's was the gathering place for most of the male cliques of Zinnia and a large part of Sunflower County. In the early mornings, the Buddy Clubbers had the largest table in the far right corner with the merchants huddled up on the left, the farm leaders by the rest rooms, the new-moneyed folks—scandalously including two women—in the center, and the general Zinnia breakfast-eating individual or family scattered at the smaller tables throughout.

It was a place where folks came for a cup of coffee and to pick up news while pretending to read the newspaper. While the Buddy Clubbers—the elite, white male faction of the Delta—could eat at Millie's, it was considered inappropriate for the daughters of those men, the Daddy's Girls, to dine there. I'd often gone there with my father, where we sat in a booth not part of any clique. I'd always thought it was because my father was a judge and that people were afraid of him. I'd learned as an adult that wasn't necessarily the truth.

The bell on the door jangled as I walked in. Millie was behind the counter, her apron tied around a waist still small and firm for a woman her age. She gave me a smile as she carried four heaping plates to a table of farmers who were the only patrons. It was that time between breakfast and lunch when normal people were at work, or otherwise gainfully employed. I liked to stop by the café in the in-between hours. Millie and I were developing a solid friendship.

After she'd refilled everyone's coffee, she put two cups down in front of me and poured for both of us. "What's happening?" she asked.

"Tell me about Lawrence Ambrose," I requested, "after I get some hot biscuits."

She retrieved my order from the kitchen and then perched on a stool behind the counter.

"Lawrence was a great man. I sure hated to hear he'd passed on." She pushed a wisp of blond bangs off her forehead. "I know he was old, but it seemed to me he ought to last forever." She made a small face. "Hell, I'm old."

Millie was in her fifties. Lawrence would have been long gone on his European adventures by the time she was old enough to remember him. "I was hoping you knew something about him."

She shook her head. "Not like you want. He dropped by to eat some after he came home to Zinnia."

She pushed her bangs back again though they weren't close to her face. "He gave me some recipes. That short rib stew with a side of cheese grits that everyone loves—that was one of his."

I'd already eaten my biscuits, but the idea of the stew made my mouth water. Pavlov and Sweetie Pie came to mind. "Was Lawrence close to anyone in town, other than Madame?"

"Who?" She looked at me like I was crazy.

"Rosalyn Bell." I had stepped off the path and into deep cow-poo. Millie wasn't the kind of woman who would agree to call anyone madame, not even a ballet teacher.

"I hope to goodness she and your psychic buddy, *Madame* Tomeeka, don't get into a hair pulling over which one is the grandest." Millie refilled the coffee cups. "At any rate, I do remember the first time Lawrence came home from Europe when one of those professors from over at Oxford had this big to-do. It was like a Lawrence Day where the town celebrated him. There was a parade with a band and baton-twirling dancers." Her face softened into a smile as she sank into her memories.

"The first time he came home?"

"Yeah. I was little. I went with Aunt Bev. She was the only one in the family who read. She came over from Greenwood with copies of some of his books. Pissed her husband off." She laughed. "Somewhere they'd gotten an elephant for Lawrence to ride. It was hot, and I remember the elephant left tracks in the asphalt at the elementary school. That's where they'd set up for the big barbecue and party.

"After the parade Lawrence sat on a rug under this red and white striped umbrella with his legs crossed like a sultan and wrote in the books people brought by."

Again she shook her head. "It was a day that would leave an impression on any kid."

"Did anything special happen?" I was more curious than hopeful that Millie could shed light on Lawrence's past.

"He bent down and looked right at me and said, 'Someone should use your eyes to design a china pattern.' I didn't understand, but Aunt Bev told me it was a compliment."

"This would have been in the late fifties?" I was trying to pinpoint the time frame.

She nodded. "I was seven or eight. I remember my dress, a powder-puff blue organza with five starched petticoats."

"What, exactly, was the event?"

"Lawrence had come home, to write and bring prestige to the State of Mississippi." She intoned the last with great dignity before her expression changed to one of lively mischief. "He didn't stay a week. There was some big falling out with the university man. They were supposed to have a job for Lawrence, and when he went over to start teaching, none of it had actually come through. I don't know where the fault lay, but the upshot was that Lawrence went right back to Paris, but not before he created a big stink in the newspaper. It was a scandal, but I don't remember the details."

The word "motive" was flashing behind my eyelids like a neon Christmas wreath. "Would your Aunt Bev?"

"She might. She spent a summer with Lawrence and some others up at some lake." Millie's blue eyes focused sharply on me. "What are you up to, Sarah Booth. Is this a new case? Something about Lawrence?"

I didn't show a single emotion. "As you know, my work is confidential. Even if I had something to tell you, I couldn't."

She squeezed my hand. "Call Aunt Bev. She lives over in Greenwood. Call her." She wrote the telephone number on a napkin for me. "Tell her I said I loved her."

I put the money for my breakfast on the counter. "Thanks, Millie."

"Thanks aren't necessary, but I sure would like to know what you're working on."

"I'll tell you before I tell anyone else," I promised.

"Well, if you need backup." She put one hand on a hip.

"I'll keep that in mind." And I would. Millie had proven herself tough and reliable when she'd been kidnapped by Veronica Garrett and Pasco Walters. I could go a lot farther and do a lot worse, as Jitty would say.

Since I was already downtown, I stopped by the bakery, selected the largest and cheesiest Danish, and headed for the newspaper. Cece was too young to remember the scandal, but she could give me access to the newspaper files.

Several reporters who had once ignored my very existence perked up as I walked through the room.

"Working a case, Sarah Booth?" Garvel LaMott called out.

"Your mama," I said with a fake smile. I'd gone to high school with Garvel and he had been quite the successful snoop, sniffing out cigarettes in the bathroom and Wild Turkey in the book lockers. Unfortunately, he was also a tattletale. I hurried into Cece's office—the only private one—and closed the door.

"Sarah Booth, dahling, you look . . . robust."

"I see my tenure as your own personal Florence Nightingale did nothing to reduce your venom. Thanks instead of insults might be in order," I said with annoyance, dropping the pastry sack on her desk. Robust was not exactly the same as calling me Peggy-porker or Little Miss Ham Hocks, but it was close enough.

"Touchy about our weight, are we?" Cece stood up and ran her hands down her svelte hips. One advantage of having been a man was that she would never suffer from middle-age spread.

"What is this royal plural crap? And that dah-ling." I drawled it out. "You stole that from Lawrence."

She sat back down and studied me. "I didn't steal it. He gave it to me." A single tear dribbled out the corner of her eye and she batted it away. I noticed that for all of her perfectly applied makeup, she was still a little pale.

I sank into a chair, ignoring the fact that it was stacked with old newspapers. "Are you really okay?"

"It was just an anxiety attack. It's just so awful about Lawrence," she said, accosting another tear before it could leave track marks. "When I came back from Sweden, after the surgery, he came to see me. My own parents wouldn't speak to me but this famous writer appeared at my door with an armful of paper whites and daffodils that he'd stolen from mean ole Mrs. Hedgepeth's sidewalk." She started laughing. "He took every single one of her flowers, and he made me put them in a vase in the window so she could see them."

We were both laughing. "You didn't know him before that?"

"Of course I knew who he was. I'd read all of his books. I learned to cook with his recipes. But I'd never met him until that moment. I was shocked." The laughter was gone and the tears were dangerously close to the surface again, but she continued.

"When I was well, he dropped by with some net gloves and a black hat that he said Audrey Hepburn had worn in a movie. He told me they'd bring me luck and always, whenever anyone tried to hurt me, to visualize myself wearing them and to use the royal plural. And he said he wanted me to use his trademark 'dahling' so that it would continue after he died."

"You never said a word about any of this," I accused.

Cece spied the pastry bag on the corner of her desk. She snagged it, opened it, and peered inside. "I never had a reason to say anything. Until now. No one ever accused me of *stealing* a character trait. Until now."

"Okay, so I'm fat *and* bitchy. What's your point?"

"No point. I just like to keep you in line."

"Practice sex alone," I whispered, leaning forward.

Cece laughed, biting into the Danish with a show of her former good appetite. "So are you looking for a writing assignment or working something else?" She took another large bite of the pastry. "You can talk until I finish eating, then I have to work. Deadline at eleven."

It was ten-thirty, so I had to talk fast. "Do you remember any gossip about Lawrence coming home from Paris in the fifties?"

"The time Ole Miss didn't have the teaching job for him?"

"That would be it."

"Check the files. Lawrence never said anything to me about it, but I've heard stories. There was something in the paper, some sort of literary feud going on. I don't really remember." She took the last bite. "You know where the files are. Tell Glenda that you're looking up something for me."

"Thanks," I leaned across the desk, "dahling."

Her eyes narrowed in calculation. "There was something about a death threat. Some dark secret, a hidden past." Her forehead furrowed. "Let me know what you find. I'm doing a story for Sunday's paper on Lawrence. I've heard rumors that some people believe Lawrence was murdered. Is this a new case, Sarah Booth?" Curiosity glinted in her eyes.

I smiled and shrugged. Cece was crazy as a run-over dog if she thought I'd stoke those fires.

She swallowed the last of the pastry. Her gaze dropped and I could tell she was about to cry again.

"He seemed very fond of you," I said, failing utterly at comfort.

"He called last night to check on me, after you'd fallen asleep. I think he genuinely cared."

"What time did he call?" I asked as innocently as I could.

Her gaze lifted in a smooth motion—radar. "You *are* working on a case." Her eyebrows arched. "I can't say exactly, but it was after midnight because he said something about it being Christmas. And I'll tell you something else. He said the party was over, but I don't think he was alone."

7

The last time I had to go searching in the morgue of *The Zinnia Dispatch* I'd been lucky. My quest had taken me back into the late seventies and early eighties and the information was still in bound volumes. When I put my request before Glenda, the morgue librarian, she pointed me in the direction of the spools of microfiche. The year I sought was 1958, summer. With Millie's hints about elephants and umbrellas it didn't take long to discover that the Barnum and Bailey Circus was in town in June, hence the availability of an elephant in the Mississippi Delta. Although the circus was the headline news for the day, Lawrence's arrival home was bottom of the fold, front page.

The whiz of the printed page made me dizzy as I rolled the film through the viewer. It was a week later, June 15, 1958, that the vitriol began to spew. The first salvo was on the editorial page, where Lawrence had written a letter. It was a masterpiece of wit and whiplash. The gist was that he'd been promised a job, which upon his arrival had been withheld because of his lack of "formal" education. My favorite part of the letter went "as if the gatekeepers of the hallowed halls of learning could recognize a truly educated man. These academic pretenders give evolution a bad name. Indeed, the monkeys in the jungle are howling disclaimers of any kinship to these rogues."

I was laughing out loud. Dean Joseph Grace made the response for the school almost a week later, pointing out that Lawrence had led them to believe he held a degree. I read his rebuttal, hearing in my mind the pompous drone that had drilled my ear like a woodpecker at the dinner party. "When it became obvious that Lawrence was not formally educated," Grace wrote, "the decision not to offer the position was unavoidable. The criteria for excellence in teachers at Ole Miss could not be lowered, not even for such a fine writer."

Right. Somewhere between the offer and Lawrence's return to Zinnia, someone had decided to slam the door in his face. Degrees had nothing to do with it. I made a note to check the policy at Ole Miss.

It was in the next issue of the paper that Lawrence volleyed back with a front-page interview in which he challenged the university dean to a public display of knowledge—a match—to be performed in the Zinnia High School auditorium with the whole town in attendance to judge who was the most learned man. Lawrence said that if Grace bested him, he would drop the issue and never speak of it again.

A brilliant and sneaky gambit! I loved it.

Grace declined, saying that it was beneath the dignity of a full professor to indulge in public displays. Yes, indeed, the trump card for cowards—a claim to dignity.

It was almost too delicious but ultimately useless. So

far there was no hint of dark secrets. The two men had obviously patched up the dispute because the dean had been a guest in Lawrence's home. I'd observed them closely, and there had been no open animosity that I could detect.

No sooner had I thought that than I turned to the next issue of the paper and saw the banner headline. "Author Threatened By Vile Caller."

There was a photograph of a very handsome Lawrence coming out of the courthouse. Though debonair, Lawrence was clearly shaken. I read the story with interest.

Lawrence, upon his return to Zinnia, had been put up in the Sunflower Hotel, a Delta luxury establishment during the fifties. It had still been in operation when I was a little girl. My father went there in the mornings to sit in the shoeshine chair and let Old Mose buff up his shoes before he went to the courthouse. The lobby of the hotel was marble, and there were huge columns and always fresh flowers. I particularly remember the artwork, strange sculptures of men who were half beast. Centaurs and satyrs, my father had explained, reminding me that it would be rude to climb up on one and try to ride it.

I never saw one of the rooms. By the time I got old enough to consider the benefits of a hotel room, the Sunflower had burned and been razed. But I had heard frequent stories about the elegance of the rooms with draped beds and bath towels kept in warmers. It was a place Lawrence would have enjoyed.

This time the reporter, one Sarah Gillespe, had gone into great detail. The focus was the death threats Lawrence had been receiving, always late at night, always from a man, who threatened him with "a bullet to the brain" if he didn't "quit humiliating the university and get out of town."

Ole Miss was famous for its devoted alumni, and though the formal education there had been known to knock the rough edges off more than a few graduates, no school could be expected to completely change the genetic structure of a good ole boy.

As indicated in the story, Lawrence had taken the threats to the sheriff. The reporter went on to discuss the dispute between Lawrence and the school about the hotel bill. Lawrence refused to move to other, cheaper quarters, saying he'd been guaranteed a room at the Sunflower until his cottage at Ole Miss was available. Since there was to be no cottage, he was staying at the Sunflower until he could book passage back to Paris.

It would seem that Lawrence had them on breach of contract on two counts—if he had any of the deal in writing. Which was the crucial question never asked in the story.

There was one quote from Lawrence that stuck out. "Justice is only a word in this state. Money and power have always ruled in Mississippi, without regard to truth or right. It is a system of corrupt politics and decay."

It was not the eloquence that held me, but the fact that it didn't exactly fit in with the rest of the story. I made notes, jotting down the threats. It was apparent from the story that the sheriff, John Wayne Masters, had not shown much interest in acting in Lawrence's behalf. It was also clear that Lawrence had made the threats public as a thumb in the nose to someone.

I read the story again. There was something not right, but half a century of passing time and a lack of knowledge of the players had blurred the issues for me.

Why had Joseph Grace offered Lawrence a job and then reneged? What did Lawrence know that threatened Joseph Grace to the point that he would stir such a public stink? The bit about Lawrence not having a formal degree didn't hold water. Lawrence was a renowned and respected author and artist. He would add stature to any university program. Something else was involved, and I'd been a private investigator just long enough to realize that Dean Grace wasn't going to tell me voluntarily.

I closed my notebook and returned the newspaper reels to their slots. As difficult as my previous case had been, this one looked as if it would be harder. Lawrence's death was real and immediate even if the motive was buried in the past along with the bones of many of the people involved.

Living at Dahlia House, with the family cemetery just outside the kitchen window, I had a lot of traffic with the dead. Living with Jitty, I had a lot of abuse from the dead. Bones didn't scare me, but finding the places they were buried was a challenge.

The good news was that I had several leads. I could drive to Oxford and talk with Dean Grace, or I could talk with Madame. Or I could find Johnny Albritton, the local telephone man. Since I wasn't in a mood for ego or tears, I decided to find Johnny. We'd gone to school together, though he was a bit older.

I tracked him down at the Western Auto on Main Street in Zinnia. He was buying plumbing supplies for a new addition to his home, and he gave me a slow grin when he recognized me.

"Well, if it isn't the private detective," he said. "I read all about you in the newspaper."

"Don't believe everything you read," I warned him.

Cece had a way of exaggerating things. It worked to my benefit, but it was also a little embarrassing.

"What do you need, Sarah Booth?" he asked. "A wiretap?"

I rolled my eyes. "No, a little history."

"Now that doesn't sound too dangerous. Shoot." He was examining PVC pipe fittings as we talked.

"Back in the fifties, the old hotel in town, what kind of phone system did it have?"

"It would have been a central switchboard. If I recall, it was still in use in the early seventies when it burned. Now, that was a tragedy. They don't make buildings like that anymore." He looked at me through a two-inch fitting. "You haven't changed since high school, except maybe to look a little prettier."

"You always were a smooth talker." Johnny had been a standout on the basketball team and, though handsome, was so shy he hardly spoke to anyone. The joke around high school had been that he had to get his best friend to ask a girl for a date for him. "What would happen on the switchboard if a call came in to someone staying in the room?"

"The operator would plug in the call to the room and put it through." He put the pipe down. "Are you asking if the operator could listen in?"

"That, and could a call be traced?"

"Yes and yes." He braced one hand on a shelf and gave me his full attention. "What's this all about?"

"I'm writing a book," I told him. "I had an idea for some phone calls. Threats, you know, that kind of thing."

"Uh-huh." He picked up the same piece of pipe and dropped it in a basket at his feet. "There wasn't such a thing as a private call where a switchboard was involved. The operator could listen in whenever she chose. Not much has changed today. Almost every call can be traced, if you have the right setup and enough pull with the law."

"Thanks, Johnny."

"You're welcome, Sarah Booth. Let me know where I can buy this book you're working on."

His sarcasm pushed me down the aisle. Funny, back in high school I'd never suspected that he had wit. But I'd found out what I wanted to know. Sheriff Masters either had a good reason not to investigate Lawrence's complaints, or he didn't believe they were real. Or perhaps he had investigated and knew exactly who'd made the calls! John Wayne Masters was long dead or I could just ask him. That was a big problem with this case. A lot of people who had answers were six feet under.

Outside on Main Street, the sky had thickened with dark rolling clouds. It was perfect weather for watching daytime television, but I had a check for ten grand from Madame that was financial proof that she'd bought my time and energy—even if I never intended to cash it. I got in the Roadster and headed for Oxford. It was the day after Christmas, and I knew school was out for the long holiday break, but Grace had to live somewhere around the campus. He'd been in Zinnia the night before at Lawrence's party; perhaps I could catch him before he took off to visit relatives or whatever academicians did on holiday break.

The drive to Oxford covers more than distance. It is a metaphysical journey. The Delta is left behind, and the woodlands of Mississippi rise up tall and mysterious. In the Delta, life is simpler. Or at least the parameters are. There are the rich and the poor, the privileged and those who serve. Though the stark clarity is often cruel, I preferred it to the oak-shaded avenues of that venerable old state institution. I'd spent my time at Ole

Miss. I knew that intellect was touted as god, but social position was still the determining factor. The quality of education couldn't be challenged. It was the social order that I could never accept.

I drove through the campus for old times' sake. I had forgotten the beauty of the trees and the gracious lines of the buildings. At the Lyceum I stopped the car, thinking about the young girl I'd once been. I'd gone to college with such expectations of what I could accomplish. My mother, before her death, had led me to believe that I could be anything I wanted. Aunt LouLane had taught me the machinations to accomplish the only goal a woman *should* want—matrimony. I could only wonder what both of them would think of how I'd turned out. PI work certainly wasn't a career option either would have considered.

I avoided the dormitories and made it to the English Department, which was locked tight. Everyone was on holiday. I happened upon a janitor, who unlocked the door and allowed me to snoop long enough to find Dean Grace's home address. God bless janitors and the urge to get even with those who have three-week holiday breaks.

I stopped at campus security and asked directions. Grace's home was out past Rowan Oaks. Long ago, on a hot summer night, I'd gone with a date to Faulkner's home. We'd both been callow enough to think it would be romantic to spoon beneath the huge oak trees that marked the spot where the writer had created characters driven by lust and greed and the gamut of primal human emotions. Whatever we'd anticipated, the reality had been vastly different. Sitting beneath the oaks in Lamar's convertible, I'd suffered an infusion of Satoris angst. It was not a night that added to my reputation as a hot date.

Dean Grace's home was three miles beyond Rowan Oaks, a two-story clapboard with a porch and modest gingerbread trim. It looked bookish. Very suitable for a man of his station. Even the pea gravel in his parking lot was uniform. There were two cars in the drive, a Volvo and a Sebring convertible. I had no difficulty telling which one belonged to the missus.

If he was surprised to see me, he didn't show it. He wore a burgundy cardigan, buttoned, with leather patches on the elbows, and a black and white checked tie. His hair was sculpted into that long sweep that bespoke his vanity even more than his natty attire. He answered the door, hesitated, then called out to his wife to make coffee.

I stepped inside the house, which smelled of cinnamon and cedar. Without looking back he led me to a living room dominated by a giant tree decorated with red ornaments and—incredibly—small blond dolls. It was the eeriest thing I'd ever seen in the annals of decorating. A hundred pairs of light, glassy, blue eyes watched me as I walked to the fireplace and warmed my legs. The little dolls were all dressed in red and green outfits, but it did nothing to detract from the feeling that they watched me with a certain malice.

"What brings you to Oxford?" Grace asked without preamble.

I detected more than a hint of hostility. "History."

"I'm afraid you're barking up the wrong tree." He smiled at his colloquial acumen.

"I wasn't barking," I said softly. "Not yet."

"What I meant was that my specialty is Chaucer. *The Canterbury Tales,*" he added, as if I needed the clarification. "History would fall more in the domain of Clarence Moore. He's"—he checked his watch—"still at home. I'm sure he would be glad to talk with you."

"Personal history," I said, and saw, with gratification, that he frowned.

"Tilda and I are getting ready to leave," he said, checking his watch again. I noticed it was a handsome sterling Rolex. He was a man with expensive taste.

"I won't keep you long," I assured him, casual yet determined. "It's about Lawrence."

"I heard he'd passed on. Excellent timing. One grand dinner party and then an exit with Hollywood attending. He couldn't have planned it better."

"It wasn't a shock, then?" I asked before I grasped what he was suggesting. "You think—"

"Lawrence was many things but clumsy was never one of them. He was a realist about the publishing world. Other than getting a celebrity to write the book, which he did, his best guarantee for a big audience was to die."

The audacity of his remark stunned me. Before I could respond, the sound of tapping heels signaled the entrance of Tilda Grace. I recognized her from Lawrence's party, but I was shocked to discover that she was Grace's wife. She carried a tray laden with coffee, two cups, and handmade chocolate treats. She didn't look at either of us as she put the tray on a table.

"Do you need anything else?" she asked.

Her accent surprised me. European. German or Swedish. I hadn't noticed it at Lawrence's party. She was one of those women who usually faded into a corner at a social event. I looked at her more closely and saw her ancestry in her square face and gray-blond hair. She was younger than her husband and could have been a beautiful woman. Instead, she'd chosen to subvert her looks with her hair pulled severely back in a ponytail and a gray dress that hung off thin shoulders.

"That will be all, Tilda." Grace said. "Are you packed?"

"Yes," she answered, casting me a nervous look.

"I won't delay you for long," I said to her. "Do you teach also?" She was about to flee the room, and for some reason I wanted to detain her.

"Oh, no," she said, blushing. "I only have my bachelor's. In printmaking. I couldn't possibly teach."

"Tilda is too busy to have a job." Grace clasped his hands in front of his belt. "She has all the talent in the world, but there just doesn't seem to be time to use any of it."

Although I'd suspected as much, I was shocked by the cruelty. I waited for her to make some response.

"I'll make sure there's nothing in the refrigerator that will spoil while we're gone." She slid from the room, a shadow.

"If you have something specific you need, you'd better tell me." He checked his watch again. "We're going to be late."

"Why did you renege on the contract with Lawrence when he returned home from Paris in 1958?" Okay, little Napoleon, let's line up the soldiers and charge.

"Lawrence violated the terms. He led the school to believe he held a terminal degree, but he had very little formal education." He picked up a cup of coffee and waved at me to do the same. Though I wanted to throw the cup at him, I picked it up and sipped daintily.

"Lawrence recognized that he was wrong, and we settled that dispute long ago. What makes you interested in it?"

"I'm always interested in breach of contract."

"He signed a release, relieving me and the school of any legal repercussions."

"Charming," I said. "And smart. How much did it cost?"

For the first time Grace smiled. "That's none of your business. In fact, I can't see where any of this is your business. I have to be going. It was lovely of you to visit, Miss Delaney. Come again soon."

It was a tacky maneuver, but one I wasn't ashamed to employ. I let the coffee cup slip from my fingers and crash to the floor. China and coffee flew around my ankles. "How clumsy of me," I said, bending to pick up the pieces. The cup rim was broken, and the jagged edge sliced through the tender skin between my finger and thumb. Blood spurted.

I grabbed a napkin and pressed it against the wound. When I looked at Joseph Grace, he was staring at the broken cup and the blood with pure horror.

The scene of Lawrence's death came back to me, full force. The broken glass, the blood.

The sound of the accident brought Tilda on the ready. "Are you okay?" she asked, taking my hand and examining it. "Just a nick. See, it's already stopped bleeding."

"I'm fine," I agreed, kneeling beside her as she blotted the coffee. "I'm very sorry."

"Tilda can manage," Grace said impatiently.

"I wouldn't dream of leaving such a mess." I smiled at him.

"I have some calls to make." He stormed out of the room, a tiny field marshal thwarted.

"Have you been in Mississippi a long time?" I asked, knowing the answer as all good PIs and lawyers are supposed to do. Though her accent was foreign, it was tainted with a drawl.

"Nearly thirty years," she said. "I was eighteen when I met Joseph. He was studying in Vienna."

"It must have been a difficult change to come here."

She shook her head. "Regret is for the foolish." Her smile was tentative. "It was a decision I made long ago."

I put the shards of the coffee cup on the tray. "Are you going to visit your children?" The doll-laden tree made me think perhaps it was done up for their grand-children.

"We are childless," she said, and her gaze dropped to the floor. "Not even the best doctors here could help us."

Tilda had no way to understand that her affliction would be the highest form of womanhood if she'd been born into the circle of Southern gentility. An accident of birth had turned an asset into personal shame.

She pressed her thin body down on the towel she was using to blot the carpet, allowing the task to absorb her so completely there was almost no one left. I touched her shoulder. "I'm sorry I didn't get a chance to talk with you Christmas Eve. At Lawrence's party."

Her blue gaze met mine. "I don't like such parties."

To my further amazement, large tears welled up in her eyes and one slipped down her cheek before she could turn away. "Lawrence encouraged me in my art. He said I had talent. He was very kind to me when we met in Paris. If he had never started talking about this stupid biography." Her voice grew lower and more powerful. "So stupid. To say that he was going to write everything."

I rocked back on my heels, thinking fast how not to spook her away from what I wanted to know. "You knew Lawrence in Paris?"

"Oh, yes. He introduced me to Joseph. He did not expect that we would marry." She slowly got to her feet, lifting the tray as she did so. "I have to go. Joseph doesn't like to wait."

"Did Lawrence talk to you about his book?" She knew something, and I realized the question was an awkward fumble when her eyes darted toward the door Grace had left through.

"To me? No. I was always on the fringes of Lawrence's life. Just another young person who wanted to paint. He said nothing to me." She held the tray rigidly, gaze shifting beyond me. "You must go. Joseph gets angry when his schedule is interrupted."

There was nothing to do but leave—with more of a mystery than when I'd arrived.

"Tilda?" I hesitated. "Who would want Lawrence dead?"

Her blue eyes were clear and unflinching when she finally looked into my eyes. "The book he was working on, his biography. It would damage many people, my husband among them. But others, too. Lawrence was filled with secrets, the dark acts of others. People were afraid of what he would reveal." She smiled the most curious of smiles before she continued. "Even me."

She walked past me, and when I turned to watch her I saw what she'd seen the whole time—Joseph Grace's shadow as he stood outside the door and eavesdropped on us.

8

The one thing I'd learned from my last case was that at a certain point in any investigation, everyone is a suspect. One of the things I'd learned from my undergraduate years in psychology was that given the proper motive, a person is capable of anything. My problem with this case was that it seemed the list of suspects and motives was endless.

The theft of the manuscript indicated that Lawrence had, indeed, written something damaging. But to whom? Everyone seemed to have a motive for not wanting the book to see print.

The only other component necessary for a crime was opportunity. And from what I could tell about Lawrence's manner of living, just about anyone who happened to drive up to his home had opportunity.

Unless, of course, he had simply died from a severe cut on his hand that was accidentally inflicted. Accidents are the most common cause of death in the United States, but Doc wasn't satisfied that Lawrence's death was accidental. Only the autopsy would prove anything concrete.

The possibilities of the case perked and bubbled in my brain as I drove home. It was a relief to see the bare sycamores that marked my drive—at last I could get out of the car and away from my fruitless speculations.

I saw the first dog when I was halfway down the drive. It was a small creature that looked like a cross between a greyhound and a Brillo pad. He was sitting patiently beneath a tree and watching the front porch with such intensity that he never acknowledged the passing of my car. As I pulled around the house, I saw six more, a motley crew of shaggy and slick, big and little, black and white, and all in-between dogs. They were simply sitting, watching the back door.

I'd never seen so many dogs in one place. I got out of the car with some trepidation only to discover that whatever they were interested in, it wasn't me. The doggy portal that Harold had sent a carpenter to install in the kitchen door burst open and Sweetie Pie bounded down the steps in one single leap.

"Sweetie," I called out, glad for the welcome. She shot past me and headed for the pack. It took all of fifteen seconds for me to realize what was going to happen.

"No!" I rushed for the garden hose and made all efforts to run the dogs away, but Sweetie had no intention of allowing her suitors to depart. Dropping the hose, I went for the phone.

Harold, at least, had the decency to be at his desk at the bank. "I thought you had Sweetie Pie spayed," I accused, breathless. Outside the kitchen window, every dog was having his day.

"She was," he said.

"It wasn't successful." I turned my back on the orgy.

"I've never heard of such," Harold said, and there was the hint of laughter in his voice. "How can you tell?"

Had I not been well trained by Aunt Loulane, I would have given him the graphic details of how I could tell. "She's in heat," I said. "Trust me. I recognize the condition."

"Yes, I suspect you do."

I felt a sudden throbbing in my thumb, and for a split second I was no longer in my kitchen in Dahlia House but beneath the oaks at Harold's. I felt his mouth close over my thumb and the corresponding surge of desire. "You have to do something," I said, and my voice sounded rough to my own ears.

"I like a woman who makes her demands clear," he said.

"The dog, Harold," I said, striving for a tone of affronted dignity.

"Oh," he gave a silky chuckle. "Take her back up to Dr. Matthews. I'll speak with him."

"I don't want puppies."

"And you shall not have them. You have my word. Baxter removed her uterus, Sarah Booth. She can't have puppies."

"Right." I put down the phone and confronted the scene in the yard. Sweetie Pie had no intention of listening to any advice I had to give, so I decided to make a pot of coffee and wait until passions cooled. It had been a long, hard day.

I didn't hear Jitty until she pulled out a chair and sat down at the kitchen table. "That dog is creatin' a spectacle right there in the yard. I tol' you it was a mistake. Folks see all that goin' on in the yard and they gone be talkin'."

"So what? She's spayed." I was banking on Harold's seed of hope. She did have a scar on her abdomen.

"Somethin's wrong with her." Jitty's eyes widened, emphasizing the golden brown shantung of her sleeveless tunic. I gave her a closer inspection. Her attire was chic for a woman of the fifties, and it showed off her lean arms to advantage. For the first time I noticed she was wearing pants. Tight pants. Clamdiggers. And little flat black shoes that were very cool. It was a striking outfit—more movies and Bacall than tepid television. Though I thought Jitty's interest in the decade of bomb shelters and Ike was repugnant, I wouldn't mind borrowing those clothes.

"Nice outfit. What happened to the whalebone corset, pointy bra, and cinched waist?"

"I'm going out this evening," she said. "Business. Even in the fifties a businesswoman is allowed to look good."

"Right, all ten of y'all." I sighed. I would be left alone with a dog in heat and the holiday blues. I'd have no recourse except to plug in the Christmas lights and play Mother's old albums. I was in a Garfunkel funk.

Jitty smirked. "Don't go feelin' sorry for yourself, Sarah Booth. You took the dog against my advice." She leaned closer, her dark eyes dancing with mischief. "Ask that veterinarian man to check that hound for a Delaney womb. That must be the problem. She's been here three days and already developing the tendencies that kept this bloodline running for five generations." She gave a hearty laugh and evaporated before I could think of an insult to hurl back at her.

Sweetie and I sat on the porch as dusk fell over Dahlia House. Dr. Baxter Matthews had determined another surgery would be necessary to diagnose Sweetie's sudden enchantment with reproductive activities, but we'd decided to wait until the new year. So now I held her on a leash as she softly bayed under her breath at the dozen dogs who waited patiently in the yard. She sang to them in the softest of doggy tones, a siren lure to the panting pack. Only the firecrackers I kept throwing out in the yard dampened the ardor of her new friends.

It reminded me of old stories of Great-Aunt Cilla, who was known across five states as a tease and heartbreaker. It was family legend that she'd violated the rules of womanhood and refused to marry young. During her twenties, she'd had men lined down the driveway in cars waiting for the chance to take her for a drive. Cilla, too, had suffered from some womb disorder. Father had been kind in his diagnosis, saying she'd been a spirited woman. Aunt LouLane, who was her sister, had been more to the point. Nympho was the word she'd used, saying it through lips so tightly drawn that her mouth had looked like a coin slot.

"Ooo-ooo-ba-ba," Sweetie moaned softly.

Holding my moaning hound and thinking about Harold, Hamilton, and Willem, I couldn't help but wonder what diagnosis my family would put on me. The possibilities made me squirm.

A pair of headlights came down the drive toward the house, and I felt a vague stirring of curiosity. I was anticipating no one. I wasn't certain I was in the mood to entertain. Still, any company was better than my own.

Anyone except—Brianna Rathbone.

She got out of her car at the front steps, a tall, willowy beauty that made Sweetie Pie's hackles rise.

The male dog suitors took one look at her and scattered.

"Smart move," I called out to them. "She eats her mate."

"How like you, Sarah Booth, to sit on your porch all alone and talk about breeding habits with a pack of dogs. Desperate doesn't begin to describe you, does it?"

"What brings you here, Brianna? Cannibalized the male population of Zinnia already?"

"If that were the case, how long would it be before you noticed? A month? I gather you don't have a lot of male callers."

Ah, she was quick. But I had a trump. "Willem was here yesterday. A very amusing man. He told me about his aversion to silk. He said it reminded him of waking up in the cocoon you'd spun around him."

"Willem." She sighed. "A talented man in the bedroom, but not enough substance in a conversation."

Brianna's idea of substance had to do with listing the most precious jewels in order of their monetary value, or perhaps the most current stock index. "What brings you to Dahlia House?" I asked again. I wasn't about to ask her in, even though the light was fading and it was growing too cold on the porch. I knew the rule about vampires and invitations.

"I hear Rosalyn hired you to investigate Lawrence's death."

I was surprised by her knowledge of that fact, though I was careful to show no emotion. "What business is it of yours?"

"I thought you might want to do a little additional work, for me."

"Sorry, conflict of interest."

She looked at me, perfectly defined eyebrows crashing together. "Are you saying I'm a suspect in a murder?"

I couldn't stop the smug look at her use of the word

"murder." "There's no conclusive proof that Lawrence was murdered," I said. "But if it should prove that he was, I'd say you're the number one suspect."

"Ridiculous." She spat the word, pacing the porch.

Sweetie growled low and throaty.

"Shut that creature up," Brianna snapped. "Why would I kill the golden goose? Lawrence and I were going to make a fortune on his life story. I wouldn't do anything to jeopardize that deal."

"Perhaps you can make more money alone, and have more license. Lawrence wasn't exactly happy with you. He told me you'd lost the right . . . focus." It was a small lie. A perfectly legitimate PI lie.

She whirled. "What did he say?"

The light in her eyes was sharp, demanding. It's one thing to consider someone capable of murder and quite another to confront that reality. Now, with the last pink light of a winter day in her eyes, I believed it. She was the ice queen, a woman of no emotion and total greed. The cold hand of self-preservation tickled my back and warned me not to provoke her too far. We were alone and I didn't have a witness.

"Damn you, Sarah Booth, don't play coy with me. What did that old man really say about me?"

Sweetie Pie shifted into position beside my leg. She wasn't a rottweiler, but she had teeth and a spasming womb. A match for Brianna. "Where were you on Christmas Eve, after the party?"

"None of your damn business."

"You don't have an alibi." I felt a thrill, which quickly turned to a chill when she took a step toward me.

"That old man was my meal ticket. He was doing most of the work. All I had to do was sign my name to a lucrative book *and* movie contract and then go out and sign autographs. I needed him alive." She stepped closer.

Sweetie bared her teeth.

"Lawrence had the power to expose you for the liar you are," I said. Backing down was the smart thing, but then again Delaneys were known for activity in the nether region, not the brain. "You didn't write that book. You *thought* you were going to take credit for it. But Lawrence lost his faith in you and changed his mind. So you killed him. What made him lose his trust, Brianna?"

I'd never realized how large her hands were until she lifted them. I thought she was going to punch me, but she halted the motion.

"Lawrence was a difficult man. We had a disagreement—stupid, really—about the scope of the book. But our deal was firm. We had a legally binding contract."

"I'd like to take a look at that," I said.

"Bite my ass." She clenched her hands and turned abruptly. "I don't know why I'm even talking to you, Sarah Booth. You're jealous of me. I'll find the manuscript myself, and then I'll do exactly what I want with it. By law, it belongs to me."

Her words were like a slap. The clear implication was that she didn't have the manuscript or even a copy of it. Impossible! There would certainly have been multiple copies of such a thing.

I thought back to Christmas morning when I'd first entered Lawrence's cottage. In the wake of the party, it was hard to tell if Lawrence's home had been tampered with. But Madame insisted things were stolen. If Brianna didn't have the manuscript, who did?

"Brianna," I called out, stopping her at the bottom step. "Are you saying you don't have a copy of the manuscript?"

"My, aren't you the brain? That's exactly what I'm saying. Lawrence insisted it was a big secret. He wanted a grand moment, when it was complete, and it was almost there."

"You didn't have a copy at all?" I was incredulous, and she was dumber than I ever thought.

"Read my lips," she said, furious. "He wouldn't give me a copy. I had to agree to sign my name to whatever he wrote. Or that's what he thought." Her smile was sly, and she lifted her chin, a gesture that a camera would have loved. "Lawrence was a cat toying with mice. You saw him, the night of the party. That book was bait. He had some scores to settle, and he was tossing out little bits of that biography, making the rats dance. If you want to find whoever killed him, find who he was tormenting." Her full lips curled into what some would have thought a smile. "Maybe that's why Willem is still hanging around town. Lawrence had something on him. Something juicy."

"What?"

"You're the investigator. You find out." She opened the door of her Porsche. "I have no faith in your talents, Sarah Booth, but if you happen to find the manuscript, remember it belongs to me. That's the law and Daddy will make you obey it. Should you feel inclined to quibble, I'll give you thirty thousand for it. Cash. No tax forms, no questions."

She got in the car, slammed the door, and spun out of the drive. As soon as she was gone the male dogs came slinking back through the soft gray dusk.

9

Dahlia House was silent. I'd taken a hot bath, eaten a salad, and lit a fire in the front parlor. I liked the contrast between the bright burn of the neon Christmas lights and the flickering flames of the hearth.

I sipped a little bourbon and patted Sweetie Pie's head. She was exhausted from all the activity she'd recently been having.

Soon the tree would have to come down. There remained great debate among the Daddy's Girls about the proper time to de-trim, but the Delaney tradition held firm. No later than December 31. To leave the tree up would bring untold bad luck. It was a violation of superstitions almost as bad as washing clothes on New Year's Day, which was a sure way to kill off a family member. Trouble was, you couldn't pick the member you wanted to die.

Tradition—a word that haunted and yet defined much of my life. I'd fought the concept tooth and nail only to discover that I held on to it even as I struggled against it. In college I'd sneered at the sororities Aunt

LouLane had worked so hard to have rush me. Of course, my mother had gone me one better by becoming a socialist in her youth.

I'd shunned traditional studies, throwing myself into the dramatic arts. Theater was far removed from the respected life of a Delta belle. One of my other distant relatives had already gotten the drop on me in that regard, too. No matter how I tried, I'd never be as untraditional as cousin Talullah. And certainly not as successful, either.

By not marrying, I was following a long line of spinster Delaney women. Cilla, though reported to be one hot mama, had never married. The family had moved her to Atlanta, where rumors of her lovers were muffled by distance and the roar of the city.

But I was hemmed in by one last tradition—that of bearing an heir to carry on the Delaney name. Cilla and the others could dodge that particular bullet. I could not. I am the last of the line, the end of the Delaneys. If I don't produce a child, Jitty will have no one to haunt, and Dahlia House will certainly fall to the development mentality that is now raping the South.

Tradition is a heavy burden on a cold December night when the fire is flickering and Bob Dylan is wailing on the record player. Brianna would never let family or tradition stand in her way. It seemed not even legal or moral issues held her back from her pursuit of whatever she wanted.

To avoid my own gloomy thoughts, I got out a pad and began to make a list of leads to follow in my case. Brianna's visit had unleashed another round of possibilities.

Knowing the cunning nature of the beast, I instantly suspected that Brianna had stolen the manuscript and was only trying to throw me off the trail. Nothing was too Machiavellian for the mind of Rathbone. It would be just like her to point suspicion at Willem by implying he had some dark secret to hide. He'd dumped her. There was a score to settle there, and what better way than to sic me on him. Two birds with one stone. I toted up the evidence against her with growing pleasure.

But there had been the lingering smell of cigarettes in the house. Willem, for certain, smoked. Brianna had smoked in high school, until she learned it could prematurely age her skin. My belief, though, was once a smoker, always a smoker. Reformed smokers were only those who hadn't backslid yet.

That put Brianna and Willem squarely in the zone of suspects. Joining them was Joseph Grace. Whatever Lawrence had on him, it had to be good. Tilda had tossed her own name into the hat as a suspect.

There were countless possibilities—everyone he might have included in his book. Since I hadn't read any of it, I had no idea how damaging it might have been. Tilda said that Lawrence was the secret keeper. I remembered the howling stink that followed on the heels of Truman Capote's biting tell-all. Lawrence had never struck me as that kind of person, but I couldn't swear to it.

There was, indeed, a certain appeal to score settling in one final, conclusive book. I'd lived a short and uneventful life compared to Lawrence Ambrose, but given the opportunity to thumb my nose at my enemies as I tweaked them on their exposed asses, I knew I'd be very, very tempted. And if Brianna wasn't lying, then Lawrence was doing exactly that—letting each person know what he was about to do to them. If she wasn't lying . . . about a lot of things, including her *relationship* with Gustav Brecht, the publisher who'd failed to appear at the party.

The only thing I was positive about was that Lawrence hadn't deliberately cut his hand, as Grace had suggested. Lawrence had not committed suicide—he wasn't the type.

I picked up the phone and dialed Madame. "What is it?" she asked, weariness in her voice.

"Lawrence's manuscript covered his years in Paris, right?"

She hesitated. "What's this all about, Sarah Booth?"

"*If*, and that hasn't been established yet, there was foul play in Lawrence's death, I'm trying to compile a comprehensive list of suspects." When she didn't respond, I continued. "The guests at the dinner party could be on the list. But he knew everyone. The rich and famous, the talented and wannabes. He could have written something about one of those people that caused them to sneak into Sunflower County and kill him."

"Brianna killed him."

There was no arguing with Madame. She'd made up her mind.

"Don't waste your time and my money looking for anyone else," she commanded. "Brianna did it. You know it as well as I do. Just figure out how she did it and make her pay."

Beneath the commandeering attitude was deep grief. "How are you doing?" I asked.

"I miss the old fossil." Her voice cracked but she regained control. "The police won't tell me anything. They've locked up his cottage. I can't get in to tend to his personal affairs. Even the cats are shut out. He would be furious."

Madame was in a mood and subverting her was tricky. "Several people mentioned Lawrence's 1958 return to Zinnia. Why *was* he denied the job at the university?"

"Jealousy. Plain and simple. He had talent and they didn't."

"But wouldn't his talent reflect back on the school?"

"Oh, certainly that. What you don't understand, Sarah Booth, is that Lawrence had connections to the world of talent and glamour. He could pick up the phone and talk to Marilyn Monroe or Clark Gable, Judy Garland or Groucho Marx. He didn't even have to call them, they called him and told him their secrets, their sorrows and joys.

"He worked with all of the famous European film directors. That access gave Lawrence power. He would have become *more* powerful than the other faculty, so they all ganged up against him. They're inferior intellects and they thrive on mediocrity. What they couldn't stand was the idea of someone coming in and upsetting the balance of power."

Explained in those terms, I could see where Lawrence might stir a rebellion. "Why didn't he push it? Why didn't he sue?"

"You didn't know him, Sarah Booth." Madame's voice was worn and thin as onionskin. "You wouldn't ask that question if you did. He was a proud man. He wouldn't force his way into a job, even if he had a right to it. Times were different then. It was 1958. People didn't go to court at the drop of a hat."

"He should have," I said.

"Today, yes. Back then, no. He did the right thing. He had another twenty years in Paris. That was where he belonged. The one thing that might have made his life here tolerable was denied him."

Sweetie put her head on my feet, sighing deeply in her sleep. "Why did he finally come back to Zinnia?"

"Money. He ran out." Her laugh was dry, like rustling leaves. "Lawrence attracted people with talent and money. He introduced people, sponsored young writers and artists. For many, many years he lived exactly as he wished. Then the world changed and he was forgotten. He came home."

Her tone had turned pensive, and so I decided to risk another question. "Would this book have put him back in the literary limelight?"

"Undoubtedly. He was a brilliant writer. This was his final effort, the culmination of all of his years of living and writing. It would have been hailed not only as an incredible look at a specific period of literature, it would have been a work of art."

"Even under Brianna Rathbone's name?" I pressed.

"That's exactly what I finally made him understand," Madame said. "That's what got him killed." She took a deep breath. "Enough talk. This won't bring Lawrence back. Quit diddling and find the evidence we need to put that woman behind bars. I'll call you tomorrow and see what you've found."

The phone went dead in my ear, and I laid it on the table beside my chair. I was about to pick up my drink when the phone rang. The unexpected shrill made me jump, which caused Sweetie Pie to leap to her feet, a lanky tangle of legs and snarl that sounded vaguely like something from *The Exorcist*.

"Easy, girl," I said as I clicked the on button. "Hello."

"You aren't the first woman to stand me up, Sarah Booth, but I must say you're the fastest." Willem's voice was deceptively smooth and rocked by Latin rhythms.

I sat straight up. I'd completely forgotten that I was to take him for a drive.

"I was out of town. On business." I offered an explanation rather than an apology until I could gauge the depth of his anger. It was a trick I'd learned from my friend Tinkie. Never overapologize.

"I would have ridden over to Oxford with you, if you'd asked."

"How did—"

I didn't even get to finish the question before he was chuckling, a sound that reminded me of silk rubbing against silk. He was a man who stirred my imagination in tactile ways.

"You aren't hard to track down. Was your trip fruitful?"

"How did you know I went to Oxford?"

"Don't get overwrought," he said. "Cece told me."

"How did she know?"

"I didn't ask. I was more concerned at why you didn't bother to call and cancel our date."

I should have felt guilty, but there was something about Willem that offset any tendency toward regret. He was too confident that he would ultimately win game point. It was not regret I was feeling but the thrill of the chase. "I thought it would do you good to wait and wonder."

His chuckle was soft and intimate, like his lips on my palm. "So often women yield to me, Sarah Booth. I quickly grow bored with them. You're not like that, are you?"

"Yielding isn't one of my finer talents." I sipped the bourbon, enjoying the verbal sparring more than I wanted to admit.

"Shall we try for a drive tomorrow?"

"You must want to spend time with me badly." Aha!

"Perhaps. Or it could be that I want a chance to return the favor." He laughed again.

"Tomorrow, then. At two."

"I'll pick you up." He paused. "Don't disappoint me."

The phone went dead and I put it down, left with a cool feeling in the pit of my stomach. Willem was fun to play with, but I didn't have to be told that he could cuddle *and* bite.

I went to bed with the jitters and dreamed of Jitty. She was at the head of a long mahogany table, the shantung tunic shimmering in a slant of golden sunlight. White, cat-eyed sunglasses concealed her eyes, but her lips were turned up in happiness. Every seat at the table was taken by a man in a handsome business suit. Twelve sleek heads, twelve pairs of dark sunglasses. They all smoked.

It was a dream of textures, as if I didn't see but felt the elements. No one spoke—there was the sense of anticipation—as if some great event were on the verge of unfolding. Only Jitty seemed to know the score, and she wasn't saying a word. As the dream faded, I awoke to a bright sun and a blanket of purest snow.

I'd barely stretched when there was a rapping at the front door. It had been weeks, but I recognized the pitter-patter of little fists and knew that my old friend Tinkie Bellcase Richmond had come acalling. By the rhythm of her pounding I could tell she was also in a snit.

"Hold your horses," I called as I grabbed a robe and ran down the stairs.

"It's freezing," Tinkie said as she sailed in, a small bundle of quivering fur clutched against her chest.

"Hello, Tinkie. Hello, Chablis," I said to the toy Yorkie who was the seed of my detective agency. In desperation, I'd dognapped Chablis and returned her for ransom. In retrospect, it seemed a low-down thing to do, but it had saved Dahlia House. Besides, I wasn't totally responsible; Jitty made me do it.

"Coffee," Tinkie demanded as she sailed toward the kitchen.

"Oh my God," she said, stopping so abruptly that I ran into her back. Luckily she's a bit shorter than I am, so no serious damage was done.

She pointed at the neon. "I've never seen anything so tacky."

"Willem says it's artistic." I cut her short.

She put it in high gear again and headed to the kitchen. "I'm desperate for caffeine," she said, pushing open the swinging door. "You can't imagine what's been going on. Oscar is about to—" She froze.

In the Delta young girls are trained to handle any situation. Whether it is a heart attack in the middle of a dance or a terrorist demanding your diamond Rolex, DGs don't freeze. I peeked around her shoulder. Sweetie Pie stared back at me, tail wagging.

"What *is* that?" Tinkie asked.

There was no time to answer. Chablis leaped from her arms and scrambled across the tile, six ounces of raging fur and fury. The little spitfire was jealous!

"No-o-o-o!" I made a dash for the furball. She wouldn't be but a mouthful for Sweetie. That hound had eaten bigger hams.

"Chablis!" Tinkie finally sensed the potential for real disaster and leaped after me. We landed in a tangle, just in time to see Sweetie's mouth open and descend on Chablis.

With five feet separating us and the dogs, there was nothing we could do but watch. Sweetie's long pink tongue came out and licked Chablis so hard the little fluff was scooted back within my reach. I pulled her to my heaving chest.

"Chablis," I said, now wanting to wring her scrawny neck for frightening me nearly to death.

Tinkie's hands closed over the dog. We all managed
to gain our feet just as Sweetie came over. Her happy
tail whipped hard against Tinkie's knees and made her
dance.

"What kind of dog is that?" Tinkie asked again.

"Red tic hound," I said. "Sweetie Pie is my new
dog."

Tinkie sighed. "Oh, Sarah Booth, there's so many
other ways to show your rebellious streak." She backed
away from the dog. "She's so ugly, I don't want to
touch her." She looked up at me, a frown forming.
"Does that make me shallow?"

"Shallow and in danger of getting clobbered. That's
my dog you're calling ugly."

"Sorry." She pulled out a chair and sat at the table.
"I'm sorry. I'm so flustered that I don't even know how
to behave."

"What gives?" I put on some coffee.

"This whole thing with Lawrence Ambrose has everyone in a tizzy." She pointed to the last of the fruitcake, wiggling a finger to let me know the need was
urgent. I cut her a slab and put a coffee cup down for
her. Because she was Tinkie, I used the china with the
Delaney crest.

"Back up to the beginning," I said, eyeing the fruitcake. It wasn't even eight o'clock. If I started now, I
could probably eat six thousand fruitcake calories before noon. It was a definite challenge.

"You know Harold was named executor of
Lawrence's estate."

I didn't, and I got up and poured our coffee, hiding
my sudden shock. Madame was certainly going to be
angry. I kept my coffee black and cut Tinkie another
wedge of cake.

"Oscar got a call this morning at seven. Layton

Rathbone's hired a lawyer for Brianna. She's suing the bank!"

"I thought he went back to Geneva or wherever he lives."

"They have phones in Europe, Sarah Booth. And bank transfers."

I wasn't fully awake, but I was alert enough to know that at seven in the morning, no courthouse was open so no suit could be filed. And I'd never met a lawyer that prompt or efficient.

"Lawrence's death has created a lot of gossip. I wouldn't jump the gun." I stifled a yawn. This was a typical Daddy's Girl maneuver—to get her papa to call in the hired guns.

Tinkie shook her head emphatically. "It's true. Just wait and see. At nine this morning, Boyd "Catfish" Harkey is going to file suit against the bank."

"What's the Bank of Zinnia got to do with any of this?"

"Brianna is claiming that Harold has Lawrence's manuscript locked up in the vault. She's demanding that the vault be searched—and if it isn't found there, then every safe deposit box in the bank will be opened. *Until the manuscript is found.* Oscar was wild. He said this would destroy faith in the bank."

Such a search might cause problems. Serious problems. But I wasn't certain even Brianna Rathbone and Boyd Harkey could force it. "How can you know all this?" I asked.

"Boyd's sixth wife. You remember Angela Rhee Finch, of the old Finch line. You know, some say that Harper Lee took the name for Atticus from her family. They settled the Delta back in the early eighteen—"

"Tinkie!" I well remembered the Finch family and especially Angela Rhee. A quiet girl with navy eyes and dark secrets. "Angela married Boyd? He's forty years older than she is."

"What's your point?" Tinkie gave me an exasperated look.

I'd forgotten the mantra of the Daddy's Girl. Security-security-security-security. Boyd Harkey was filthy rich. Old money, new money, drug money, dirty money. He had some of all of them. But Angela, married to the lawyer who resembled nothing more than an old and cunning catfish? It was disheartening.

"Angela called to tell you what her husband was planning?"

"This morning. She could hardly wait until Boyd went to eliminate. She has no loyalty to him. After all, he never stays married longer than five years. She's vested in the marriage pension now, so she doesn't have to mind her Ps and Qs so much."

I let that whole worm box of marital loyalty pass right by. "Did Oscar say the manuscript was at the bank?"

Tinkie shrugged. "No, he didn't say one way or the other. And no one can find Harold this morning. Oscar's frantic."

10

Tinkie finished her coffee and fruitcake and finally decided that a visit to Madame Tomeeka was in order. Tomeeka, or Tammy Odom, was Zinnia's answer to Jeane Dixon. We'd been friends in high school, though she was a few years older, and I was honored to have her granddaughter named after my home. Even as I thought of baby Dahlia I felt a twinge in that mysterious region where the womb resides. Dahlia was the kind of baby that made motherhood seem like a viable career.

I saw Tinkie to the door and then rushed upstairs to dress. I wasn't exactly worried about Harold. He was a capable man. That was more the area in which my concern lay. He *was* capable. And eligible. As well as desirable. Brianna would see all of those things as clearly as I. And few men could resist her. She was beautiful and still maintained the aura of her modeling celebrity. I was dying of curiosity, well seasoned with a sprinkling of jealousy. I left the house and drove straight to Harold's.

As Tinkie had said, he wasn't home. His car wasn't in the garage. There was no hint that he'd been home the night before—I climbed the magnolia tree in old Mrs. Hedgepeth's yard next door and used my new binoculars to peep into his bedroom window. The bedspread was unrumpled.

Since I was out and about, I stopped by the hospital and checked with Doc Sawyer. No official word on the autopsy, so I moseyed on down to the newspaper and took Cece some Danish. She was conducting an interview and had no time to talk. I left her pastry and decided that a visit to Tomeeka might be a good idea for me, too.

I didn't believe in Tammy's powers to predict the future, but I didn't strictly disbelieve. As a student of psychology, I understood the *need* to believe in such things. As a child orphaned by a tragic and senseless car wreck, I had felt the whiplash of fate. Tammy held out the slim hope of controlling fate. The appeal was enormous. Perhaps she had no line on the future, but she was the best at dream analysis that I'd ever met—a match for Jung.

The dream about Jitty troubled me. Twelve men, sleek and stylish. Jitty at the head of the table. It was nothing like the dreams I'd had about dove fields, but I was curious to see what Tammy would make of it.

I slowly drove through my hometown, noting that the Bank of Zinnia was doing a steady business and that Harold's Lexus was not yet in the parking lot. I'd never known him to miss a day of work since I'd come home to Sunflower County from New York. Where could he be?

With the swiftness of a gut-kick, I hatched a strong hunch. I swung a hard left in my little Roadster and headed north toward Memphis. I didn't have far to go, but as I drove I tried to argue myself out of believing what I already knew.

Rathbone House was on the outskirts of town, a two-hundred-acre estate where Brianna had hosted high school dances, tennis parties, horseback rides, shuffleboard tournaments, skeet shooting matches, and other soirees. Brianna had been the high school princess, the girl with everything and a father who doted on her every whim. Layton denied his daughter nothing, even when he should have. I remembered him in polished black boots that matched the Tennessee Walker he rode through the vast expanse of his fields. Pamela Rathbone was also a looker, but she faded beside her husband and daughter. The power of their illumination completely overshadowed her. When Brianna took her face to New York in the mid-eighties, Layton and Pamela transferred their address to Lifestyles of the Rich and Famous. As far as I knew they never returned to the Delta. Rathbone House had been closed until Brianna's most recent return.

The wrought iron gates were locked, and Brianna had neglected to give me the code to open them. No matter. I parked on the side of the road and climbed over the fence.

The white shell drive, imported from Biloxi, showed fresh tire tracks. I scrunched down to it, not bothering to be discreet. I wasn't going to pay a call, I only wanted a look. I was halfway to the rambling stucco house with its Mediterranean terra-cotta roof when I saw Harold's Lexus. It was parked under a grouping of leafless walnut trees. The house, surrounded by a blanket of fresh snow, was like a postcard image of some faraway fantasy. I blinked several times, then had to accept the evidence. Harold had spent the night with Brianna.

My thumb gave a feeble pulse, and I turned around

and headed back to the road. There was absolutely nothing I could do for him. He was drinking the spider's nectar. I knew too well the fatal appeal that Brianna had for men. But I'd always thought Harold too smart to fall for someone like her. I'd given him credit for putting the Big Head in command. It was another bitter lesson in the unreliability of men, and right on top of my disappointment with Hamilton. Yeah, Merry freakin' Christmas.

I made it to Tammy's just in time for lunch. The sight of Harold's car at Brianna's house had effectively killed my appetite, but Tammy put a plate of barbecued ribs, cole slaw, and turnips in front of me, and my taste buds revived.

We talked of Lawrence. Due to psychic–client privileges, she wouldn't discuss Tinkie's concerns with me, but Tammy was an avid fan of Lawrence's writing. She'd never met him, but she knew his work and was far better read than I.

"When I was pregnant with Claire, I read *Weevil Dance* about a thousand times," she said. Her smile was sad. "There was such magic in that book, such life. It gave me comfort, to allow my fancy to be led by his words. And he made history so romantic. Sad but romantic."

"Rosalyn Bell believes someone murdered Lawrence."

"I know," Tammy said. She got up from the table and walked to the window over the sink. The light from outside was bright, sun reflecting off the snow, which would be gone by the end of the day, melted into the gumbo of the soil. "Mrs. Bell hired you, didn't she?"

I didn't see the harm in telling. "Yes."

"And what do you believe, Sarah Booth? You saw

the body." She still had her back turned to me, which was vaguely troubling.

"He didn't cut himself deliberately." That was the only truth I knew for sure. "I don't *think* it was an accident." I shifted in the chair so I could at least glimpse her profile. She was staring studiously out at the snow, as if it might explain everything.

"He was seventy-six and had lived quietly and alone for the past twenty years. If someone was after him, it had to be about his biography," she said.

"Is that a psychic revelation or a hunch?" I meant to be funny.

"Neither." She turned to face me. "You're the detective. I don't even know why I said anything. So, who's having the big New Year's Eve party in the circle of Daddy's Girls?"

I let the conversation drift, and we gossiped aimlessly for a few minutes. Brianna's name came up, and I told her of my recent discovery of Harold's assignation, doing my best to play it off as an amusing tidbit. As Tammy refilled the tea glasses, she didn't bother to hide her scrutiny of me.

"What's wrong with you?" she asked as she sat down across from me, finally holding my gaze. "You're not in love with Harold. You had a chance, and you picked Hamilton."

True. But facts had nothing to do with this. "She'll eat him alive."

Tammy arched her eyebrows. "That's not your concern, Sarah Booth."

True again, dang her. "I thought the future was your forte, not the present."

Tammy gave me a long look. "Now, that's a statement worthy of a Daddy's Girl."

Thrice true. "Ouch!" I rolled my eyes. "Accept my apology and let me tell you about my dream."

Jitty would have been impossible to explain, so I substituted myself in her role. Tammy listened attentively, asking a few questions about the color of the sunlight—pale yellow; the color of the men's hair—all darkened by a hair cream and combed back from the forehead; the arrangement of the room—very balanced, six men on each side of the table and Jitty in the center.

"The religious implications aren't lost on you, are they?" she asked. "Twelve disciples."

I shook my head. "I got the feeling that at any moment the entire cast might jump up and do a Broadway dance number. Not religious in tone."

She put her hand over mine. "Just testing, Sarah Booth." She grinned. "It's really pretty simple. There's an aspect of you that's trying to conduct your emotional life like a corporate board meeting. You dress your men in success, line them up, and then try to pick one like you would a stock. The sense of waiting is exactly that—once you choose, you think life will start. The dance will begin, and what a glorious number it will be. The band will swing, and you'll know all the dance steps." She squeezed my hand. "But the sunglasses mean that you're blind, as are the men. But this blindness is deliberate, self-imposed." Her grip tightened. "Be careful, Sarah Booth. Be wise with your heart and your body."

Wisdom is a passing thing, especially for a female Delaney. Tammy could counsel me all she wanted, but when I left her house I was no closer to an emotional or investigative conclusion than I had been before I arrived.

I was getting out of my car at Dahlia House when I heard the approach of another vehicle. Willem was coming down the drive, promptly at two, wearing his ten-million-dollar smile. It made me regret that I wasn't wearing something other than jeans and a sweater. I had the cutest red wool miniskirt. Willem was the kind of man who made me think of wearing such things.

"*Hola*," he said, getting out of the car. He came straight to me and lifted my hand for a kiss.

"*Hola* to you." I was glad to see him. Harold's defection to Brianna had left a wound that needed the balm that Willem was a master at applying.

"Shall we drive?" He crooked his arm.

"We shall," I said, putting my hand on the bend of his elbow and allowing him to escort me to my seat. Ah, the sins that can be forgiven for the pleasure of good manners.

It was a luxury to sink back into the car seat and let Willem assume command. This is a sensation wasted on young girls, or true Daddy's Girls. These females live under the guardianship of a male. They can never fully appreciate the release involved with dropping the torch of independence, even for the brief interlude of a drive.

We headed out between the crisp fields of snow. The afternoon sun was already melting it in patches, but for long vistas there was only sparkling white so bright that it made my eyes ache. Far in the distance the snow picked up the lighter blue shadings of the sky so that the horizon was indistinguishable.

"Tell me, Miss Delaney, how someone of your beauty became an investigator. You have to admit, the image is usually one of sharp-eyed men with the shadow of a beard."

It was blatant flattery and I loved it. "Circumstance and a genetic predisposition to nosiness."

"Have you discovered any evidence in the matter of Lawrence?"

"Nothing concrete." I had no desire to discuss my suspicions.

"I really must find that manuscript."

The veneer of manners had slipped, revealing firm determination. I glanced over at him. "You and everyone else. Where do you suppose it is?" I baited him.

"I was hoping you could help me there."

I shook my head. "Lawrence didn't confide in me."

"And Mrs. Bell? She's offered no hint?"

"Even if she had, I couldn't divulge such information." I glanced out the window, wondering how to pump Willem about his secrets. It was at that moment that the car slowed and I realized we were turning down the drive to Lawrence's cottage at Magnolia Place. So much for yielding the helm of the ship to a man. I knew better than to disturb a crime scene.

"Will you help me find that manuscript?" Willem asked. "I have no one else to turn to but you, Sarah Booth. I'm desperate. Please help me."

I couldn't help but be turned on by his twinkling eyes or feel deeply touched by his words. Willem was a man who knew the right buttons to punch. But I was also older and wiser than I'd been a holiday before. "This isn't a good idea."

He stopped the car in front of Lawrence's cottage. The yellow crime scene tape fluttered around the front porch in the breeze and he turned to me, waiting. "I must see what he's written. The manuscript has to be inside the cottage, unless someone else took it. Lawrence was going to show it to me."

I hadn't ruled Willem out as a suspect, but he was

rather convincing in his talk of searching for the manuscript. It stood to reason that if he'd murdered Lawrence, he would have it.

He got out of the car and walked around to open my door, as if I were waiting on him to perform the male duty. It was reluctance, not manners, that kept me in the leather seat.

"You have some official capacity, Sarah Booth. If you're caught, no one will punish you. I'm a foreigner. Worse, a Latino." He leaned so close his lips brushed my hair. "A former soldier for socialism. A Sandinista." There were just enough Ss in the sentence, whispered against my ear in that Spanish rhythm, that I couldn't control the chill bumps. My God, if he could achieve this effect with talk of politics, what could he do to me with compliments?

"Coleman will put me in jail as fast as he would you if I disturb a crime scene." True enough, and I didn't want to go inside and confront the scene of Lawrence's death.

"If you find the manuscript, you can solve the murder." He arched his eyebrows. "I'm certain those memoirs are the basis for his murder. Lawrence made it clear he intended to reveal secrets. He just didn't understand how dangerous that could be."

"If I find the manuscript, you'll try to take it."

He shook his head. "Lawrence wasn't a cruel man, and as an artist, I respect his right to tell his story. But I have to be certain of what he knew, what he said. I won't try to take it. I simply have to know."

He was the epitome of sincerity. I wanted to believe him, but I needed more. "What are you afraid he wrote?"

He looked down the drive, focusing on the beautiful

oaks still frosted with a dazzle of snow. "My father assumed the name Arquillo. He was not Nicaraguan."

I remembered the spiteful comment at the dinner party. "He had a past to hide."

He nodded. "He started a new life in Nicaragua with my mother. He was very young during the war, a young man. Mistakes were made, but nothing so terrible. Still, my mother is alive. To have the secrets of the past printed . . . If they are in the book, I must prepare her. That's all I ask."

"Why would Lawrence include such things in his book?" This spoke to the heart of the matter. I'd watched Lawrence and Willem together. There seemed to be a genuine fondness. Lawrence had been instrumental in getting Willem's work accepted in several big galleries. He had, in fact, championed the artist.

"I don't believe he did, but I can't risk it. I came here expressly to ask Lawrence about this. My mother is dying." His eyes narrowed. "Sometimes death comes as a friend. Other times it is a goad, a stick that beats a person hard. When it is this way, the reaction can be fear and a desire to lash out." He turned abruptly. "Such things I've witnessed with my own eyes. My mother is terrified. She is obsessed with this book. I must do this for her to die in peace."

Never in my wildest dreams had I thought to feel pity for Willem Arquillo. Yet I did.

"What if we find the manuscript and you discover that Lawrence has written something . . . about your father?"

"Then I will prepare her for it. We can prepare together." He walked up to the crime tape and touched it. "Do not think me uncaring when I say that she may die before the manuscript is published. There are times when the gods show a moment of kindness."

"You won't feel compelled to try and change what Lawrence has written?"

He turned back to face me, the whiteness of the snow all around him contrasting with the golden tan of his complexion. "If Lawrence has written about my family, he has put down only the truth. You must understand that it is death which has caused my mother to lose her nerve, to want to tidy up a past that is not agreeable to neatness. I learned, long ago, never to fear the past. Once you do, it becomes a hobgoblin that grows larger with each passing night."

His eyes were the most striking color of gray and his gaze held me, making sure I understood. I nodded slowly. "If the manuscript is in the cottage, you'll read it and then give it to me?" Of course, Harold would have to be contacted. As executor of the estate, he would determine the ultimate fate of the biography. But it wouldn't hurt one whit if we looked at it.

"I want to know what to prepare for."

"Okay." I ducked under the crime tape and signaled for him to follow. Willem had touched my soft side, but there was one irrefutable fact. If I found the manuscript, I had an excellent chance of catching Lawrence's killer.

The front door opened at my touch. I noticed then, for the first time, that the lock was broken. When I'd found Lawrence's body, the door had been unlocked, but intact. We stepped into the room and I stopped. There was movement in the kitchen, and I put out a hand to halt Willem. It was an unnecessary precaution. He, too, had seen something.

Stepping in front of me, he moved toward the kitchen. I reached out to halt him, but he was already five paces across the room, moving with a speed and stealth that made me think of James Bond. Willem had not lied when he'd said he had been a soldier. The training showed.

A scuttling sound came from the kitchen, and I almost cried out when the small creature rushed out toward us.

Willem scooped the cat into his arms in a fluid motion. "Ah, Apollo," he whispered to the cat, chuckling softly. "You stole at least a year of my life." He came toward me with the cat in his arms. "Lawrence's favorite terrorist cat."

"Apollo," I whispered, unwilling to speak aloud. I scratched the cat's ears and was rewarded with a purr. "Madame said that the cats weren't allowed in the cottage. She said the sheriff put them out." The others were nowhere in sight.

"I heard that Lillian Sparks came and took them. She couldn't find this one." Willem transferred him into my arms. "I know he misses Lawrence."

It was an unexpected sentiment. I held the cat as I turned slowly about, examining the room.

"What is it?" Willem was staring at me.

"It's just that this place is so empty. All of the paintings, the books. Everything that was once so vivid. It's all fading."

"Lawrence is gone." He stepped away from me. "Where do you think the manuscript might be?"

I gently put Apollo on the floor. "Let's try his study. If it's there, it shouldn't be hard to find."

"I disagree. If it were easy, Brianna would already have it."

"Why are you so positive it was her?"

"Of all of us, she has the most to lose. And like it or not, her celebrity and her father's wealth give her a certain privileged status. Do you really think a local sheriff could stop her?"

That was a point I didn't want to argue. Coleman Peters, the sheriff, didn't seem the type to be cowed by Brianna's fame. But I'd seen too many other men fold beneath her demands. Instead of replying, I led the way into the study. We had to pass the hallway where the chalk outline of Lawrence's body was still on the floor. Mercifully, someone had cleaned up the blood. Willem stopped to look at the outline. "He deserved death with dignity. Not an ending as he scrabbled for the telephone."

Once again, Willem's sensitivity surprised me, but the reality of what we were doing had begun to set in. I wanted only to conduct the search and get out. It was as if I was peeping into a private place.

I found two boxes of manuscripts, most of them sent to Lawrence by other writers for him to review or edit. In a smaller plastic container were poems and plays, riddles, and the beginnings of three novels. There was no sign of the manuscript. If it had ever been in the cottage, someone else had taken it.

I stopped my work long enough to find Willem, who was poking through the pigeonholes of an old desk.

"It would be hard to hide a manuscript in that small a place," I noted.

He shut a small drawer. "Yes, a paper manuscript. But what if Lawrence had put it on computer disk?"

"There's no computer. Just an old electric."

Willem restacked a bundle of magazines. "Lawrence hated the idea of computers. It took him decades to use an electric typewriter. Only after arthritis began to hurt his fingers. But he wasn't a fool. He didn't want to learn new technology, but since no one has found his manuscript, I suspect he may have paid someone to put it on a computer disk for him." He opened another small drawer and poked through it with his finger before shutting it. "Even so, I don't believe it's here."

We'd worked in our coats and gloves because the cottage heat had been turned off. He pulled off his gloves and beat them against his leg to knock off the dust.

"I'm sorry," I said, as disappointed as he was.

"We tried." He lifted my gloved hand to his face, leaning into the palm. "I owe you, Sarah Booth."

"Don't be silly. I wanted to find it as much as you."

"I always repay my debts. It's a matter of honor."

He was so serious. "I like a man who talks of honor." I tried to lighten his mood.

"I should get you home. It's getting late."

Indeed it was. The light in the cottage had gradually dimmed as the sun had begun to fall below the oaks. We put everything back as we'd found it and started out of the house.

"Meow." Apollo called to us from the kitchen.

"We can't leave him," I said. The cat would starve in the cottage, and the idea of him being there, alone, waiting for Lawrence to return, was too sad to bear. I felt tears sting.

"Will you take him?" Willem asked.

"I have a dog."

"Yes, I recall." He bent to pick up the cat. Apollo arched his back and spit, one front paw striking out with lightning speed. Willem drew back his hand with a cry of surprise.

"Willem!" I grabbed the injured hand. The cat's claws had raked the back. He was bleeding. "Let me put something on that."

He shook his hand, pulling a handkerchief out of his pocket and binding the wound. "It's nothing. Let's get the cat and get out of here."

But when we tried to find Apollo, he was gone. Vanished. And darkness was falling.

"I'll come back for him tomorrow," I said. "We should go."

Willem took my arm and together we left the cottage, taking care to close the door behind us.

On the drive back to Dahlia House we were mostly silent, but it was not uncomfortable. Willem was deep in thought, his attention focused on some inner landscape.

"I'll call you tomorrow," he said as he stopped the car in front of the house. "Forgive me for not walking you inside."

He waited until I was up the stairs and opening the front door before he drove away. Thank goodness he missed the sight of Sweetie Pie rushing out of the house with such vehemence that she almost flattened me with the door.

"Sweetie," I called after her, but she was gone, vanishing into the darkness. There were several excited yelps, and I knew she was out for the evening. Ah, foolish youth. I would have to wait up for her. Alone. I decided to employ the long hours by working on the case.

Madame was right about one thing. I didn't know Lawrence. The best way to narrow the field of suspects was to get to know him a little better.

My mother had been an avid reader, adding her own books to the established library of the Delaney clan. I trotted into the library, and because it was so cold, I gathered up an armload of Lawrence's books and took them back to the parlor, where I immediately lit a fire and put on some Mozart. The cover of *Weevil Dance* caught my eye and I opened it to the title page.

"To Rosalyn, who taught me the lessons of life." The

dedication didn't surprise me, but the publication year did: 1942. Lawrence had been a very young man.

It was with a tingle of anticipation that I discovered that the setting of the book was Moon Lake, the very real locale where Lawrence, Madame, and several others had spent a summer.

After that initial observation, I was swept up in the story. The record player stopped, the fire burned low until I buried my body beneath the comforter on the sofa, and yet I read on. Lawrence transported me back in time to a lodge on the edge of a resort lake where illegal gambling was the order of the night and where four youths lost their innocence in a series of events that seemed to foretell the future.

It was four in the morning when I finished and knew with dead certainty that Lawrence Ambrose had been murdered.

11

I struggled out of a dark sleep with the sound of baying outside the parlor window. It was full light, and as I blinked myself slowly awake, the copy of *Weevil Dance* fell off my chest and onto the floor. For those few seconds of waking, I was not in the parlor of Dahlia House but caught in the glamour of a beautiful, secluded lake and the impetuousness of youth during the summer of 1940 when the world was radically changing. Lawrence had so vividly created the setting of Lula, Mississippi, the last gasp of the Great Depression, and the magic of a lost time, a desperate time, that I had dwelt there in my sleep. Lingering with me still were the consequences of an action taken in innocence. That it had all happened in the pages of his novel didn't matter. The characters were alive in my brain, and though I knew on some level that the crying I heard was my own Sweetie Pie, it was somehow confused with the characters of Lawrence's book.

"That hound of yours is howlin' to wake the dead."

Jitty was sitting on the end of the sofa, giving me the evil eye.

I rubbed at my face, a little unsure of my surroundings. I was half tempted to return to sleep and the rambling of my imagination. "Wake me in an hour," I requested, already envisioning the mirror-clear surface of the lake and the small rowboat coasting along beneath the overhanging cypress limbs.

Jitty demanded my full return to the present. "I saw you drive off with that artist man. What happened?"

Sleep was not going to be an option with Jitty in the room. I shifted to a sitting position and gave her a brief rundown of Willem's and my search for the manuscript.

"Breakin' and enterin', huh? That's what your boyfriends get you to do? What happened to the good ol' days when it was makin' out in the backseat of a car?"

I yawned, stretching one arm out from beneath the comforter. There was an annoying rasp, rasp, rasp and I realized the record player was still turning.

"No harm was done," I said. "Where were you last night?"

"Takin' care of nocturnal events. I tol' you I had a business meetin'."

I remembered my dream and sat up a little taller, giving Jitty the once-over. Business meeting, my ass. She was infiltrating my sleep and trying to send subliminal messages. I inspected her, hoping for a clue to her game plan from her attire. She was wearing a sweater set and wool skirt. Classy, professional, a change from the housewife attire of June Cleaver. Rather Hepburnish, Katharine, that is. Perhaps there was hope for Jitty. "Stay out of my dreams," I warned her.

"If it weren't for me, you wouldn't have any dreams." She stood up and began pacing. "Sarah Booth, you go around actin' like a hoodlum, that's the kind of man you'll attract. I was thinkin', maybe you should join that big Baptist church over in Greenwood. They got a bowlin' alley and a theater. It's a regular Disneyland. And they got classes for single people. It's sort of like a Datin' Game thing where they help people like you find a mate."

The suggestion was so out of left field that I almost choked. "I need coffee." I crawled off the sofa, turned off the record player, went to the front door and admitted Sweetie, who did not smell sweet, and headed to the kitchen. I put the coffeepot on and slumped into a chair to wait. Only the aroma of the brewing coffee kept me upright.

Jitty had the decency to wait until I had swallowed half a cup before she sat down beside me. The silver bangles she'd worn only a few weeks before had given way to a delicate, ornate wristwatch clasped to her arm with two black silken bands. I remembered a similar watch that my Aunt LouLane had worn each day, marking off the hours and the chores in her daily routine. My aunt had loved me greatly and had done her best to teach me the ways of a female. Responsibility and a constant awareness of time were hallmarks of "a great woman." That and a delicate womb. I was a failure in all regards.

"It's quarter after nine," Jitty said with a hint of disapproval. "Half the mornin' is gone already."

"I read all night," I said. "I was doing some research." As the coffee began to encourage my brain cells to move a bit, I was beginning to formulate a plan of action. "I think I need to go and talk with Millie's Aunt Bev."

"What's Millie got to do with this?"

"Her aunt was up at Moon Lake when Lawrence and Madame and one of Harold's relatives were there, along with Tennessee Williams. Lawrence's book *Weevil Dance* was based on that time. I know it's fiction, but I think the answer to all of this is buried up at Lula. The book has a story about a murder, a sheriff's brother who was involved in land scams. He used his brother's power to drive poor people off their land when they couldn't pay taxes. Then the sheriff killed his own brother. Maybe there's something there."

Jitty ignored the entire book idea.

"Speakin' of Harold, your time would be better spent with him than a book. I've done some hard thinkin' on this. Sarah Booth, a man isn't interested in a woman who reads. That's where a lot of your troubles come in. You think too much. Men find that unattractive."

The audacity of that remark so stunned me that I didn't reply.

Jitty must have mistaken my silence for compliance, because she continued. "I know your Aunt LouLane was doing the best by you she could, but I see now that sendin' you off to that college was a big mistake. You were already a handful, and all you did there was date weirdos and fill your head with ideas that kept you from focusin' on learnin' to please your man."

I carefully put the coffee cup on the table. The words threatened to spew out of my mouth, but I had to control them. Jitty was not trying to devil me. She was terrifyingly sincere. "I have no desire to please a man," I said stiffly, thinking that Jitty was a polar opposite of Kate Hepburn.

"Honey, you aren't tellin' me a *secret*. You broadcast that fact loud and clear. The problem is, all the men know it, too."

"Why should I want to please a man? Why shouldn't he want to please me?"

Jitty's eyes widened and she pointed a finger at me. "See there! That's exactly what I'm talkin' about. You somehow got the whole system turned upside down. It had to of happened in college, 'cause your Aunt LouLane surely knew better."

"Mother never felt she had to please Daddy." I dared her to deny this. Double-dared her.

Jitty's head rocked up and down, her lips pinching at the corners with satisfaction. "You're seein' it, girl. You're finally seein' it. They were aberrations. Your mama and daddy were a different case. They came of age in the sixties. That whole time was a fluke." She swept her arm in a wide circle. "The normal way of doin' things was thrown right out the window, and for that one generation, the upside down worked fine. Honey, this is a new century, and the pendulum has swung back. You can't keep pretendin' this is the sixties."

"I don't pretend anything," I said. "I'm a private investigator. I have a career and a home. If I decide to share my time with a man, it'll be because *he pleases me*."

"That's why you sleepin' with a book." Jitty pushed back her chair and stood up. She paced the kitchen, ignoring Sweetie Pie, who'd eaten her dog food and fallen asleep by the stove. Looking at the dog, I envied her. She went out and took her men as she found them, then came home for me to feed and love her. And best of all, she didn't have Jitty gnawing on her.

I decided on a different tack. "You think Harold is so wonderful, you should know that he spent the night before last with Brianna. And before you can get started, Brianna went to college. She's educated." I couldn't bring myself to say she was smart.

"She may have gone to college, but she didn't let it

ruin her. How many husbands did she catch? Four?
Five? I rest my case—Harold spent the night with her,
not you."

"He may sleep with her, but he won't marry her."
There wouldn't be enough of him left to slither down
the aisle to the altar. She'd suck him dry in two weeks.
But I wasn't going to say that to Jitty. Somehow she'd
find that a virtue in Brianna.

"Well, she's one up on you. You get an engagement
ring out of Harold, but you never consummated the
deal."

"Jitty! I thought you'd gone over to the right-wingers
and the hue and cry for family values."

"That's where I'm trying to take you. Nothin' wrong
with sealin' an agreement, though. Harold gave you the
ring. You shoulda pleased him, Sarah Booth. With just
a little bit of effort, you coulda had him eatin' out of
your hand."

"I should have deceived him and slept with him,
right?"

"You should have taken him up to that big ol' bed
and made him think he'd died and gone to heaven."

"And the next morning I could have polished his
shoes, cooked his breakfast, and sent him off to work.
While he's at his desk at the bank making money, I
could get dressed, do my makeup and hair, and then
spend the whole day preparing his favorite dinner and
wondering what dress he'd like for me to wear."

"Sounds to me like all that might take an hour. That
leaves seven to do whatever you want."

"What if what I want is to please myself?" I'd finally
circled the wagons on her. She was trapped.

"Then you got the life you want. Alone." She
stopped her pacing and leaned on the table with both

hands. "Nobody gets it all, Sarah Booth. Nobody gets to be Wonder Woman and Mama while playin' out Gypsy Rose Lee in the bedroom. There's not enough of a woman to fill all those roles. Not even you. All I'm sayin' is to make a choice. At thirty-three, if you want a child, maybe you'd better start thinkin' about a man who wants the comfort of a wife who pleases him—a home where he wants to be at night."

I swept the coffee cup off the table, shattering it against the cabinets. "That's stupid." I stood up so fast my chair spilled backward. "I put up with your seventies lectures and your attempts to get me pregnant, but I won't listen to this crap. I won't give up myself just to have a man. That's asking too much."

Jitty sighed. "Maybe in givin' up a little bit of yourself, you might find the rest."

"Damn you." I wanted to choke her, but she was already dead, and besides, she'd begun to fade. In a matter of seconds, I was sitting alone in the kitchen with a broken coffee cup and a bitter taste in my mouth.

A long soak in the tub improved my frame of mind but not by much. I put on some gray wool slacks and a black turtleneck and was ready for the drive to Greenwood when the phone rang. I was still suffering from the aftereffects of nearly losing Dahlia House, so I hadn't spent the money yet on caller ID. It was a choice I regretted as soon as I picked up the receiver and heard Harold's voice.

"Sarah Booth, I need to speak with you for a moment. Do you have time?"

I couldn't believe he still had the strength to speak in

a normal voice. I thought for sure Brianna's legendary ministrations would have left him with a weak, whispery rasp.

"Sure, what's up?" Never in a million years would he know that I was aware of, or upset by, his defection.

"Mr. Harkey is in my office. He claims that you and that artist, Willem Arquillo, were in Lawrence's house yesterday. He says you were working for me. For some reason, he believes that as executor of the estate, I gave you permission to enter the house and encouraged you to steal Lawrence's manuscript."

"He's nuts." It was a broad, general statement that covered the situation without a direct lie.

"That's not an exact answer, Sarah Booth." Harold's tone conveyed strained patience.

Drat him, he was expert at slicing through verbal vagaries. Boyd Harkey obviously had the goods on me—it was pointless to lie. My tactic was to hold admissions to a minimum. If Harold wanted to get picky, he could turn me over to Coleman for violating a crime scene. Sure, Coleman had a crush on me, but then he'd been good friends with some of the boys he'd crushed on the football squad when he'd been the number one linebacker for the Zinnia Panthers. In other words, his affections didn't get in the way of his job.

"I went in the cottage, with Willem," I confessed in an innocent voice.

"May I ask why?" There was a harshness in Harold's voice that spoke of his disapproval.

"We were looking for something."

"Obviously. What?"

"The manuscript."

There was a long silence. "I think you need to have a talk with me, Sarah Booth."

"I have an appointment right now."

There was another pause. "When?" he asked tersely.

"This evening? Say seven?" I'd have to catch him before Brianna latched on. I didn't want to spend time with a husk.

"I'll stop by Dahlia House. I want to say hello to Sweetie Pie."

"I'll be here." I hung up fast, and a little rudely.

I was eager to get on the road, but I couldn't find my wool jacket. I hunted through the hall closet to no avail. Madame's check was in the pocket—not a big issue since I didn't intend to cash it. The coat was somewhere in the house. But if I was going to talk with Beverly McGrath before noon, I had to get going. I settled for my leather jacket, picked up my keys, and went outside.

In the strange shift of weather that is accepted as winter in the Mississippi Delta, the day was balmy. The rise in mercury had melted the snow. It was nine o'clock and warm. On the spur of the moment, I let the top down on the Roadster and invited Sweetie Pie along for the ride. She wasn't exactly the type of dog that might be expected in a Chinese red Mercedes Roadster, but I found an old pair of sunglasses and a scarf, and Sweetie Pie was transformed into Connie Francis in *Where the Boys Are,* one of the beach movies Jitty had lately been brainwashed by.

We made a stop by the hospital first, and I was relieved to see Doc Sawyer standing out on the emergency ramp smoking a cigarette. His white hair caught the sun behind him, giving him the impression of a large dandelion that was about to combust.

"Hey, who's your friend. She's cute," he said, pointing to Sweetie Pie as I walked up to him.

"She's a movie star who's traveling incognito."

"Came to Zinnia for a little cosmetic surgery, did she. Nose job and ear trim?"

"Maybe a tummy tuck." For all of his humor, I saw there was something wrong. "What is it?"

He looked back at the hospital as if he expected someone to be watching him. "Let's take a walk." He put his arm around my shoulders and we walked down the ramp and across the gravel parking lot toward the incinerator where the hospital disposed of all types of surgical leftovers and other horrors.

"The initial tests are back on Lawrence," he said.

"And?"

"And he had some unusual things in his system."

I forced myself to wait. Doc wasn't a reticent man, but he was a cautious one. He was weighing what he wanted to say with great care.

"Lawrence had a thyroid condition, something he'd lived with for a long time, Sarah Booth. I wasn't surprised when the report came back showing Synthroid in his bloodstream." He looked for a long time at the yellow-brick building that housed the incinerator. "There was another drug. A derivative of Coumadin."

"Which is?" I prompted.

"An anticoagulant. Warfarin is a common enough prescription drug for patients with arteriosclerosis. The drug thins the blood so that it can pass more easily through the narrowed arteries."

"Did Lawrence have a heart blockage?"

Doc reached into his shirt pocket and pulled out another Salem. "None that I found. His heart was as strong as an ox and his arteries were amazingly clean for a man his age. There was some liver damage. Actually, his liver was a mess."

I was confused. "So he died of natural causes?"

He looked at me. "No, Sarah Booth. He bled to death. The combination of the warfarin and the thyroid medication was deadly once he was cut. He must have known what was happening and tried to call for help. The blood rush was too fast. He died before he could make the call."

"So it was an accident?"

Doc signaled me to walk a little farther with him. We made it to a stand of willows beside the river where the hospital had put up a picnic table, for the families of patients, I supposed.

"I've called Lawrence's family physician and ordered his medical records. I should have them this afternoon. but"—he looked down at the slow swirl of yellow river—"he wasn't taking warfarin. At least not on doctor's orders."

"Then why?"

"Someone was poisoning him. Coumadin is often used in rat poison. It's easy to get, easy to hide in food. Judging from the condition of his internal organs, I'd say he'd been taking it in small doses for something like a couple of weeks."

It was my turn to stare into the muddy water. "Have you told Coleman yet?" I asked.

Doc shook his head. "I just got the lab reports about ten minutes before you drove up. I'm going in to call him now." He turned and started to walk back.

"Doc? How sophisticated would a person have to be to know about Coumadin?"

He stopped and turned back. "Anybody who's ever talked with an exterminator could know. It's one of the selling points in rodent eradication. A large dose of Coumadin will weaken the blood vessels until there's massive leakage. The rat craves water. In the quest for water, the rat leaves the house. End result is no decaying rats in the house." He shrugged. "The interaction with the thyroid medication would take a little more knowledge. Then again, maybe they didn't have to know that."

I watched him walk back to the hospital, a man carrying the burden of ugly knowledge. I was weighted down with a strange form of grief. I'd just finished one of Lawrence's novels. His brilliance was undeniable, and yet unacclaimed in his latter years. He'd shone brightly and then faded, and finally been extinguished in a deliberate act. And now the only person who cared was an old woman.

And me.

And dammit, it wasn't enough.

I heard Sweetie Pie's gentle baying, and I felt a rush of kinship with the dog. She somehow sensed my sadness and was commiserating with me. It was good to have a dog, even if she was dressed as Connie Francis.

I walked back to the car only to discover that Sweetie's sweet and sad singing wasn't meant for my ears. Standing with his front paws on my expensive car was a strange black dog with one thing on his mind.

"Sweetie," I said softly as I got in the car. "You've got to stop this. I can't get a date, and you have every dog in the county hot after you."

"Ooo-ooo-ahh," she cried softly as we drove away and left her latest conquest in the ambulance bay, a victim of unrequited love.

12

Silt-loaded Delta rivers surround and sweep through the old town of Greenwood, Mississippi. Near the heart of the city, the Yalobusha is joined by the Tallahatchie to form the Yazoo.

The rivers bear the names of Indian tribes long removed from their native soil, a reminder that a particular culture is imposed on the land for only a brief time. Of course the damage done by chemicals, fertilizer, and removal of natural foliage may well be permanent.

There's a graciousness to Greenwood that has always pleased me, and I drove through the business district, enjoying the old brick buildings. I'd decided against phoning Beverly McGrath. I would take my chances and show up on her doorstep. Of course Millie might have alerted her of my impending visit, but I didn't think so. Millie was eager to help me probe Lawrence's death. She was certain that if her aunt had something to tell about Moon Lake, Aunt Bev would be delighted to talk.

I wasn't so sure, but I parked at the curb, left Sweetie

Pie snoozing in the front seat, and walked up the side-walk to the front door. Beverly McGrath's home was a neat clapboard painted white with green shutters. An old cypress swing hung from chains on the front porch, which was free of leaves and debris. Although there were no plants blooming in the yard, the shrubs were neatly trimmed and the earth bordering the sidewalk had been freshly tilled. Aunt Bev was eager for spring.

The neighborhood was older and had the air of a place long settled and loved. When I was a small child my parents had taken me to Meridian, to visit the Booth side of the family. Grandpa Lowell Booth was a banker, and the neighborhood had the same air. Solid, safe, a place where families rode the tide of life with grace and dignity.

Beverly McGrath answered the door almost as soon as I knocked, and I could see a good bit of Millie in her blue eyes and bottle blond hair. She was a slender woman who gave the impression of meeting life head-on.

She didn't know me from Adam's housecat, but she gave me a warm smile as she asked how she could help me. Though she spoke with a drawl, it was different from any I'd ever heard. There was a hint of some other influence I couldn't put my finger on.

Her puzzled look told me that Millie hadn't alerted her to my visit. I introduced myself and followed her into a living room stuffed with antiques. "What lovely things," I said, touching the plush brocade of an old rocking chair.

"Some are family things, some I picked up at estate sales. I had a refinishing business when I was younger." She stood, hesitating. "Would you like some coffee and plum pudding?"

I'd resisted fruitcake for two whole mornings. I had a choice between feeling sanctimonious or indulged. "I haven't had plum pudding since I was a child and my Aunt LouLane would bring it with her when she came for Thanksgiving." It was a peculiar memory, because it occurred to me that once LouLane took over the job of mothering me, she never made plum pudding again.

"I didn't know your aunt personally, but I've heard so many nice things about her," Bev said. "Let me get us some refreshments."

I examined the room while I waited, noting the handsome portrait of a man over the mantel. Family patriarch, no doubt. Whoever he was, he was rugged with a sharp eye. I knew that look, and the laugh lines that marked his face. Millie Roberts, née Wells, came from a strong gene pool.

"What brings you to Greenwood, Sarah Booth?" Bev asked as she came into the room bearing a tray laden with coffee, pudding, and some homemade cheese straws. I had to swallow before I could answer.

"Millie was telling me some stories about the past, and she said that you'd spent some time up at Moon Lake."

She was placing the tray on the coffee table. Her toe snagged one of the table legs and she almost stumbled. I grabbed the tray, and she was able to right herself. I couldn't be certain if the dismay was due to her near fall or my reference to Moon Lake. Whichever it was, she recovered quickly.

"So clumsy. I have to wear these big old shoes now. To accommodate my corns and hammertoes and all the other wages of sin." She laughed at the expression on my face.

"Fashion sins, Sarah Booth. Yes, I was up at Moon

Lake for a summer. It was 1940, and I can tell you honestly it was the best time of my life. I never took a step unless it was in five-inch heels, and I loved every minute of it. Oh, I was nimble then. And had a figure that made men stop and stare, if I do say so myself. Once George Reeves, you know he played Superman on television years later, anyway he came up on the stage with me and proposed. It was incredible." She sighed.

"For ten short weeks, I lived a dream. Sometimes, when I think about it now, it seems that I must have read it in a book. Every night there was dancing, and lights out on the lake. So many famous people stayed at the resort." Her skin had actually flushed with pleasure. "It isn't possible that I had such excitement and glamour in my life. But I did."

Whatever I'd anticipated, it wasn't this Hollywood memory. I'd assumed, after reading *Weevil Dance*, that Bev would be somehow scarred. In the book, four young people witnessed a murder. I was positive something sinister had actually happened at Moon Lake that summer. Something other than gambling, gangsters, and teenage adventure.

"You were there with Lawrence Ambrose and Rosalyn Bell." I watched closely for her reaction to those names.

"I was indeed," she said. "Rosalyn got me the job, actually. She knew I could sing." When the folds of her face finally did sink into sadness, her age was revealed. Until that moment, she'd been able to hold the illusion that she was much younger. "Such a pity about Lawrence. He was seventy-six. My age." She reached to pick up the coffeepot and her hand shook. "My husband has gone on, fifteen years ago. I lost one of my boys when he was an infant. And it nearly killed us all when my niece Janice was murdered. Soon it will be my turn to die, and I have to say that with each passing year, the prospect seems more and more attractive."

That wasn't a statement to be easily refuted, but it was one that left me very curious. Bev seemed in good health, and she certainly lived in comfortable surroundings. Why would death seem appealing?

"Did you stay in touch with Lawrence or Ma— Mrs. Bell?"

Bev finished pouring the coffee and held a cup out to me before she answered. "No." She put cream and sugar in her coffee and sipped it. "I was brought home from Moon Lake before the summer ended. My father came up and got me. It was a humiliating scene." She put the coffee down, and once again her hand shook. "He dragged me out of the casino by my hair." She looked up at me. "I mean that. It was horrible. Lawrence tried to intervene, and my father beat him savagely. I was so ashamed . . . I didn't answer their letters or talk to them. They came to visit me three times, and it was a difficult journey back then. No one had a car or gas, but they came. And I wouldn't answer the door. My father thought it was because he'd scared me into obeying him. He was so satisfied with himself." The lines around her mouth deepened, and I understood that it didn't matter that sixty years had passed. She was still angry. "I just couldn't face them. That's why I didn't open the door."

"I'm so sorry." I held my coffee cup and didn't know what to say. "I didn't mean to—" What? Drag up the past? But that was exactly what I'd come to do. "I'm sure they understood."

"You young people today are so lucky. You chart your own futures, and you don't even realize how different things were one generation before you. I wanted to be a torch singer. I didn't have great expectations. I thought maybe a small club in Memphis, or even New Orleans. Some place exotic where I could have an apartment and sing at night. I didn't expect to get wealthy or become famous. I only wanted to sing." She looked me dead in the eye. "Not a terribly big dream, is it?"

I started to say that sometimes having a dream was more important than achieving it, but before I blurted it out I realized how utterly stupid that platitude was. It's one thing to fail at a dream, and quite another to have it choked and suffocated.

"How did you find out that Lawrence was dead?" I changed the course slightly, wanting to spare her further digging into that particular tar pit of memory.

"I read the paper. Every day. And Millie called. She remembered the day I took her up to meet him. That left an impression on her."

"I only met Lawrence a few days before he died, but he left an impression on me, too. He was extraordinary."

"Brilliant," Bev said, and her face took on that internal light. "He wrote and directed our little productions up at the Crescent, that was the name of the casino. We had a special production every Friday and Saturday night. You wouldn't believe the people who came to see us. Rosalyn was a fine dancer, and she knew some very unusual routines. If some of those men had realized that she was barely sixteen . . ." Bev laughed out loud. "We were a scandal, but everyone thought we were legal."

It was so easy to follow Bev back into the past. Part of it was because I'd read *Weevil Dance* and I had everything set up in my brain. Another part, though, was her vivid recollection.

"I know this is going to sound like a strange question, but did anything untoward happen up at Lula that summer?"

It was almost as if the expression froze on her face for a split second. I couldn't be positive that I'd seen anything, because she immediately recovered and drew her eyebrows together in thought as she handed me a serving of plum pudding.

"There was that murder, of course."

"Murder?" I played innocent.

"That awful man was killed. It couldn't have happened to a more deserving guy." She waved a hand in a quick gesture that gave me a glimpse of the girl she once had been. "Lawrence and Tom, that's Tennessee's real name, had all of us in a high state of nerves, predicting that all hell would break loose because of Hosea's murder."

I slowed the hand that was shoveling plum pudding into my mouth and swallowed. The pudding was delicious, and I was caught up imagining Lawrence and Tennessee Williams embellishing a murder. But I needed the facts, not some imaginary version. "Tell me exactly what happened," I said, pointing at the pudding with my spoon. "This is the best I've ever had."

"My great-grandmother's recipe. A family secret. The only person I ever told was Lawrence." Some of the enthusiasm had faded from her face, and once again she looked old and worn. "Hosea Archer was the man who was murdered, the son of Senator Jebediah Archer. It was a big scandal, and there was some speculation that his daddy would come down to Mississippi and shut the Crescent down."

"A U.S. senator could have such influence on a place in Mississippi?"

"Don't be so naive," she said, but gently. "A word from Senator Archer and the doors of the the Crescent would have been nailed shut. Gambling was illegal back then, and the only way the casino stayed in business was because it had protection."

"There must have been a lot of money." I *was* naive. It had never occurred to me that someone in Washington would have his finger in a Mississippi pie. Mississippi had always been the bastard stepchild of the nation. The Crescent must have been a truly high-stakes house where big money changed hands.

"Several senators were connected to the Crescent. Mississippi had some powerful men then. Old men who knew how things worked. The casino was a perfect place for the rich and powerful to come and play without the eyes of the world on them. It was secluded, a private little hideaway with the benefit of a few celebrities hanging about. Hollywood and Washington have always been in bed together, you know. Kennedy wasn't the first and he won't be the last."

I was getting the picture. Lawrence had hinted at undercurrents of power in his book—even drawn strong parallels—but Bev was laying it on the line.

"Anyway, after Hosea was killed, there was a week or so when everyone tiptoed around, but nothing came of it. The gamblers kept coming, and the riverboats drifted around the lake. The liquor flowed, and we kept our jobs."

"Who killed Archer?"

"As far as I know, no one was ever arrested." She shook her head. "Hosea was caught cheating in a card game up in the Yukon Room. It was a magnificent room decorated with a huge stuffed bear and moose heads. Teddy Roosevelt loved that particular room, I was told. It was where the high rollers played cards."

I spooned the pudding into my mouth, alternating with a sip of coffee. By this time, I honestly didn't care what Bev told me as long as she kept talking. She knew some fascinating history.

"Let me get back to Hosea, though. He was not much older than we were, but he acted like he was a big man. He had this attitude, because his father was powerful, that he could treat everyone like servants. For a Southern boy, he was horrible to the Negro girls who worked in the kitchen and laundry. Arabella told me and Lenore that he pushed her face down on his bed when she went up to change the sheets and tried to sodomize her."

"What a creep."

"He was indeed. On the staircase one time he passed me and grabbed my breasts." Her hands went up in a defensive gesture. "I grew up with brothers, though, and I knew a thing or two. I jammed my knee right between his legs and pushed him down the stairs backward. I was terrified he'd tell on me and get me fired, but he never did anything."

"No wonder somebody shot him." This bore a resemblance to Lawrence's novel, but only in the vaguest sense of plot. And perhaps in the reaction of the four young people. My disappointment was keen. I'd assumed that the story Bev would tell me would somehow parallel actual events. I'd conveniently forgotten that Lawrence was a fiction writer.

"Yes, he probably deserved to be shot, but it was a terrible shock. I was taking a round of drinks up to the room when the alarm went off, alerting the gamblers that a raid was in progress. I heard the shot and a lot of scrambling. When I opened the door of the Yukon Room, there was the body. He'd flipped backward in his chair and was lying there, cards scattered everywhere and blood seeping out onto the carpet."

Since he was shot during a poker game, he was probably shot by a man rather than one of the women he enjoyed abusing. Unless I was badly mistaken, women weren't allowed to play poker with the men unless it was in a movie or out West.

"Was there actually a raid?" In Lawrence's book, the killing had been an inside job. The raid had been a setup.

"Yes. There was a system of bells set up in each gambling room. It was a truly remarkable place. Each room had a theme and a different game of chance. There were several high-stakes poker rooms, roulette, craps, blackjack, all of that. But down at the front desk, hidden beneath the counter, were buttons. It was an old system that was put in back when the local sheriff used to bust the card games.

"If there was a raid or trouble, the clerk at the desk could reach under the counter and press all the buttons. Up in the gaming rooms, the bells would sound and alert the gamblers that a raid was in progress. They'd mostly have time to grab their money and hurry down the back stairs."

It was an amazingly simple system, but one that would work.

"How many raids when you worked there?"

"It was strange because the local sheriff was paid off. He kept clear of the Crescent, except to come eat a fancy dinner and listen to our show. He had something of a crush on Rosalyn."

"The sheriff led the raid?" I was interested in Hosea

Archer's murder only because it was so blatant—and so thoroughly uninvestigated.

Bev nodded in response to my question. "It was a Tuesday night, which were generally slow. The weekends were the busy times, when folks came downriver from Memphis and upriver from New Orleans. On weeknights, Rosalyn and I took turns entertaining. Either she'd dance or I'd sing. Lawrence directed and sometimes played the piano. Lenore, though, was usually the pianist for me. She could play those old songs beautifully."

"What about Tennessee Williams?" I couldn't help but ask.

"Oh, he was too shy to perform. He was a little older than us, and a hundred times more reserved. He and Lawrence wrote songs together and skits, but he'd never put a toe on the stage. He just stood in back of the curtain and watched. Lenore was shy like that, too, and didn't like to perform. She sewed all of our costumes. And she played a guitar, too. It was something of a scandal, a woman with a guitar. But she was very talented. Very popular with the guests. Maybe a little too popular." Pain crossed her face, and I wondered if she was thinking of Lenore's suicide.

Lenore was an Erkwell. Even though the family had been hit hard by the Depression, they were still considered upper-crust. If Bev's father was so opposed to her working at the Crescent that he dragged her out by the hair, I wondered about Lenore, a society girl.

"How did Lenore Erkwell manage to get permission to be at the Crescent?"

Bev brightened. "Her folks thought she was with relatives in Tunica. Lenore was shy, but she was very strong-willed. Of the four of us, she was the one who came up with all the plans. The whole adventure in Lula was her idea." Her voice grew hesitant. "I never knew what her life at home was like, but she had no problem doing whatever she wanted. Either her parents were stupid or they didn't care as long as she didn't cause trouble."

Still, it was a daring lie for a young girl. "Tell me about the night of the murder. What did you see?"

Bev's gaze focused on a middle distance where the past was most easily seen. "It was my night to sing, so I did my numbers and then went into the bar to help out. That's what we did. We were the performers, but we also helped serve drinks, and if the dining room was really busy, we'd serve there, too.

"That's when I got the call to take the drinks up to the Yukon Room. All the other waitresses were running their feet off, and I always liked to go up and serve the men playing poker. It was exciting, that big pile of chips on the table, the smoke, the intensity. And, of course, the tips."

Lawrence had described a game in the book, and it was easy to picture the scene as Bev talked.

"Like I said, I was outside the door when the alarm went off. I could just hear it through the closed door. There was the gunshot, and when I opened the door, Hosea was lying on the floor."

"What about everyone else in the room?"

"They went out the window and down the back stairs."

"Who was in the room?"

She shook her head. "I never saw them."

"But there had to have been talk. A man was killed."

She looked down at the floor. "There was talk. But that's all it was."

My heart rate began to increase. "Who was supposed to be in that room?"

"You'll laugh."

"Try me."

She met my gaze. "J. Edgar Hoover."

"The head of the FBI?"

She lifted her eyebrows. "I knew you wouldn't believe me."

I didn't disbelieve her, it was just that Hoover was almost a mythic figure. The control freak head of the FBI who cross-dressed. It was almost too much. And now he was involved, or at least a witness, in a gambling murder in Mississippi. "Did you ever see him in the hotel?"

She put her coffee cup down abruptly. "You'd think one day I'd learn. No matter how many times I've been looked at like a fool or a liar, I still open my mouth. If you have to know, I did see Hoover at the Crescent. He was there on at least two occasions that summer. Fishing in Moon Lake. Lawrence took him out in the boat and paddled him to all the fishing holes."

"I'm sorry, Beverly," I said, reaching over and grasping her hand. "Hoover is almost like a joke to someone my age. I didn't doubt you, it's just that he's almost like a fictional character to me."

She gave me a long look. "Lawrence said that exact thing. He said he could never write a character like Hoover because no one would believe it."

"You honestly think he was in the room when Hosea was killed?"

She cleared her throat. "I believe that and more. I think Hoover may have shot him. Or at least he knew who did."

That got my attention. "Why?"

"I don't think the shooting had anything to do with gambling or money. There was something else going on. Look, the sheriff was in the casino. He came up,

questioned me to see if I'd seen anything, which I
hadn't. They loaded up the body and hauled it away.
That was the end of it."

"Where was Lawrence when all of this was going
on? Did he see anything?" Perhaps he'd witnessed the
shooting. It was possible that someone from far in the
past had a lot of reason to fear what Lawrence might
write.

"No, Lawrence didn't see a thing. He was too busy
with Lenore's boyfriend. He was outside on the front
porch, playing the role of big brother. Or trying to.
Lenore was . . . involved with a man. There was serious trouble brewing."

"And Lenore?"

"She was outside, chasing that man like white trash.
It was quite a scene. Lawrence got into a terrible fight
with the man. A bloody fight." She shook her head.
"I've never seen a woman more obsessed."

"You're positive neither of them saw the murder?"

"Positive," she said firmly.

"Mrs. McGrath, Beverly, you've helped me more
than you can know," I told her as I prepared to leave.
"A million thanks."

"Tell Millie to come by more often. And be careful.
If someone hurt Lawrence for poking into the past, they
might not think twice about hurting you."

13

All the way home I pondered the questions Bev's conversation raised. Sweetie Pie, drowsy from her beauty nap, enjoyed the wind through her ears as we sped across the flat reaches of the Delta.

The scenario Bev had created with Hoover, whether accurate or not, had begun to color my own thoughts. Lawrence had not written about the murder at Moon Lake—at least not in any factual way. But there were parallels between the facts and *Weevil Dance*. It was possible that someone powerful was afraid Lawrence might write the truth about that long-ago murder. A wealthy and powerful person might have hired a killer to make certain that Lawrence never published a whisper about the incident.

The flaw in that scenario was the time frame Doc Sawyer had imposed. Lawrence had been given small doses of Coumadin for at least two weeks. Not a technique a gun-for-hire would use. I still believed he was killed by someone he knew.

Bev McGrath's recounting of history made it clear to

me that Lawrence was more than capable of playing with facts—and doing it with great literary skill. Using the magic of imagination and talent, he'd woven his own tapestry out of the tragedy at Moon Lake. But it was also clear to me that Lawrence had known the true story. It was very possible someone hadn't wanted to see what pictures Lawrence could paint if he published his autobiography.

Hoover's presence at Moon Lake was both fascinating and horrifying. He was obviously the character Donald Bathos in *Weevil Dance,* a man of great power who provides the cloak of protection for the murder to take place, a political necessity. So Hoover had visited Moon Lake and the Crescent casino. Gambling at that time was illegal. Though Prohibition as a national event had ended, liquor was still illegal in Mississippi. Hoover enjoyed every vice the average American was denied, and based on my limited knowledge of his predilections, perhaps a few more.

Hoover, in his time, was incredibly powerful. His vindictiveness was legendary. He was not a snake I'd want to poke with a short stick. Had Lawrence decided to reveal the Moon Lake incident in his biography? That would put a whole new spin on people who might want to stop publication of the book.

But Hoover was dead, and his reputation already tarnished by revelations of corruption, perversion, and criminal behavior. Moon Lake was a long time in the past, and a book now wouldn't exactly blow the cover off his past.

Still, it would be interesting to see if any official documentation of Hoover's Mississippi visit existed. I knew better than to think I could waltz into the records department of the FBI and turn up a travel voucher for such a trip. From what I knew of politics, powerful men always thought they were above the law. They made sure to leave no official tracks.

No, if I dug around this story, I'd have to start with Hosea Archer and his father. There should be plenty of local print on the honorable Jebediah Archer, U.S. senator from Clarksdale, Mississippi. My state, like most others, had a long record of electing crooks and ne'er-do-wells. Many prominent Mississippi politicians, unfortunately, were also stupid. Statesmanship hasn't always been a high priority, in the past or present.

Bits and pieces of my limited memory of Senator Archer were coming back. He'd retired before I was born, but my parents had mentioned him. It was not in a flattering light. I just couldn't remember if he was simply a crook, stupid, a racist, or all of the above. It would come back to me after a little brain food.

Although I'd eaten two servings of plum pudding, I was starving when I pulled into the driveway of Dahlia House. It was late afternoon, and soon I would have to deal with Harold. I hadn't really given a lot of thought to what I was going to tell him. Or how I was going to hide the fact that I was on to him and Brianna. He'd hardly had time to recover from Sylvia Garrett throwing him over and going to Paris and he was already bedding Miss Most Photogenic Succubus.

As much as I didn't want to talk to Harold about my visit to Lawrence's cottage, I had some questions about his aunt Lenore. Strong-willed and yet a suicide. The character trait seemed to defy the fact, but then again maybe it was only strong-willed people who were capable of taking fate into their own hands. It wasn't an issue I'd given a lot of thought, but I was certain that if I brushed off my psychology texts, I'd be able to find theory and case studies. Just another lead to follow in this already complex case.

Winding down the drive, I dodged the stag line of dogs and parked. In her Connie Francis disguise, Sweetie slipped by them, and we went into the kitchen and made a peanut butter and jelly sandwich. Since I was knife deep in the nut-butter, I made Sweetie one, too. We stood at the kitchen sink and dined together. Sweetie was totally absorbed in her food, but I kept a wary eye out for Jitty. Eating at the counter was "white trashy." Jitty had nailed me on it several times, pointing out that it was a convenient excuse for me to eat: too fast, too much, and without satisfaction. She was right—therefore I gobbled faster before I got caught. I didn't have time for the niceties.

The red light on my answering machine blinked like a tiny little pulse of possibility. I didn't catch Lillian Sparks's voice at first, but when she started talking about Lawrence's cats, I knew who it was.

"Apollo is still at the house," she was saying. "He must be brought to me immediately. Rosalyn has paid for your services; bring me the cat. I shall be home this afternoon and expect you to do your duty."

I rolled my eyes. Lillian was like a blackberry briar. Once you were in it, there was no way to get out without losing a little skin. The good news was that she wanted Apollo. Or at least she was willing to assume the responsibility for him. I had Sweetie, and that was enough, especially since, lately, she was the most popular bitch in town, outshining even Brianna.

Seeing as how I was already in Dutch with Harold about visiting Lawrence's cottage, one more trip wouldn't hurt. Although Sweetie whined pitifully to go, I left her home in deference to Apollo. It took fifteen minutes for me to drive to Magnolia Place. I slowed under the trees, caught by a sense of loss that, for some reason, made me think of my parents.

The crime tape was still up, the door still unlocked, and Apollo cried from within the house. I hurried to the kitchen and began to open the cabinets, looking for cat food. The poor animal had to be close to starvation.

"Kitty, kitty," I called as I searched. There had been some Seafood Delight in a cabinet. I remembered it from my and Willem's search. I cursed myself for not being thoughtful enough to open a can and leave it for the cat the day before.

"Aha!" I saw the can in the back of the pantry and reached for it. A three-can stack of tinned smoked oysters toppled over. I halted in mid-reach. A brown plastic-coated bag of rat poison was sitting right beside the cat food.

I picked up the food and opened the can. Apollo magically appeared at my ankles, winding back and forth between them. I put the food on a plate and put him in the sunroom where I could easily shut the door. Then I went back to the pantry. I'd searched the damn thing myself, looking for the manuscript. The poison had not been there the day before. I would have seen it. I couldn't have overlooked it. Yet there it was.

Lawrence kept a stack of brown paper sacks beside his cabinet and I used salad tongs to put the rat poison in a bag. I put it in the trunk of the car and retrieved the cardboard box I'd thought to bring. I didn't mind holding Apollo, but cats are not always rational when it comes to cars. He would be safer in the box than in my arms.

Apollo was surprisingly agreeable. I made sure to cover my tracks, taking the cat food can and plate with me. I was about to start the car when I was struck with a terrible thought.

One of Lawrence's cats had recently died. I vividly remembered Lawrence sitting in my parlor, insisting that the cat had died of natural causes. My instincts told me there was another, uglier possibility. I was deep in thought as I drove to Lillian Sparks's to deliver Apollo.

True to her word, Lillian was sitting in her parlor window, one eye on the street and one eye on a German novel. She opened her front door and urged me to bring Apollo into his new home.

Lillian had grown up on a horse farm east of Zinnia on the Tallahatchie River. Her family had once been very wealthy, and Lillian had studied languages at the Sorbonne. As a child she'd followed her father around the world, buying such exotic horses as Akhal-Teke, Paso Finos, Connemaras, Belgian warm bloods, and big Irish Drafts. Vernon Sparks had hoped to breed the perfect sports horse.

He'd gone bankrupt in the process, and Lillian had clung to the only bit of real estate that wasn't encumbered by debt, the family house in Zinnia. I'd visited her in the past with my father, and as soon as I stepped into the room, I remembered the bookcases that stretched floor to ceiling around a huge stone fireplace.

For a time Lillian had worked for the World Health Organization, traveling through Third World countries as if they were the familiar roads of her home state. And then she'd come home to Zinnia and begun a twenty-year crusade to preserve, protect, and cherish the history and culture of her hometown. My mother, the socialist Peace Corps worker, had loved her.

Lawrence was part of that history and culture, and so were his cats.

"Ah, Apollo," she said, lifting the cat out of the box and cuddling him, though he didn't seem particularly interested in affection. After a moment she put him down and watched as he examined the room. As if by magic the other three cats appeared in the open doorway to the huge central hall. Apollo never looked back as he took off to be with them. "He'll adjust," she said. "They miss Lawrence, but they have each other."

For a woman who'd held children dying of diphtheria, she'd amazingly managed to retain her soft side.

I bent down to pick up the box. I didn't want to appear to be rude, but I wanted to talk to the veterinarian. The business about Lawrence's dead cat was worrying me.

"Have you found any conclusive evidence to bring Brianna to justice?" Lillian asked.

Her question startled me, but then I remembered that she and Rosalyn were good friends. It was an odd alliance, the poor dance teacher and the very sophisticated woman who'd once had great wealth.

"Nothing conclusive."

She motioned me to a chair and sat back in her own. I noticed then that her feet were terribly swollen. Having known her as an indomitable force, I'd failed to see the changes time had wrought.

"I'm worried about Rosalyn," she said. "She's obsessed with proving Brianna guilty."

I didn't say anything. Client–investigator code of ethics. The best I could hope was that escape would come sooner rather than later.

"Tell me, Sarah Booth, do you believe Lawrence was murdered?"

The answer was yes, but I'd learned that a nonresponse often triggers more reaction. "There's nothing conclusive."

"What have you learned about the missing manuscript?"

Obviously the gossip was all over town. "I'm following some leads," I hedged.

"I hope it's gone. Nothing good could come of it."

I was surprised. Lillian was the strongest supporter of the arts in Sunflower County. She'd always been an advocate of Lawrence's work. This book, whatever else it was, would be of literary interest since Lawrence had written most of it.

"Did Lawrence tell you what he was writing?" I asked. If she knew what the book contained, it would certainly help me focus my investigation.

"I didn't know a thing about it until his dinner party. When I heard he was going to let Brianna Rathbone take credit for writing it, I was horrified. Now that he's dead, I hope the wretched thing has vanished forever."

"Why?"

"Only a young person can ask such a question. Imagine, if you can, what it might feel like to have the follies of your youth in black and white for everyone to read."

"Are we talking about your follies, or Rosalyn's?" I asked. Though she covered well, I could tell I'd hit a nerve.

"You're smarter than I thought, Sarah Booth, but I won't be drawn into this discussion. No one lives without regrets."

"Then may I ask another question?" I hadn't anticipated that Lillian might have information that would bear on the case. Now I thought she might.

"I reserve the right not to answer."

"Why did Rosalyn stay here in Zinnia, teaching dance to untalented and ungrateful young girls?"

She considered a moment before she answered. "Rosalyn changed that summer up at Moon Lake. She went up there a young girl with dreams of dancing across Europe. She came back to Zinnia a different young woman, much subdued. Of course she did a stint in New York, but I believe she'd lost the heart to really reach. Of all the arts, dance is the most demanding mistress. Time is so brief. She came back to Zinnia because it was home."

Her answer had been carefully phrased. "What about Lawrence?"

"Oh, he was a talented boy."

"That's not exactly an insight, Lillian."

"What do you want me to tell you?"

"Did Lawrence change that summer? Was it possible he witnessed something . . . dangerous?"

"He was thrust into a world of gambling and powerful men. The rest of the world was engaged in war. France fell to the Germans that summer, Sarah Booth. The world as we knew it was changing. Lawrence was fully aware. He changed, undoubtedly. After that summer he went to Paris, a correspondent for a national magazine. He was there when he wrote his first novel. That summer at Moon Lake was the turning point for a lot of things. It was the last idyll of youth, I believe, for all four of those young people."

She was a foxy old lady who knew how to dance. "I wouldn't exactly call the scene of a murder idyllic," I said flatly.

"Yes, the murder of Hosea Archer in a card game. You've dug that up, have you? The common sentiment around the Delta was that he got what he deserved."

Lillian had shown far more compassion for Lawrence's cats. The reference to Hosea Archer had hardened her mouth. It made me decide to press.

"Do you remember Senator Archer?"

Her hands tightened on the arms of her chair, a reflex she wasn't even aware of. "Too well. You're too young to remember, but my father had dealings with him."

"I understand Archer was something of a high roller."

"Indeed. He rolled over anyone who got in his way. My father had this idea of creating a national stud service in Mississippi. Along the lines of the Irish stud. Senator Archer was supposed to help him." Her face was well schooled, but it was her voice that gave her away. She hated the man. "The senator decided at the last minute that he couldn't support the idea. Father had been counting on his help. Without it, the entire plan collapsed. We lost everything except this house."

To quote a wise old country person, this pile was old but the stink was still on the turd.

"What about his son, Hosea?"

"I doubt if even his mother grieved his death. He came out to the horse ranch a few times. He was a misanthropic little sadist. It's a blessing he wasn't allowed to reproduce."

So much for epitaphs. "His murder was never solved. Did Rosalyn ever say anything about it?"

"This isn't an avenue you should pursue, Sarah Booth. Hosea Archer was trash. Let it go at that. No one cared when he was killed in 1940, and certainly no one cares now."

In the background I could hear the cats running about in another room. That reminded me of the somewhat gruesome task I needed to complete. Lillian took my momentary silence as an opportune moment to rise and indicate I should leave.

"Thank you for bringing Apollo. I'll take good care of him."

She walked me to the door, and just as I was leaving,

she put a hand on my arm. "Your parents were wonderful people. I'm not so sure they would approve of your new trade."

"Rosalyn hired me," I reminded her. "I'm working in her behalf."

She ignored my parry. "I'm glad you came home to save Dahlia House."

"I hope I can."

Her smile was sad. "I hope you can, too. You never get over losing your home, Sarah Booth. Never."

I went over my list of friends and realized no one would help me with my task. Putting the spade in the trunk of the car, I made sure the box was there also. Dr. Matthews was not excited by the prospect, but he'd agreed that if I would exhume Lawrence's cat, he would do an autopsy.

Lawrence had claimed the cat's body from the vet's office, so I knew it would be buried somewhere near the cottage. For the third time, I made the drive down the oak-lined drive and parked. This time I walked around the cottage to the backyard.

It didn't take long to find the patch of freshly turned earth. Lawrence had buried his pet beneath a wild grape arbor, and I worked carefully until I unearthed the towel-wrapped body. I moved it to the box and drove back to the veterinarian's office.

"It'll take a day or two," he said. "I have to send the tissues off to the lab."

I wondered if it was the same place that had evaluated Lawrence's tissues. "Check specifically for Coumadin," I requested.

His eyebrows lifted. "You think someone deliberately poisoned Lawrence's cat? Why?"

"It's just a hunch," I said, not willing to say what I really thought. That someone had been poisoning Lawrence and that the cat had simply gotten into it by mistake. "Call me."

"How's Sweetie Pie?" he asked.

"Entertaining the troops. If there was a USO show for dogs, she would be the main attraction."

He laughed, good-humored in the midst of my dog's hormonal woes. "Bring her in first thing next Wednesday. We'll take care of whatever ails her."

"Any ideas what that might be?"

He shook his head. "I took out two ovaries and a uterus. What's happening with her defies logical medical explanation. Therefore I reserve comment until I check her out."

"Call me with the results on the cat."

I had just enough time to make one more stop before I had to get ready for Harold. Even though this was a business meeting, I intended to make him rue the day he'd chosen Brianna as his new playmate.

"You want me to do what?" Coleman Peters asked, leaning against the counter so that he was only inches from my face.

"Fingerprint the bag." I pointed to the poison I'd brought in and deposited on his desk.

"Why?"

I looked around to make sure no one was eavesdropping on us. "To see who might have touched it."

"I know how fingerprinting works, Sarah Booth. The why refers to why do you want to know?"

I didn't want to tell him I'd taken the bag from Lawrence's. That would justifiably make him annoyed.

Coleman liked me, but not enough to forgive me for mucking up his investigation. "It's a hunch."

He eyed me, and behind the blue eyes that so often held only a pleasant light, I saw the intellect of the young high school boy who'd calculated his odds and moved from football hero to sheriff. Coleman had married the head cheerleader, a perky little thing who was an asset on the campaign circuit, and from what I heard, a nag in between.

"I hear you've been a mighty busy woman," Coleman said. This time he didn't bother to hide his accusing glare.

"I don't get paid to watch soap operas."

"There's busy good and busybody. I hear you've been the latter."

He knew I'd been in Lawrence's house.

"I heard you and that artist searched Mr. Ambrose's cottage. Did you remove evidence from a crime scene?"

"Not a single thing." That was true. Sort of.

"What's the significance of the rat poison?"

"Coleman, I brought it to you. I could have taken it to Memphis and found a lab to do simple fingerprints. If something shows up, then I'll tell you everything. If it doesn't, then there's no point starting a bunch of suspicions."

He didn't budge, and his blue gaze never flinched. "Don't put yourself in a position of working against me."

"That wasn't in my game plan." It truly wasn't. I liked Coleman and thought he was honest.

"I'll run the prints for you right now." He pushed back off the counter so fast I slumped forward. He disappeared in back and came out with a kit. In a matter of moments he had out what looked to be minuscule particles of the same stuff used in magnetic drawing boards, a dark gray powder.

"Plastic is a pretty good surface." He dusted the sack with what looked like a big blush brush. Magically, the dust seemed to adhere to several prints. I felt a rush of excitement.

"Look! A print. Two of them!"

"Uh huh."

I gave him a look. He was awfully blasé, but then he didn't realize where I'd gotten the sack. Or at least he couldn't prove it.

He went to the back and came out with a 35 millimeter camera that had a macro lens attachment. He set up a small tripod, carefully took aim, and photographed the prints.

"Will you match them off the photographs?" I'd seen this on television.

"I'll run them," he said, lowering the camera and looking at me. "You're forgetting one small thing, Sarah Booth. If the person these prints belong to doesn't have a criminal record, we won't be able to match them."

14

"Damn! Damn! Double damn!" I pulled at the stocking, trying to straighten the line up the back of my leg. The stupid thing was twisted, but that wasn't what was bothering me.

"Why don't you just get an ice pick and stab it?" Jitty said from the doorway of my bedroom. "You want to put a run in it, that'll be a lot faster and easier on you."

I stood up and glared at her. I had ten minutes before Harold was supposed to arrive. I'd decided on secret underwear—my private weapon. Harold might not know I had on my sexy black garter belt and stockings, but I would know and it would give me feminine powers. So far, though, the stockings were more than I could contend with. How was it possible that mankind could live in outer space but couldn't invent a silk stocking that went on without twisting?

"You look wild-eyed," Jitty said, plopping down on the foot of the bed. She began to rifle through the pile of clothes I'd tried on and rejected. "Anything left in the closet?"

"Where've you been all day?" The only way to deal with her sarcasm was to ignore it.

"Busy. Is Harold taking you to dinner?"

"We're having jerked butt, and it's going to be mine."

"I'm sure you can persuade Harold to be a little forgiving." She stood up and came to stand behind me, staring into the mirror. "I've seen you be highly persuasive."

"Harold's involved with Brianna. I don't want her leftovers."

Jitty lowered her chin so that her eyes bored into me. "You afraid to go head-to-head with her, aren't you?"

For a moment I simply stared back at her. "I'm not afraid of Brianna Rathbone on any terms."

Jitty's grin was sly. "Then spin a little silk, do your own sexy little spider dance, and lure him over to *your* web."

"You make him sound like an insect." I finally got the stocking hooked to the garter. I let it go with a snap that made me jump. "I thought you were against wanton sex and into marriage and family values."

"Once you get ahold of him, he'll pop the question again. Besides, I just want to see if you got what it takes."

"I won't be dared into laying snares for a man."

Jitty chuckled. "That's an interestin' statement. I'll keep that on file. So what are you gonna wear other than black lace underthings?"

I pointed to the black wool skirt with a slit up to my hip and a white silk blouse. My black wool coat was still missing, but I had a red one that would work. "Demure, yet—"

"More of a business slut. You musta got that in one of those secondhand shops in New York."

She was right on the money. "Illusions was the name of the shop. I've never seen anything like it."

"I wish I could shop in one of those places."

The wistful tone in her voice made me realize that in all likelihood Jitty hadn't been off the home place since she died. Maybe never.

"Have you ever been out of Mississippi?" Sitting down at my dressing table, I watched her in the mirror.

"New Orleans. Once. Right before the war. It was glorious, too. I've never seen a place so alive. Your great-great-grandma Alice took me with her when she went to meet the ship that brought a lot of the furniture for Dahlia House."

It was almost impossible for me to imagine how much effort had gone into the building and furnishing of my home. There had been no trucks. Every stick of furniture, every piece of hand-cut glass for the windows and chandeliers had been carried upriver by barge and then overland by mules and wagons.

"We had to love every stick of that furniture to work that hard to get it home." Jitty ran her left hand over the smooth finish of my bedstead. Her face was turned down, her attention on her hand brushing the polished wood. "Yes, indeed. Lots of hard work went into your home, Sarah Booth, and if you don't find you a husband and start a family, it'll all be for naught."

I gave her an evil glare. She'd sucked me right into the palm of her hand and then clapped. "You can leave now," I said. "And send in my dog. I want some good company."

"Wear those wicked black shoes you bought for Harold's Thanksgiving party. They put a good angle on your calf."

"Anything for Harold," I said.

"Don't get my hopes up, Sarah Booth." She walked back over and leaned closer. "Whenever you doubt your abilities, remember you have one thing that Brianna Rathbone can never get."

"What's that?"

"The Delaney womb," she said in a stage whisper. "Now that's a deadly weapon."

The doorbell rang and I slipped into my clothes. The skirt was an excellent choice.

"I'm coming," I called down the stairs to the front door. "Just a minute."

There wasn't time for any more primping. I went down to let Harold in. He was barely over the threshold when Sweetie Pie launched herself at him, nearly knocking him over.

"What are you feeding that dog?" he asked, eyeing her critically.

"Why?" I felt a surge of guilt at the peanut butter sandwich. Not to mention the fruitcake. I did hate to eat alone.

"She's put on ten pounds, at least."

I stepped back, unwilling to let his flesh-appraising eye dwell too critically on me. "She needed a little fattening up. Her ribs were about to poke through her skin."

Harold lifted an eyebrow. "She's a hound, Sarah Booth. She's supposed to be lean so she can run."

"Sweetie Pie has other uses for her energy these days."

"Yes, I saw the dogs when I came in. There must be fifteen of them out there. Well, it's a warm night. They won't freeze."

"Come in and I'll make you a drink. Bourbon?"

In the foyer mirror I saw Harold's gaze catch on the

slit in my skirt as I moved away from him. His lips tightened slightly, and I felt a tiny little thumb pulse in response. Brianna might have snared him, but he wasn't firmly caught.

"Perhaps we should talk before we drink," he said, following close behind me. "What I have to say is serious."

I didn't like the sound of that, but my Daddy's Girl training had taught me not to disagree with a man. At least not in a head-on manner. I simply went to the sideboard and made our drinks while Harold watched. He was too well mannered to stop me. When I offered him his glass, he took it with a look of wary amusement.

"What *were* you doing at Lawrence's with Willem Arquillo?"

"What part annoys you the most?" I sipped my drink slowly, never taking my eyes off his. "That I was at Lawrence's or that I was with Willem?" Ah, there was a rush of color to his cheeks.

"Both. Both of you should know better. Especially you, Sarah Booth. You claim to be a private investigator. Surely you've bothered to learn a few of the rules. Such as don't disturb a crime scene."

"We were looking for the manuscript. Willem had agreed to turn it over to you. He just wanted to look at it."

"And I'm going to dance *Swan Lake* in downtown Zinnia tomorrow."

I put my hand on my heart. "Madame will be delighted. She could never find men to perform in the ballet."

His gripped my arm firmly. "This isn't a game, Sarah Booth."

I locked gazes with him, fascinated, and a little fearful of the sudden intensity in his pale blue eyes. Harold was a man who veiled strong emotion in manners. Even when he'd proposed to me, he'd been so carefully controlled. Now I saw passion, a hint of exactly how hot the opposite of his ice control could be, and I liked it.

"Willem's mother is dying. He was afraid there was something in the manuscript about his family. He wanted to know so that he could prepare his mother. And if it wasn't in there, perhaps allow her to die in peace."

Harold's hand slipped down my arm, warmth sliding over the cool silk, but his gaze didn't falter a millimeter. "You believe that?"

"I did." Doubt suddenly plucked at me. "I do." Vacillation is a deadly sin in the Daddy's Girl rulebook. To err is human. To vacillate is begging for trouble.

"If such a thing were in the manuscript, why would Willem allow it to be printed?"

"How could he stop it?"

Harold's eyes narrowed. "I always took you for a bright woman."

I would accept his grilling, but I wasn't about to take an insult from a man who slept with one of the sexually undead. "Just because I don't spend my days foreclosing on poor widows and orphans doesn't mean that I'm soft or stupid. Willem made a promise to me. I have no reason to doubt that he would live up to it. Besides, what if he found the manuscript and took it? You've got that copy at the bank." I decided to try a bluff.

Harold went to the neon Christmas wreath, his finger touching the warm buzz of the lights. He sipped his drink and studied the neon as if he'd never seen it before. When he finally turned back to face me, his glass was empty. "There's no copy of the manuscript at the bank."

"What about Lawrence's safe deposit box?" I'd

assumed there would be a copy there. It had to be there. "Maybe not the actual pages, but a computer disk?"

He shook his head. "Don't repeat that to anyone." As he walked to within a few inches of me, I caught the scent of his aftershave. Whatever it was, no one else wore it like him. "I've looked everywhere and I can't find Lawrence's work. I'm afraid it's been destroyed."

"I didn't—we didn't—take the manuscript from the house."

He nodded. "I believe you." He reached out and brushed his fingertips across my cheek. "I'm sorry I said you were dumb."

I looked down in my glass and found the decency to meet his gaze, far gentler this time. "I'm sorry I said you put widows and orphans on the street."

His chuckle was soft, amused. "You don't fight like the other ladies of your group. You go straight for the ba—"

"No need to point out my weaknesses," I interrupted. "If we went out to the family cemetery, we'd probably discover the ground all disturbed. That would be Aunt LouLane turning in her grave."

"She tried, Sarah Booth."

"She did indeed." And I had never felt more like a failure, at least in her eyes.

Harold held out his glass. "So what did you and Willem find, poking through Lawrence's things?"

I made us both another drink while Harold lit a fire. We settled onto the sofa. I was tempted to tell him about the rat poison, but something held me back.

"Someone had been in the cottage before us."

He tensed. "Are you sure?"

"The cat, Apollo, was in the house. Rosalyn said the cats had been left outside." If confession was good for the soul, I had more. "I went back to the house and got

Apollo and took him to Lillian." I was on a roll. "And I
went back again and exhumed a dead cat."

By now, Harold had firm control of his expressions.
"You've been a busy girl."

"I think the cat was poisoned." It was the perfect
moment to tell about the rat poison, but still I held
back.

"Any suspects?"

Oh, yeah, the woman providing the bounce in his
mattress. Again, I held back. Restraint had never been
my long suit. Perhaps private-eyeing was teaching me a
lesson of ladyhood that Aunt LouLane had said I would
never learn.

"It's hard to make a guess without knowing what's
in that manuscript."

"You really think the motive was Lawrence's book?"
For a split second, there was flint in his eyes. It disappeared in a blink, but I'd seen it and I knew that he,
too, believed the motive for murder was Lawrence's
words.

"That's a logical assumption." It was time to turn
the tables. "Who do you suspect?"

He got up to poke the fire. "It wouldn't be fair for
me to say, since I have no evidence."

My pulse increased. Harold had a suspect! I was
dying to know who it was, but I also knew he'd never
tell me.

"Sarah Booth, what were you doing in Mrs.
Hedgepeth's magnolia tree the other day?"

His question caught me by surprise and I almost
choked on a swallow of bourbon. By the time I caught
my breath, I was still unable to come up with a convincing answer. What was I going to do, confess that I'd
been peering into his bedroom window with my binoculars? The answer was yes, because there was no other

possible reply. He'd nailed me. Dang Mrs. Hedgepeth and her busybody ways. She probably had her own field glasses.

"Tinkie was worried about you. She said you weren't at work and Oscar was looking for you. She asked me to find you." It was almost the truth.

"Yes," he said, without giving a darn thing away.

"You weren't at home."

"Yes," he said again in that annoying fashion.

I pulled out the big gun. "Your bed hadn't been slept in."

"No." He poked the fire again.

"So where were you?" Let's see how good he was at evading a direct question.

"I had some personal business. I was away for the night."

I wanted to turn to him and say "I know that! And I know where you were!" Restraint. Restraint. I heard the drumbeat of Aunt LouLane's command in my head, and I managed to force a tight smile onto my face. "I hope it was satisfying."

He gave me a sharp look. "We have to find that manuscript."

As much as I wanted to torment him about Brianna, his sudden inclusion of me as a partner stopped me dead in my tracks. There was one question that had to be asked. "Harold, have you actually seen this manuscript?"

"There's a nearly completed autobiography," he said with certainty. "Even though Brianna's name was going to be on it, Lawrence actually wrote it."

"How can you be sure?"

He came to stand directly in front of me. "I read his will. There's something you should know, Sarah Booth."

His eyes were so pale a blue that they looked like the deep, deep interior of an ice crystal. "What?"

"The night of the dinner party, Lawrence called me back to the cottage. All of the guests had gone. He had written a new will. He gave it to me—in case something happened to him."

"You were there, at the cottage, after everyone else had gone?"

"I was. He gave me the will and named me as executor."

"And the manuscript?"

"He told me it was finished and that he'd decided to publish it under his own name."

"Where is it?" I was ready to jump out of my seat.

"I don't know," Harold said so softly that I thought I'd surely misunderstood him.

"What do you mean?"

"He handed me the will in a stack of papers and asked that I not read it, unless he died. Right then I should have picked up on his concerns. He suspected he was in danger, and I didn't even notice."

"Who would have considered murder?" I said softly. "Lawsuits, yes. Murder, never."

Harold's sad smile showed his thanks. "Lawrence said he'd made arrangements to safeguard the manuscript, and that I would know where to find it. He quoted a line of poetry—'Ah, distinctly I remember it was in the bleak December; And each separate dying ember wrought its ghost upon the floor.' " Harold watched me intently. "I haven't been able to make head nor tail of it."

"That's it?" Though the words were chilling, they weren't much of a clue. "There must have been something in the papers."

"I've looked through everything a dozen times. There's no mention of where the manuscript might be."

"The publisher! Maybe he sent it to them."

"I've contacted Bainbridge Publishing. They don't have the book. I spoke with Gustav Brecht. He was expecting it but it never arrived."

"And Brianna, did he know her?"

"He knew her." Harold's gaze slipped to the floor. "I couldn't determine what his relationship with her or Lawrence was, except that he'd been waiting for the manuscript."

"Could Lawrence have sent it to another publisher?"

"I've called every publisher Lawrence ever worked with. No one has the book."

We looked at each other.

"Brianna doesn't have it," he said with such deliberateness that I knew, even if I wanted to argue it would be pointless. I agreed with him anyway. If she had it, she'd be rushing to New York, not hanging around Zinnia. Unless she was interested in Harold as something other than a boy toy.

"That's another small complication," he said. "Lawrence's new will was never witnessed. There's the possibility someone might contest it." His hand brushed a strand of my curly hair out of my face in an unexpectedly tender gesture. Before I could say or do anything, he was on his feet. "I must be going," he said.

"I wanted to ask you something." I truly did. But I also wanted to know what that touch had implied. Harold wasn't the kind of man to hop from bed to bed.

"It'll have to wait." He checked his watch. "I'm late."

Because Harold was not a man to pull a pout on, I rose to my feet and walked him to the door. "Your aunt

Lenore," I said. "Did she ever tell you anything about Moon Lake that might have come back to haunt Lawrence? There was a boyfriend, a fight—"

He stopped abruptly, a move that allowed Sweetie Pie to shoot between his legs and into the pack of waiting suitors.

"Sweetie!" I made a lunge but missed. "Primal drive," I said. "Your aunt—"

"I wouldn't worry overly much about Moon Lake. That's the distant past, and I'm certain Lawrence had no interest in writing about it. Now I must be going." He turned and walked away. I watched for a moment as he skirted the tangle of sniffing and snorting dogs and disappeared into the night.

15

I went to sleep in a tangle of unanswered questions and unresolved emotions. Sweetie Pie, all of her needs and urges met, snored beside my bed. The gentle whuffle of sound coming from the dog should have been comforting, but it was only a counterpoint to my own noise-making—the incessant ticking of my biological clock.

When I finally drifted into a restless sleep, I found myself in a long luminous hallway. It was an endless corridor of white, wide and inviting, but perfectly empty. I could go left or right, but neither direction seemed to recommend itself.

Far in the distance was soft music, an acoustic guitar played with great skill. It was something in a minor key, sad and filled with longing. I started walking, hoping to find the musician, or anyone who could tell me where I was.

I walked and walked for what seemed like hours, until I came to a white wooden door. The knob was crystal, glowing in the radiant light that filled the hallway. The music was still with me, no louder than before. I turned the knob and opened the door, stepping through hesitantly.

A garden awaited me, filled with bright flowers and the sound of water running. A brick path forked in front of me. This time I took the left-hand fork and followed it to a cul-de-sac where two benches had been placed, back to back, beneath a willow tree.

I was tired, so I took a seat on the bench with a view of the lake that suddenly appeared. I could see there were two piers leading to two different sailboats. Both were equally beautiful, their bright spinnaker sails ballooning in the quickening breeze. Filled with despair, I started to weep.

I woke up slowly to sunshine streaming through my window. Not the white light of my dream, but the pale yellow sunlight of a Delta winter morning. I lay in the warm bed for a few moments, replaying the dream. I didn't need Madame Tomeeka to interpret this one. Choice. One choice leads to another. There is no end, no final conclusion. It is only a series of decisions, moving endlessly until death. Each time we choose we leave behind untold possibilities. Each time, our path narrows. Because we cannot see further down the road, few choices are based on anything other than intuition and hope. There are no guarantees, only the grand lotto of life. Until the end.

Perhaps I'd have a choice whether to stay dead or come back as a ghost. It was the perfect thought to shake me out of the depression of the dream and onto my feet. Wouldn't it be exquisite to come back and haunt Jitty?

"What you smilin' like a mule eatin' briars for?"

I hadn't realized she was in the room, but I should have been expecting her. "When I die, will I have a choice about becoming a ghost?"

She arched her eyebrows. "Depends on whether you do your duty in this life."

This sounded vaguely familiar with that ring of religious fanaticism. Duty being the operative word. "Meaning?"

"Get you a husband and produce me an heir."

There was the sound of sharp knocking on the front door. I closed my eyes for a split second, and in typical Jitty fashion, my haranguing ghost disappeared. I was left to rush downstairs and answer the door. The familiar rat-a-tat-tat was as insistent as ever. It was becoming a regular morning pattern—to serve as Tinkie's chef.

"Coffee," she said, breezing past me. She put Chablis on the floor and followed her into the kitchen where Sweetie greeted both of them with writhing tail wags as she offered her stomach up for belly rubs. The dog was shameless in her needs.

"Do you think we might have some costumes made for that dog?" Tinkie asked, eyeing Sweetie. "Something brocade."

"She isn't a sofa." I put the coffee on. "What are you doing here at daybreak?"

"It's after seven. Oscar went in early to talk to Harold. They're having a teleconference with Boyd and Layton. Naturally, Layton is off somewhere—Tokyo, Tunisia, somewhere with a major time difference. It's a big deal."

She was about to bust a gut to tell me the rest. "What kind of meeting?" I agreeably prompted. I sort of enjoyed waking up to Tinkie's chatter.

"I couldn't help but overhear. Brianna *has* filed suit. Angela Rhee was telling the truth." She gave me a thin-lipped look. "I told you so."

I shook my head. "I'm surprised at you, Tinkie. A

well-brought-up Daddy's Girl would never, ever resort to telling someone so."

"That's true. I'd never do it to another DG. But you're a fallen angel, Sarah Booth. I can do it to you and it doesn't count."

"Thanks. Want an omelet?"

"With sausage, please." She put sugar in the coffee I put in front of her and settled in for a long chat. "There's more."

As I broke the eggs with one hand, I gave her an inquiring look. "What's going on with you, Tinkie? Normally I'd have to bribe all of this information out of you."

She put more sugar in her coffee. "I want to be your assistant, Sarah Booth."

I almost crushed the egg I was holding. "What?"

"Oscar will never let me study hair design. You know, my dream. But he can't stop me from picking up little tidbits of gossip. It just happens naturally, like lint in a man's navel."

I was dumbfounded, but I could see by the sparkle in her eyes that she wasn't kidding. "I'm barely hanging on to Dahlia House. I only have one client, who doesn't really have the money to pay me." I had a stab of guilt about Madame's check in the pocket of my coat, which had gone missing. I was going to have to find that thing today. "I can't afford to pay you."

She waved a hand. "Money doesn't matter. Daddy and Oscar won't ever let me realize my dreams. Heck, they won't even let me talk about hair. But they're generous with money." Elbows on the table, she wrapped both hands around her coffee cup and held it in front of her chin. "I need this for me, Sarah Booth. And I can be a help."

"Arr-rrrr." The tiny growl came from under the table where Chablis had Sweetie's long, silky ear and was tugging at it. Sweetie wagged her tail.

"Me and Chablis," Tinkie amended. "You know that little fool barks every time I go by your driveway."

That was it. The final element of guilt. It was the ransom money for Chablis and Tinkie's subsequent faith in me that had gotten me started in the PI business. I simply could not deny her. "Okay, you're hired."

"Oh, Sarah Booth!" She jumped to her feet and rushed me. Her hug was strong and enthusiastic. "I've never had a job before. I can't believe it. I wish I could tell the other girls. They'd be green with envy."

I was glad that, what with her face crushed into my shoulder, she couldn't see my expression. She'd never had a job. None of her friends had ever worked. Not a lick. Females were to be taken care of, to be guarded, protected, and totally dependent on their fathers and then their husbands. There were times, when I was desperate and afraid, that I was jealous of such cradle-to-grave safety. Then again, I could never have borne the heel of male authority on my neck.

"Tinkie, I suggest you keep this job to yourself." It was meant to be kind advice. One of the other Daddy's Girls, maybe inadvertently or maybe deliberately, would spill the beans to *her* husband, who would then call Oscar, and that would be the end of that. Somehow, I didn't think Oscar, or Tinkie's father, bank president Avery Bellcase, would view private-eyeing as a suitable pastime for someone of Tinkie's social status. They'd put the kibosh on it instantly.

"I won't tell a soul. I'll be like a secret agent," she said, sitting back down as I put a heaping plate of eggs and sausage in front of her. "What's my first assignment?"

Somehow I managed not to roll my eyes. "What other gossip did you overhear?"

"Oh, Oscar and Daddy are furious with Harold. They told him if he couldn't get Brianna to drop the suit, they were going to fire him."

I sat down across from Tinkie. "Why? Why are they blaming Harold? It's Brianna who's filing the suit."

Tinkie swallowed a mouthful of eggs and daintily wiped her mouth with a napkin before she spoke. "They think Harold hid the manuscript in the bank, thereby putting the bank in danger."

"But Harold said the manuscript wasn't in Lawrence's safe deposit box."

Tinkie nodded. "That's true. It wasn't. Coleman Peters was there when Harold opened the box. There were some papers, financial things, some old photographs, deeds, letters, a few pieces of jewelry. That's all."

Those were the normal things kept in safe deposit boxes, as far as I knew. "No computer disks?"

She shook her head. "Oscar had already thought of that."

"Did anyone check *Harold's* safe deposit box?"

Tinkie lifted an eyebrow. "He voluntarily opened it. Nothing pertaining to Lawrence."

"So how can they blame him?" I was a little worried for Harold. He took his job very seriously.

"I don't know, but they do."

"Can Brianna really force the bank to open safe deposit boxes of other patrons?" This sounded like a violation of privacy or civil rights or something.

"Probably not, but the publicity itself will damage the bank. Or that's what Daddy and Oscar say." She finished off her eggs and pushed her plate back a little.

"Personally," she added, her eyes glittering. "I think it's because Harold is courting Brianna."

I schooled my face into a bland expression. "Are you certain?"

"He was there last night. It's hot and heavy."

I got up and poured us more coffee, mostly to avoid her curious stare. Damn Harold. He'd left my house and gone straight to Brianna. Another appointment my butt. He had a date.

"Aren't you going to eat?" Tinkie asked.

My appetite was effectively squelched. "I don't have time. I've got some running around to do."

"What's my first assignment?"

The question irritated me. I wasn't certain what I should do, much less Tinkie. But I had to come up with something, and there was an area where Tinkie could be far more effective than I could. "What do you know about Senator Jebediah Archer?"

"He's about a hundred and ten, but he still lives outside Clarksdale. There was talk that he had a child out of wedlock, a girl who takes care of him. Juicy, juicy scandal. Daddy knows him. They've been involved in some things together."

I'd hoped for some political insight, but scandal was almost as good. "How about you have lunch with your father and pump him about the senator. I'm particularly interested in what happened up at Moon Lake in 1940, the year the senator's son was killed in a card game."

"Perfect," Tinkie said, scooping Chablis into her arms. "I'll get Daddy to meet me at The Club and we'll have a few martinis. He'll talk. Gin makes him gregarious."

"J. Edgar Hoover was at Moon Lake that summer. I want to know what brought him down to Mississippi."

Tinkie nodded. "Should I save my receipt? For tax purposes?"

It was a noble question and one that made me smile. Tinkie honestly thought I'd make enough money to file a long form. "Sure," I said. "Do that."

Researching the senator had been my next chore, and now I was left trying to decide how to proceed. My case was a mess. There was the distant past, the past, the book—all potential motives for the murder of a writer. There were a half dozen solid suspects, and maybe fifty more, depending on the scope of the book, which was still missing.

If I had ever doubted that the manuscript was the motive, I no longer did. Madame, Harold, even Lillian had indicated it was the source of danger. I had to find it.

I went upstairs, bathed and dressed, donning a peplum-cut wool jacket with a black velvet mandarin collar and some black wool slacks. The pants were tight, but I was finally over my fruitcake binge. All would be well in the end.

Jitty was conspicuous by her absence, but I didn't have time to worry about her. She was up to something. Whatever it was, I wouldn't have to wait long. We both shared the trait of impatience.

My first stop was the bakery in town, where I bought two coffees and three Danishes, which I promptly took to *The Zinnia Dispatch* society editor's private office. Cece eyed the white paper bag and licked her perfectly outlined, tawny lips. She'd obviously fully recovered from her panic attack.

"For me?" she asked even as she reached.

I gave her the bag, watching as she bit large into the cheese Danish that was her favorite. "Wonderful. Thank you, Sarah Booth. I was starving."

"My pleasure."

"So what do you want?"

There wasn't any point in trying to disguise the fact that I only stopped by when I needed something—an excuse to attend some function as her minion or some information. "You knew Lawrence pretty well, right?"

She took a smaller bite of the Danish. "We became friends."

"Does he have any family?"

She chewed and stared. "You know, you're the only person who's asked that question. I did his obituary, and he has no one. Not that I can find. By the way, his burial is today at two o'clock."

Strange, but I'd never considered that there would be a funeral. The finality of it was startling. It was the first time Lawrence's death fully registered.

Cece pushed a copy of the newspaper across her jumbled desk to me. The memorial service was front-page news. "Literary Figure Laid To Rest." The byline was hers. "Most investigators at least make an effort to keep up with the news. Especially when their friends work for the newspaper."

I ignored her jabs and scanned the story, growing more amazed with each paragraph. The acclaimed French filmmaker Ramone Gilliard was coming to Zinnia to give the eulogy. He was an old man, and ill, but he was coming to say goodbye to his friend. And the list of other notables was astounding. John Irving, John Grisham, T. R. Pearson, Dolly Parton, and Boy George, not to mention several famous artists.

"This is incredible." I leaned forward in my chair

and pulled a Danish out of the bag. I hadn't intended to eat one, but I had to have some sustenance to help absorb this news.

"I know." Cece grinned.

"Where did you get all this information? Is it confirmed?"

"Harold told me about Ramone. Apparently Ramone and Lawrence had a pact that whoever died first, the other would do this. And I have a friend who does reservations at the airport in Memphis. There's no other place they can fly into."

"Brilliant." I was as impressed with Cece as with the list of names she'd come up with.

"Would you like to work as my photographer at the memorial service?" She grinned wickedly.

"I'd love it." Once again, Cece had come through with the perfect entrée for me.

"You do know how to use a camera, don't you?"

"Sure." I did, in a fashion. How hard could it be? "I studied photography in college. And I made an A." True, as far as it went. I had shown what the professor called "artistic flair," even if I was a little shaky on the technical aspects.

"I'll see you at one o'clock, at the chapel. We need to set up and discuss the shots. Father McGuire is officially in charge, and this is one of the biggest things that's ever happened in Zinnia. I'm counting on you not to screw this up, Sarah Booth."

"Yeah, sure. Lawrence was Catholic?"

She shrugged one shoulder. "It doesn't really matter. The priest is agreeable, and he loved Lawrence's books."

"At one. I'll be there. Bring the camera." I crammed the rest of the Danish into my mouth, picked up the second cup of coffee, and left. There was a lot to do before the service.

Harold's car was not at the bank. I didn't intend to stop by to see him, but I hadn't been able to resist checking on his whereabouts. Dark images of what Brianna might be doing to him snaked through my brain.

I pushed them aside as unworthy of mental energy and drove to the sheriff's office. The courthouse was in a dither as secretaries put up notices stating that they were closing for the funeral. If celebrities hadn't been coming to town, I wondered if Lawrence would have gotten this kind of attention.

There was a carnival air in the rotunda, with laughter echoing off the old tile as I made for the sheriff's office. Coleman, at least, was sitting at his desk, lounged back, with a steaming cup of coffee on the blotter in front of him.

He sat up when he saw me, then stood. For a moment we stared at each other. There was something he wanted to ask, but he was calculating his odds. Apparently he decided against a direct question because he signaled me into an empty interrogation room, nodded at a chair, and closed the door.

"Coffee?"

I shook my head. "No thanks. I had some with Cece."

"I wish she'da held off on her story until after the fact. Everyone around here's gone crazy."

"I saw."

"It's a memorial service for a man most of them didn't know. All they want is to rub up against someone famous."

Coleman was put off by all of the hoopla. "I wonder
how Lawrence would feel about all of this," I said.

"I didn't know him very well, but I don't think anyone would want this commotion." He waved his hand
toward the door.

We talked a minute about traffic and how two of his
deputies were already locating parking for the hordes of
rubberneckers. Burial was to take place on the grounds
of Magnolia Place, where he'd lived for the past twenty
years. The Caldwell family had offered a place in the
small cemetery there, and Harold had agreed to it. That
part, at least, would be private. I forced myself to sit
still in my seat, waiting for Coleman to come around to
the point we both knew we had to talk about. Instead,
high school days cropped up, and we chatted a minute
about that. It was clear he'd decided to outwait me.

Patience was never my strong suit. "Did you find any
matching prints?" I asked.

He folded his hands on the table that was between
us. "No. We got prints, but they didn't match any we
had on file. None in the national registry. I didn't think
we would."

It was a long shot, but I'd been hopeful. Now I was
disappointed, and I didn't bother to hide it. "So we
don't know who handled the bag. What a bust."

"We do know that Lawrence didn't touch it."

If he didn't touch it, he didn't put it in the cabinet.
Which was interesting in and of itself. "How did you
find that out? *His* prints were on file?"

He shook his head. "I went over and fingerprinted
the body."

It was a grotesque image, but I was grateful to
Coleman for his thoroughness. He'd also earned my
respect. He'd figured the bag had come from

Lawrence's home or else he wouldn't have gone to the trouble to check the prints.

"So that leaves us nowhere."

"Maybe, maybe not." He went to his desk and got his coffee, coming back into the interview room and sitting down. He stared into his cup as if the secrets of the universe might be revealed. Damn him, he was playing me like a cheap harmonica. He knew I couldn't stand the role of patient waiter.

"What?" I demanded.

"Harold Erkwell is hosting a reception after the funeral."

A flash of annoyance shot over my skin, causing a flush. Coleman noted it but said nothing. Harold hadn't bothered to invite me. Hadn't mentioned it. Neither had Tinkie. I'm sure she'd assumed I was invited, but I wasn't.

"Are you going to it?" Coleman asked.

"As a photographer for the newspaper." Thank goodness for Cece.

"I know Erkwell, and he won't be serving in paper cups. If you could snag a few of the glasses that people drink out of . . ."

I didn't know whether to be flattered or put out that Coleman would think me capable of such a thing. I decided on flattered. "I can. Whose prints would you want?"

He smiled slowly. "You're the PI, you tell me."

"No suspects of your own?" I countered.

He held his smile but it was by an act of will. "You're not going to like this, but I do have a suspect."

"Who?" I was all ears.

"Harold Erkwell."

I almost gasped. "Harold?"

Coleman nodded. "I've always liked Harold, but his connections to the case are too strong. His aunt was involved with Lawrence all those years ago. There was a murder then, a senator's son. Harold is claiming to be the executor of the estate, although there are no witnesses on the document he purports to be the final will. He visited Lawrence's home the night of the murder—as far as I can tell, he was the last one to visit. Toting up all the evidence we have, Harold has a bigger stack than anyone."

"He isn't a killer, though." Harold really wasn't the kind of man who would do such a thing. He had ethics.

"Maybe not by himself, but he's involved with Brianna Rathbone."

I knew by the way he said her name that he wasn't overly impressed with Brianna. Maybe Coleman remembered her from high school, though boys seldom remembered the same things that girls did. I'm sure Brianna never gave him the time of day. Coleman was a farm boy, one with keen intellect and athletic prowess. But he didn't have a trust fund or a fancy car. In Brianna's world, he didn't exist.

"You suspect Brianna?"

"If I had to guess, I'd say she was behind it. But I'm afraid she's the kind of woman who always finds a man to do her dirty deeds. Harold seems like the perfect fall guy to me."

16

Doc Sawyer sat on the slanted emergency ramp at the back of the hospital and lit up a Salem. "Coumadin is probably the easiest poison to obtain this day and age. Like I said earlier, it's a big selling point with exterminators because the critters don't die in the house, causing such a stink."

"Do you have to sign for it when you buy it?" Back when I was a child, local pharmacies sold strychnine to poison "nuisance" animals such as raccoons. The purchaser had only to write a name in a book, signing for the poison. As a system of accountability, it was pathetic. Any name would do—no one checked.

"Not as far as I know," Doc said. "Buy it off the shelf or buy it from an exterminator. It's legal stuff."

"How fast does it work?" I looked longingly at his cigarette, the smoke curling upward from his fingers in a dancing pattern. Since I couldn't make any progress on my case by working on motive, I decided that opportunity was the angle I'd take. I already knew that Lawrence had been taking the poison for a couple of weeks. Now I needed to find out exactly how the stuff worked.

"A high dosage actually causes the blood to thin so rapidly that internal hemorrhaging occurs rather quickly. It's the internal bleeding that drives the rats toward water. An act of final desperation."

He pulled hard on the cigarette, making the ash glow red and burn long. He didn't look at me. When he lowered his hand, I saw that it was shaking.

"I haven't had a drink today," he said. "Hard on my nerves, but I think it's time to quit."

I wanted to put my hand on his arm or somehow convey a sense of encouragement, but I didn't want to presume. In my own family, I'd seen the ravages of alcohol. Cousins, uncles. Some were legendary, like Uncle Lyle Crabtree and my great-great-uncle William Carter Delaney, who survived fighting in the War Between the States only to break his neck in a fall from a horse while riding drunk through the countryside jumping fences with a naked whore on the back of his horse. The whore, luckily, was uninjured. My great-great-uncle had made the accurate pronouncement that "she had a lot of bounce."

"Family propensity," was all I said. In the long run, what I thought or felt about his decision had no merit in the grueling fight he'd have against the demons of the bottle.

"I am, therefore I drink." He chuckled and I knew it was okay to let it go.

"In the end, could you tell if Lawrence had been given a massive dose of the poison?" I forced my voice to remain level, professional. There had been so much blood. I blocked out the memory of Lawrence, a man of such charm and grace, lying in a pool of it. Instead, I made myself hang on to the fact that the bag of rat poison was gaining in importance. I had discovered an important clue.

"No, he'd ingested small doses. That's the problem here. Coumadin is also used in high-blood-pressure medication. Remember, I told you warfarin is frequently prescribed for patients."

"But Lawrence wasn't taking high-blood-pressure medicine?"

Doc shook his head. "Not according to his medical records. Only Synthroid, and occasionally something for arthritis. Other than that, nothing. Lawrence preferred his cure in a bottle, same as me. He always kept his drinking under control, though. Never let it get the upper hand."

"So he was poisoned." I wanted to be clear on this.

"An autopsy can't tell that, Sarah Booth. Coumadin was in his system and had been for some little time." He lit one cigarette off the butt of the other. "Lawrence wasn't the type to take medication. It was hell to make him accept his need for Synthroid. He resisted the notion that he needed to take anything, except a little port or Jim Beam, on a regular basis. Whoever did this is very clever."

I'd given up smoking, but I felt a real craving for one of Doc's Salems. Nicotine and menthol, a bolus of bad health factors but oh, so satisfying. I bolstered my resistance and focused on the case.

"I'll check with Coleman and see if he found a prescription for, what was it, warfarin?"

"Coleman didn't find one."

"How can you be so certain?"

He cast me a sidelong look. "He didn't need a blood thinner. I autopsied him, remember. Besides, thyroid medication and Coumadin don't mix. A doctor wouldn't have prescribed it. Coleman had all the medicines from Lawrence's house. I looked through them."

I tapped my heels against the cement ramp, beating out the rhythm to Elvis's classic "Suspicious Minds." "How would the poison be given?"

"Small, regular doses."

"In what?"

"Food or drink. Same as rats."

"This was definitely premeditated."

"No doubt about it. It would have to be someone who had access to Lawrence's food or drink on a regular basis."

So this was the reasoning behind Coleman's theories about Harold. If this scenario was accurate, then it would have to be someone in Zinnia. Someone who was around regularly. But Harold wasn't the only potential suspect. Brianna had been in town for a month or so. Her celebrity status had made her arrival a newspaper headline. "Beautiful Brianna Comes Home." There had even been a parade, for God's sake. And Willem had been in town for a while. Joseph Grace was within easy driving distance. In other words, it didn't *have* to be Harold.

"What about the cut on Lawrence's hand. He wouldn't have died without the cut, right?" I asked.

"He wouldn't have died Christmas Eve. The cut was the underlying cause of death at that particular time. The Coumadin, combined with the thyroid medication, was the pathology."

"Was the cut accidental?"

He stubbed out the cigarette and turned to face me. "This is the crux of Coleman's problem. I believe the cut was administered deliberately. It was made from a jagged shard of glass, the one in the kitchen sink. But I can't state conclusively that he didn't accidentally cut himself."

"Then unless Coleman can prove the cut was inflicted by someone else—"

"He has no murder case."

"But the Coumadin—"

"Wasn't the cause of death. The cut was. Unless Coleman can connect the cut to the murderer, the best he can hope for, if he catches the poisoner, is attempted murder."

"Damn!"

Doc gave me another sidelong look, this time with a smile. "Makes you want a drink, doesn't it?"

"It does." Reaching out a hand I touched his shoulder. "I've heard that walking helps. If you ever need someone to walk with you . . ." I slapped my thigh, "I could use the exercise, as well as the company."

Doc's hand, well manicured but showing the ravages of time and hard drinking, shook as he reached and caught my fingers in a gentle squeeze. "You sound just like your mama," he said. "Your father would have offered a paid vacation down to Briarwood Center, but your mother would have suggested a walk. I thank you, Sarah Booth. And if it comes to it, I'll call."

I had time either to eat lunch or go home and change into a funeral dress. After my talk with Doc, I was in a rebellious mood. I decided to do neither. My pants were tight and I didn't need lunch; besides, a dress and high heels would be a liability as a photographer. My black leather boots were perfect.

I rode through Zinnia once again, this time spotting

Harold's Lexus at the bank. Wherever he'd been, he was back at work. I wondered why he wasn't at home, preparing for the reception. But then why should he? He had Brianna to serve as his hostess. Perhaps they were cooking up another murder. It was a thought born of jealousy, and instantly I knew it was wrong. It seemed impossible, but my ugly mood blackened.

Harold. I'd given him more credit than he deserved as a male specimen. He'd fallen into Brianna's clutches without a whimper. No matter how I twisted the facts, though, I couldn't connect Harold with Lawrence's death. He wasn't a murderer.

But someone had murdered Lawrence Ambrose, and because of a stupid loophole in the law, they might get away with it. When I passed Lillian Sparks's home, I saw her on the sidewalk, waving at me. I pulled over to the curb and let the window down.

"Rosalyn is terribly upset," she said, her breath coming shallow and fast. "Someone's done the most horrible thing. They desecrated the grave of his beloved cat."

I closed my eyes. "Where's Madame?" This was going to be bad. Really bad. I should have called and warned her.

"She went to make sure the grave diggers had the right plot."

"I'll go there now." I checked my watch. I had enough time before my appointment with Cece.

"Who would do something so cruel?" Lillian asked.

Who indeed. It was a guilt-laden drive to the cottage. I found Madame sitting on Lawrence's front porch, the crime tape broken and fluttering in the breeze. She wore a solid black dress with a hat and veil, an interesting effect so that her expression was somewhat hidden from me. Her posture told me the degree of her distress.

There was no point trying to soften the blow. "I dug up the cat and took him to Dr. Matthews for an autopsy."

She rose slowly to her feet. "You? You took Rasmus?"

"You said yourself the cat didn't die of old age. I'm sorry, I should have called you."

She sat down heavily. "I thought it was vandals. What did the autopsy show?"

"I'll know tomorrow."

"If Lawrence had only listened to me." She looked down the drive as if she saw him somewhere in the distance. "I never understood when someone said they were ready to die. Now I do."

I was shocked. Madame was indomitable. She was unstoppable. In the eight years I took ballet classes from her, she'd never accepted an excuse or a whine. Quitting was anathema to her.

"I miss him," she said, her eyes dry. "We shared so much of the past, even when he was in Paris. I went to visit him often. He made my life here bearable."

"Lawrence wouldn't want you to give up," I said as gently as I could.

She gave a half snort of agreement. "He would loathe the idea of me sitting out here, whining. But here I sit. He's gone and left me, Sarah Booth. He promised he would never do that."

I took a seat in another rocker beside her. There was bourbon in the house, and both of us could use a shot, but I resisted the idea. I didn't want to fall into the private investigator stereotype by drinking at noon. I also didn't want to shake Madame's faith in me. She had enough on her plate.

"Tell me about Moon Lake. About Hoover and the murder of Hosea Archer. Was Lawrence going to include it in his book?"

"If he'd put in everything he said, the book would have been a five-volume set."

"What really happened?"

"Hosea was a little monster. A bully and quite stupid. He was killed for cheating at cards. His death isn't an issue."

"It might be," I insisted. "His murderer was never brought to justice. If Lawrence knew the real murderer—"

"Lawrence knew nothing. We had no interest in the secret conversations that buzzed about that casino. There were many powerful and wealthy men there during the summer. I was sixteen and I wanted to dance. Lawrence was performing. We were artists. Nothing more."

"But Hoover was there. A man was killed right under the nose of the head of the FBI and nothing was ever done about it."

"I don't know." Her mouth hardened. "Perhaps no one cared because they knew how horrible Hosea could be." She checked her wristwatch. "We should be going. I'm disappointed in you, Sarah Booth. You're wasting all of this time and effort on something that's unimportant. Brianna killed Lawrence. Forget the past and focus on her. If you're not willing to do that, then perhaps I should hire someone else."

The coldness of her voice, her refusal to look at me, touched off my temper. "I haven't deposited your check. If I don't solve Lawrence's murder, I'll give it back to you." I knew it was my pride speaking, but I didn't care.

She rose to her feet and walked to the railing of the porch. She was old, but she was still lithe. She leaned against the railing with a grace that reminded me of her routine of limbering up before a dance class. "I have to get ready for the funeral service." She walked off the porch and got into her car without ever looking back.

The rocking chair creaked as I moved slowly. I was ten minutes late to meet Cece, and Madame had taken the wind out of my sails.

Cece was furious when I finally arrived at the funeral home. When she handed me the camera, it was abundantly clear that I'd never used such a sophisticated piece of equipment. The photography class I'd taken in college had come under the heading of Art. The cameras we'd been told to use were basic—to give us the latitude for artistic expression. This camera had more bells and whistles than a computer.

"You said you could do this," she hissed at me, pulling me behind a stand of fake fronds that the funeral parlor used for a setting. The smell of the place made me dizzy.

"I can do it," I said, tugging the camera from her hands. "Just give me a minute to look at the damn thing."

"I'm calling Ralphie," she said angrily. "You're fired."

"Cece!" I caught the sleeve of her alpaca sweater and held firmly enough so that she'd stop. Cece was careful with her expensive clothes. When she finally turned back to face me, I stared her dead in the eye. "I can do this. Don't panic."

"If you mess this up, it could ruin the biggest story . . . Look." She nodded toward a man with a pad who was being followed by another man with several fancy cameras hanging off his neck. "That's Allan

List from *People* magazine, and his photographer. Look
at the television camera crews. I can't afford not to have
photos of this in tomorrow's newspaper."

"I can do it." I made the vow even though my stomach was curdling. Cece knew how to put the heat on an
imposter.

It was, luckily, a moot issue at this point. The funeral
director asked everyone to take a seat. Cece cast me one
black look and moved to the front. I joined the other
photographers moving about and snapping photos of
the rich and famous.

Harold sat in the front pew with Brianna at his side.
She, too, wore a black veil that hid her face. Sniffles, no
doubt fake, issued forth from behind the veil.

Madame arrived and sat on the other side of Harold.
The small chapel was filled with other faces I recognized from magazine covers and television. Everyone
from the town of Zinnia was trying to cram into the
chapel, but one of the funeral home employees was
holding them back.

An old man got up and went to the podium. Ramone
Gilliard. I was shocked. He had none of the joie de
vivre that had been so much a part of Lawrence's
charm. He was a thin man, exuding almost the same
attitude of the academic aesthetes who'd taken over the
third pew of the chapel.

"Lawrence was my friend."

With those first words and the ones that followed, I
changed my mind. Appearances aside, this man had
heart.

I forced myself to take pictures though I wanted only
to sit and listen to the eulogy that brought Lawrence's
Paris years to life. Ramone Gilliard described a young
man whose door was always open to other writers and

artists. He spoke of the magic that Lawrence could create with a cheap bottle of wine, fresh bread, olive oil, and his lively intellect and humor—"a repast for all of the senses." He spoke of Lawrence's passion for creativity and his eye for talent, his involvement with politics and the human condition. Before he finished, I was blinking back tears while others were openly sobbing. Someone remarkable had passed from this earth.

Ramone gripped the edge of the podium as he concluded. "It is an irony that in first coming to Paris, Lawrence felt that he had chosen the city out of desperation. He had come to the place where others like him had found a haven. I remember our first meeting. He'd left behind the land and all he loved—all except his belief in the trinity of art, political involvement, and truth. He was so passionately in love with his country, so despairing of the horrors of the war. And so afraid for his friends. But it was not long before I realized that Lawrence had not chosen the City of Light for his home. Paris had chosen him. I honor him as an artist of the world. I miss him as a friend. I remember him as a man of great talent."

It was over. The casket was wheeled out to the car, and the funeral procession formed for the short ride to the cemetery. Madame, followed by Harold and Brianna, led the way.

At the grave side I assured Cece that I had the photos under control. The techniques that I'd studied at Ole Miss came back to me with surprising ease once I'd adjusted to the new camera. I continued to snap away as the final words were spoken by Father McGuire.

It was a crisp winter day and the cemetery plot at Magnolia Place was surrounded by the leafless trees of a pecan orchard. The scene was bleak—perfect for the photos of the black-clad procession. I did my job, watching carefully for an expression or look that might give the murderer away. In truth, though, I saw only sadness on the faces of those in attendance.

Madame placed a rose on the coffin, followed by others, and the small crowd slowly walked away as the grave diggers prepared to lower the coffin and fill in the dirt. Harold glanced at me, a speculative look. I suffered a tiny stab of pain when he put his arm around Brianna and escorted her to the waiting car.

I lingered a moment, struck by the sense of a time long past in the worn faces of the two black men who waited beneath a pecan tree with shovels.

As soon as everyone was gone, they came forward and began their work. They seemed not to notice me, but I should have been warned that we weren't alone when I saw them look up and then at each other. They tucked their heads lower and dug faster.

The grip on my shoulders was unexpected and made me gasp.

"What do you know about that missing manuscript?"

I recognized the planter tones of Boyd Harkey before I even turned around. I had to crane my neck to look up at him. He did, indeed, bear a strange resemblance to the creature from which his nickname derived. I suddenly wondered if he enjoyed the fact that everyone called him Catfish. His bristly mustache played to the name.

"Mr. Harkey," I said with wide-eyed surprise. "What makes you think I'd know anything about a manuscript?"

"Don't play the ingenue with me, Sarah Booth. I know you've been plundering Ambrose's home. Rumor has it that you and that filthy Nicaraguan took off with the book."

"Rumor is seldom accurate." I didn't like him. He was probably the most famous lawyer in the Delta. *Rumor* had it that only his poor clients found a new home in Parchman State Prison. *Rumor* had it that Boyd Harkey would get a client as much justice as he could pay for.

"Let me make this very clear. That book belongs to Brianna Rathbone. If you have it, you're a thief. If you have it and don't return it immediately, I'll see that you're prosecuted to the fullest extent of the law. Then I'll buy Dahlia House and see that it's bulldozed to the ground."

His threat made me breathless with fury, but Aunt LouLane's rigorous training saved me. "Brianna must have paid you handsomely. If I liked her more, I'd warn her against wasting her money on a third-rate lawyer."

His lips stretched into a smile, and I no longer thought of a catfish. He was definitely more shark. "Listen to me, you little fool. I'm trying to give you a chance to return the manuscript. Give it back and no charges will be filed."

"I wouldn't give you spit," I said, stepping back from him.

"Willem Arquillo is a man with a past. Don't let your hormones overrule your brain, Sarah Booth. You'll regret it. You don't have a clue what's at stake here."

My DG training was running short. I wanted to say something crass and vulgar, fortified with a hand gesture. Instead, I turned away and went to my car. Cece was expecting me at Harold's gathering.

Boyd Harkey yelled after me. "This isn't about celebrity or a few scandals. You're in over your head on this one."

17

As usual, Harold's reception was beautifully elegant. The front porch was filled with pale yellow baskets of blooming calla lilies, and inside there were a dozen arrangements of red roses. In a masterful touch, Harold had put out his collection of Lawrence's work. I found myself examining the books, paintings, and several smaller sculptures with renewed respect. I'd been aware of Lawrence's diversity, but I'd never been confronted with the sheer weight of it. He'd written four cookbooks on Southern cuisine, a how-to on puppets, several plays, music—comic and serious—six volumes of poems and the novels. Not to mention the magical figures he'd created from stone and clay.

I looked up from a particularly witty poem about a young woman who was famous for her charm and deception to find Cece headed for me like the *Titanic* toward an iceberg.

"Put the books down and circulate," she commanded while maintaining a smile. "How much film do you have left?"

"Four rolls. I've shot ten, and I'm getting great shots."

"You're late. Where were you?"

"Boyd Harkey and I had a tête-à-tête at the cemetery."

Her interest was immediate. "And?"

"He said I couldn't be president of his fan club."

She gave me an exasperated look.

"I'll tell you later," I promised. "Did *you* see anything unusual?"

She quirked her mouth. "We'll talk later. I need photos of everyone at the party."

"Sure." I lifted the camera and began to drift around the room. I saw Joseph Grace and the bookstore owner, Bailey Bronson, over in a corner. In their absorption with each other, I was able to snatch their empty wineglasses and store them in my camera bag, per Coleman's request.

I eavesdropped on their conversation, which centered around themselves, of course. Joseph's wife, Tilda, was noticeably absent, as was Willem. The artist had missed the service and now the reception. Something else to check on.

Brianna was stuck to Harold like glue. I captured them on film just before I added their wineglasses to my collection for Coleman. The reception would have to be rated flawless, and Brianna was laying a languid hand on Harold's arm and trilling as if she were at her Pulitzer acceptance party. I moved on, aware that watching them together only made me feel more alone.

Tinkie was at the hors d'oeuvres table, and she lifted one eyebrow and winked. I eased in that direction, and together we slipped into Harold's spacious kitchen. The catering staff ignored us as we maneuvered in the lee of the big refrigerator.

"What did your father say?" I asked.

Tinkie rolled her eyes. "He went ballistic. I've never seen him so overwrought."

Tinkie's news took me by surprise. Avery Bellcase wasn't a man who was known as a regular gossip, but what Tinkie was asking was old, old news.

"He told me to mind my own business and that if he heard I was annoying old man Archer, he'd cut off my trust."

"Did you act like you were going to visit the senator?"

Tinkie shook her head slowly. She bit her bottom lip, and finally let it pop out. "I just said that I was reading some stuff about Lawrence, and that the summer at Moon Lake had come up and what about Jebediah Archer and his son. I was cool, Sarah Booth. I didn't botch this, I swear."

I put a hand on her shoulder. Tinkie couldn't take both her father and me chewing on her in one day. "It's okay. I wonder what set him off."

She shook her head, her blue eyes wide.

"He won't cut off your trust." He wouldn't either. He might get mad at Tinkie, but she was his only child. In his own way, he adored her. Tinkie had lived up to every expectation. She was beautiful, well groomed, a tempting bauble for any man to have at his side, and she'd married well, never causing gossip or a scandal by dating bad boys. Her only flaw was that she hadn't produced a child, which I suspected was Oscar's doing. Oscar was so tight he'd squeeze a nickel until the buffalo screamed. A child, what with private schools and college, would be an incredible expense.

"It's not my trust. Daddy won't disown me. He can't. I'm all he's got," Tinkie said slowly. "I saw his eyes, Sarah Booth. He knew something. And that scares me." Her bottom lip disappeared into her mouth as she sucked it in concentration. "What really went on up at that lake?"

I'd talked to everyone I could who'd been at Moon Lake that summer and was still alive. Everyone except Jebediah Archer and the people who ran the Crescent casino. It was time for a road trip.

"I intend to find out, Tinkie."

"Sarah Booth!" She squeezed my arm. "Behind you."

I turned to find myself face-to-face with Brianna. She wore a black designer gown and five-inch heels, which put her at six-four. She had the height advantage, but I had the moral low ground.

"So, you decided to lurk in the kitchen with the help. How appropriate," she said. "Harold thought he saw you sneak off, and he asked me to come and see what you were up to. I think he was afraid you might be trying to steal the silver."

I *was* collecting the crystal, but I wasn't about to admit it. "If Harold's so concerned about what I'm doing, maybe he should come and check himself." It was a pitiful rebuttal, but the best I could do with my head full of Moon Lake.

"Harold's too busy to be bothered with the likes of you." She turned to Tinkie. "And I'm shocked at you, cowering back in a kitchen corner. What's Sarah Booth doing, blackmailing you?"

"Sarah Booth is my friend." Tinkie stepped forward, and for a split second I was reminded of Chablis. They were both petite, and they both had a lot of heart.

"You always did take up for the underdog." Brianna's lip curled. "One day you're going to get bitten, Tinkie. Remember the old saying, 'Lie down with dogs, get up with fleas.' "

"Fleas are curable, Brianna. Stupidity isn't."

Score one for Tinkie!

"If you can drag yourselves out of the corner, Harold's going to make a toast. I'd like this particular photo to be on the society page." She looked at me. "Chop chop, Sarah Booth. You are working, you know."

"I'd like to plant my shoe right up her butt," Tinkie said as Brianna pushed through the door into the dining room.

I held up my hand for a high-five. "But you were terrific."

"Let's go hear this toast, and then I want to go home. My feet are killing me, and Oscar's threatening to fire the maid. I have to get home and keep the peace."

The duties of a wealthy wife. I grinned at her. "Let's go. And I have some evidence I need for you to sneak out for me." Tinkie would be the perfect person to haul out the wineglasses. After the fingerprints were removed, I'd figure out a way to get them back to Harold.

"Sure," she said, giving me a curious look. "Whatever you need."

I did the obligatory party shots as Harold toasted Lawrence's literary accomplishments and his humanity. His final words made me lower the camera and look at him.

"Lawrence was a man who held his friends and their secrets dear."

When I felt Harold staring directly at me, I lifted the camera to my eye and went back to work.

Cece nodded to let me know I was fulfilling her needs. At last it was over. I waited on the porch and gave Cece the camera and rolls of film I'd shot.

"You did great," she said. "I never really doubted you."

"Right." I grinned to let her know I didn't blame her. "Let me know how they turn out."

"I will. Where's the camera bag?"

I had a fib ready since I'd sent it off with Tinkie, filled with wineglasses. "I left it in the car. I'll run it by tomorrow."

She gave me a long, curious look before she hustled away, eager to get back to her story for the paper.

I was standing on the porch alone when Harold came out the front door. "I'd hoped to have a word with you," he said.

"Brianna isn't much use for intelligent conversation, is she?"

"Sarah Booth, I'm shocked at you," he said, barely able to hide his amusement.

"I'm shocked at you."

He lifted his eyebrows. "She's a beautiful woman."

I found my throat suddenly jammed. To my horror, I realized it was a lump of jealousy.

"I hear I'm the number one suspect in the murder," he said.

His abrupt change of topic derailed my green-eyed monster. I looked directly into his crystal gaze and tried to fathom what he was thinking. His mask of complacency was carefully in place.

"I don't believe that's exactly true," I hedged.

"Don't bother denying it. I've had a long talk with Coleman. He's a direct man."

If he valued directness, I'd give him a shot of it. "It's Brianna and the will. The *unwitnessed* will." I let that hang long enough for him to understand how easy it was to draw the wrong conclusion. "By the way, who does inherit Lawrence's things?" I'd heard that the Caldwells allowed him to live in the cottage free because he had no regular income.

"I inherit everything."

That was surprising, and it required all of my facial strength to keep my mouth from dropping open. "I didn't know you were that close," I said as casually as I could muster.

He shrugged. "There're lots of things people don't know."

Beneath that shrug was something else, something that glimmered with a patina of pain, but it was gone before I could pin it down.

"Is there anything of real value?" Mostly a rhetorical question, I asked it because I realized that of all the motives for murder I'd toted up, monetary gain from inheritance hadn't even made the list.

"Yes, quite a few things."

Another surprise. This time I didn't bother to hide my reaction. "No kidding. What?"

"Lawrence often encouraged young artists, as you know. When he had money, which was sporadic, he frequently bought artwork as part of his support system. Of course he had a fabulous eye for real talent. There's a storage facility in Memphis with quite a collection of early Warhols, Dalis and Monets, and some younger artists who are now very valuable. Not to mention some unpublished short stories of Faulkner's. Along with some other, lesser-known writers who achieved a certain amount of literary fame."

It was a good thing the porch railing was there and strong. I grasped it tightly and held on until my head quit spinning. "He had all of this stuff in a storage bin. Is it ruined?"

Harold put a hand on my shoulder and gave it a

gentle squeeze. "Nice jacket. The cut emphasizes your long legs."

"Screw the jacket! What about the paintings and stories?"

He squeezed a little firmer, moving his fingers in a way that suddenly made me sigh with pleasure. "It's a climate-controlled storage vault. The artwork is well preserved."

"You paid for the storage, didn't you?" A place like that would cost several hundred dollars a month. Lawrence could never have afforded it. "That's why he left them to you."

He shook his head. "He left them to me because he knew that I'd see they were properly placed. The Lawrence Ambrose Collection. It sounds nice, doesn't it?"

"You're giving them to a museum?" My stomach fluttered.

"Yes. To a place that will preserve them, along with Lawrence's reputation as a writer and artist. It's the best way I know to make sure he isn't forgotten."

With that kind of money, I could restore Dahlia House and then turn my hand to the life of a liberated Daddy's Girl. Imagine the mischief I could get into with my highly polished attitude *and* some money.

His hands working the tendons of my shoulders brought me back to reality. "Maybe, Sarah Booth, it would be best if you let the past rest."

Those words undid all of his massage. My neck tightened and I stepped away from him. "Why?"

He met my gaze. "Half a century has passed. Not even the ghosts are interested any longer."

"You're forgetting one small thing, Harold." I was having difficulty breathing. Harold was asking me to drop my investigation into Lawrence's murder.

"No, I'm not forgetting. I'm accepting. And Lawrence would prefer to let it drop. You have to trust me on this."

"Even if I let go, Sheriff Peters won't."

"Coleman has other things to occupy his time. It wouldn't be improbable for Lawrence's death to be ruled accidental. He cut his hand washing dishes."

There was a pain in my chest. I knew it wasn't medical but emotional. "Lawrence trusted you." The words were an accusation of his betrayal, if not more.

"I wish you would, too."

"He was poisoned." Each word was a deliberate stab at him.

"Sarah Booth, he's dead. There are other people who are alive."

I backed away toward the door. "I don't believe this."

He remained where he was, sadness slicing over his face once again and then disappearing in the carefully controlled mask. "You'd better. For your own sake, stay out of the past and away from Moon Lake."

I hadn't heard Brianna come up to the door, but there she was. Her smile was victorious. "You tell her, darling."

18

Tired of pacing, I sat at my bedroom window and watched the sun push back the blackness of the night. It was going to be a gray day, one to match my mood. Although I'd gone to bed early, I hadn't rested. The case was working on me.

Ramone Gilliard's words at Lawrence's funeral were like tiny little digs of a sharp knife. Someone wonderful and unique had left this earth, and he'd been taken away before his time. Greed, fear, the protection of an old and moldy secret—whatever the motive—Lawrence had paid with his life. And half the town was saying to forget about it. Even Harold. Especially Harold.

I stopped at my window and looked out into the grayness. Normally the view from Dahlia House of the surrounding fields soothed me. This morning, the vista held a strange emptiness.

"How important is this case to you, Sarah Booth?"

I'd been expecting Jitty—her question was no surprise.

"It isn't the case." My eyes burned from lack of sleep.

"Maybe you should just drop it."

I rounded on her. "I can't."

"Sure you can. Just call up Madame and tell her you quit. You're not keeping her money anyway. Let Coleman tend to it."

I leaned my head into my hands and closed my eyes. I was bone weary. "I can't."

"Sarah Booth, I know you don't want to disappoint her, but think of what's at stake."

I'd spoken briefly with Jitty the night before, telling her of my conversation with Harold. What I hadn't been honest about were my fears. I'd never truly considered that Harold was involved—in any way—with Lawrence's death. I still didn't believe he'd done anything evil. But he was protecting someone who had. And betraying Lawrence in the process.

"I know what's at stake." I rose slowly. "Harold."

"Can't you just let it go? You don't want to take on the role of that Greek girl who opened the box."

I turned to look at her, and for a brief instant I wanted more than anything to find my place in the world she offered. I knew then why she chose to spend her time in the fifties. Women weren't allowed to risk. Father knew best. Men assumed the burden of responsibility. Women nurtured and accepted. I didn't want to completely yield to male dominance, but God, I didn't want to risk—at least not so much.

"What if you find out Harold *is* involved?" she persisted.

That was the question that had kept me awake all night.

Jitty took a seat on the bed and stared at me. "What

will you do?" she repeated, this time with a degree of sympathy.

"I don't know." But I did. There had never been real doubt about what I'd do. All through the night I'd been haunted by another ghost, that of my father.

As if she shared my thoughts, Jitty spoke. "I remember when your daddy took the bench. He had reservations about sittin' in judgment on other people. Most men would have thought only of the power, but he was more worried about the possibility of makin' an error. Many a night he paced the bedroom floor, hashin' out the particulars of a case with your mama."

"He never walked away from his responsibilities."

The silence grew between us as the sun climbed higher in the sky, filtering weakly through the bedroom window.

"Sarah Booth, whether you like it or not, there's a difference between men and women."

"Jitty, not now," I begged. "Please."

"I'm not tryin' to devil you, girl. I'm tryin' to help."

I shook my head. "Like it or not, I have to do what's right. My gender doesn't excuse me from it."

She sighed. "I wish your daddy was here. He'd know what to say."

I swallowed back the rush of emotion that her statement brought on. I would give five years of my life for a conversation with my father. I longed to have him beside me, right now, to help chart my way through these difficult troubles. He would dispense wisdom in a quiet, calm voice that I remembered with such an aching desire that it made me dizzy. I closed my eyes and tried to force him to appear. Jitty was here, why wouldn't he come back to me?

And then I knew what I was doing was wrong. Like

the old fifties sitcoms that Jitty watched incessantly, my memories of both my parents had taken on the sharpness of black and white. They were good and noble. Infallible. Death and the passage of time had stolen their humanity and their ability to err.

With the best of intentions, I was reducing them to less than what they'd been.

The fact was that I had to make this decision alone. And then I had to live with it. This case was no longer a game of cops and robbers, of figuring out a puzzle. Lawrence Ambrose had been murdered. Harold was at risk, and though I wasn't certain how deeply I cared for him, I was certain that I cared.

I went to the closet and began pulling out clothes. I settled on a suede suit that I'd bought in New York several years before when I'd gotten a small part in a play. It was a golden green, a nice contrast to my hair.

"Where you goin'?" Jitty asked softly.

"To Clarksdale."

"Going to see that old senator?"

"Yes." I turned to her, still wanting approval but trying hard not to let it matter. "I have to, Jitty. Even if I quit now, this would always be in the way. For me and for Harold."

She nodded, standing and smoothing her hands down her pale blue shirtwaist. In the weak morning light, she looked like a monotone television character. I had a vision of Loretta Young descending a staircase with perfect poise. She had obviously been practicing her deportment. "Be careful, Sarah Booth."

"I will," I promised.

"Take the dog."

I smiled. Sweetie's protection value was in her size and the fact that she'd knock a person down trying to lick them. "You keep her company. She has to go to the vet soon."

"Not soon enough. Any day now you gonna get a bill from some of those other dog owners. She's 'bout killed a couple of 'em."

"The honor of the Delaneys is upheld," I teased.

"You watch your back," Jitty warned. "Old folks are mean by nature, especially one who's lost all the power he once had."

If the Archer home had ever been named, there was no trace of a plaque or marker. It was a beautiful old ante-bellum style house that had once been the center of plantation life. But Clarksdale had grown up around it, encircling it with paved streets and upper-middle-class neighborhoods. All that remained of what the house had once been was the driveway made from baked-clay bricks hand-fashioned by slaves.

To create the driveway, which was at least a thousand feet, there must have been sixty thousand bricks. Untold man-hours. The Archers had been, and still were, wealthy people.

Jebediah Archer wasn't expecting me, and the young black woman who opened the door wasn't thrilled with my presence, but she let me in and told me to wait in the hallway after I'd introduced myself and asked to speak with the senator.

She was a beautiful woman who moved with the stealth of a cat, and the same arrogance. I had the strangest sensation that I'd run across another species of Daddy's Girl.

While she was gone I had time to examine the hall-way, checking my makeup and outfit in the large mirror, inspecting the lush red leaves of the poinsettias that graced a marble table, snooping over some carved ivory figures of amply endowed women. Fertility goddesses, if I had to guess. Interesting.

"The senator will see you."

She'd slipped up behind me and caught me with one of the figures in my hand. Removing it as if I were a naughty child, she replaced it exactly where it had been. She made it clear that she thought I might try to steal it.

I followed her down the hallway past what I presumed would be the formal parlor and into a room that had been furnished as a study. A huge mahogany desk gleamed in the pale light that filtered in a large window hung with damask draperies. The walls were lined with books and the ghoulish heads of lions and tigers and bears. The senator was a big-game hunter. I wondered if he'd made his kills on safari or on some of the canned hunts in Texas where declawed animals, often former pets, were shot in cages as trophies. Either way was reprehensible.

"What is it you want, Miss Delaney?"

I hadn't seen the senator. He was sitting in a large leather chair that faced the window. When he turned around, I was startled.

He was older than dirt, at least a hundred, his face creviced by wrinkles and the raw patches where skin lesions had been removed. When he looked at the black woman, fury sparked in his eyes. "Get out."

She said nothing, just left the room. The door closed behind her with a soft click, and I had the desire to follow on her heels. Malice seemed to ooze from the old man.

"I don't have all morning. What do you want?"

"To talk about the past." It was a fumbling start, and one I knew I'd pay for.

His laughter was sharp, a bark of anger rather than mirth. "I have no future, but I won't dwell in the past. That makes the present a very miserable experience."

For a very miserable man, I could have added. But I didn't. "Moon Lake. Nineteen forty."

I expected him to tell me to leave. Instead he leaned forward. "The summer my son was murdered."

"Yes," I said. "The summer J. Edgar Hoover visited Mississippi."

He sat back in his chair, putting his face in shadow. "Sit down," he said. For all of his meanness, he was smart. His eyes, so old that all color had faded, were alert, cunning.

I took a seat across the desk from him and waited. Moments ticked by. The room was oppressively warm, and my suede suit was becoming uncomfortable. Still, I waited. He was trying to unnerve me and force my hand, but I didn't give in to the urge to explain.

"I knew your father," he finally said.

Of all the opening gambits I'd expected, this wasn't one. "Yes, he knew you, too." My voice was cool. "He was—"

"A weakling."

If his intention was to make me angry, he accomplished his goal. It took all of my restraint to remember that this wasn't about me. Or my father. I stood up. "Integrity is often viewed as weakness by someone who has none. Moon Lake. Nineteen forty," I repeated. "Your son was murdered and nothing was ever done about it. Why?"

"Sit down. You came here to get something. If you want it bad enough, you'll stay."

His game was to insult, anger, and abuse me, and ultimately he'd give me nothing. He'd lost every bit of power, except to inflict suffering. "You're mistaken." I picked up my purse. "I heard your son was a bully. I see he came by it honestly."

He laughed. "Don't go home and cry because the world is such a mean old place. Wait fifty years, then see what hard reality is like. Deloris! Deloris!" He shouted the woman's name with a gusto that left me terrified he was having a stroke.

The door opened and the black woman returned carrying a tray with a decanter and glasses. She put it on the desk, ignoring his bellows. Without a word she walked out again, closing the door firmly behind her.

"Who is she?" I asked.

"I thought you came to talk about the past." He leaned forward and poured the bourbon over the ice in the glasses.

It was only nine o'clock, and I had no desire to share a drink with this man. I ignored the second glass.

"Her name is Deloris Marsales Archer."

"Your wife?"

"My daughter," he said, draining the glass and pouring another. "She's counting the moments until my death."

I was still standing, purse in hand. This was surely hell, or as close to it as I'd ever come. I started to leave.

"No grit, girl. Maybe you should go home and bake cookies. That's a woman's job. Domestic chores."

His life was obviously comprised of hurling insults and hoping that one of his victims would rise to the bait. I took a page from Deloris's book and kept walking to the door.

"You want to know about that summer. They were all a bunch of fools and degenerates. My son. Hoover. They were disgusting."

Whether it was the same fascination that makes people watch tragedies on the six o'clock news or the hope that he actually knew something, I didn't walk out the door.

"A good man has been killed. Lawrence Ambrose. Something happened at Moon Lake that may have played a role in his murder. I want to know what."

"Sit down."

It was a command, and I considered ignoring it. But if Archer knew something, I wanted it. I did not want to come back to this place ever again. I returned to my chair.

"I remember Ambrose." His lips stretched into the design of a smile, but there was only cruelty there. "He tried to come home. Thought he was going to get a teaching job, bring all his cultured ideas and ideals back home to Mississippi. Hah! He went packing back to Frogland, where he belonged."

"*You* stopped him from getting the job at Ole Miss?"

"With one phone call." He chuckled, and it was the sound of old bones rubbing. "It wasn't hard to convince those ivory tower fools to work with me. Rabbits. That's what they are. They'd eat their own young to keep from sharing."

"Why?"

He moved forward suddenly in his chair, and I had the impulse to jump out of mine. He saw my revulsion and grinned.

"He betrayed his country. All of them, those prancing young people who thought they knew so much. Those singing, dancing whores, all eavesdropping for bits and pieces of information." He poured another drink and belted it back. "They thought they were so sly, but I was on to them. Hosea, that damn idiot, mixed in there, thinking he was so clever. He was worse than stupid."

My heartbeat had almost doubled. So Lawrence had been on to something at Moon Lake. Hanging around the wealthy and powerful, he'd learned secrets. He was going to put them in his book. All I had to do was find out what Lawrence had known. Find out and then stay alive.

"What happened that summer?" It wasn't the greatest question, but I was feeling my way forward.

The sharp old eyes flattened out of focus for a moment. I was wondering if he was truly insane when he spoke again, and I realized he'd slipped into the past. "Hosea didn't have the backbone of a tadpole. He could have been an officer in the army. Lazy coward! That life was too harsh for him. He said if I made him sign up, he'd humiliate me, ruin my name. He was going to buy the Crescent casino." Jebediah's laughter rang out against the walls. "Buy it! 'With what?' I asked him. He didn't have two dimes to rub together. The Depression had ruined his big scheme to sell cars. No one wanted a car. They wanted food. Gambling was his ticket home, he said. And when I wouldn't give him the money to buy the casino, he decided to sell information to my enemies. Steal it from me, his father, and sell it to the Germans. He was an imbecile."

I was mesmerized by his venom. I couldn't stop myself from staring at him. "That's why he was killed?"

"My son was killed in a card game, a tragedy." He poured another drink, holding the glass this time as he met my gaze. "You came here for the truth, didn't you? Well, here it is. I found out what Hosea was up to. I got Hoover down there. *I* had the local sheriff raid the

Crescent. *I* paid him to do what he'd been paid by others not to do. But there were no arrests. No gamblers were busted, no charges were filed. One shot was fired, right into Hosea's heart."

I braced my hands on the arms of the chair. "Hoover shot him?"

"I shot him. I gave him life and I killed him. He wasn't fit to live. He should have been drowned at birth."

His eyes never left mine, and I knew he was feeding off the horror that I felt.

"You've finally got the truth, Miss Delaney. Now what are you going to do with it?" He downed the liquor. "Not a damn thing, that's what. Not a damn thing. Good riddance to Lawrence Ambrose and all of those traitors. I knew what was going on back then. Tom Williams writing his trash, holding up the South to criticism so that everyone who saw his plays viewed us as products of incest. And your Lawrence Ambrose, stirring up trouble. He lived longer than he deserved, and he finally came crawling home to Mississippi."

The contrast between the two old men was a measure of extremes—Lawrence so generous and filled with life; Jebediah drowning in his own venom. "I don't believe anything you've said, except that you probably did kill your own son." I stood up slowly, not trusting my rubbery legs. "I'll remember this day. I'll mark it as the day I encountered true evil."

My legs shook, but I made it to the doorway.

"You think so much of all those artistic types. Ask Rosalyn Bell what she has to hide." He laughed. "Ask her how much money a dance teacher in Zinnia makes. When you get the right answers, maybe you'll quit poking around in the past before you get hurt."

I walked straight down the hallway. The front door was open, and I walked through it. Stepping onto the porch, I sensed someone beside me. Deloris stared at me, unflinching, from a swing.

"Don't bother calling the police. They won't do anything." She rose to her feet, a motion fluid and controlled, just like her voice. "Everyone thinks he's crazy, because of the cancer, but he's not. He's just mean. And he's dying and terrified." Her smile was contented. "It'll be over in a matter of months. The fear will kill him if the cancer doesn't."

"He's your father." A wind had blown up, skittering dead pecan leaves across the freshly painted boards of the porch.

"I am the daughter of his blood." Her lips drew tighter, revealing perfect white teeth. "I am exactly what he deserves."

She walked back inside and closed the door in my face.

19

Instead of going straight to Lula, I took a detour, needing the solitude of a drive. A steady rain had begun to drench the empty cotton fields that stretched on either side of the road, and when I rolled the window down to get a better look at a shotgun-blasted road sign, the odor of the rich, rain-soaked soil wafted up to me. Nothing in my life had ever smelled so much like wealth. Not money, but wealth. It was something that not everyone understood.

I'd gone miles out of my way to drive along one of the older highways, a little-used thoroughfare that hugged the tall levee that restrained the Mississippi River. Three stories high, the levee is a man-made swell that rises out of the Delta and from a distance looks like a green and shimmering wave. At the base it's maybe a hundred feet wide. At the top, thirty. The old road I traveled, Highway 1, runs straight north and south, parallel to, yet separated by several miles from, 61 Highway, the route the blacks took during the great migration to the Northern cities back in the twenties and thirties. 61 Highway, always styled in that fashion, is also the long, dusty road blues musicians took to the North, where the sexy, sad, and dangerous songs they created were recognized and recorded as an original new sound, the Chicago Sound.

61 Highway is a four-lane now, a quick ride north to Memphis and Chicago. My narrow little road was much closer to the river, much closer to the past. I followed it through four-way stops that marked what had once been a small community. Now the dormant kudzu vine, waiting patiently for the warmth of spring, clung to the old bricks of a deserted service station, a small grocery. With the first encouragement of sun, the vines will quickly claim the crumbling bricks, burying them beneath the lush green leaves. In a matter of years, the past will be covered from sight by a vine that, to the outsider, looks strangely beautiful. I know differently.

I turned left on a dirt road and drove on top of the levee. The other side, the western side, is a wilderness of breaks, ponds, and woodlands—a hunter's paradise.

On the eastern side of the levee, cattle grazed and old shotgun shanties eroded in the shadow of the huge man-made bank. Only a few yards distant were the cotton fields, wide open so the crop dusters can spray with ease.

In 1927, the old levee broke. Hundreds of thousands of acres flooded. Hundreds of people and thousands of animals drowned as the river the Indians had named Father of Waters swept over that flat, flat land. The Corps of Engineers built the new, improved levee, and the wild spirit of the river was contained. For the moment.

Like all things regarding nature, the levee is a solution with a price. Without the flooding, the rich soil of the Delta is not replenished.

I stopped the car on top of the levee and listened to the rain pounding on the roof. The weather reflected my thoughts, and it was with grim satisfaction that I realized that I needed a dose of Denise LaSalle. Or Muddy Waters. Or B.B. King. To truly enjoy the pleasures of a good depression, you have to keep one finger on the pulse of vital life, which is exactly the point of the blues. I found a tape and slotted it into the player. Robert Johnson, one of the most mysterious of the bluesmen, sang about trading his soul to the devil at the crossroads for a talent to play the guitar. There were plenty of people who believed that the young singer and guitar player had done just that.

After Jebediah Archer, I, too, believed that a man might sell his soul for power. This case had taught me that some people sold their souls for a lot less satisfaction than being able to play the blues.

At any rate, I'd spent enough time searching the rainy Delta landscape for answers that would not be found in the fallow cotton fields. I'd needed the time to absorb what had transpired in Clarksdale. Now I had to move on.

The grand mystery of who killed Hosea Archer was solved. Hosea's father, a man with enough power to escape prosecution, had set up a bust and then taken the opportunity to destroy the child he'd created. Instead of outrage, I felt a sickening pity. Jebediah had lived longer than anyone ought. And he'd lived in a hell of his own creation. That he had undoubtedly destroyed everyone whose life had intimately touched his went without saying. But his punishment was meted out minute by minute, day by day. Nothing I could do to him would be worse. I eased down on the gas and negotiated the steep, muddy road down the levee and made it back to pavement.

The truth struck with deadly force. Harold had known all of this, as had Tinkie's father. How, I didn't know. It was part of doing business in a small town and a poor state, the secrets and weaknesses of those who had money and those who needed it. This kind of knowledge was part of the power, the world of men. Women were excluded. Being the fragile flowers of the South, we needed protection from harsh reality.

This was a train of thought as depressing as the rain. I realized I'd been sitting at an intersection for at least ten minutes, the only vehicle for as far as the eye could see. Way across the cotton field to my right was a tiny white church. It seemed to have sprouted from the field, unprotected in the vast expanse of land. From a distance, it looked abandoned, and I'd passed enough of these churches to know that if I drove to it, the cement block structure, painted white, would bear a name like Mt. Zion Free Church or Mt. Sinai Tabernacle. For a land that didn't contain a hillock for a hundred miles, the namers of churches were big on Mounts.

I'd lost my taste for Lula and the long-buried secrets of the Crescent casino. Back in 1991, Mississippi voted in legalized gambling. Big developers out of Nevada and New Jersey docked riverboats in Tunica and wiped out any chance that a small, independent operation like the Crescent might still exist. The new state law required that all dens of gambling be "on the water." Which meant that a land-based operation such as the Crescent, if it had somehow managed to survive, was still not legal. Going to Lula was bound to be a pointless exercise, but I had to take a look. My job was far from finished.

I turned the car eastward, away from the river, and headed inland toward the huge old Mississippi River oxbow lake that was shaped like a crescent moon.

The narrow asphalt road clung to the outer rim of the lake, a beautiful drive and movingly solitary, except for the small clusters of civilization where homes had been built on the water. As I drove along, stretches of steel gray water flashed through the trunks of cypress and tupelo gum. The rain had slackened a bit but was still falling, and a mist was forming in the center of the lake.

It was going to be an evening for ghosts, and I regretted my decision to drive to Lula all over again. Senator Archer had spooked me. He'd made me understand the past was a dangerous place.

My destination was less than four miles away, though, and I'd be damned if I was going to turn back now. I drove on, passing a few tiny dining establishments and finally coming upon a grand old building that faced the lake with a series of wraparound porches on three levels. I'd never seen a building look so much like a beached riverboat. There was no question that this was the old Crescent casino, though it now bore the name of Quarter Moon Lodge.

Even in the fading afternoon light it was clear that the lodge had seen better days. The paint was peeling and the parking lot was almost empty. This was not a holiday hot spot.

New Year's Eve was less than forty-eight hours away, a thought that sent my depression level down another ten degrees. I'd make this quick—a cursory questioning of the current owners.

The young woman behind the counter looked startled to see me. I noticed the glass of wine and burning cigarette, and the open magazine. *Vanity Fair*. She was keeping up with the outside world even if she was stuck on the back side of nowhere.

"Is the owner around?" I asked, giving my professional smile.

"Maybe." She took a drag off her cigarette. "Who wants to know?"

I explained that I was interested in the history of the lodge. Her attitude didn't bother me—she was sharp-eyed and alert.

"What are you doing, writing a book?" she asked.

It was the lie that launched my career, and I smiled wide as I embraced it once again.

"Must be an epidemic going around. Johnny said some other fella stopped by yesterday while I was buying groceries. Anyway, enough shit's happened around here, you could write a series." She stabbed out her cigarette and pulled another from the pack. "It's a good thing this place has a past, otherwise it would be a fucking pit of limbo. Nothing happens here now." She waved me into a seat at the counter.

Behind her the swinging door inched open and a young boy's head peered through. "Mama?"

"Finish your sandwich, Johnny," she said. "I'll be there in a few minutes."

"Cecil wants to know if he should stay to cook or go home."

The boy was about eight or nine, a handsome child with straight dark hair that was cut just above beautiful eyebrows, exactly like his mother's.

The woman gave me a look. "Are you eating or just talking?"

"Eating," I said, suddenly realizing that I'd missed a meal—a true sign of depression—and that I wanted to talk to this woman. "I'd like a glass of wine, too, please."

She reached under the counter and produced a wine-glass and a bottle. "Unless you want to go in the dining room and eat all by yourself, you can stay here, and I'll tell you all about the grand and notorious past of my current establishment and how I came to live in this backwater."

"I'm happy to be here," I said, scooching my chair up closer to the counter so I could lean on my elbows.

"Cecil makes an excellent grilled catfish with sautéed squash, peppers, and andouille sausage."

"Perfect," I agreed.

"Tell him the catfish, Johnny. Make it two." She grinned at me. She was probably about my age, but when I'd first seen her she'd looked younger. "What evil wind blew you in here?" she asked. "Mostly we get the geriatric set trying to dredge up memories of the past."

"My book." I shrugged nonchalantly.

She nodded. "A lot of writers used to hang out here. Tennessee Williams, that guy who just died, something Ambrose. Lots of actors, too. Some pretty famous ones in the past. We still get a few, during duck season." She looked around at the empty place. "If I can hang on another couple of weeks, I can make it another duck season."

"How'd you end up here?"

"Family inheritance." Her laughter was good-humored. "Can you believe it? I was living the good life in Kansas City, working as a graphic designer in a big advertising agency. Then my great-aunt somebody dies, and I inherit this place. I'd never even been here, but it sounded so romantic. I was hooked quicker than a bream on a cricket."

Listening to her talk I'd had an opportunity to look around the front desk area. It was exactly as Millie's aunt Bev had described it. I wondered if the buttons that would alert gamblers to a raid were still under the counter.

We sipped our wine and Edy Lavert told me about

her family and the lodge. The gambling rooms and bed-rooms had been preserved, as had most of the rest of the establishment. The kitchen had been remodeled in the seventies.

It wasn't hard to steer her to the summer of 1940, and by the time I did, the catfish had arrived. One taste of the delicate fish and I was in no hurry. I ate at the counter and she sat across from me. We finished the first bottle of wine and started on the second. Edy was obviously delighted to have a peer to talk to.

"What's so special about 1940?" she asked.

"Part of my book takes place then."

"There are some scrapbooks upstairs. Want me to get them?"

I could have fallen out of my chair. "That would be perfect."

We'd finished the main course and were waiting on bread pudding for dessert. "Come on," she said. "Take a look around."

I needed no second invitation. We climbed the stairs to the second level, which featured a huge wraparound room, all golden wood that glowed in the circles of illumination cast by the antique lamps she turned on to light our way.

"Back when the casino was in full swing, the band would set up at this end," she pointed, "and the dance floor was here. I think the front was open, but some-where along the line it was walled in. I guess when air-conditioning came along."

She motioned to the wall behind us where a series of closed doors caught my eye. There were name plates on the doors, and I walked closer. Jungle Room, Flapper Room, Yukon Room. I stopped there. "In 1940 a young man was murdered in this room," I said.

"Yeah, a senator's son." She nodded as if she'd finally caught on to the real thread of my interest. "That was the summer the nest of troublemakers worked here."

"Troublemakers?"

She laughed out loud at my reaction. "The way the story came down to me was that Tennessee was always busy writing, but that Ambrose, he was always stirring up trouble with the wealthy guests, talking politics and civil dissent. It must have been something. From what I've been able to tell about Mississippi politics, these kids must have been extremely unusual. One time they did a benefit show to collect money for the starving children in Europe."

She led me to a framed photograph on the wall that clearly showed Lawrence and Madame in costume performing before a hand-lettered banner that said "Dimes for War Children."

"That crowd was way ahead of its time. A foreshadowing of the sixties."

The photograph captured Lawrence as alive and vibrant as I remembered him. Madame was stunning, a curvaceous package of verve and bounce. Several things clicked into place. Jebediah Archer's spleen was still bitter on my tongue. He'd avoided calling them communists, but he'd hinted strongly. And Lawrence had left the United States after the summer he spent here—the summer France fell and Europe was ground into hamburger.

When Lawrence had tried to come home and work at Ole Miss, he'd left without putting up much of a fight. His life had been threatened and no one had bothered to investigate. Now I knew why. He'd been tarred with the red brush—and Senator Jebediah Archer had

either wielded that brush or put it in the hand of Joseph
Grace. Anger isolated me from my surroundings, but in
a few seconds it burned away. Edy was still talking.

"Ambrose was the ringleader. Hell, you know communism was more of an intellectual calling than political. From what I've been able to tell, only a handful of
people in the entire state had a clue what communism
or any other political philosophy might be."

She was correct. Up until the eighties, the South had
voted straight-line Democratic. No questions asked; no
ideology discussed. Deputy Dawg could have been on
the ballot and he would have been voted in if he was a
Democrat.

Edy walked to a coffee table filled with old scrapbooks. She dug through them, pulling one from near
the bottom. "You'll like this," she said. "I've had a lot
of free time to go through these things. I guess in the
back of my mind I've been trying to decide what to do
with all of this stuff when I have to sell the place."

"These could be valuable." I took the book she offered, sat down in a chair, and began to turn the pages.

The Crescent casino captured in the black and white
photographs was a place of glamour and luxury. "Is
that—?"

"Clark Gable, yes." Edy laughed, flopping into a
chair.

We both looked up at the sound of footsteps on the
stairs. The little boy peeked around the corner.
"There's a car out front, Mama."

"Are they coming in?"

He shook his head.

"You want some bread pudding?" she asked him.

His smile was answer enough.

"Would you be a big boy and ask Cecil to serve us
up here, with some coffee? Tell him to bring some for

all of us and we'll talk. If he doesn't have to go straight home, he can join us, too." The look she gave me was direct, completely devoid of self-pity. "He's the best chef in this part of the state. Cecil's become like family to us, but he won't be able to stay on much longer."

"What about the man?" the little boy asked.

"What man, darling?"

"The one out front in the car. Can he have bread pudding with us?"

"If he comes inside he can," she answered.

I gave her a questioning look.

"There's a buzzer on the door. It'll ring up here. A lot of times people stop in the parking lot to look at the lake. We have the best view."

I turned my attention back to the scrapbook. It was a fascinating glimpse into the past. There were photos of Madame dancing and Beverly McGrath, a beautiful young woman singing to handsome movie stars. An excellent photograph of Lawrence and Tennessee Williams had them in conference at a table, the sunlight filtering in an open window behind them as they focused on whatever plans were in front of them.

There was a vaguely familiar photo of Lawrence, his bright eyes alive as he held a string of trout. The background of the picture had been cut out, but I remembered it had contained a clench. My gut told me I had stumbled on something significant. "What happened?"

"I can't imagine." Edy examined the book. Several additional photos had also been cut. "I don't remember this. Dammit, I'm afraid I'm going to have to have a talk with Johnny. These old albums aren't paper dolls."

The book was magic. Time was forgotten as I leafed through the pages. The casino was even more wonderful than Beverly had described it. I could see how such a summer would capture the hearts of four young people.

I'd lived in New York, hoping for just such a life. Now I saw that with the passing of the forties, true glamour had disappeared from this country. I had missed my era.

"That's my great-aunt," Edy said, pointing to a dark-haired woman in an exquisite gown. She had her arms around Lawrence and Tennessee. "That's how I knew about the communist thing. She joined up, too. It almost got the casino shut down, and she was sent out to Missouri, along with her younger sister. They met and married brothers, and that's how my branch of the family got there."

"Sisters marrying brothers. It sounds terribly romantic."

"A double ceremony, yeah. It was romantic, except both of their husbands were drafted and killed in the war. They were both left widows with a kid in the oven."

"I'm sorry."

"I don't think Aunt Kate even knew what a communist was. After her husband was killed, she became more politically active. And more radical."

There was the sound of footsteps coming up the stairs, and we paused as a short, wiry man brought up a tray of desserts and coffee. As soon as he set the tray down, Edy poured us all a cup and we sat back. The bread pudding was delicious. Johnny squeezed into the chair with his mother and we ate in silence.

"Delicious," I said. "Bourbon sauce made with George Dickel?"

Cecil smiled. "Maker's Mark. Similar in a sauce."

We all laughed and I felt the tension begin to drain from my neck and shoulders. Outside night had fallen, but in the glow of the old lamps that gave the wooden walls a warmth, I felt that time had stopped. Still, I needed to go home. I had only a few more questions.

"Did your family stories include any other activities of Lawrence and his friends. Anything that might make someone want to silence him?" It was a hard question to phrase delicately.

"Is it a book or a murder you're working on?"

She was one smart cookie, and I liked her chutzpah. "Both."

She shook her head. "The whole communism thing became a joke, you know. America, home of the free. In the forties it was a crime to be red, but not today. So what? And they were kids. I'm not certain they were anything except opposed to the concept of human beings slaughtering each other."

She put her finger on Lawrence's picture. "He was a great writer. We have a collection of his books here. He sent them even when he was in Europe. Sometimes we have a literate hunter who wants something to read, and I loan him a book."

I had a terrific thought. "Why don't you turn this place into a museum?" I sat forward with a flush of excitement. "Look at it." I swept my arm around. "Everything is perfect. You could still keep it a lodge, but it could also be a museum. You could get state and federal grants."

Her eyes widened. "Do you think?"

"I'm not certain, but it wouldn't cost anything to check it out. And all of this could be preserved. This is a page from the past, a place where people could come and see what it was like. You could hire young people to bring it to life."

I saw the idea catch fire in her eyes. She leaned forward and gripped my hands. "Thank you," she said. "Dinner is on the house."

Though I tried repeatedly to pay for the meal, Edy adamantly refused. She and Johnny and Cecil hugged me and walked me to my car. They watched as I started to leave. Except the car wouldn't start. It didn't even make a sound. It was as if the spark of life had been stolen from it.

Cecil opened the hood and looked at the engine, then closed it again. "Fancy motor. I wouldn't even begin to tamper with it. I'd do more damage than good."

"It was running fine." Stomping my foot, which is what I wanted to do, wouldn't do a bit of good. I was stranded.

"Johnny and I heard a car." Cecil's face was thoughtful. "Kids come to the parking lot to look at the lake, usually they're up to romance, not making trouble."

Great. Vandals. That was all I needed. At nine o'clock in the evening, there wouldn't be a garage open anywhere nearby. Chances were I'd have to go to Clarksdale to find a Mercedes dealer.

"You'll have to stay the night," Edy said, more delighted than disturbed by the turn of events. "As it happens, we have a vacancy."

I shook my head as I got out of the car. "I don't have any clothes or anything."

"You can borrow some from me. We'll call the Clarksdale dealer in the morning and have it towed to the shop."

There was nothing else to do. I had to give in gracefully. At the desk I made a call to Tinkie, who agreed to check on Sweetie Pie. My hound had a doggy door, but she needed food, water, and human companionship.

Edy and Johnny had an apartment downstairs, but my room was on the third floor. It, too, looked as if it had been created in the forties and left untouched.

"Sorry about the lack of television," Edy said as she brought fresh towels and a nightgown designed for a sex goddess. There was nothing kittenish about this piece of lingerie.

"It's an antique," she said, laughing at my look. "I thought you'd enjoy the whole experience. Maybe someone famous like Lana Turner left that gown here."

My fingers slid over the rippling coral silk, and I knew it was possible that it had once graced a famous body. What fun.

"How about a good book?" Edy asked. "Not exactly the right companion for that gown, but the best I can do on short notice."

I accepted the collection of Tennessee Williams's plays she held out to me. "Thanks. Can I look through the scrapbooks some more?"

"Help yourself. I hate to do it, but I'd better turn in. We start breakfast at five, and that's our moneymaker. Cecil doesn't come in until lunch, so I have to cook."

It was a long day for her, and it was already late. "Get some rest, I'll be fine."

"There's an old record player on the second floor. We can't hear a thing in the apartment. Feel free to enjoy." She went to the door. "One more thing." Her dark eyes sparkled. "I didn't tell you about the ghost."

I had an image of Jitty, waiting at Dahlia House for me to return, and smiled. "What ghost?"

"Old man Rutledge. You'll know him. He drags a leg. He was shot in a card game by a deputy sheriff. They say he was cheating."

"And he haunts the third floor?"

"They hid him up in one of the bedrooms for a week before he died. He was only shot in the leg. If they'd gotten the doctor, he would have lived."

"Why didn't they get a doctor?"

"He didn't have any money left to pay for one. That's why he's so pissed off."

She was having a good time with me. I nodded wisely. "I'll be on the lookout for him."

She was gone, and I was left with a book, a bed stacked with throw pillows, and my own thoughts about Lawrence and his friends. Communists. It had been an age of innocence.

I wandered around the third floor, peeping into the other empty rooms. It was a big place, and very dark. The lodge itself was secluded, and Moon Lake had passed from the fancy of the rich and famous. I examined the scrapbooks on the second floor by the light of the old antique lamps. And finally, I went to bed. I had to get home to Dahlia House. I had a few questions for Madame. She should have mentioned the communist thing. It was no big deal. Lots of artists had dabbled in different political systems—and still did.

I shut off the space heater and crawled between the thick comforter into a bed heated by an electric blanket. I was going to be warm and toasty all night. When sleep finally claimed me, I was dancing a waltz with a handsome man who reminded me of Matt Dillon, the actor, not the marshal. He was quite a good dancer. Moon Lake glittered in the background as he held me and we spun around the room. We were going so fast that I grew dizzy, finally tumbling into the blackness of deep sleep.

Step, step, step, pause. Step, pause.

I awoke with a start, my heart pounding at the noise outside my room. Edy's little ghost story came back to me with a vengeance, and I grasped the heavy comforter and pulled it to my chin. I'd turned off the room's space heater before I went to sleep. Now I could see my breath condensing in the air, a halo of silver caught in a shaft of moonlight. The storm had passed and a beautiful crescent moon hung just outside my lacy curtains. In the distance, Moon Lake glittered through the furry limbs of the cypress trees.

Step, step, step, pause.

The sound was distinctive. Someone was walking outside the bedroom doors—walking and then stopping to listen. I, who lived with a ghost, was suddenly terrified. Edy had said that in her apartment, two floors away, she couldn't hear a thing. Even if I screamed, no one would hear. And along with no television, the rooms didn't have a phone.

I tensed my body, willing myself deeper into the bed. The sounds of the steps came again, stopping one door to the left of me. Through my terror, I realized that the thing outside my door was not limping. It wasn't old man Rutledge come to spook me. Unless, of course, wounds were healed in the afterlife. That was something I'd failed to consult Jitty about.

Step, step, pause. He was right outside my door. I pulled the covers up to my nose, praying that this was all a dream.

The tap at the door was so soft I almost didn't hear it over the pounding of my heart. Tap, tap, tap. It came again.

Damn! He knew I was there.

"Sarah Booth."

Double damn! He knew my name! The whisper seemed to seep through the thick wooden door, which I had taken the precaution of locking. But what did that mean to a ghost?

"Sarah Booth, let me in."

This couldn't be happening. It couldn't. All I had to do was click my heels together three times and wake up.

"Open the damn door."

Would Mr. Rutledge speak with an accent? Suddenly I was out of the bed and at the door. "Who is it?"

"Willem. Let me in. Quickly."

I recognized his voice then and slid the thumb bolt free. I cracked the door, catching only the silhouette of a tall, well-built man. "Willem?"

"Who did you think it was, James Bond? Let me in."

I opened the door. In the soft moonlight, he was breathtakingly handsome. Not exactly Sean Connery, but a nice second choice. "What are you doing here?"

"Hunting for you," he said. "I found the manuscript."

20

The breath squeezed out of my lungs, making my heart pound harder than ever. I didn't know whether this was a result of his words or his hands on my bare shoulders as he grasped me and moved me away from the door so he could enter. He closed and locked the door behind him, as if he expected the hounds of hell to come bounding up the stairs after him.

"Where?" I asked, my mind wrapped firmly around the location of the manuscript.

He didn't answer. Instead he rushed to the window and peered outside. "You're safe here, I think."

"Where's the manuscript?" I asked again, at last getting my pulse rate under control.

"It's safe. That's all I can tell you."

It was anger this time that made my heart pound harder. "Willem, I'm not in the mood for games. You burst into my room and—"

He stood in shadow, but as I began to talk, he stepped forward to join me. In the soft glow of the moonlight I saw his face shift. His gaze swept over me, lingering and moving on, then shifting back for another taste.

"Sarah Booth," he said, a low rumble in his voice. "My God, you look like a movie star."

Ah, the power of great lingerie. Although I'm a private investigator by choice, I'm a woman by birth. I couldn't help but respond. Vanity slipped to the forefront—the low, revealing forefront—and I wished I'd had time to put up my hair in one of those loose, rumpled looks where a few tendrils slipped free. I could just imagine Willem removing the pins and allowing the weight of it to tumble down to my shoulders. Juvenile fantasy, perhaps. Inappropriate, definitely. Irresistible daydream, without a doubt.

With great reluctance I stepped out of the moonlight and into the shadows. Playing with fire was fun, but Willem claimed to have found the manuscript and now he was holding out on me.

"Willem, where is it?" I meant business.

"It's safe. Very safe," he said, stepping closer. "I was worried about you. Look, you're cold." His fingers brushed my arm with electric friction. "Let me light a fire."

He'd just done that, a near case of spontaneous combustion, but I had to focus on the case. "How did you know I was here?"

"Your partner, Tinkie." He struck a match, and in the light his smile was both sexual and highly amused. He bent to light the space heater. "Tinkie was very eager to tell me all about your new business relationship and the case."

I was going to have to have a talk with my partner. She wasn't supposed to tell every Tom, Dick, or Harry where I was snooping.

"She was worried about you, too," Willem added, in a more serious tone. "This case isn't exactly what it seems." He reached out and his hand circled my wrist. Very gently he pulled me back into the pathway of light that fell from the moon. His gaze slid from my eyes, slowly moving downward, then back up to hold me for a long moment. "You're truly beautiful."

His palm tenderly caressed my cheek. "Under different circumstances . . ." He took a breath and walked over to the window where he watched the play of moonlight tipping the lake with silver.

The next move was up to me. I could go to him, touch him, and initiate the thing we both wanted. It occurred to me that having the power of a sex goddess was useless unless the goddess knew what she wanted to do with it. Suddenly I was unsure.

"What are you really doing here, Willem?"

He turned back to face me, hesitating for an instant while his gaze swept over me, before he came forward. "I was concerned for you. Tinkie told me you were at Senator Archer's, and from there I followed you here." He hesitated. "There was another car following you, too."

My passions had cooled to a mild simmer, allowing for a trickle of blood flow to my brain. I'd been so deep in my own funk that I hadn't even thought to look behind me. Willem had followed me. Hell, half of Zinnia could have been in a parade behind me and I wouldn't have noticed. The reality of my carelessness was unnerving. "Did you recognize the car?"

"No." He shook his head. "Mississippi plates. A boxy car, the kind matrons drive."

Probably a Mississippi matron headed for groceries. No one had a reason to follow me. "Why weren't you at Lawrence's funeral?" I asked. The room was warming, but I shifted closer to the space heater. The warmth on the back of my legs was delicious.

"I was searching Harold's house. It was the only time I was certain he wouldn't come home."

While I'd been snapping pictures of the rich and infamous, Willem had been solving my case. "You found the manuscript!" My heart was racing. If I could read that book I'd be a lot closer to finding Lawrence's killer.

"I know where it is."

I felt my eyes widen. "You didn't get it?"

He shook his head. "But it does exist. I know where it is."

"Where?" I demanded.

"We can go for it together," he said. "I'll protect you, Sarah Booth. We'll retrieve it together."

I began grabbing my clothes, preparing to dress. "Did you know that Lawrence and Madame were communists? There are some fabulous scrapbooks here."

"I don't think you could honestly consider them to be communists," Willem said. "They were activists. How well do you know your history, Sarah Booth?"

"I made it out of college."

"Vague at best," he concluded. "In the summer of 1940, Europe was at war. Terrible things were happening, which Americans chose to ignore. It was inevitable that America would join the Allies, but the country was greatly divided. There was much to be gained—or lost."

It was nearly midnight, and I wasn't in the mood for a history lesson. "Yeah, yeah, I know it took the bombing of Pearl Harbor to push us into war. Let's go get the manuscript."

"You said there were scrapbooks?"

His question caught me off guard. "Yes, on the second floor." I had my clothes in my hand.

"Let's go look at them." He took my hand, removed my clothes, and led me out of the warm room and into the freezing hall. He slipped out of his jacket, a nice leather one, and draped it over my shoulders but kept walking, heading straight for the stairs as if he'd been in the lodge a hundred times.

When he'd settled me into one of the large, overstuffed chairs, he lit the nearby heaters and sat down on the arm of my chair, his hip brushing my shoulder. "Let me get a blanket from the room," he said.

"Willem!" I was ready to get going.

He disappeared for several minutes, returning with a heavy blanket he wrapped around my legs. "Which book?" he asked.

I picked up the one I'd been looking at earlier and flipped the pages.

"I have to tell you something. A confession. The complete truth this time," he said.

My finger was on the butchered picture of Lawrence standing at the lake. As impatient as I was to get moving, something in Willem's face made me hold still.

"As I told you, my father was in Germany during the war. He was a doctor."

My stomach knotted, hoping he wasn't headed where I thought he might be going. "A doctor?"

"In one of the concentration camps."

I closed my eyes. "So this is what you didn't want Lawrence to put in his book."

"It's what my mother wished to conceal. My father did nothing wrong. Nothing. He treated the victims of the pogroms. He was a kind man, and when the war was over, he was allowed to emigrate to Nicaragua without any difficulty."

"I see." I wondered if this was a family fabrication, something that Willem had heard and wanted so desperately to believe that he'd deceived himself, or simply the truth. "Why is your mother afraid of this story?"

"There were experiments conducted on prisoners. Though my father never participated, his name was put on research papers. He never knew this. It wasn't until he was dead and unable to dispute the journals that my mother learned about this. It almost killed her."

"And how did she find out?" I was afraid I knew that answer, too.

"Lawrence told her."

I didn't say anything. My finger moved across the face in the photograph. Lawrence was a handsome man with kind eyes. Surely kindness was the motivating factor in what he'd done. "Is there anything in his biography about the experiments?"

Willem's hand brushed down my shoulder. "I don't know. There's something else. Did you ever wonder why Lawrence was so encouraging of my art?"

I didn't follow him. "What do you mean?"

"I was in medical school when I took up painting to relieve the stress of school. I enjoyed painting, but my dream was to be a doctor, like my father, to go into the small villages and heal. Lawrence urged me to drop medicine and become an artist. He wrote me letters every week, encouraging me, giving me introductions to influential people in the art world. In a manner, he seduced me away from medicine and into art."

I couldn't tell if he was blaming Lawrence or not. "Do you regret becoming an artist?"

"No," he said. "He was right. In my dream, I was a hero. Self-aggrandizement isn't a good reason to become a doctor." His smile was self-deprecating, and worth at least two million bucks. "But I can't help but wonder if he understood what would happen to my medical career if my father's past became public. I would have been ruined. The taint of such things is never forgotten."

I wondered, too. "How far along were you in school before you quit?"

"I finished, I just never practiced. The week after I got my diploma, Lawrence arranged a huge showing for me in Paris. Friends of his friends. I sold every painting I had, and received several commissions—the kind of money that a young artist fantasizes about. I was a celebrity in a world of beauty and glamour. No disease or sickness. No maimed or hungry children. I embraced that life, and I had no time to think about medicine. But that life is costly. There were times I was overextended. Times I used Lawrence's name as a ticket. Times I acted . . . unethically. Even illegally."

His confession and the implications didn't shock me. He'd bent opportunity to his needs. Hadn't I done the same when I'd kidnapped Chablis?

He shifted so that he faced me.

"Willem, I—"

Before I could offer my own confession, he interrupted me. "Don't say anything," he said softly. He went over to the old record player, selected an album, and put it on the turntable. "As Times Goes By" was a song my parents often danced to, a song that called for dim lights and a crackling fire, for the sound of their soft whispers and the lilt of my mother's laughter in response to something my father said.

Willem came to stand in front of me, in the edge of the light cast by an old lamp. Beyond him, out the window, Moon Lake glimmered.

"The song suits your gown," he said, his finger pushing aside the lapel of his jacket and tracing the narrow strap of coral satin. His hand closed over my wrist and lifted me to my feet. His jacket fell to the floor.

He drew me into his arms. "For just a few moments, forget who we both are and live what this place used to be. We share many things, Sarah Booth. A love of family, a love of the land. We are much alike. Forget everything else for the time of one dance."

There was no hesitation as he swept me into the rhythm of the song, leading with a strength and sureness that left only the music, the movement. My body pressed tightly against his, the nightgown offered little protection from the sensation of flesh against flesh.

I had been freezing earlier, but I was flushed with sudden warmth. I closed my eyes and yielded to the subtle pressure of his body against mine, the timeless pleasure of dance.

The needle moved into the final groove with a repetitive scratch, scratch, scratch that broke the spell. Willem put his hands on my shoulders as he stepped back from me. "Ah, Sarah Booth," he said. His lips brushed my forehead, then grazed my ear. "We'll go to Memphis and examine the art vault. That's where the manuscript is hidden."

I was surprised that Willem knew about the storage facility in Memphis, but since he was an artist, Lawrence had probably told him about it. "Okay. We'll get it together." I frowned up at him. "What did you tell Harold to make him give you the key?"

For a moment he said nothing. "I thought you had it. Brianna said you were going to Memphis to open the vault." Willem looked puzzled. "Why would she—"

"You talked to Brianna about Memphis?" An alarm was ringing.

Willem stepped back from me. The cold seemed to move in closer, as if it had been waiting. "I have to leave." He put words to action and started down the long room toward the stairs.

I jumped up and followed after him, my bare feet lightly slapping the freezing floor. "Willem!" I caught him on the stairs. "You can't leave me here. My car isn't working."

"I have to get in that vault. Right away."

"How do you know the manuscript is there?"

On the darkened stairwell he had to look up at me. A hint of moonlight slipped through a landing window and seemed to linger in his eyes. "It's the only place Harold could have hidden it so successfully."

He hurried down the stairs, leaving me standing in the cold in a movie star's borrowed nightgown.

21

For the rest of the night I replayed the hour I'd spent with Willem. He'd hornswaggled me with his charm and Latin movement—and then left me high and dry. I suspected him of crippling my car. I gratified myself with visions of revenge, and then moved on to Harold.

The idea that Harold knew where the manuscript was—had deliberately concealed it—my mind balked at such deception. Yet Harold *was* romantically linked with Brianna. It was possible that somehow she'd sucked his brain slam out of his head. Whatever technique she used to send normally intelligent men off the deep end, it was an awesome talent.

I took a shower, carefully folded the nightgown, left it on the bed with a shivery tad of regret, and went downstairs where Edy and Johnny were having breakfast. The dining room was open and there were half a dozen big, burly men eating. All conversation halted at my entrance. Something exciting was going on.

"Lucas," Edy pointed to a man in a flannel shirt and

overalls eating a plateful of bacon and eggs, "fixed your car. Someone had unhooked the spark plug wires."

I walked over and thanked him, shaking his hand and offering to pay him, which he refused. When I returned, Edy had breakfast in front of me.

"What's going on?" I asked her. Conversation was still hushed.

"A body washed up at Harbo's Landing. Some fancy-pants."

"Fancy-pants?"

"Tourist, more than likely. It happens two, three times a year. Local folks don't normally drown in Moon Lake." She finished her eggs and poured us both coffee. "Whatever it is you're up to, be careful. Those spark plug wires didn't jump off your car. That was deliberately aimed at keeping you here."

My effort to pay was again flatly refused. It was with some reluctance that I said goodbye to Edy and the lodge. There was something very special about the place. The car started perfectly, and I headed for home through a bleak winter day. In the summer, the Delta days are long and monotonous, the heat broken only by an occasional afternoon thunderstorm. The winter is another story. A fairyland of ice crystals can melt and give way to a day as balmy as spring. Or the sky can lower in a gun-metal gray so that it touches the horizon like a prison wall. It was this latter kind of day I drove into.

I dug out my Townes Van Zandt tape and pushed it into the stereo, a sad songman for a day that begged for bed, bonbons, and bourbon. Unfortunately, I had no window of opportunity to indulge in my three preferred pastimes. I pressed down on the accelerator and sped toward Dahlia House.

Sweetie Pie greeted me with a yodeling bark that brought a baker's dozen suitors out from under the porch. "Slut," I whispered to her as I caught her collar and dragged her into the house with me. No matter that she was just following her natural instincts. I, too, am instinct-driven—as much an animal as my hound, yet I must subjugate my urges. All except for nosiness. Which, so far, was the one instinctual drive that was saving my home.

Once inside the house, with a resisting Sweetie Pie in tow, I heard the television. The sound of laughter stopped me in my tracks and I listened for a moment. The television in my bedroom was going full blast.

"Rick-y!" came a woman's wail.

"Lu-cy!" was the shocked response, in an accent that made a shiver touch my spine as I remembered dancing in Willem's arms.

I crept up the stairs to my bedroom where I found Jitty sitting on a chaise lounge by the window intently watching an episode of *I Love Lucy*.

In the soft gray tones of television, Lucille Ball looked both elegant and comic, a neat trick. Desi Arnaz glowered handsomely at some caper she'd pulled.

"Welcome home, traveler," Jitty said over her shoulder.

"Busy morning?" I replied, going to the closet to find some clean clothes.

"Tinkie left the television on to keep the hound company last night. These *I Love Lucy* episodes are pretty good. Did you know Desi Arnaz developed the split screen technique of showing two sequences simultaneously?"

That comment stopped me dead in my tracks. "What are you up to, Jitty?"

"Watching the tube."

"You are not that innocent, and I am not that stupid." There was something different about Jitty, but I couldn't discern exactly what. It was only when she moved her legs, curling them up beneath her that I saw the red toenail polish. June Cleaver would never wear Red Passion toenail polish. And false eyelashes! My God, they were as thick as a broom.

"Updating your image?" I asked.

"Close your mouth or you might catch a fly," Jitty responded.

She rose slowly to her feet, and I was given the full effect of the tight black pants overlaid with a fitted gold jacket that flared from her waist into a calf-length skirt. With the stand-up collar she looked like a cross between the wicked witch in *Snow White* and Mrs. Jetson.

I heard the rush of my breath through my open lips, and I snapped my jaw shut before she pointed out that I was little more than a mouth-breather. I almost choked when I saw the shoes—stiletto heels, backless, and with a clear strap across the ball of her foot. She looked like some designer's dark vision of vixen hell.

"Wow," I managed.

"Deadly, huh?" she asked, pleased by my reaction.

"I thought you were into a family values mode."

"I am." She did a little turn, giving me the view from all angles. "Desi and Lucy were married *and* worked together."

Somewhere along the track my train derailed. "What are you talking about?"

If all of this reverted to her obsession with wholesome families of the fifties, I didn't have time for it. I was trying to unravel a murder and build the foundation for a life in the new millennium—a life with some form of companionship other than the company of a ghost.

"Lucy and Desi are evidence that family and glamour aren't mutually exclusive," she said, preening in front of my mirror.

I snatched a pair of jeans and a sweatshirt from the closet. Harold Erkwell was the man I needed to see, and pronto. "Real life isn't television, Jitty."

"That's where we got it wrong, Sarah Booth. We thought that solid family values came along with rigid conduct and rigid underwear. Watching *I Love Lucy* I realized that wasn't true. She was beautiful and glamorous and Ricky loved her. They created a dynasty together."

It was all I could do to keep from rolling my eyes. "They fought like cats and dogs. They divorced, Jitty."

She followed me into the bathroom, where I began running water. "They had years of happiness, Sarah Booth. And children. Years and years together. Your track record is what, six dates?"

"And that long only for someone who really, really interests me," I replied. She was about to hurt my feelings.

"You can do it, Sarah Booth. I've been giving it some thought, and if that Nicaraguan artist isn't a murderer, maybe you should go after him." She was staring at herself in the bathroom mirror and batting her eyes. I wanted to smack her, but she was talking to her image in the mirror.

"Willem Arquillo is handsome and single. After listenin' to Ricky Ricardo, I've developed a yen for that Latin accent. Very sexy."

She had a point. Willem could seduce the petals off a flower just by talking to it. I slipped out of my clothes and got into the bath. The water felt delicious and I sank beneath it. When I came up, Jitty was still standing there.

"Maybe you should add a little comedy to your datin' routine," she said, finally pulling her gaze away from herself and over to me.

"Comedy?" Maybe my ears had clogged with water.

"Pranks, pratfalls, the lighter side of life. You're terribly serious, Sarah Booth. Men like a woman who makes 'em laugh. They want to be the hero. It doesn't hurt for a woman to be a little silly, a little foolish, and let the man come to the rescue. I've been watchin' these old shows, and—"

"Jitty, those shows are idealizations of a time that never existed, except in Hollywood. It's a television show." I thought I'd pop with frustration.

"You ever listen to the news? Everybody's torn up today about the violence on television affectin' children. If that's true, if watchin' violence can make children violent, then why can't watchin' these old shows make families happy?"

"Because it's television! TV doesn't make anything happen. Even if I were willing to suck up to a man to make him feel like a hero, it wouldn't last. I'd be pretending!"

"What's wrong with that? Seems to me like a little nice pretendin' would go a long way in this old world."

"Jitty, those shows are all about what a man needs. Don't you see? The women look good, fix dinner, keep the house clean, and are always there with a smile when someone needs nurturing or a kiss."

"That don't sound too hard."

I could feel my righteous indignation heating the water. I climbed out and began to dry off. "I'm not interested in that kind of life."

"But what if being loved was the payoff?"

Give the devil her due—Jitty had a way of defending her side of an argument. I pulled on my jeans and the

black sweatshirt that gave me an artist look. "I don't
know that being loved is enough. I want to be respected
and valued as a person."

"You think *I* been brainwashed by TV—who *you*
been talkin' to?"

I finally saw the humor in the situation and began to
laugh. "I don't have time for this. I've got to find
Harold."

Jitty's eyes brightened. "Harold's good. Stable, local,
a man with a secure future. Now you're talkin'. But put
on a dress. Men like dresses. You gone pry him out of
the clutches of that female barracuda, you better use
everything you got in your arsenal, includin' that black
garter belt."

"This is business," I told her.

"The wise woman makes an opportunity where none
exists."

"Is that a Lucille Ball quote?"

"It's a Jitty quote. And don't you forget it." She
viewed me up and down. "It's almost New Year's Eve,
and you don't have a date, yet you're goin' into town
dressed like a derelict."

"I may have to move fast," I replied.

"Yeah, 'cause the fashion police gone come and put
you under the jail."

"Later." I took the stairs two at a time, halting in the
foyer when I saw the red light of the answering machine
blinking in the parlor. There were four messages.

I rewound the tape and listened.

The first was from Dr. Matthews. "Sarah Booth,
stop by the office, please. The results are in on Rasmus.
The cat was poisoned. Looks like some form of
Coumadin. Could be he got into some rat poison, but
not at Lawrence's house. You know he wouldn't even

use flea spray, much less rat poison. When you come, I think you should bring Coleman with you."

I stopped the tape and replayed it just to be certain I heard correctly. After hearing it again, I let the machine continue to the second call.

"Sarah Booth, I just don't think you should go off and leave that dog again. She's ugly as homemade sin, but she still has feelings. Why, she was so excited to see me and Chablis, I thought she was going to wag herself to death. Why are all those other dogs in the yard? There were at least twenty of them. My God, Sarah Booth, you haven't become one of those humane society ladies, have you? You know if you start bringing home all those strays you'll end up with some man who looks just like one of them. But it's in your blood, isn't it? Oh, Sarah Booth! Folks will think you're craz—eccentric like your aunt Elizabeth. How many cats was it? Fifty-four? We'll have to discuss this when you get home. Think how bad it would be for business. People won't hire our agency to solve mysteries if they think you're a kook. Maybe we can get someone to help with a shelter for those dogs. I'll ask Daddy. You know, Daddy can be a little uptight about things. But don't worry, I'll handle it. By the way, I hear Harold's taken a vacation! Can you imagine? He hasn't gone anywhere in years. Call me."

My stomach was in a complete knot. Harold was gone! I set the tape in motion again. The next call was from Cece.

"The photographs you took at the wake are fabulous, Sarah Booth. Marvelous. New assignment, dahling. Very you. Call."

It took me a moment to recognize the voice of the final caller. The remnants of her German accent gave her away, and I checked the time of the call—two o'clock this morning.

"Ms. Delaney, my husband has been missing for two days. I'd like to hire you to look for him. Please call me at 601-555-3434. This is Tilda Grace."

22

I called Tinkie first and made a valiant attempt to cut her off before she could get started. "No time to explain. Find out where Harold's gone. That's your assignment."

"Where have you been? Those dogs! I'm positive there's some kind of law against letting your dog run wild. People draw parallels between dogs and their owners."

"Tinkie, just find out about Harold. Find out where he is and if Brianna's with him." Things were coming to a head in this case, and fast.

"Okay. I'll get it out of Oscar." The momentum of her words slowed. "It's going to take some work. I could invite him home for lunch." There was a pause that hinted at her sacrifice, then her voice perked up. "He only takes an hour for lunch. Those are the rules at the bank, you know. I suppose I could tempt, tantalize, and then delay on delivery."

"Whatever it takes, do it."

"Sarah Booth! You aren't married to him."

"This is a tough business, Tinkie. Sometimes a private investigator has to lay it on the line." The tactics she used on her husband were up to her. "I'll call you after lunch. Right now I've got to go."

My next call was to Cece, who wanted me to photograph the New Year's Eve bash at The Club.

"Kincaid was going to have it, dahling, but after that awful country theme party when she pulled the costume bit at the very last minute, no one wanted her to host the biggest party of the season. Then Angela Rhee Finch said she and Boyd would be delighted to have it at their country home. Very elegant, you know. But Boyd said absolutely, positively never. He's afraid someone might get drunk, have a wreck on the way home, and sue him. Only Boyd would think of that. Probably because he's considered doing it to someone."

Cece was in rare form, already moving on from Lawrence's funeral to the next big story. I'd begun to see her emotional hardness as the coping mechanism reporters had to learn. They couldn't afford to linger in a tragedy. It might dull their lust for the facts.

"I have a small complication," I said, thinking of Joseph Grace's disappearance.

"You couldn't possibly have a date," she continued. She wasn't being malicious, but it still stung.

"No date," I admitted.

"Good, dahling. One can't focus on work when one is focused on a man. I know."

"Right." Even if I drove over to Oxford, I could be back in plenty of time for New Year's Eve. And working for Cece as a photographer was a lot more appealing than singing "Auld Lang Syne" with Jitty and Sweetie Pie. "I've got to do some running about this afternoon, but I'll make the party."

"No problem, stop by the office."

"Do you have the photographs from the wake?"

"Right on my desk. Dahling, you sound awfully rushed. Is something going on?"

"I'll tell you when I see you," I promised, once again cutting off the connection.

Dr. Matthews was easier. I told him I'd be there in fifteen minutes, and he said he'd call the sheriff to meet us. The next call I made was to Tilda Grace.

I let the phone ring twelve times before I accepted that she wasn't going to answer. Or couldn't.

I headed out to the vet's office with a sense of dread. Coleman was already there when I arrived. The look he shot me let me know he was angry, but I followed him and the veterinarian into the back, hoping the cat's body wasn't going to be our focal point. I was in luck. We went into an empty exam room, and Dr. Matthews closed the door.

"As I told both of you, the cat was poisoned," he said. "A dose of Coumadin. There's no way to tell if it was accidental or deliberate."

"I'd like a copy of the lab reports." Coleman cut his eyes at me as if he expected some statement. I bit my lip in Tinkie fashion, showing what I hoped was wide-eyed innocence.

Oblivious to the undercurrent, Dr. Matthews nodded, easing one hip up on the edge of an exam table. "Lawrence loved those cats like his children. I hope you find out who did this."

"I hope so, too," Coleman said, giving me another look. "Thanks, Dr. Matthews." His hand clamped around my arm, and he escorted me out into the parking lot.

"Hey," I said, trying to shake him loose.

"You can talk to me now or you can talk to me through the bars of a cell," he said, maneuvering me toward the patrol car.

"What?" I tried for innocence but found it hard to reach. Coleman was not a fool, and he wasn't buying my dumb brunette routine.

"That bag of rat poison. Where did you find it?" His blue eyes narrowed. "I just want to hear you say it, Sarah Booth."

"In Lawrence's pantry."

"You violated a crime scene." He reached toward the back of his belt, and I thought he was going for the cuffs. Instead he pulled a notebook out of his pocket. He studied a page for a moment, then he looked at me again. "I searched that cottage. There was no poison there."

"I didn't see it either when Willem and I searched. I found it when I went back to get Apollo. Lillian Sparks asked me to pick the cat up and deliver him to her."

My response mollified him somewhat because he flipped the notebook shut and put that hand on his hip. "I probably shouldn't tell you this, but I matched the prints on the bag."

Instead of arresting me, he was going to give me information. My eyebrows rose in anticipation. "Whose?"

He stared directly into my eyes, and my opinion of Coleman rose another notch. He was determining how much to tell me, evaluating how much I could be trusted. I suddenly felt a rush of anxiety. Those prints belonged to someone I knew. "Tell me," I said, this time not bothering to hide the dread I felt. "It's someone I care about, isn't it?"

"Do you know where Harold Erkwell might be?"

The implication was more than clear. "Not Harold."

My reaction was instant and sincere. I wasn't defending Harold because I liked him. He simply wasn't a murderer. Out of the darker regions of my brain I suddenly heard Willem's parting shot about the whereabouts of the manuscript and Harold. I knew I should tell Coleman, but I had no proof, only Willem's accusation.

"Harold's and another set."

"Brianna?" I breathed the name. She'd finally done it. She'd pulled him down the rat hole with her.

His mouth tightened as if he thought about refusing to answer. "Not Brianna. But she and Harold are both missing. I'll ask again—do you know their whereabouts? And this time, Sarah Booth, I won't sit still for your interfering."

Coleman was a fair man, and one with a slow temper. A fool could see that I'd lit the fuse. "Tinkie just told me Harold had gone on a vacation. She's supposed to find out from her husband where he went."

"And you'll call me right away?" His hand was still on my arm, and he made me aware of it.

"I can't believe Harold would have anything to do with hurting Lawrence. Or anyone else." But he might protect someone he cared about.

"Money is a great motivator. Folks will do a lot of things you wouldn't expect." His fingers gentled on my arm. "In a lot of ways, Sarah Booth, you're pretty naive. I think it works for you in some instances. Not this time, though. Whoever is behind this has killed once already. Don't think they won't do it again, and let me just be frank and say that you can aggravate a person to the point of wanting to do something rash."

I ignored his insult because I recognized the seed of truth in it. "Who did the other set of prints belong to?"

Once again his mouth drew into a thin line. "You're going to like this even less."

"What do you mean?"

"The second prints belong to Rosalyn Bell."

Once, when I was about five, my parents took me to the beach at Gulf Shores, Alabama. Wading out into the water with my father, we were caught by an unexpectedly big wave. The water crashed over me in a dizzying whirl. My hand slipped from my father's grip, and for one horrifying instant, I felt the primal force of the water grab hold of me. I felt that same sensation as I stared into Coleman's eyes.

"Easy there," he said, and this time his hand on my arm was as sure and steady as my father's had been when he pulled me from the frothing water. "Take a breath."

I did and felt better—and a little ashamed of my weakness. A private investigator doesn't get lightheaded. "I'm okay." I looked down at my shoes, noting the toes needed a good polish. Jitty was right. I looked like a derelict.

"Sure," he said, but he didn't let me go. "When you hear from Tinkie, you call me," he said, his hand sliding down my arm until the contact was broken. "I want a promise."

"I'll call," I said, and meant it. "There's something I should tell you." Coleman had been more than forthcoming. I was, after all, a woman of honor. If he was going to share with me, I owed him. "If there's someone in the sheriff's office over at Oxford, you might want to check and see if a missing person report has been filed on Joseph Grace, the dean of Arts and Sciences at Ole Miss. His wife left me a message saying he'd disappeared. She sounded upset, and to be honest, I had him figured as a possible suspect in Lawrence's murder."

"Would you mind telling me why?"

There was no condescension in Coleman's tone, so I

told him everything I'd learned on my trip to the senator's house and to Moon Lake. And my suspicions of
Grace's role in the academic politics of Lawrence's past.
I told him everything except about Willem's unexpected
visit.

"Would it do any good if I asked you to go home
and stay there?" His fingers strayed to the handle of his
gun.

"Rosalyn paid me—" I halted. "Damn, I've got to
find that check. I can't remember where I put my coat."

Amusement touched his mouth. "Tinkie might make
you a good business partner," he said. "I'll bet Oscar
taught her how to account for every penny."

I needed his humor, and I knew that he was trying
hard to ease me over the shock I'd suffered. He'd also
put my mind on another issue. "So, you've heard about
Tinkie?"

"It's all over town," he said. "Folks at Millie's Café
were buzzing. It's not every day that two society
women decide to become sleuths."

"I'm not a society woman," I protested.

"Ex," he amended. "Though you always were a little
different than the others." He finally gave me a full
grin. "That's a compliment, Sarah Booth."

"Thanks, I think." But my mind was on the case.
"What are you going to do about Harold?" I was fi-
nally able to look that fact straight in the face. "And
Madame?"

"I'm on my way to pick up Rosalyn and bring her in
for questioning."

"Coleman . . ." I stopped because I didn't know
what I wanted to say. "Are you sure?"

"They matched the prints on the wineglasses you
brought in. Unless you made a mistake . . ."

I'd been careful, snatching the glasses and then

marking the base with lipstick before I turned them over to Tinkie. I didn't say anything. I didn't have to, he read my face.

"Maybe there's a good explanation," he said slowly. "The only way to find out is to ask."

"Madame will have a good explanation." This was spoken more for myself than Coleman.

"I'm sure she will," he said, no longer meeting my gaze. "Tell me, Sarah Booth, what exactly is Harold's relationship with Brianna Rathbone?"

I couldn't tell if he wasn't looking at me because he'd heard of my interest in Harold and was trying to spare me, or if he was concealing his own thoughts. "I believe they're involved. Romantically." I said it as if it didn't bother me.

"So you wouldn't be concerned that she's disappeared at the same time that he's gone on vacation?"

I wanted to take his face in my hands and force him to look at me, but I restrained myself. "The only thing odd about it is the timing. Harold has to execute Lawrence's estate, and with all of this business about . . ." I faded to a stop. "Are you saying I should be concerned about Harold? That maybe Brianna has done something to him?"

"I was thinking more along the lines that Harold may have taken Brianna. Possibly against her inclination to go."

"That's ridiculous!" The words jumped out of my mouth. "No one makes Brianna Rathbone do a damn thing she doesn't want."

He shook his head. "I'll tell you a secret. I don't care for Ms. Rathbone and all of her haughty ways worth a damn. But an old man is dead, and the evidence points to the fact that someone killed him. I intend to bring that someone to justice."

I sighed. "I never expected anything less of you." Coleman was a man who'd learned balance, in his handling of others and in his treatment of himself. It was a lesson I needed to absorb.

"I'll check on the dean. And I'll keep an open mind." He walked around his car, got in, and drove away.

23

The pale sunlight of a perfect winter day struck the white trunks of the bare sycamore trees that lined the drive to Dahlia House as I headed home at top speed. Nine o'clock—the day was getting away from me.

I left the Roadster in front of the steps and dashed upstairs, jumping a sleeping Sweetie on the way. She lifted her head and gave me a mournful look from bloodshot eyes and then collapsed back into her doggy stupor.

"Don't expect me to feel sorry for you," I called over my shoulder as I cleared the final step. "If you weren't out all night carousing, you wouldn't be tired." I realized suddenly that Sweetie Pie was leading the life Denise LaSalle, the dynamic blueswoman, advocated. Sweetie was loving the one she was with—again and again, and changing partners at fifteen-minute intervals.

Stepping over the clothes I'd left on my bedroom floor, I went to my closet. "Where is that darn jacket?" I slid all of my clothes to one end of the rail and began the laborious process of looking for the black wool coat I'd worn to what I'd anticipated as a charming brunch with Lawrence Ambrose. I remembered tucking Rosalyn's check into the coat pocket.

Since my former dance teacher was now being interrogated as a suspect in Lawrence's murder, I decided my role in the case had shifted. Now, instead of trying to prove Brianna guilty, I was going to focus on proving Madame innocent. And Harold to boot. Whatever he'd done in an attempt to protect her, it was under Brianna's influence. Harold was not the first dumb man to fall under her seductive spell. Somehow, I would save them both.

Madame needed her money for a lawyer. The little bungalow where she lived in a residential section of town pointed to the fact that money was not something she had to throw around. I still had enough cash from my first case to pay the bills for a few months. Madame was a fixture from my past, a woman whose rigid adherence to routine and practice had been a lifeline to a young girl who lost her parents. How amazing that I saw with such clarity that Madame's demands, her relentless harping on perfection, was her method of being kind to me. Though I had no real talent, she'd continued to work with me, pressing ever harder until that forced concentration became a place of safety.

I went through my clothes in one direction, sliding each hanger over the metal rod, then reversing the order. The coat had to be there.

"Lack of organization is a sign of sloth," came the dark voice from behind me.

I didn't slow down or turn around. Since Jitty's closets were in some ghostly beyond, I had no way to examine them and compare. "Help me hunt or get out," I said.

"My, my. Sounds to me like you need a Calgon bath."

Out of the corner of my eye I saw her step over the suede suit I'd earlier discarded, shaking her head at my messiness.

"That's one thing I like about you, Sarah Booth. You put your own personal style on a room. I'd call this *boudoir pigsty*. Yes sir, any man would find this an enticin' little love nest, if he didn't break his neck tryin' to get to the bed."

"Jitty," I warned. "I'm not in the mood."

"What, exactly, are you lookin' for?" she asked.

I described the coat as I began my third pass through the closet. The coat wasn't there, but I wasn't giving up.

"Honey, wear that cute suede outfit if you're goin' back out. It does wonders for your eyes. 'Course you've already walked on it this mornin'."

"I need the coat." The last hanger slid over the metal pipe. The closet didn't contain the black wool, and it wasn't going to appear no matter how desperately I searched. "Damn it all to hell."

"Cussin' is the sign of a weak vocabulary," Jitty said archly.

It was exactly what Aunt LouLane would have said, and in exactly the same tone. Suddenly it struck me as funny. Jitty and LouLane weren't what I'd normally consider a team. But since Jitty's decision to join the conservative fifties, she was acting more and more like my dead aunt.

"I'll bet I could teach you some cuss words that would improve your vocabulary," I said, finding satisfaction in needling Jitty. There was a closet downstairs where I sometimes hung my coats. I signaled her to follow.

"It's not that I don't know those words. I choose not

to use them. And so should you," Jitty said in her best prim tone as she followed on my heels.

Sorry that I'd started a lecture by teasing Jitty, I stepped over Sweetie and went to the closet under the stairs.

"What's so important about that coat anyway?" she asked.

"Ten grand." That would get her attention. "There's a check in the pocket."

"Let me help," she said, moving up to my elbow.

The closet yielded no secrets, and no black wool coat. The damn thing had disappeared. I remembered wearing it to Lawrence's house. I'd come home, changed clothes, and gone out to play with Sweetie. Then Willem had driven up. Unless the handsome artist had a fetish for women's coats, it had to be somewhere in the house.

"Exactly what kind of detective are you that you can't find your own coat?" Jitty asked.

"One who's sick of being gigged by an uppity ghost." I closed the closet door. The coat was gone, and I had no more time to search for it at this particular moment. Tilda Grace was the woman I needed to see, and since she wasn't answering the phone, that meant I had a drive ahead of me.

I went to give Sweetie a goodbye pat and discovered as her pillow one of my fabulous high heels that I'd bought at Steppin' Out. "Sweetie," I admonished. "You've got to stop stealing my shoes."

"Maybe if you picked your things up off the floor, the dog wouldn't have to play maid," Jitty said.

Car keys in hand, I ignored her. She was stuck in the groove of nag. "Think about what I should wear to the New Year's bash," I told her. "I want to make an impression."

"You gone do that, goin' without a date."

"Men have always gone to parties stag. They're considered playing the field. Women have the same right. Maybe I'll meet someone interesting."

"Like that Felix guy. The convicted felon who changed his name. He was real interestin', as I recall." Jitty had me there. I'd made a few dating faux pas.

"Just think about what I can wear." All the Daddy's Girls would already have rushed out for a new dress, but I had my entire New York wardrobe of secondhand fashions that no one in Zinnia had ever seen. Nothing like wearing the remnants of a past life to ring in a new one. "Think festive," I ordered as I opened the front door, determined to track down Tilda Grace.

The ringing of the telephone stopped me. My impulse was to go on, to ignore the ting-a-ling summons. On the chance that it might be Tilda Grace calling again, I answered.

"Sarah Booth, thank goodness." Harold's voice came over the wire, tired and desperate. "You've got to help me."

"Harold!" At my elbow Jitty made a victory sign.

"I'm in Memphis and I need your help."

"Where's Brianna?" I asked, suddenly wary.

"Listen to me, Sarah Booth. Several of Lawrence's paintings have been switched. The originals have been taken."

Art was nice, but I truly didn't give a damn. Harold was under suspicion for murder and kidnapping. Paintings could wait. "Coleman thinks you had a hand in killing Lawrence, and I'm sworn to tell him your whereabouts. You'd better get back to Zinnia and straighten this out."

There was a pause. "You don't believe I'm guilty of such a thing, do you?"

"Guilty of stupidity in getting mixed up with Brianna Rathbone." I was very angry with him. "Not guilty of murder," I added grudgingly.

"Thank you for that, Sarah Booth."

Something in his voice made my thumb give a weak throb. What did he care what I thought? He now belonged to the queen spider herself. By the time she finished with him, he'd be little more than a crusty husk. Whatever chance we might have had as a romantic couple was long over. "My opinion isn't the one that counts. Coleman is looking for you, and he's serious. He doesn't want to believe you're guilty. But the evidence . . ." I was on the horns of a dilemma. I wanted to tell Harold about the rat poison, but it would be the worst betrayal of Coleman. "Listen to me. Coleman has physical evidence. You'd better get home and talk to him. Now!"

"Two of Lawrence's Pleshettes are missing. They were original works, valued at somewhere around half a million dollars. The security team at the art storage vault found where someone had, unsuccessfully, tried to break into the place. That means the paintings were switched before Lawrence died. Someone very talented did this. The art appraiser just left. He's positive the Pleshettes are excellent frauds."

The beauty and value of a painting by Rene Pleshette were not beyond my comprehension, but Harold's complete ability to ignore the danger he was in baffled me. "Screw the paintings. Coleman has—"

"I believe these stolen paintings are the key to who murdered Lawrence. I have one potential suspect."

He didn't have to say Willem Arquillo's name. I was already thinking it. Was it possible Willem had killed Lawrence over paintings? I thought back to his insistence on finding the manuscript. He could have been looking for the key to the vault the entire time. It was a sickening possibility, made more sickening by the fact that I'd aided and abetted him.

Willem's role in Lawrence's death was something to worry about, but Harold had something more immediate to deal with. "Coleman's taken Madame in for questioning. The evidence implicates her, too." That much I could tell him.

"Madame! That's ridiculous. I have to get back to Zinnia."

I heard his anger, and it was very reassuring. "Harold, do you have any idea where Brianna and the manuscript might be?"

His next question was my answer. "Sarah Booth, do you think you could get into Rathbone House?"

Harold was asking me to breach the walls of the Rathbone estate. He was requesting that I enter the spider's den and rifle through her personal things. He wanted me to violate Brianna's sanctuary and plunder her private affairs. "I'm on my way," I said quickly. "You'd better call Coleman and tell him you're headed home."

"It isn't Brianna. Sarah Booth, you don't understand—"

I didn't want to hear how I didn't understand his love for her, how it was different for them than it had ever been for any other lovers on the face of the earth, how she was misunderstood—the beauty who was never allowed to be human because of her physical perfection. Not a word of it. Zippo. "I'll see what I can turn up at her house. Just remember, if she tries to press charges against me for breaking and entering, you have to get me out of it." If he still had any pull left in town after being a suspect in a murder.

"You don't understand—"

I hung up the phone and stared directly into a pensive Jitty's dark eyes. She'd changed from her sort-of-cool polka dot pajamas into very tailored capris and a scoop-necked wool sweater in fuchsia. "Is that color allowed in the fifties? It's sort of loud. Calls undue attention to you, and we all know a woman's place is in the shadows." I was trying to forestall the lecture I knew was coming.

"Be careful, Sarah Booth," she said slowly. "Remember, a spider is good at hidin' and waitin' until the unsuspectin' fly lands in the web."

24

Getting into Rathbone House was easier than I'd ever dreamed. In her haste, Brianna had failed to shut the gate or set the alarm system. Or check the downstairs windows. Big windows which were easy enough to lift and step inside without even stooping much.

One thing I hadn't expected was a general atmosphere of neglect. The paint on the porch was peeling, and the window latches were rusted. The house had been empty for too long, and like all abandoned things, time was taking a toll on it.

As I slipped through the lacy sheers, I froze. There was a sound, as if the house sighed—or someone was softly shutting a door somewhere upstairs.

I tucked my body to the left, hiding in the thick brocade of the draperies, and listened. The sound wasn't repeated. There was the ticking of a clock, the whir of the heating system—the creaks and moans of an older home, like Dahlia House.

I cased the house once, thoroughly, to be sure I was alone, then headed back to the room that passed as

Brianna's study-library. It was a beautiful room, walnut bookshelves gleaming with leather-bound volumes and a portrait of Layton Rathbone in his striking riding attire standing beside his big black Tennessee Walker. The horse's name had been Satan. I remembered it as I stared at her father. No wonder Brianna was so beautiful. She'd had the genes handed to her on a silver platter and served with a silver spoon.

Nothing of Mrs. Rathbone had surfaced in Brianna. She was petite, dark, and very quiet. It was Layton and Brianna that I remembered so vividly, riding wildly over the cotton fields together in what could have been a snippet of a movie about the beautiful people. Brianna was strictly her father's daughter, and her destiny had been almost inescapable.

My gaze happened to fall on the telephone. I considered calling Coleman and telling him that I'd moved my portion of the investigation into Rathbone House, but he was undoubtedly busy interrogating Madame. I wouldn't trouble him. Aunt LouLane had taught me to be considerate of others. In the arduous study of transforming myself into a Daddy's Girl, I'd learned the value of a considerate spirit.

I started in the filing cabinet, hoping to discover some correspondence that might direct me to Brianna's current whereabouts—and the manuscript.

The files were mostly outdated and a mess. Although Rathbone House was not her permanent residence, it was obviously where she stored the data of her life. Several different handwritings indicated Brianna's lack of ability to keep help. Out of curiosity I pulled her modeling contracts and then wished I hadn't. For sitting in an air-conditioned room with a fan blowing her hair into tousled disarray about her perfect face, Brianna made ten thousand dollars an hour. An hour!

The sum was staggering. The date on the contract was 1984, the year we'd graduated from high school. Ten grand an hour.

I suddenly understood a little better how Brianna might have gotten a big head. In the Delta in 1984, many families didn't make ten grand a year. She was oozing money, and all because of the good fortune of her genes.

Nosiness made me scan some more current contracts. Time had definitely marched on, and in more current years her fee had dropped considerably, down to a full-day charge of five thousand dollars. For the past year there were only about a dozen contracts. It was still a lot of money for looking good, but at thirty-three, Brianna was a has-been. Not an easy fact to accept.

The gift of beauty had a hidden price tag that was steeper than even I had anticipated. For years I'd been jealous of Brianna's looks. Now i pitied her for them.

I closed the file cabinet and moved on. The minutes were ticking away from me. The wheels of justice had begun to grind, and I was certain two innocent people were tied to the tracks in front of the oncoming locomotive.

I could have spent two weeks going through Brianna's private affairs, absorbing every delicious tidbit. She'd squandered millions of dollars, some her own but plenty of it belonging to the men she'd married. As I dug through the files and drawers, I compiled a stack of pertinent documents. Numbered bank accounts, names of lawyers, that kind of thing. I wasn't an accountant, but the bottom line appeared to be Brianna's rapidly approaching financial ruin. And then I found the real bonanza—foreclosure papers on Rathbone House.

There was a second mortgage from the Bank of Zinnia. Harold had executed the loan himself.

I sat back in my chair and tried to think it through. The sum of money was staggering. Nearly a million. More than Rathbone House was worth, in my opinion. Maybe the land holdings were more extensive than I knew, but Christ, what had Harold been thinking? Brianna had no current modeling contracts. She had no training to do anything except look beautiful.

Lawrence's book had been her only hope.

The date on the loan was November 29 of the current year. Feeling slightly nauseated, I got up and moved into Brianna's bedroom. The chaos there hid nothing of significance that I hadn't already deduced—she wore designer underwear and had a fetish for ugly socks and big feet: size ten, double A.

Brianna's boudoir looked as if a cyclone had torn through the room. I wished for the newspaper's camera to document the piles of expensive clothes trampled on the floor, the drawers half closed with saucy underwear hanging out, the shoes scattered hither and yon. I would make Jitty eat the photos, since she viewed Brianna as such an accomplished femme fatale. Hah! Brianna was a bigger pig than I ever dreamed of being.

I didn't know her wardrobe well enough to determine what clothes she'd taken, but I could tell by the scattered pieces of luggage in the hallways and under the mess on the bedroom floor that she'd been packing.

Her bath held every luxury known to woman. Oils, unguents, masks, toners, tighteners, defoliants, the gamut of beauty aids, all designer names. She hadn't missed a trick in a pitched battle to hang on to her beautiful skin.

Though I sifted through her things, I was on the alert

for something to show Harold's tenure of residence at Rathbone House. Perhaps he'd always planned on bailing her out financially by purchasing the place for her. Once, not so long ago, he'd indicated his willingness to save Dahlia House for me.

Saddened by that memory and how far things had progressed down a slippery slope for Harold, I moved into the guest rooms. It was there I found evidence of Harold's occupancy—a sock under the bed, some Obsession on the dresser. Knowing his passion for neatness, it didn't surprise me that he'd chosen to store his things in an orderly room. Had he tried to move into Brianna's closet, he wouldn't have been able to hang a shirt.

My last hope was crushed. Harold had moved in with Spiderwoman, even if it was only a minimalist move. And he'd loaned her a lot of money. Money he would never recover if she went to prison for murder. Perhaps that was why he'd proven such a willing helpmeet for her. Duty, obligation, an attempt to recoup the money he'd loaned her—anything was better than the possibility that he was actually in love with her.

Opening the guest room dresser drawers, I came upon a handsome leather briefcase embossed with Harold's initials. I flipped the snaps up and stared. A single page of typewritten, doubled-spaced manuscript rested in the bottom. I scanned it quickly. The implications were so complex I reread the entire passage:

By the time my book has blown up a storm gale of denials and outrage, I'll be long dead and buried. There is no art in telling secrets. The art is in keeping them. For all of these years I've harbored the truth, giving it a safe place to rest, until it was time to tell it. This was my last promise to Lenore, the thing she asked—no begged—of me when she was huge with child and learned that they would take the baby from her.

It was the last thing she asked of anyone before she took her own life. So now I, the man who loved her and could never win her, have told the truth, finally and ultimately putting it all down for future generations to read, or not.

Rosalyn will forgive me. I never judged her for actions I wasn't forced to take. It was not a hospitable world for women in the summer of 1940. The common sentiment was that she got what she deserved for daring to have ambition, for possessing talent. Who can blame her for turning a cruel tragedy into a means of support? Certainly not I. Hopefully not the reader.

Our only true flaw was our youth and naïveté. We went to Moon Lake with two simple desires— to enjoy life and to perform. We stayed that summer and developed a political conscience. It was an experience that shaped each of us, molded us into the people we became. That summer informed us of the treacheries of life and the intricacies of human nature. It was the seed for fiction and the spur to action.

If my friends are still alive, they'll know that I await them in a place where the desire for life, the joy of creation, and the heady thunder of applause is given freely. When we're all together again, the curtain will rise once more.

The End

My hand shook as I held the page and let the words wash through me. Lenore had been pregnant just before she took her own life. She'd given birth to a child that

someone subsequently took from her. Odd that neither
Bev nor Rosalyn nor Harold had mentioned such a
thing. Odd and disturbing. Lenore had been in her early
forties when she'd given birth. A grown woman who
was bullied into giving away her child—an act that re-
sulted in a suicide. What was it Bev had said? Something about how Lenore was the quiet one, the
instigator, yet too shy to enjoy performing herself.
She'd returned to her family home in Greenwood after
that summer and slipped from view.

And Madame. "A cruel tragedy into a means of support." What could it mean? I examined Lawrence's
words again, wondering how this single page had been
left. Who would steal a book and leave the last page? It
didn't make sense.

I considered returning the page to the briefcase when
I noticed something else, a dusting of fine, white pow-
der. Cocaine was the first thing that came to my mind.
The second possible explanation was worse. Poison.

Still holding the damning page, I backed out of the
room and stood in the hallway, the sound of my breathing harsh in the silent house.

My formal training as a private investigator is rather
sketchy, but I'd always been a good observer of the
people around me and a student of human nature.
Harold had been in my gunsights for a long time. I
found myself thinking of his image and wondering if
somehow I'd failed to learn him at all.

Good people can become diseased. The Christian religion has a single name for evil—Satan. In psychology,
cruelty is called by a number of names, most describing
aberrant mental conditions.

There is a process in both psychology and religion
where good becomes corrupted, where the strong are
brought to weakness. Whether one believes it's the

work of Satan or a process of mental deterioration, the end result is the same—suffering.

For the first time I accepted that Harold Erkwell, the man I'd known as a good businessman, an educated man with a sensitive side that I'd never anticipated but definitely appreciated, the man I'd considered—on more than one occasion—crawling into bed with, was someone I didn't know at all.

The sound of something sliding came from downstairs. It was a soft, subtle noise. Very much like the shush the window had made when I opened it to slip inside the house. I'd taken care to park my car in the barn so that no one who happened up would know I was here. Now my only choice was to pick a hiding spot and employ it.

I snatched the page and out of some misguided loyalty I grabbed Harold's Obsession, his sock, and the briefcase, and dove under the guest bed. It wasn't a position of strength if someone wanted to harm me. The ugly truth was that there wasn't a hiding place in the house that would protect me if someone meant to get me. Sucking in my gut I crept to the center and listened.

There were two of them—both creeping up the stairs in slow, stealthy movements.

"What makes you so certain the manuscript is here?" one asked.

I gripped the carpet. I recognized that voice. It was Cece Dee Falcon!

"Because Willem said it was here."

And that was Tilda Grace. I started to wriggle out from under the bed, then thought better of it. They'd broken and entered into Brianna's home. They'd come to look for the manuscript, and they had to have good reason for such a search. The two of them together. It was a twist in the case I hadn't expected. If I stayed under the bed and remained perfectly quiet, maybe I'd learn something useful.

The two women stopped in the doorway of Brianna's bedroom. "My God, what a mess," Cece said.

"Come on," Tilda ordered, her voice stronger than I'd ever heard it.

They continued closer.

"Why did you ever send that information to Lawrence?" Cece demanded in a voice roughened by emotion. "I never did anything to you. I didn't even know about you until you walked in that door. He was my teacher. I never thought to ask if he was married."

"I never blamed you." Tilda spoke with amazing calm. "You're as much a victim of a monster as I have been."

"But if this gets out, if this scandal is started, I'll lose my job. No one will ever hire me again. You don't know—" She broke off.

Tilda's sigh was deep. "I'm sorry. If I had it to do again, I wouldn't. But I was so angry, so hurt. He was so cruel to me, furious that I'd dared to enter his private world. He'd made me believe that I was less than a woman, someone he married out of pity but could never love. His cruelties were immense. Then I walked into the room and saw you both. He'd destroyed me so that he could have his life exactly as he wanted it."

"Why didn't you leave him?" Cece asked.

"I was afraid. I had no place else to go, no family, no money, no job. On the very day that I found you, a young man, with my husband, I should have left. But I didn't. When he said that we would never consummate our marriage and never have a baby—I didn't leave him, as I should have done. Instead, I wrote it all down and sent it to Lawrence."

I had to work hard to regulate my breathing. It felt like the box springs of the bed were pressing down on me, and the revelations that I was hearing made me want to inhale sharply.

"Why?"

"Lawrence was my friend. I see now he'd tried to warn me against marrying Joseph. He hinted at things, but I didn't understand. I was naive and young and so very desperate to find someone to cling to. Somewhere to go to escape my family."

Now Tilda sounded as if she were crying. I closed my eyes, regretting that I had overheard such intimate details. Sorry that now I had reason to suspect both Tilda and my friend Cece in Lawrence's death.

"We have to find that book," Cece said. "What did Willem tell you?"

"He said Brianna had called him. He said she'd found the book and taken it, and that she was going to publish it and that it was filled with things that would ruin us all."

"If Brianna's gone, then the book is probably gone, too. That bitch'll find someone to publish it and everything I've worked so hard to leave behind will be head-lines again."

"We can't give up. We have to look," Tilda insisted. "We're here, so let's look. The bastard probably has the book and Brianna. They were so cozy-cozy lately."

They opened the door of the guest room, looked in, and moved on. I slowly exhaled after I heard their foot-steps moving down the hallway. My inclination was to crawl out from under the bed and talk to them, but I held back. Based on what I'd read of Lawrence's book, a single page that would wreck at least two lives, it was highly probably that Joseph Grace and Cece, who had been Cecil while attending Ole Miss, would be served up as appetizers. If Lawrence didn't spare his childhood friends, he'd think nothing of torpedoing Cece.

But there was the off chance that he'd left out that chapter. And if he did, I never wanted Cece to know that I knew. She'd kept her secret for so long, there was no need for her to ever worry that I might reveal it. No matter how much Joseph Grace deserved punishment for what he'd done.

I followed their search by the flow of their sporadic conversation. When they were in the study, soon to become as absorbed by the details of Brianna's life as I had been, I slipped from beneath the bed. The study was on the far side of the house. With a little luck and good timing, I could make an escape.

I folded the page of the book and slipped down the stairs. They'd left the window open, so my departure went without a sound. The barn was far enough from the house that when I started the car, I knew they wouldn't hear. There was an old farm road that led to the now empty pastures and I took it, trusting that since all of the horses had been sold the gates wouldn't be locked.

I glanced back at the house once in the rearview mirror. A curtain in a third-floor room dropped quickly back in place. They'd seen me after all.

25

The Christmas decorations glittered in the noonday sun as I drove through the empty streets of downtown Zinnia. Without all the cars and people, it was easier to see the decorations. Lillian Sparks was right. The old tinsel and lights that were strung along the telephone lines looked tacky in the daytime. But I loved them still, and in the flutter of the silver tinsel, I hung on to Christmases past and a sense of something bigger than myself.

The conversation I'd overheard had greatly upset me. If Joseph Grace had stepped off the curb in front of my car, I wouldn't have even tried to brake. And what I had to confront was going to be even harder.

I took a right and headed for the Sunflower County courthouse. The stately old red-brick building was adorned with huge red ribbons on the white columns. Holiday pranksters had be-wreathed the statue of the bedraggled Johnny Reb that guarded the front entrance. I had no intention of stopping, but I wanted to see who was at the sheriff's office. Harold must have driven from Memphis with his foot on the floor. His Lexus was parked beside the jail.

I took a couple of left turns and pulled into Madame's driveway. A leafless crape myrtle framed the porch where she sat in the swing, a plumed hat on her head, her gloves and handbag in her lap.

My emotions had been slammed, jammed, and brutalized, and I wanted some straight answers. But just when I needed it most, my anger abandoned me. Madame looked old and tired and worried. I found myself walking up to her porch with a lump in my throat.

It wasn't necessary to say anything. I pulled the folded page from my jeans pocket and handed it to her. She was a tough old lady. Her expression never changed as she read the page and handed it back to me.

"I never dreamed Lawrence would actually write it," she said, "and in such a sanctimonious tone. His years in Paris, when he and Ramone Gilliard were so involved with the French Resistance. That would have been plenty for a book. It begged to be made into a movie. I honestly never thought that Lawrence would trade on his friends for a few moments of glory."

If I'd had her check in my pocket, I would have torn it up in front of her. I wasn't angry anymore, but she had betrayed me by not telling me the truth. She was upset because Lawrence had told her secrets, and yet she hadn't hesitated to lie to and deceive me.

"What does this mean?" I asked, lightly shaking the page. "What is Lawrence talking about?"

The edge in my voice made her stare at me. It was a long stare, one that probed for the old weaknesses she'd tried to dance out of me.

"Your mother would be proud of you, Sarah Booth. I thought when your parents died that you might not make it. I was afraid you'd fold. But you didn't. You've grown to be your own person, a rare luxury."

There had been a time when I would have groveled at her feet for such words of praise. Even now they affected me, but I refused to show it. "What is Lawrence referring to here, this tragedy turned to support?"

Very slowly she took her hat off. As she did so, she regained some of her posture. She sat up in the swing a little straighter, with a little more pride. "Hosea Archer raped me that summer at Moon Lake. It was a vicious rape that required a hysterectomy. His father paid me not to press charges." Madame's dark eyes were flinty as she laughed. "The loss of my health and innocence were of little consequence to Jebediah. What mattered was that he not come under scrutiny."

"I was right all along. That summer at Moon Lake." The words were like a dark chant. "It all started then."

"For the most part," she agreed.

"Why did Jebediah kill his son?"

"It's complicated, but time has a way of simplifying things. It all started with the rape. Lawrence was out of his mind with rage. One night Lawrence followed Hosea out on the lake. I honestly believe he planned on killing him. Instead, Lawrence learned a secret."

"What?" Moon Lake still exerted a powerful magnetic pull on me. I was enthralled with Madame's tale.

"That night Hosea was paddling instead of using the little outboard motor. That in itself was strange, Lawrence said, because that boy never did a lick of physical labor if he could avoid it. Lawrence followed him into a cypress cove, one of the hundreds of little inlets on the lake. Lawrence hid so they didn't see him. But he watched. Hosea met some men there. Not Germans. Americans who supported the Third Reich and wanted our country to stay out of the war. Money changed hands." She leaned back in the swing and pushed it gently with her toes. "I swore I would never tell that story. So did Lawrence. We made an oath."

"Jebediah Archer paid for your silence. And Lawrence's, too?"

"Oh, no. Lawrence never took a penny. He left the country and went to fight against the Axis powers. He and Ramone Gilliard were very active in the underground. Lawrence did some very brave things that no one will ever know."

"But the senator paid you."

"Yes, and he's continued to pay me all this time, a small monthly allowance. It's how I've managed to live."

Very slowly I sat down on the top step. Words were inadequate, and I had sense enough to know it. So I'd learned the big secret of Madame's past, of why she'd come home to Zinnia, of why she'd never married. I suddenly thought of Jitty and the safety and repression of the decade she'd decided to embrace. What must it truly have been like for women in the forties and fifties? What had Madame and others like her suffered because they wanted to dance on a stage, to revel in movement and beauty? What would she suffer now?

She reached her hand out for the page, and I gave it to her, watching as she read it yet again. "I simply can't believe he did this," she said. "Not Lawrence. You have no idea how he took care of me that summer, how he nursed me back from the brink of insanity." She shook her head, lowering the page to her lap. "And then Lenore. My God. We were wild. Young and wild and completely unaware how the decisions we made then would affect us in the years to come."

"What about Lenore?" I had to ask though the words

tasted of ash as they passed my lips. I didn't want to hear more secrets. I didn't want the burden of knowing.

"She was having an affair with a married man. A prominent man. She was desperately in love."

"Who?"

Madame looked past me out into the street. She must have seen the Thunderbird coming, but she made no motion to indicate she saw it. "Sarah Booth, there are secrets I won't reveal. If they're in that book, then Lawrence must accept the blame for telling them. I'm an old woman, and though I'd prefer to avoid the label of blackmailer, I have only a limited number of days left to endure such censure. Long ago I gave my word. That has to mean something."

The crunch of the tires made me turn around. Willem Arquillo got out of the Thunderbird and walked toward us. This time his million-dollar smile was missing.

"Let me offer apologies for what I'm about to do," Willem said in that lovely voice. "I need the key to the storage vault, Miss Bell. Please give it to me now."

"It's too late, Willem," I answered for her. "Harold knows the Pleshettes are fakes." For someone who was solving a mystery, I found no satisfaction in delivering the coup de grâce.

Willem's posture loosened, and he sat heavily on the front porch. "I know you might not believe this, but I meant to get them back before he died. I needed the money. My mother's care, the doctors . . . I was careless with my own success. Lawrence never looked at his collection, never showed them to anyone. So I painted the frauds and made the switch. I've got money now. I can buy them back and replace them as I always meant to do."

"You followed me to Moon Lake because you thought I had the key to the art storage vault."

He didn't deny it. "I'm sorry, Sarah Booth. Give me credit that I left you, untouched. I could not deceive you to that extent."

What should I say, thanks? I swallowed the bitter taste of disappointment.

"Have a seat, Willem," Madame said, holding out the page to him. "You might as well give it up. Lawrence obviously finished his book and spared no one. He's known for years about the switched paintings. He told me. But he always knew you meant to make it right, and he wanted to give you the chance. That's why he invited you to Zinnia for the holidays. He was hoping you'd recover the real paintings and make the switch. That was his intention, before he was killed."

Willem held the page but didn't read it. He looked over it at Madame. "He knew?"

She nodded. "He just never let on. He understood, I think. And until this morning, I always believed that he forgave you. Forgave all of us our sins."

I'd hardly known Lawrence, but I was finding it difficult to imagine how he'd sat down and written things that would destroy everyone he'd seemed to care about. Willem read the page and then slowly lowered it to his side.

"What did he write about me and my family?"

Silence stretched before I answered. "I found only that one page. The rest of the book is still missing."

Willem leaned back against the pillar that supported Madame's porch roof. He tapped his beautiful head against it several times before he spoke. "There is a saying about writers. When you sleep with one you put your most intimate life on the page. I never would have believed it of Lawrence."

"Maybe the book is truly lost," Madame said.

"Brianna has it. I'm sure of it. She called to rub it in."

If possible, Willem's shoulders slumped a little more. "It's pointless now. I'll be revealed for a thief and the worst kind of betrayer. Lawrence trusted me to buy the paintings for him, to spend his money on quality work. And I cheated him. I cheated my friend."

I faced Willem. "Did you kill him?" I asked.

Willem's dark brows slammed together. "How can you ask that? I'm a thief, not a killer."

I stood up and looked at Madame. "Did you? The bag of rat poison had your prints on it."

She made a sound in her throat, a soft yielding. "No," she said. "I didn't kill Lawrence. I did buy the rat poison. There were mice in the cottage, and Lawrence didn't approve of poisoning things. It was a health issue, but who will believe me? Coleman confirmed that Harold and I are the prime suspects." She gathered herself and her lips turned up in a crooked smile. "Ironic, isn't it? The woman I tried so hard to stop now has the book and the best possible method of publicizing it. Not only is Lawrence dead. He was murdered. And the woman who loved him for the past five decades will go to prison for it."

The injustice was almost more than I could bear. "We have to find Brianna," I said, rising to my feet. "Willem, you said she called. Where was she?"

"She didn't say." Willem was morose.

"I'll be back," I promised as I stepped around Willem's long legs.

"Where are you going?" Madame asked.

"I know just the person to help me with Brianna's phone call. Keep thinking and I'll be in touch."

Johnny Albritton was watching a ball game in his den when I knocked on his front door. If he was surprised to see me, he didn't show it. Based on the way he pushed the screen door open and invited me in, it would seem that I stopped by all the time.

"What's shakin', Sarah Booth?" He sipped a beer and gave me his attention.

"I need a favor. A big one. Can you trace a call?"

"Local or long distance?"

"I don't know." I forged ahead. "The call was made to Willem Arquillo. He's staying at Ruth Anne's bed-and-breakfast."

He nodded as if he were considering and I felt my hopes begin to rise. "Have you asked Ruth Anne?" he asked.

"Do I have to have her permission? It wasn't a call to her."

"No. But she's got caller ID. Maybe if she hasn't erased it you could just check her box. Might tell you right off where the call came from. Of course that won't work if it's a cell phone or out of an area that doesn't have caller ID."

I didn't have time to waste, but I went to him and took his hand. "Thanks, Johnny."

"You'll get the hang of this PI business. Don't give up. And don't watch those television shows. They get it all wrong." He walked me to the door, his gaze already straying back to the television.

Ruth Anne Welsh had gone to Zinnia High but we'd traveled in different circles, not to mention different grades. She was a bit younger.

She was in the kitchen cooking something that smelled heavenly, a gumbo of some sort. She eyed me skeptically while I told her what I wanted. I thought I'd won her over until she put one hand on her hip and balked.

"I'm sorry, Sarah Booth, but this sounds too much like an invasion of privacy. How do I know that Mr. Arquillo said you could do this? How do I know it's even his calls you're really interested in."

"Because I said so?"

She rolled her eyes. "That's exactly the sort of thing Tinkie Bellcase would say."

"You know Tinkie?" I felt a pulse of hope.

"She talked to her husband and helped me get the loan for this bed-and-breakfast. After Howard left me with two kids and no means of support, nobody in this damn town would give me a job or a chance. I'd done some catering for Mrs. Bellcase, and she went right down to the bank and stood at her husband's desk and told him exactly how he was going to give me the loan."

"God bless Tinkie," I said, already moving toward the door. "I'll have Tinkie come over and explain this to you," I promised.

"Now I'd believe Mrs. Bellcase. You just send her on. I'd like to send some of this duck gumbo home with her anyway. It was always one of her favorites."

I started to ask to borrow her phone and give Tinkie a call right on the spot, but then I remembered something. I checked the wall clock in Ruth Anne's kitchen and saw it was nearly two o'clock. Lunch was over. Tinkie had sacrificed herself on the altar of her marriage in an attempt to discover where Harold Erkwell had gone—and he was sitting at Coleman's office. I'd neglected to call my partner and save her.

"You got indigestion?" Ruth Anne asked. "You can't see my phone, but I will give you an Alka-Seltzer."

"Not yet, but I'm going to have a terrible earache," I said as I headed back to my car.

I felt like a worm. Most of the rules and regulations of a Daddy's Girl I'd been able to put behind me, but there was one supreme rule that I'd always revered— one Daddy's Girl never left another in a bad situation out of carelessness. It didn't matter that I was used to working alone; or that Tinkie was married to Oscar and a little nooner probably would work to Tinkie's advantage in the long run; or that I had no way of knowing Harold would call me from Memphis.

Rationalizing would not make this right. I had done a bad thing.

So I decided to go home and call Tinkie from there and do what I could to repair the damage—and see if I could get her to go to Ruth Anne's. I had to get that phone number.

My home was like a beacon of safety as I left the main road and cruised onto the drive. I'd been home almost a year and still the sense of perfect wonder that came over me as I turned down the drive was as fresh and magical as it had been when I was a child. Home. It was a word that filled me with good and solid emotions.

I coasted by the front of the house, going slow to avoid the milling crowd of dogs. Sweetie Pie had her own fan club going. I wondered if it was her gentle baying that won such devotion from her boys. My genial thoughts skidded to a halt as I saw a flash of black, russet, and tan streak down the front porch steps. She hesitated just long enough for me to recognize the fabulous square-heeled, strappy, extra-sexy shoes I was planning on wearing to the ball.

I jammed the car in park and dove over the side as I went in hot pursuit of dog and shoe.

"This is it, Sweetie Pie. You're going to the gas

chamber," I yelled after her as I crawled on all fours under the house. She had the height advantage on me and disappeared in the darkness. She'd gone to that nest she was building. For a dog without ovaries or a uterus, Sweetie had a real thing about preparing for puppies.

Rocks bruising my knees and cobwebs clinging to my head, I scrabbled after my dog. When I finally got to her, I reached into the darkness for my shoe. I found it—and a host of other things. It was difficult to tell in the dark, but I pulled out two more shoes, not mine, a plastic shovel, a roller skate, a wool coat, three towels, and a tin pie pan.

"This has got to end," I told her as I clutched her stash to my chest and hobbled toward the light.

It wasn't until I was outside that I recognized my black wool coat. Now I remembered hanging it on a tree limb when I was playing fetch with Sweetie. No wonder I couldn't find it. Now I wasn't certain that I wanted to. It looked pretty disreputable. Not even the cleaners were going to be able to save it. But the pockets were intact. Reaching into the left one I found Madame's check and another scrap of paper.

Walking up the steps I unfolded it, wondering where it had come from. It was a bad habit of mine to stuff things in my pockets. Usually I found them in the washing machine. Lipstick, gum, things that weren't meant to be washed.

The handwriting stopped me, a beautiful, flowing copperplate. An old school kind of writing. The first word, which was Harold's name, stopped me in my tracks. *"Harold, I hate to be mysterious (actually, I love it) but this manuscript is the best I've ever written. Take care of Brianna, and be wary. Should anything*

*happen to me, you'll be able to find the book where
tears of stone fall on Brianna's past. Be sure that it's
published. Many thanks, Lawrence."*

"Boll weevil!" I whispered, using the curse Aunt
LouLane had taught me as the vilest thing a lady could
possibly say. "Boll weevil and a plague of locusts." I
threw the biblical image in for emphasis.

"Is that the black coat you been lookin' for?" Jitty
asked, fading in beside the front door.

"Yeah."

"You'd better give it back to Sweetie. No help for
that thing now."

"No, you're right." I let the coat slide from my grip
and fall on the porch.

"Girl, what's wrong with you?" Jitty put a ghostly
hand on my forehead, just the slightest whisper of
something cool touching my skin. "You got a fever?
This is the first time you ever agreed with anything I
had to say."

"How did Brianna find the manuscript?" I asked,
looking at Jitty with eyes that didn't actually see her.
"How did she get her mitts on it?"

"Maybe she called the psychic hotline."

I ignored Jitty and went to the phone. "Can I have
some privacy. I'm about to eat crow."

"And just when you were beginning to lose some
weight," she countered before she walked out of the
room.

I dialed Tinkie's number. The voice that answered
was throaty, a little confused. There was a loud, rhythmic noise in the background.

"Tinkie! Are you okay?"

"Oh, it's you, Sarah Booth. I was just taking a little
nap." She came more awake. "Just a minute. Oscar's

snoring hard enough to suck the wallpaper down. Let me get in the bathroom." There was a pause, and she came back on the line, alert and energized. "I found out where Harold is. He's gone to Memphis. Not much of a vacation, if you ask me."

"Did you have any . . . trouble getting the information?"

"Sarah Booth, can I tell you the truth?"

How much of this did I want to hear? I was already bogged down in guilt. "Sure." The least I could do was commiserate with her sacrifice.

"Oscar and I really had a good talk. I mean, not like you'd think. I sent all the help home and I made us a bite of lunch. Nothing fancy, just some BLTs and iced tea. Oscar was a little suspicious at first, but once we started talking, it was like back when we were in high school. He told me things— Never mind about that. I felt kind of bad. He didn't have a clue I was working him to find out about Harold. It never entered his brain. And I guess that made me feel a little guilty, so I was nicer to him than I planned. And he was nice back to me. And then we got to laughing and carrying on. We just wore ourselves out having a good time. He even said he'd heard the gossip that you and I were working together, and he said he didn't care. He thought it would be good for me to have an interest."

"Happy New Year, Tinkie." I felt as if I'd just dodged a bullet. "I've got another assignment for you."

"Great!"

"You sure you want to leave Oscar in there snoring?" I couldn't help but tease her a little bit.

"He needs his rest." Her giggle was young and happy. "You know how men are, Sarah Booth."

"Yeah, I've got a vague memory."

She laughed again. "I think you're going to get a big surprise tonight. Once Oscar got to talking, he just didn't want to stop. He told me a big, big secret."

"About the case?"

"No, silly. Something else. Something that's going to knock you right out of your shoes."

"Sounds divine, but right now we'd better focus on the case."

"Just tell me what you want me to do."

So I did. And with Tinkie on her way to Ruth Anne's with a request to call me back as soon as she saw the caller ID, I went upstairs to select my dress for the New Year's Eve dance at The Club.

Without Jitty's nagging and interference, I made my selections in a matter of minutes. By some stroke of fate, Sweetie Pie hadn't damaged my shoes. Everything was neatly stowed in my carryall when the phone began to ring. Tinkie didn't even wait for a hello.

"You're not going to believe this, Sarah Booth, but that call was made from Lawrence Ambrose's house. Do you—"

I didn't wait to hear the last of it. I dropped the phone, vaulted over my sleeping dog, and rushed out into crimson sunset of the last day of the year.

26

Driving to the courthouse, I had one thing on my mind—to find Harold. He was the only one who might possibly be able to interpret Lawrence's note.

Coleman was at his desk, and when I asked about Harold, he rose slowly to his feet. "He's in the jail," he said.

My opinion of Coleman rose in equal measure with my concern. Putting a man like Harold in jail was not a politically savvy move and one for which Coleman might pay a high price. The idea of Harold behind bars was bitingly painful. "I have to see him," I said, taking tough over pleading.

"He's had his phone call." Coleman sat back down and picked up some paperwork. He, too, was playing hardball.

"Brianna's still in town." I had bait and I knew how to cast.

He lowered the paperwork. "How do you know?"

"I'll tell you, if you let me see Harold." Bartering with Coleman was a dangerous game. He could easily pop me into a cell and I knew it. "You know Harold isn't capable of murder."

"Maybe not, but he's capable of being stubborn as a mule. I'll let you see him if you can make him talk."

It was an offer I couldn't refuse. "I have my ways."

Instead of taking me back, Coleman opened the door to the jail and motioned me through. Impeccable, as always, Harold rose from his cot as I approached the bars.

"Sarah Booth," he said in that deep, modulated voice. "I'd hoped to ask you for a dance tonight. I suppose that's out of the question now." He reached toward me but stopped. "Thank goodness you're okay. Did you find anything at—"

I leaned forward, pressing my face between the bars. I didn't want him to let on where I'd been. "You've got to make Coleman let you out of here."

Coleman had come up behind me. "All he has to do is answer a few questions. But my patience is wearing thin. With both of you."

I zeroed in on Harold. "Tell him what he wants to know."

Harold's ice-blue eyes held a spark of amusement. "Shouldn't you be getting ready for the party at The Club?"

"Stop it, Harold." I could take a little teasing, but this simply wasn't the time. "I've got something to show you, something meant for you. When you read it, you have to tell the truth. You can't protect her any longer."

It was as if ice had formed in his irises. "I don't have to do a solitary thing. Let's make that perfectly clear."

"He's one stubborn son of a bitch," Coleman said with disgust. "He must like his cell, because with an attitude like that he's not getting out any time soon."

I pulled Lawrence's note from my pocket, waving it slowly.

Harold recognized the handwriting instantly, and despite himself there was eagerness in his voice. "Where did you get that?"

Whatever religious nutcase said confession was good for the soul had obviously never done anything wrong. I knew I was going to be in trouble with both men. "I picked it up off the floor at Lawrence's. When I found the body. I didn't read it until today because I tucked it in my coat pocket and Sweetie Pie stole my coat and dragged it under the house." I said it all really fast in the hopes that some of the details would slip past them.

Harold's hands grasped the bars, and Coleman's hands grasped my shoulders.

"You what?" they both said in unison.

"Read it. Out loud." By diverting attention to the note, which I handed off to Harold, I hoped to keep Coleman from arresting me.

Harold hesitated, then did as I asked. When he finished he lowered the page and stared at me. He knew what Lawrence meant. It was plain on his face.

"What does that mean—tears of stone on Brianna's past?" Coleman demanded.

Harold walked to his bunk and simply stood there.

"Harold, tell us," I pleaded. "I found a page of the manuscript. It's awful. Madame will be destroyed. So will your aunt Lenore. We have to find that book and . . . and . . ." I stopped, because not even I could suggest what needed to be done.

"It's too late for Lenore. It was too late for her years ago." Harold faced us. "The irony of this is that Lawrence began his biography with the idea of helping her. The book was part of his big plan."

For a man who mostly communicated in binary language, Harold was certainly being oblique. Coleman's glower told me that Harold wasn't helping his case for freedom.

I jumped in with both feet. "I read the last page of the biography, and I'm here to tell you it's cold, hard, cruel, life-destroying fact. It isn't designed to help anyone at all. Now where's this place where tears of stone fall? We have to get there before Brianna."

Harold came up to the bars and wrapped his hands around them, one still clutching the note I'd given him. He leaned his forehead against the metal. "Sheriff, what do you want to know?"

Coleman spread his feet for balance and looked Harold squarely in the face. "How did that rat poison come to have your fingerprints on it?"

For a moment I thought Harold wasn't going to answer. Then his distinctive voice began. "I found the poison in a linen closet the night of Lawrence's party. He wasn't feeling well and called me over to help set up for the party. I was looking for napkins and found the poison instead. I suspected that Madame had been poisoning the mice in the cottage, and I knew it would infuriate Lawrence. He disapproved of all poisons. To prevent a serious fight between Madame and Lawrence, I took it."

"When did you take it?"

"That night. I put it in my briefcase in my car."

"And how did it get back in Lawrence's house?" Coleman asked quickly.

I knew the answer to that. "Brianna stole it out of Harold's briefcase and took it back to the cottage to frame him." From the look on Harold's face, I knew that I was right. "The only problem is that she implicated Madame, too."

Harold talked over me. "*Someone* took it. I have no proof it was Brianna."

"Stop defending her, Harold." It tore me up to see that he was still in love with Brianna, still trying to find an out for her, a way for her to avoid punishment.

Harold's eyes flashed fire. "Be careful, Sarah Booth. You don't know what you're treading on. This isn't as tidy as you'd like to make it."

"I don't care," I answered hotly. The image of Madame, so deflated and old. The memory of Cece's voice, her fear that a difficult past would rise up to haunt her. The burden of that was on my shoulders. "There are other people getting hurt here, not just your precious Brianna."

Coleman ignored the escalating anger between us. "Do you know where the manuscript is?" he asked Harold.

"Yes, I believe I do."

Coleman held up the cell key. "Where is it?"

"Greenwood," Harold said. "At my aunt Lenore's grave."

"Coleman, please." I put my hands on his strong forearm. "Let him out. We'll go get the manuscript and bring it back. You have my word."

Coleman stared at me. "We had a deal."

"You bet. Brianna's at Lawrence's cottage." It gave me great pleasure to rat her out. "She called Willem and I traced it via caller ID."

Harold's hands reached through the bars and caught my arms in a grip that conveyed passion and anger. "It isn't Brianna. Brianna is my cousin, Sarah Booth. She's Lenore's daughter."

The tension of the moment was shattered by the ringing telephone.

"Let him out, Coleman," I said, trying to detain the

sheriff. Coleman ignored me and went into this office. I wanted to say something to Harold, but I didn't know what. I couldn't even look at him.

In a moment Coleman was back. He went to the cell door and opened it, waving Harold out. "I'm trusting the two of you," he said. "Find the manuscript and bring it back. I have some doubts about doing this, but I don't have a choice. I've got to get Brianna and my deputy's got to go up to Moon Lake."

"Moon Lake?" Harold and I said in unison.

"They identified the body of a drowned man up there. It's that college dean, Joseph Grace. Folks up there are beginning to think it's a murder instead of a drowning."

Our journey across the Delta was mostly silent. For company I had my own thoughts and judgments—and a healthy dash of regret—and Harold had his.

I was still gnawing on the fact that Brianna was Harold's cousin. Over the past week I'd spent a lot of time trying not to imagine what they might be doing to each other. Now it was as if I'd been creating a pornographic film in my mind.

Cousins!

It was like some bad parody of the South. All I needed was August humidity, kudzu, a run-down plantation, and a heroine of virginal innocence. Hell, I had all of it—except the virginal innocence. Which I wasn't certain was actually a necessary ingredient anyway. Faulkner managed without it.

"It was good of you to come to the jail to get me out," Harold said, breaking the hour-long silence between us. It was a nice opening, but the only thing it accomplished was throwing wide the door of my anger.

"Why didn't you tell me she was your cousin? Everyone in town thinks you're sleeping with her, Harold. They know you've been staying at her house."

He kept his gaze on the flat, straight stretch of road that was bordered by fallow cotton fields. "I'm not responsible for the conclusions to which people jump. Lawrence charged me with an obligation, and I had to see it through. As well as I could."

He was so damn proper. Even his diction. Anger buzzed in my head. "How long have you known about her?" Scenes flipped through my mind. Brianna at his reception after Lawrence's funeral, Brianna at the door, goading me. I truly wanted to throttle him.

"Lawrence told me the night he died. I was as shocked as anyone. I have such a vivid memory of Aunt Lenore. How could I miss the fact that she was pregnant?"

"How did the Rathbones manage to adopt her? I mean she looks just like—" I swung my gaze at him. He didn't respond, just kept his eyes on the road and his hands on the wheel. "Layton Rathbone is her father. He and Lenore were lovers long ago. She never got over him."

"You've got the mind of a true romantic, Sarah Booth. For some reason that comforts me."

The whole thing was suddenly so clear. The ultimate betrayal to Lenore. "It was after Layton and his wife agreed to take the child that your aunt hanged herself. From the wrought iron fence of the church cemetery."

"Lenore had spent her life dreaming of the day when Layton would come for her. Lawrence never said, but I believe Lenore deliberately got pregnant, hoping to force the issue. She would either be an unwed woman or the wife of a divorced man. She hoped an honorable marriage would be her family's choice. She never considered that they'd hide her until delivery and then give the child away."

"Why didn't he marry her?"

"Layton was married. Divorce wasn't a possibility. Passion or love didn't exist as a real issue for my grandparents. Duty and propriety were the boundaries that marked their days. They would not tolerate a divorced man as a son-in-law." Most of this was said by rote, as if he'd memorized it. But his voice changed toward the end. "Lately, I've begun to suspect that he wouldn't have married her had he been single."

We were arriving at the city limits of Greenwood, a town of three rivers with conflicting currents. My anger had dissipated, my heart softened by the plight of Lenore Erkwell. To have loved that deeply. A portion of me envied her that passion, but another, saner part of me couldn't ignore her suffering.

"It's hard to believe that Lenore's parents would have sacrificed her happiness for the sake of propriety," I finally said. My parents would have accepted Sam the Sham, if he'd been the man I loved.

Harold laughed softly. "Spoken like a girl who had her parents' unconditional love and approval. You had a rare and wondrous childhood, Sarah Booth. Never forget that, and never believe that others shared it. Especially not Brianna. I know you believe her to be a criminal, but can you imagine what it must have been like, growing up with a mother who took every opportunity to show that she didn't love you? And never knowing why."

Harold was pushing his luck. I would not feel sorry for Brianna Rathbone. No way. "She didn't know about this?"

"She still doesn't."

"What?" I was astounded.

"I didn't tell her. I couldn't."

He wouldn't have to. "She'll find out soon enough if she reads that manuscript. Judging from the page I read, Lawrence pulls out all the stops."

"Lawrence would never do anything to hurt Brianna. Or anyone else." Lawrence slowed the car to the point that he could really look at me. "This is important, Sarah Booth. Lawrence's last promise to Lenore was that he'd keep an eye on Brianna. He meant to take this secret to the grave. That's one of the last things he said to me."

"I'm afraid you're wrong about that."

"The biography only concerns his years in Paris. Nothing else is mentioned. It was because Brianna kept pressing him to include his earlier years that he began to have second thoughts about his deal with her. Rosalyn made him see that Brianna's idea of a good book involved scandal and titillation. That was never what Lawrence intended. When he caught Brianna repeatedly going through his private papers, he knew he had to withdraw from the book deal. He truly had too many secrets to hide, too many damaging things."

Harold was right about that, but he was wrong about Lawrence's decision not to include them. I'd seen it with my own eyes.

"The night Lawrence died, he and Brianna got into a terrific argument. She had a legally binding contract, but Lawrence didn't give a damn. She couldn't finish the book without him, and he had nothing to lose. Nothing except his art collection, which is why he told all of this to me. He wanted to donate everything to a museum, and he wanted it done immediately—before Brianna filed suit against him for breach of contract. She'd already contacted her father. Once Layton got the gist of the book and what was happening, he came back to Zinnia. I think Lawrence had hoped to find an ally in him."

"Layton wanted the past revealed?" What man would want his sexual sins spread out on the pages of a book, especially a book written by his daughter?

Harold shrugged. "Layton had never been able to deny Brianna anything. Not even when he should have. I doubt, too, that he had any idea how much of the past Brianna had been able to ferret out. Lawrence knew she'd uncovered some things, but not her lineage. And there was the matter of finances. Even a Buddy Clubber gets tired of pouring money down his daughter. Brianna had some serious financial woes."

"No kidding," I said. I didn't mention the little loan he'd engineered for her. It could wait until she was behind bars. And I still wasn't buying that Lawrence was a complete innocent in the biography, but now wasn't the time to bicker. We were both wounded enough, and the ultimate proof would be the manuscript itself.

"There's the cemetery." Harold pointed toward a sloping meadow shaded by beautiful live oaks and marked by elaborate gravestones. Cemeteries weren't exactly my favorite place. I had one in the backyard where I often imagined my dead relatives spinning in their graves at my behavior. It wasn't large, but some of the graves were very old, and as I gazed at it, I was touched with a sense of serenity.

"It's lovely," I said.

"My family is buried here. Unlike the landed gentry, we didn't have family plots."

"And you get perpetual maintenance. But if you miss the lawn care, you can come to Dahlia House and pull weeds."

"I might take you up on that." Harold parked the

car and we got out. The sun's last grip on the sky was a vivid swirl of pink and purple and mauve, mingled with a dash of gold and blue. Against the sky the gravestones took on a solemn trust. There were angels and lambs and cherubs, all looking out with stony eyes. Suddenly I was awash in sadness. This is where love took Lenore Erkwell.

"Sarah Booth," Harold said gently as he took my elbow and turned me to face him, "she's been dead a long, long time."

"I know. That makes it even sadder."

The tears were cold on my cheeks and Harold gently wiped them away. "I should have known where the manuscript was hidden by the line of poetry he quoted me. It was Poe. 'The Raven.' The poem for a lost love, Lenore."

A Daddy's Girl would have dissolved in tears and allowed Harold the masculine privilege of comforting her. That was the only thought that saved me. I was no DG, and Harold had no obligation to shore up my womanly emotions. Straightening my back, I gave him a smile. "Let's find that book. I'm freezing."

To my surprise his lips brushed my cheek, a whisper of warmth on my cool skin. "It's your independence that really makes me admire you."

With that he began to move through the graves until we came to a strange figure, a woman's torso, head, and arms with a swan's wings and lower body. Granite tears seemed to slip down the woman's lovely cheeks. "How remarkable," I said. The stone was a work of art, a masterpiece. "You know it looks like those statues that were in the Sunflower Hotel. They were from Greek mythology, my father said."

"Yes, and this one, too. Leda and the Swan. Do you remember?"

"Zeus came to her as a lover in the guise of a swan. Leda was hideously punished by Hera, Zeus's wife." I did remember. "And the sculptor?"

"Lawrence. He made it for her himself."

The earth felt as if it had turned slightly, tilting to the right. I knew it was only the emotional power of what I'd just discovered. "Lawrence was in love with Lenore, wasn't he?" Bitter, bitter the twists and turns of life.

"He loved my aunt all of his life." Harold put his hand on the face of the statue. "Once she met Layton, I don't think she ever had a clue about Lawrence. He was too much of a man to tell her." His palm rested on the angel's face, as if he might bring warmth to the coldness for just a few brief seconds. "That's why he decided to champion Brianna. He followed her career, helping out whenever he could with phone calls to his friends. When he wouldn't pull a string to help himself, he called in favors for her. And when it was clear her modeling was over, he decided to help her. She was about to lose everything. He came up with the plan to let her take credit for the book and launch a new career."

"She can't write," I pointed out.

Harold shook his head. "Lawrence had nothing else to offer her. He wanted so badly for her to contain something of Lenore, some glimmer of her personality. As did I."

The last warm colors of day were fading from the horizon. There was a finality to the sky that was as potent as the conclusion of the lives of these people I'd come to care about. It gave me no pleasure at all to say what had to be said.

"She killed him, Harold. You know that."

"I fear she did."

He bent to the statue, to the granite foundation that looked as solid as the rest of it. It took a bit of effort, but he removed a slab and pulled out a plastic-wrapped bundle.

He handed it to me and in the last rays of the December day, I peeled back the plastic to the title page. *The Romantic: The Life of a Writer, Artist, and Spy* by Lawrence Ambrose and Brianna Rathbone.

Harold's voice held pride. "Lawrence's work will be revived. His novels will be reprinted."

His hand reached out and touched the manuscript that I held, the fingers moving across the title as if he were feeling the words, connecting somehow with the man who wrote it.

I shivered in the darkness and clutched the manuscript to my chest. "We should have gone after her with Coleman. She's probably skipped the country by now."

Harold put his arm around me and led me back to the car. "In a way, I hope she is gone. Nothing we do to Brianna will bring Lawrence back."

All along Harold had underestimated Brianna's capacity for self-preservation. She still had Lawrence's notes and journals. Instead of anger I felt only regret—and a terrible thought. Brianna couldn't write, but someone could. Whoever had written that last manuscript page had been adept with language. More than adept, very skilled.

And Dean Joseph Grace was very dead. Drowned in Moon Lake.

For Harold, there was no good ending. But there was justice, and Brianna Rathbone had a judgment coming her way.

27

Driving up to the courthouse where I'd left my car, Harold and I both saw Coleman standing outside, a big, solid man framed in an overhead light. To the west, a full moon hung behind the courthouse rotunda. It was huge and pale, a winter moon to mark the ending of a year.

Brianna had escaped. I could read it in Coleman's posture, and I knew that Harold, by stonewalling in the jail for so long, had deliberately given her the time to flee. He was determined not to believe the worst of her, no matter what the evidence showed.

"Go home, Harold," I told him as I opened the door of his Lexus. "Don't tempt fate by getting in Coleman's face."

"Can you understand that Lawrence wouldn't want her put in prison?"

It didn't matter if he was protecting her because he thought that was what Lawrence would want him to do, or because she was blood. Coleman wasn't going to be happy with either reason. It would take a while for me to sort through my feelings on the subject.

"Go home," I said gently, putting a hand on his arm.

He caught my fingers and held them. "Lawrence loved Lenore his entire life. I'm sure there were other loves, but none like her."

"And Madame loved Lawrence." I sighed at the bitterness that came of drinking from the cup of love. "Good night, Harold." I leaned over and kissed his cheek.

His hand caught my wrist and stayed me. "Do you think we're always destined to make the wrong choices with our hearts?"

I couldn't tell if he was talking about the past or the present. We were both guilty of bad choices. "I don't know," I answered honestly.

"You've been a better friend to me than I deserve, Sarah Booth."

"That's where you're wrong, Harold. Very wrong."

"You thought me guilty and yet you kept trying to protect me. Why?"

"I thought you were guilty of caring about Brianna. I feared you might have done something to help her cover her tracks. Protecting the person you love isn't a sin in my eyes."

His hands slipped along my wrist to my hand. He brought the palm up to his face and held it against his cheek. "Thank you, Sarah Booth. When we've recovered from all of this, I want to have a serious talk with you."

I got out of the car and stepped back. Coleman didn't change positions as Harold drove away, and I walked up the cement steps as he watched me.

"How much of a lead has she got?"

"I wasn't even within sniffing distance."

"I really didn't know."

He opened the door and held it as I walked inside the courthouse. The hallway was still warm, a welcome respite from the freezing night outside.

"Where do you think she is?" I asked.

"The house was ransacked. It depends on whether she got what she was hunting for or not. Any guesses as to what she was after?"

"Scrapbooks, documents, photographs, anything that might give her material for her book. We found Lawrence's autobiography, and it was confined to 1940 to 1979, his years in Paris. Harold will keep it safe," I assured him. "The page I found, that must be something of Brianna's concoction. I'm pretty sure she was looking for more secret stuff in Lawrence's cottage. At any rate, Harold thinks he can stop publication."

Coleman snorted, which about summed up my opinion. "We'll get her. Eventually. I put on a fresh pot of coffee, come on in and have a cup." He held open the door to the sheriff's office and I followed him inside.

"I have to photograph the dance at The Club, but I have time for one cup." It seemed that a cup of coffee with Coleman was becoming a tradition at the conclusion of my cases.

"I found the system of delivery for the poison. Or I should say Doc Sawyer did."

I almost didn't want to know. "Tell me."

"A bottle of Jim Beam. I guess she figured it was the surest way to dose him, especially since he must have given his cat some food that she'd tried the poison in. I suppose everybody in town knew he had his five o'clock bourbon and branch."

"And if someone else had a drink of it?"

"One or two drinks wouldn't hurt. It was the cumulative effect."

I braced against the counter and closed my eyes for one brief second. It was all too sad.

Coleman's hand was warm on the back of my neck. His strong fingers kneaded the tight muscles for just a moment. "This is no time to quit. Better get yourself home, get into a dress, and go do your job. Cece gives you too many opportunities to meddle for you to let her down."

"Thanks for the pep talk, you silver-tongued devil." I accepted the cup of coffee.

Coleman laughed out loud, a resonating laugh that made me smile. The telephone shrilled loudly, and he answered it.

"You've got a phone call," he said. "It's your partner, Tinkie. She says it's urgent."

I picked up the black receiver. "Tinkie, what's going on?"

There was a sob at the other end. "Oh, Sarah Booth, I'm so sorry."

There are moments when time is telescoped. Those words mean only one thing—tragedy. I instantly knew that I'd lost someone dear to me, even if I didn't know who.

"I went by Dahlia House to see if you were back, and I found her in the drive. There was blood, so much blood."

"Who?"

"Sweetie Pie. She's at Dr. Matthews's. He's had to perform surgery. He said he'd wait at his office for you to get home."

Coleman's face registered concern as I hung up the phone, still unable to draw a deep breath.

"It's my dog. She's been hurt. Dr. Matthews has her."

"Want me to take you?" Coleman offered.

I shook my head, the tears threatening with relentless pressure. "I'll be fine," I assured him as I hurried out.

The lights were on in the vet's office, and Dr. Matthews was at the front desk filling out blood work forms when I went in. His smile was one of the best things I'd ever seen.

"Well, what you've got is a hound who's a medical miracle," he said, rising slowly to his feet.

"She's alive?" I hadn't dared to believe she might be okay.

"Alive and recovering. With remarkable alacrity."

"What happened?" I followed behind him as he led the way to the sick bay. Even as he opened the door I heard the familiar beat of her metronome tail.

"I can't be certain." He hesitated as he examined me. "It was a puncture wound in the abdomen, Sarah Booth. She must have fallen on something sharp, though how she managed that I can't figure out. It was a deep wound."

The caution of his tone registered. "You don't think she was hurt deliberately, do you?"

"It's impossible to tell but I wouldn't let her roam."

"She'll stay in the house," I promised before I was caught in the moment of seeing my dog, a thick white bandage around her middle. She slowly got to her feet and gave me the softest, sweetest, yodeling bark.

"Sweetie!" I rushed to the kennel and opened the door. She was a little unsteady on her feet, but her tongue was as warm and effusive as ever. "Oh,

Sweetie." I hadn't realized how much I'd grown to care about that dog.

"She's going to be okay, Sarah Booth. In fact, you can take her home. Just keep an eye on her and make sure she drinks plenty of water and goes to the bathroom."

"No permanent damage?"

"It was pure luck, but nothing vital was severed. And while I was making the repairs, I also took a look around. I have to say that Sweetie is a remarkable creature."

"How so?" I fondled her silky ears and urged her to come out of the kennel.

"I spayed her myself, and as I said, I removed a uterus and two ovaries. But when I opened her up, there they were. Two ovaries, just as pink and healthy as I've ever seen. Lucky for you the uterus didn't regenerate or you'd be a grandma a dozen times over."

"They *grew* back?" I looked up at his face to make sure he wasn't pulling my leg. "My tonsils did that once."

"The only thing I can figure is that they somehow regenerated. It's a case that deserves major study. I've already sent the tissue off to a lab for evaluation."

"It's a sign." If there had ever been any doubt, there was none now. "Delaney womb," I said.

"What?"

"Nothing." It would be impossible to explain. But Sweetie Pie was a Delaney. And it was time to take her home.

"Thanks, Dr. Matthews. Whatever I owe you, I'll get straight."

"No charge, Sarah Booth. But I am writing that dog up for a medical journal. I hope you don't mind."

"Feel free." When I stood, Sweetie Pie came out of the kennel. She was still a little woozy, but otherwise just fine.

"Bring her back in ten days to get the stitches out."

"Sure thing."

"And Happy New Year, Sarah Booth. I think we can both make it home in time for a glass of champagne and a kiss."

I drove home slowly so Sweetie Pie could take a little air. The brisk cold seemed to revitalize her, and when we arrived at Dahlia House, she greeted her male admirers with a gentle woof.

"Not tonight," I told her, taking care to snap on a leash and make sure we got safely inside. I still had to photograph the dance for Cece, but I was certain I could do my journalistic duties and be home in less than two hours.

Once we were inside I took her into the kitchen and made her a cozy nest. She was restless, pacing the kitchen and whining at first the back door and then the dining room door. If I hadn't given my word to Cece, I'd move my pillows downstairs, collapse into them, and call it a year.

I made sure the doggy door was shut, and I latched the swinging door to the kitchen. Sweetie was feeling better, but she didn't need to be running around the house. As I made it up the stairs, her whining increased sharply. Then came the scratching. And finally barking at the top of her lungs. She wasn't happy about being detained, but it was for her own good.

Thank goodness I'd picked out my wardrobe. I hurried up to my room, wondering why Jitty wasn't around. She probably had a haint party to celebrate the new year. Her social life was far more active than mine.

I dialed Tinkie, to thank her and also to reassure her that Sweetie was fine. Thank goodness she'd stopped by the house. Otherwise my pooch might have bled to death. I got the answering machine and left my message, reminding her that I'd see her at The Club at eleven.

The bathtub looked inviting, but I opted for a quick shower. Even as I stepped beneath the spray I heard Sweetie barking. She was sincerely unhappy.

The hot water, followed by a splash of cold, gave me the energy to finish up the night. I didn't have the heart to think about my case. I'd found the murderer, but she was still on the loose. And if Harold was right, she was probably somewhere in Europe. She had money, looks, and Lawrence's journals and notes. And there didn't seem to be a thing I could do about any of it.

I hadn't bothered to turn on the heat in my bedroom—a good motivator to dress fast. I slipped into the black velvet gown with the three tiny little straps from shoulder to derriere and felt a hit of satisfaction. The zipper sailed up as smooth as silk. Once I'd donned my glittery stockings and sexy black heels, I took a moment to admire the results. Too bad I hadn't had time to get my hair done. But I pulled up the curls with a few rhinestone combs and set to work on makeup. Even though I was working and didn't have a date, I wanted to look my best.

Makeup is a woman's best defense against lack of sleep, fatigue, stress, and the other evils of aging. I had a deft hand with base and eyeliner. It took only a few moments to change from tired and pasty to cool beige with highlighted lashes. I bent toward the mirror to apply my Show Girl Red lipstick. A movement in a corner of the room made me pause.

It was almost as if I were dreaming. Lean and lithe, Brianna Rathbone stepped out of the shadows and toward me. In her hand was a short-bladed knife stained a brownish red.

"Sarah Booth, this isn't what you think."

It had the vague ring of something Harold had kept saying—"you don't understand." I wondered if speech patterns were genetic. On a more important level, I wondered if she was going to hurt me. A tube of lipstick is not a good defense weapon. I lowered it slowly to the dressing table, aware of Sweetie's frantic barking in the kitchen. She'd been trying to warn me all along.

As Brianna came closer, I realized that Sweetie Pie hadn't fallen on something sharp. She'd been stabbed. The crazy woman slowly headed my way had stabbed my dog. Any lingering doubt that she might try to hurt me vanished.

"Don't make any sudden moves," Brianna said, her voice so soft it was hardly more than a whisper. "I'm not alone."

Right. She was not only mean, she was crazy. My gaze dropped to the knife. Yeah, and that was just a big, old, sharp letter opener.

"All I want is Lawrence's manuscript. I know you and Harold found it. Give me those things and we'll leave."

She was within ten feet of me, and I could clearly see the manic light in her eyes.

"Your mistake was killing Lawrence. Leaving might not be as easy as you think." I slowly stepped away from the dressing table. If there was a chance of dashing out of the room, I was taking it. It was eleven o'clock.

No one would even think to get worried about me for another hour. It was up to me to figure out an escape route and to use it.

"I didn't kill the old pack rat. But it doesn't matter. He's dead. That's that."

Give her credit, she'd learned to tidy up her past, at least in her own mind. I had to keep her talking. "It matters to me, and a lot of other people. You poisoned him."

"Just enough to make him sick. I wanted him weak. I had to make him dependent on me. Yes, I was giving him blood thinner in his bourbon, and it was working just fine. He thought he was dying, that he was slipping into senility and infirmity. I'd come over and have a drink or two with him and wait. When he slipped into a nap, I had free rein to go through his papers. I was going to make us both rich and famous. I didn't have a thing to do with the idiot cutting himself."

"You can't begin to understand what you've done." I was sincerely at a loss. Lawrence was dead, and Brianna's take on the matter was that it was an inconvenience to her. That she'd been a contributing factor to murder—that she'd framed Harold and Madame—didn't even register. But it did make me wonder if she was crazier even than I thought. Or less guilty. If Brianna hadn't cut Lawrence's hand, who had? I had to probe.

"Everyone he knew was terrified of what secrets he might reveal. Did you find any of them, Brianna?" I inched a little closer to the door.

She hefted the knife and widened her stance. "You're not going anywhere, so just relax. Lawrence really was an old pack rat, wasn't he?" She shook her head. "So many, many secrets. There was no way I was going to confine the book to his Paris years. What stupidity. Sam

Rayburn was correct. It's the broad scope of an artist's life that shows his development. I wasn't going to cheat my readers."

Brianna had crossed the line into *The Twilight Zone*. Somehow, she'd begun to believe that she was a writer. She'd even begun to talk like one, and it gave me another avenue of buying time. "Where did you get the idea of using Lawrence? It was his life, not yours. Why would you think—" And then I knew. Joseph Grace. A chill ran up my nearly naked back.

"Of course I don't have the literary ability of Lawrence."

"That's probably the most profound understatement of your career." I decided to goad. I'd calculated the dimensions of the room and my only chance to make it to the door was to get her to move toward me. I already knew she had a bad temper; she shouldn't be hard to bait.

"I don't need writing talent. Joseph is helping me. In fact, he's waiting for me at the Jackson airport. He designed that little page you found in Harold's briefcase. Pretty effective, wasn't it?" She laughed. "Joseph's interested in the project as a literary work, but his participation isn't completely voluntary. He has to help, unless he wants me to tell about his little peccadilloes with his students. He's so close to retirement, and so attached to the state tit. Wouldn't it be a shame if he got canned now for sexual misconduct?"

There were things about Brianna I could learn to admire. Like her use of the present tense when she was speaking of a dead man. It was to my advantage, though, that she didn't know Joseph Grace was dead! And I had no intention of clueing her in. But I still had a few buttons I could push.

"Lawrence was murdered, Brianna. His hand was

deliberately cut. And the poison you were giving him was the agent that made him bleed quickly. That makes you an accomplice to murder, at the least." I had her attention. Fully. "If Grace killed Lawrence, you don't have to take the fall for it. Just let me call Coleman. He'll come over and you can explain. We'll find Grace and arrest him. You can clear all of this up."

For a split second, I thought she might listen to me. Then she shook her head. "You are sincerely stupid. You made that up. You've always been a liar, Sarah Booth. I want that manuscript and the rest of his journals, and then I'm leaving. I can't afford to leave that stuff lying around."

I'd known rational thought wasn't going to work. Brianna was crazy like a fox, and like a cornered fox, she wasn't going to give up without biting off a few chicken heads.

Time for a new tactic. "Maybe we should have a drink." I checked my watch. "It's almost New Year's. I hate to bring this up, but I'm late for a party. In about five minutes, someone will come here looking for me. Stabbing the dog was a big mistake, Brianna. Coleman is keeping an eye on me and my house, and he's looking for you." God, I wish I'd called Coleman.

"Chill out, Sarah Booth. You aren't going anywhere and neither am I, until I get what I came for. I didn't stab your ugly hound. She tried to attack us. There was no help for it." She motioned to the chair by the dressing table for me to sit.

Once I was seated, I knew it would take even more precious seconds to get to the door, but I had no choice. Sweetie's barking had become more frantic, and I heard her body slam against the door.

"Daddy doesn't like dogs in the house, Sarah Booth. Dogs weren't meant to live inside. People don't live

with animals. That's what Daddy says. If that hound
doesn't shut up, he'll kill her. He has no patience for
such behavior."

I was trapped in my bedroom with a Daddy's Girl
holding the bloody knife she'd used to stab my dog and
babbling about her daddy's likes and dislikes. It reminded me of a sorority party/slasher movie. It was exit
time. Brianna was taller, but I was probably stronger. I
gathered myself. Sweetie's frantic barking increased in
tempo, and then I heard something else. Footsteps coming up the stairs.

Somehow, I knew it wasn't the cavalry.

It was now or never—I darted past Brianna, through
the doorway, and onto the stairs, hoping like hell I
could get up enough speed to bowl over whoever it was
on the stairs.

"Hey! Don't do that!" Brianna made a grab for me
as I darted past her. Her fingernails caught at my dress
but not good enough to hold me. Velvet, thank God, is
a sturdy fabric. High heels, though, are not designed for
speed. I made it into the upstairs hall before I stumbled.

Just as I felt myself going down, I saw him. Layton
Rathbone was slowly ascending the stairs.

My forward momentum was too great to halt. I
plowed into him with all of my weight and heard the
whoosh of air being forced from his lungs. Together we
tumbled backward down the stairs, landing in a heap,
with me on top.

He was an old man and I was glad to see him. If
anyone could control Brianna, it was her daddy. I
scrambled to my feet. "Mr. Rathbone," I whispered ur-
gently, glancing up at the top of the stairs where I knew
Brianna would appear at any moment. "Mr.
Rathbone." I shook his shoulder and felt relief as his
eyes opened.

"Sarah Booth," he said. "Why couldn't you mind your own affairs?"

"Sir?" I thought the fall had scrambled his brain. In the kitchen I could hear Sweetie Pie pounding against the door. She was going to damage herself after all that surgery.

Layton pushed himself up to a sitting position and reached inside his coat, feeling his ribs.

"Are they broken? Do you need an ambulance?"

"Hardly." His hand came out with a gun. The barrel swung to point directly at my heart. "You're going to learn that meddling sometimes carries a very high price."

I wanted to believe that he was protecting his daughter, but deep in my gut, I knew it wasn't true. A lot of things suddenly became very clear, and I didn't like a single picture.

"Daddy," Brianna called down to us from the top of the stairs. "What are you doing?"

"Stay out of this, Brianna."

"Daddy, we need to go." She came down two steps. "Harold has the manuscript. I can get it from him. Sarah Booth doesn't have anything." She twisted her hands in front of her. "Daddy, she's lying and saying someone deliberately cut Lawrence."

"Don't pay her any attention, baby. We'll go in a minute. But not until we get that book. If Lawrence wrote about Moon Lake, we have to find it." Layton spoke softly to his daughter, but his eyes were trained, along with the gun barrel, on me. "There's more at stake here than you realize, Brianna. Just let me handle it."

I was afraid if I drew a breath he might pull the trigger, so I did my best impersonation of a tree, rooted and still.

"Daddy?" Brianna's voice was lost and childlike. "We should leave now. She said Lawrence was *murdered*, that someone cut his hand deliberately. Everyone thinks it's me. We have to go."

"We can't just leave her, Brianna. She knows. She knows about Moon Lake."

"No I don't! There's nothing in the book about it, I'm telling you. Lawrence had no intention of writing about Moon Lake," I said. "I saw the manuscript. His book is about his years in Paris. It's called *The Romantic—My Life as a Writer, Artist, and Spy.* There's nothing in there—nothing about Lenore." If I had one ace, it might be that he wanted to protect Brianna from the truth of her heritage.

"Lawrence has been a thorn in my side for years." Layton held the gun on me as he got slowly to his feet. "He should have kept his mind on writing, but he was always sneaking around, eavesdropping, snooping, prying into things that didn't concern him. He hoped that if he caught me, Lenore would stop loving me. But he was wrong. She didn't believe him. Instead of killing her love for me, the things he told her only made her more determined to love me. So determined that she thought a baby would force me to marry her."

The anger in his voice stung me like a whip, and I dared a look at Brianna. She was looking at him as if he spoke a foreign language. "What are you saying? What baby?"

Uh-oh. I held my breath. He was going to tell her!

"It's time you knew this, Brianna. You're my girl, my only child. More mine than anyone else's." His smile was tender and loving. "All mine. My beautiful, perfect daughter."

"Layton, maybe this isn't the time." They were both

unbalanced. There was no telling what Brianna might do.

He continued as if I'd never spoken, as if he didn't see the pain blooming in his daughter's eyes. "Pamela couldn't carry a child to term." His tone grew more conversational. "Lenore figured it out. She thought she'd finally come up with a way to trap me. She arranged to meet me, seduced me again, and a few months later presented me with the knowledge of my heir, the baby she carried inside her. She had the one thing I wanted more than anything else. My beautiful daughter." His voice was now almost a caress. "She gave me you, Brianna, but then she wouldn't let us go. So I had to kill her."

I listened to him, but it was Brianna I was watching. She sank down on the top step and put her face in her hands. She hadn't known.

"Daddy," Brianna said softly through her hands. She finally lowered her fingers revealing confusion and fear. "My mother is—"

"She was a selfish, conniving—"

"She was Lenore Erkwell," I interjected as gently as I could. Brianna hadn't grasped the fact that her father had killed her mother, making it appear to be a suicide. I chose not to belabor that point, since he had a gun.

Sweetie hit the kitchen door again, this time with a howl. I was afraid she'd torn her stitches out, but there wasn't a thing I could do, except keep talking.

"Brianna's right, Layton. You should make an escape while you can. Whatever went on at Moon Lake, Lawrence took those secrets to the grave with him. There is nothing in the manuscript about what happened at the lake."

"Yes, those secrets are buried with Lawrence. And

Joseph. Except for what you know." Layton pulled back the hammer on the gun. "I'm sorry, Sarah Booth. I just can't trust you."

My entire life didn't pass before my eyes as they say it does when confronting death. I had the most irrational thought—that I didn't want Fel Harper touching my dead body and that I hoped Coleman would see to it that he didn't.

I closed my eyes and waited for the bullet.

"Daddy!" Brianna rose to her feet. "You can't just shoot her. Let's get out of here."

I thought of pointing out that he'd already killed Lenore, Lawrence, and Joseph Grace, but it wasn't in my best interest to play scorekeeper. "If you leave now, you have a chance of getting away. You can go out of the country. With your money, you can *buy* a country. But I'm not kidding, Coleman will be here any minute."

"Daddy?" Brianna descended a step or two. Confusion had been replaced by the first hint of anger. "Why did you want me to help Lawrence with his book? You encouraged me to do this, and all along you knew I'd find out about . . . Mother. This book could have ruined me. I'd be a laughingstock, a bastard."

"You're my daughter. You're a Rathbone. I loved you enough to steal you, enough to kill anyone who threatened you. Threatened us. Lawrence knew too much. As long as you were working with him, I could control what he wrote. But when he broke the contract . . . well, I didn't have a choice. It's one thing for us to know, but not the world. You're famous, Brianna. My beautiful daughter, the model. Everyone would forget that and remember only that I wasn't married to your mother. I didn't want Lawrence to write about you in that way. I couldn't allow him to write about Moon Lake."

Sweetie Pie slammed into the door again. Hard. She gave a cry of pain that tore at my heart. I started instinctively toward the kitchen.

"Hey! Get back over here."

Layton's shout stopped me cold, just in time to see Sweetie Pie, her white bandage soaked with blood, flying through the air in a direct trajectory toward Layton. She hit him with all seventy pounds of hound.

The sound of the shot echoed in the foyer, a reverberation that was punctuated by Brianna's scream and Sweetie Pie's howl.

The gun flew out of Layton's hand and skittered on the black and white foyer tile. Though Brianna leapt to her feet, she didn't have a chance. I scooped up the weapon and turned it on them both.

In the distance was the sound of a wailing siren. At my feet, Sweetie Pie lay in a bloody heap.

28

Coleman wrapped me in a comforter as I sat on the floor holding Sweetie Pie's head in my lap. Layton and Brianna, cuffed and Miranda-ized, sat on the sofa.

"She's torn her stitches open, Sarah Booth, but she wasn't shot," Coleman reassured me. "Dr. Matthews is on the way, sutures in hand."

"She saved my life. Again." I was pretty certain Sweetie had been the hound who knocked Pasco Walters over in my last case. I'd begun to recognize her MO—the Baskervillish leap out of the darkness. This time, though, she might pay with her life. Her white bandage was saturated with blood.

Coleman knelt down beside me. "She just popped a couple of stitches. I've never heard of a dog more determined to protect her mistress. She may be ugly, but she's loyal."

"Yeah." I rubbed her silky ears and got a warm tongue.

"Here's Dr. Matthews," Tinkie called from the doorway. She was all dressed for the ball, her white gown glittering in the lights of the foyer candelabra.

As soon as Dr. Matthews arrived, Coleman lifted me to my feet and pointedly handed me over to Tinkie. "Make some coffee," he suggested.

Tinkie led me into the kitchen. Instead of coffee, she pulled the bottle of champagne from the refrigerator and popped the cork. "It's still forty minutes until midnight, but I think we need a head start."

I accepted the champagne and got out a stainless steel pot. I'd forgotten to put my black-eyed peas on to soak. I didn't need any more bad luck—I'd eat them tomorrow if they were hard as rocks.

"How did you know to call Coleman?" I asked her.

"I called to check on Sweetie, and Dr. Matthews asked me if I knew of anyone who might want to hurt either you or Sweetie. He said he thought the dog had been stabbed, but he didn't want to upset you until he was certain. I just put two and two together. And then Oscar, who has been absolutely spilling his guts to me ever since we had our little, uh, midday rendezvous, made the comment that Layton was about to lose Rathbone House and how appropriate it was since it had been bought with blood money. I put it together about what you told me about Moon Lake and the past. I wasn't certain how Layton fit into it, but I knew his hands were dirty."

I gave her a tired smile. "You saved my life."

"Not really. Coleman and I just effected the mopping up. You already had them both at gunpoint." She topped off my glass. "If Daddy and Oscar had just told me the whole truth . . ."

I didn't have the energy to point out that such disclosures were seldom freely given outside the circle of men. "So Layton was in cahoots with Hosea up at Moon Lake." Finally, everything made sense. "Layton's affair with Lenore was just an excuse to keep going back to

Moon Lake. He used her. From beginning to end." I sat down at the kitchen table and finished off my champagne in one gulp.

Tinkie refilled my glass.

"I don't understand why Jebediah didn't kill Layton when he killed Hosea," Tinkie said.

"I doubt we'll ever know that. Hosea was a bully, but he didn't have what it took to kill, and Layton did. It's clear he killed Lawrence and Joseph Grace." I shuddered. Coleman had told me that the photographs that had been cut from the albums at Moon Lake had been found on Grace's body. Apparently the dean had been trying to set up a blackmail scheme against Layton. Not very smart, since it had cost him his life. "Maybe Jebediah was ultimately afraid of Layton."

"What will happen to Brianna and her father?" Tinkie put the bottle in front of me.

"Brianna poisoned Lawrence with the warfarin. She confessed to me. But it was Layton who went over there and cut his hand. He's the murderer."

"Layton knew Brianna was poisoning him?"

"He was the one who got the warfarin for her. I thought it was the rat poison she was using, but it wasn't. She was crushing up pills and dumping them in the Jim Beam. When she found the rat poison in Harold's briefcase, it was the perfect opportunity to frame Harold." Once arrested, Brianna had spilled her guts in an effort to save her own hide.

"What will happen to Willem?" Tinkie asked.

"I don't know. He *was* trying to replace the paintings. And Harold said Lawrence knew about it. I suppose it depends to a large extent on whether Harold wants to press charges or not."

There was a tap on the kitchen door. Dr. Matthews came in and put a hand on my shoulder. "Sweetie Pie's going to be just fine, Sarah Booth. I sedated her and resutured. She'll sleep until morning, and I suggest that you do the same."

It sounded like heavenly advice. "Thanks. For everything."

I walked him to the front door and watched as Coleman led Brianna and Layton out to the patrol car. A couple of deputies had arrived to work backup, and Tinkie and I stood in the freezing cold on the porch as they all left.

"It's finally over," Tinkie said, putting an arm around my shoulders. "You solved your second case, Sarah Booth!"

The shrill of the telephone almost made me jump out of my skin. "I'll get it." Tinkie rushed back inside, and I followed. I felt as if I'd been run over by a bulldozer and buried in a ditch.

"She'll be there," I heard Tinkie promise.

"Be where?" I asked.

"That was Cece. She's about to have a duck. She's at The Club with the camera, and she's waiting for you."

"The dance." There was no possible way I could go to the New Year's Eve dance. Not even for Cece. I groaned and headed toward the sofa. Sweetie was sleeping peacefully beside it, the last flickering blaze of the fire Coleman had built highlighting the russet spots of her hide.

Tinkie's hand grabbed mine and she pulled me toward the door. "You have to go."

"I can't," I whined. "I really can't."

"You have to." There was determination in Tinkie's voice. "Trust me, Sarah Booth. You want to go."

"I do not."

"You do. And you're going." She went to the closet and pulled out a coat. "Put it on."

"Why?" I couldn't believe she was going to force me.

"You gave your word. Sarah Booth Delaney, private investigator, never reneges on her word."

I was beginning to regret hiring Tinkie. Sure, she'd saved my life by calling Coleman. And she'd saved Sweetie's life. I looked down at my sleeping hound and slipped into the coat. There were some things worth payback.

"I'll drive." She hustled me out to the car and in a matter of moments we were flying through the Delta night. The full moon had risen high and assumed the lead role in the sparkling night.

"We'll make it just before midnight," she declared as she burned rubber in the parking lot. "It's a new year, Sarah Booth, you can't celebrate alone."

I'd intended to sleep, but it was a moot issue anyway. I got out of the car and walked into The Club. Cece waved to me from across the room.

Someone had hired a hot band, and when the lead guitar hit a chilling slide, the skin on my bare back danced. I hadn't recognized him at first, but there was no mistaking Percy Sledge as he belted out his signature song, "When a Man Loves a Woman."

Even as tired and bruised as I was, the song moved me. A firm hand settled on my bare shoulder, the fingers tightening with just enough pressure to make me draw a sudden breath. I turned to face Hamilton Garrett V.

It wasn't possible, but in his tuxedo, he was even more handsome than I remembered. His dark hair was pulled back, revealing the chiseled jaw that I recalled so well in the morning light of my bedroom window. His green eyes burned with devilment.

"Happy New Year, Sarah Booth. May I have this dance?"

My entire blood supply shot to my head and then rushed to my skin. I went from cold to hot in a nanosecond. "Hamilton?" Surely I was dreaming.

"I couldn't possibly welcome in the new year alone," he said, easing me into his arms.

I found my face resting against his starched shirt and my body moving in tandem with his. It was a good thing because I was incapable of speech. Perhaps Layton had actually shot me and this was some kind of heavenly limbo where I could merely rest in Hamilton's imagined arms until I was called up for judgment.

"Sarah Booth!" I heard Tinkie whispering my name and I lifted my head long enough to find her. She was dancing beside me in Oscar's arms. "I told you I had a surprise," she said, giggling. "And Oscar said I couldn't keep a secret." She looked up at her husband with open flirtation. "There are lots of things I don't tell. Since I'm Sarah Booth's partner, I have to be very discreet."

They danced away and I was left with the problem of saying something to Hamilton. When I looked up at him, I found he was watching me with amused expectation.

"What, no questions? I was certain you'd have at least fifty things to ask me, most of them personal and none of them any of your business."

"And what makes you think I'd be interested enough in your business to ask a single question?" I asked, but then I couldn't help myself. "Why *did* you come home?"

Hamilton chuckled, dipping me down at the end of the song. "To see you, Sarah Booth. I found that Paris was dull without you."

Whether it was his words or the dip, I couldn't be certain, but a wave of dizziness swept over me. Luckily he had strong arms, and he pulled me upright against him. His lips whispered over my forehead. "I've missed you."

The band swung into the opening strain of "Auld Lang Syne," and everyone began the countdown.

"Why didn't you call, or at least send a card?"

"We can play sixty questions, or you can kiss me," Hamilton suggested.

I closed my eyes and offered my lips as the parters hit five-four-three-two-one. The clapping, cheering, horn-blowing crowd dimmed. There was only Hamilton.

The kiss lingered well into the new year, and I gave myself to it with complete abandon. As a slave of tradition, I realized I'd set a precedent. According to Delaney superstition, the acts committed on the first day of the year will be repeated throughout the year. It wasn't a guarantee, but it was a dynamite start to a new year.

Of course, where Hamilton Garrett was concerned, there were no guarantees or traditions. There was only the moment.

It was enough.

About the Author

A native of Mississippi, Carolyn Haines lives in southern Alabama on a farm with her horses, dogs, and cats. She was recently honored with an Alabama State Council on the Arts literary fellowship for her writing. A former photojournalist, she is active in organizations that rescue animals and promote animal rights.

Another conversation with Carolyn Haines, author of *Buried Bones, Them Bones, Splintered Bones,* and *Crossed Bones,* and her character Cece Dee Falcon

Columnist for The Zinnia Dispatch *Cece Dee Falcon has insisted on interviewing author Carolyn Haines. Cece was dissatisfied with the prior interview conducted by Jitty. The questions weren't tough enough, according to the journalist.*

Since Mississippi in the spring is a preview of heaven. Cece and Carolyn met for an afternoon mint julep on the porch of Dahlia House.

CAROLYN: How's your drink, Cece? I grew the mint myself.

CECE: The drink is fine, dahling, but you've got the protocol all backwards. I ask; you answer. You made me a tough journalist and you have to live with it. My, this is going to be fun.

CAROLYN: Give it your best shot.

CECE: Well, dahling, how does one go about becoming a mystery writer? And remember, no fibbing. I have access to your innermost thoughts.

CAROLYN: I think it has a lot to do with upbringing. I grew up in a family of journalists. Some of my earliest memories are of both my parents at the kitchen table, one at either end—dueling typewriters. I was raised with the idea of hunting for the story beneath the story.

CECE: Yes, as a journalist myself, I know what it's like to have "ink in the blood." So tell the readers of *The Zinnia Dispatch,* why did you select our little hamlet of Zinnia as the setting for your books?

CAROLYN: I grew up in a small town, and I think the interrelationships of the people in a town are often more intense. I live in a city now, and though I recognize city officials on television, I don't *know* them. In a small town, people know the public persona, but they also know the personal details. It makes for a more complex and subtle stew. As to the location of the town in the Mississippi Delta, I can only say that geography dictates character. Where else could I have found you and Tinkie and Jitty? Not to mention Lawrence and Harold. You just sprang out of that rich Delta soil like a high-dollar crop of cotton.

CECE: Tell us, how does it feel to murder a character? I mean there are people I've fantasized about strangling, but one doesn't actually follow through. But you do. How does that feel?

CAROLYN: Now that's a great question, Cece. I'm proud of you. Killing off a character is a very emotional decision. There are some folks who just need killing, as you'll discover in the next book. And there are others, like Lawrence, who live on in my mind, even though he may be dead in the pages of the book. But look at it this way. If Lawrence wasn't murdered, there wouldn't be a book. Still, there are regrets when someone I've come to like has to die.

CECE: When you begin to write the book, do you know who the killer is?

CAROLYN: Another excellent question. The correct answer would be, "Yes, I always know." But I feel that I must be truthful with you and your readers. Sometimes I *think* I know. What I mean is that I start out knowing—and then things change. You people aren't the easiest to manage, you know. While I'm sleeping or swimming or riding my horses, y'all do things I don't expect. Then I sit down to write and acts have been committed that change the whole complexion of the story. I probably shouldn't confess this because it indicates I'm not in control of my work. But then I've spent too many years trying to control things. I guess I just have to trust y'all not to lead me too far down the primrose path.

CECE: You really should give us some credit. We are quite capable of taking care of most things. I'm sure I could improve on Sarah Booth's wardrobe if you'd just let me have sway.

CAROLYN: Don't get huffy—or personal. I didn't mean to imply that you're inept. Ask me something else.

CECE: Okay, how much like you is Sarah Booth?

CAROLYN: Oh, my, now that's a very probing question. Are you trying to psychoanalyze me?

CECE: Don't get clever on me. You know I got a better education at Ole Miss than you did. Just answer my questions.

CAROLYN: Can an author ever be separated from her creation? No. Sarah Booth and I both share a love of mischief and adventure. We both love animals. We're both nosy. How's that?

CECE: You're dodging the question!

CAROLYN: Not deliberately. The thing is, all of the populace of Zinnia have things in common with me. Even the wicked characters. A writer and her creations are inseparable.

CECE: Now that's a fine bit of smoke and mirrors. I can see you're not going to give me a real answer, so let's move on. Are Sarah Booth and Tinkie going to work well together? I mean I love Tinkie to death, but sometimes she is so blond!

CAROLYN: Tinkie adds some balance to the partnership, don't you think? And someone has to keep an eye on Sarah Booth. She's prone to jump in over her head.

CECE: What's going to happen next? Are you ever going to give Sarah Booth a sense of style?

CAROLYN: What, you don't think Sarah Booth cuts a fine figure?

CECE: Maybe she could discover a relative who works in the fashion business. She could go to New York for a makeover. And she could take me! Now that would be a good story.

CAROLYN: I see where you're headed and don't go there.

CECE: Okay, so what's the next mystery? Inquiring minds want to know.

CAROLYN: I'd drop that slogan if I were you. It doesn't become you. I've crafted you to be classier than tabloid fare. I can't give away the next book, but I can give you a few hints. That way you can see what it's like to be a private investigator. If I give you the proper clues, maybe you can figure it out. There will be wealth, glamour, and horses—and a man who just needs killing.

CECE: Are the Dixie Chicks going to put in a surprise appearance?

CAROLYN: Now that's an idea. They understand why Earl had to die. I wonder if I could put them on the jury?

CECE: You'd better check their concert schedule. Now let's see . . . horses, glamour, wealth, and murder. Sounds like it could be a very social event.

CAROLYN: Absolutely.

CECE: Then of course I play a starring role!

CAROLYN: Absolutely.

CECE: Then I suppose it doesn't matter what the mystery is about. My audience will be perfectly happy just reading about me. I suppose I've devoted enough column inches to you. Writers are never as interesting as their characters are. Now get back to work. Things in Zinnia are dull when you aren't working.